Echoes from the edge

NIGHTMARE'S EDGE

Other books by Bryan Davis:

Echoes from the Edge series:
Beyond the Reflection's Edge (Book One)
Eternity's Edge (Book Two)

Dragons in Our Midst® series:
Raising Dragons
The Candlestone
Circles of Seven
Tears of a Dragon

Oracles of Fire® series:
Eye of the Oracle
Enoch's Ghost
Last of the Nephilim
The Bones of Makaidos

Pronunciation Guide:
Mictar — Mis-tawr'
Patar — Paw-tar'

ECHOES FROM THE EDGE

NIGHTMARE'S EDGE

BRYAN DAVIS

ZONDERVAN®

ZONDERVAN.com/
AUTHORTRACKER
follow your favorite authors

ZONDERVAN

Nightmare's Edge
Copyright © 2009 by Bryan Davis

Requests for information should be addressed to:
Zondervan, *Grand Rapids, Michigan 49530*

Library of Congress Cataloging-in-Publication Data

Davis, Bryan, 1958 –
    Nightmare's edge / Bryan Davis.
       p.   cm. – (Echoes from the edge ; bk. 3)
    Summary: With the collapse of the entire cosmos at hand, Nathan Shepherd, in the
company of his restored mother and two mysterious beings called supplicants, seeks
God's help as he enters the land of dreams to find his father, who holds the answers to
what Nathan must do to save billions of lives.
    ISBN 978-0-310-71556-6 (softcover)
    [1. Space and time – Fiction. 2. Christian life – Fiction. 3. Fantasy.] I. Title.
PZ7.D28555Ni 2009
[Fic] – dc22   2009000825

Scripture taken from the *New American Standard Bible*, © Copyright 1960, 1962, 1963, 1968,
1971, 1972, 1973, 1975, 1977 by The Lockman Foundation. Used by permission.

Internet addresses (websites, blogs, etc.) and telephone numbers printed in this book are
offered as a resource to you. These are not intended in any way to be or imply an endorse-
ment on the part of Zondervan, nor do we vouch for the content of these sites and numbers
for the life of this book.

Interior design by Christine Orejuela-Winkelman

Printed in the United States of America

09 10 11 12 13 14 15 • 22 21 20 19 18 17 16 15 14 13 12 11 10 9 8 7 6 5 4 3 2 1

Echoes from the edge

NIGHTMARE'S EDGE

1

WAKING UP DEAD

Nathan ducked under a low-hanging branch and pushed a dangling python out of the way with his bandaged hand. The snake hissed, startling him for a moment. With its beady eyes and flicking tongue, it seemed real, as tangible as everything else in this dim, dream-fueled jungle.

Just ahead on the narrow path, Cerulean paid no attention. After all, in the realm of dreams, even the forest was imaginary. To Nathan, however, all the details—from the thick, green foliage of overarching trees darkening their steps to the high humidity dampening his armpits—painted a three-dimensional landscape that felt as real as it looked.

Wiping his brow with a sleeve, Nathan pulled off the gray Iowa sweatshirt he had borrowed from Nathan of Earth Blue and tied the sleeves around his waist. Nathan Blue wouldn't need the shirt back, since not long ago the murderous vision stalker Mictar had burned his eyes out with a life-absorbing touch.

Nathan peered into the murky jungle. Who could tell if that killer now stalked this dream world, ready to leap out from behind one of the tropical trees and repeat the attack? And—a more immediate problem—with just a slender candle in Cerulean's grip lighting their way, how could two awake people find another one of their kind in this enormous, dark land?

He hurried to catch up with Cerulean, Earth Blue's supplicant from the misty world. Keeping his eyes focused straight ahead and the white candle from Earth Blue held out in front, Cerulean stayed quiet. Only the swishing sound of his dark blue shirt and matching trousers made any sound at all. Nothing seemed to faze him, even the images conjured by frightened sleepers. Earlier, he had ignored the twelve talking chipmunks dressed in purple tuxedos. They had been funny at first, chattering about their political ambitions and the proper way to shave an elephant, but when a six-foot-tall electric razor buzzed into view, Nathan dove out of the way. The razor flew past, chasing a three-headed elephant into the forest. Cerulean merely helped him back to his feet and pressed on without a hint of a smile. He seemed unflappable.

"So," Nathan said as they marched past an old man wrapped in golden chains who was floundering in a quicksand bog, "this dream world really isn't all that dangerous once you get used to it. Why did you insist on just the two of us coming? What's the risk?"

Cerulean replied in a calm tone. "Not everything is a dream. Jack is here somewhere, is he not?"

"True. But what other things could enter this world? No one else knows how to get here in the real world. Even you had to get Kelly to go to sleep to create a portal."

"When there are no wounds in the cosmic fabric, the dream world can be penetrated only by a supplicant or through a person's sleeping mind. With interfinity at hand, however, and many holes throughout the cross-dimensional plane, I suspect that passages abound."

"How can you tell the difference?" Nathan asked. "I mean, if that poor guy in the quicksand was real, shouldn't we try to rescue him?"

Cerulean smiled, finally breaking his stoic countenance. "As the elephant has taught you, dreams are as real as you allow them to be. Once you train your mind, you will see through them. The imagined elements in the dreamscape are transparent and whatever is left is reality."

Nathan glanced around again. "Anything real here besides people?"

"A few things stay whether someone is dreaming or not." Cerulean nodded at a bent, leafless tree in the distance, illuminated by the dreamscape's ambient light. Draped with long, hanging vines, it looked like a cross between a live oak and a tropical species from a dense rain forest. Yet, without even the smallest leaf dressing its crooked branches, it seemed frozen in winter dormancy.

"For example," Cerulean continued, "it is best to avoid the spider trees."

While Nathan eyed the tree, Cerulean pressed on. "Come. Kelly's dream has now formed in her mind. Since she sleeps at the edge of a cosmic wound, her vision will be the best place to look for Jack."

Nathan followed Cerulean's lively pace. "Whose dream are we in now?" Nathan asked.

"A mixture of several." As Cerulean passed by a leafy vine that hung from a branch, he gave it a shove, making it swing. "Dreams about jungles are often created by souls who feel lost. They struggle through vines, snakes, quicksand, and many other obstacles of their own making, thus illustrating their lives of desperation. When I saw this vision, I thought it would make sense to search for Jack here while we waited for Kelly to dream. Even though he is blind, Jack might have found his way to this place of troubled thoughts."

"Sounds reasonable," Nathan said, "at least as dreams go."

After following a meandering path for several minutes, they entered a suburban neighborhood darkened by storm clouds overhead. Now walking on rubberized streets, they passed a headless woman on a bicycle who was trying to find a place to insert her earbuds. In front of a mansionlike house on a perfectly manicured lawn, a man in a clown costume juggled a woman, three children, and a briefcase. As if on a treadmill, he ran in place, huffing and puffing, but getting nowhere.

Nathan stared at them, knowing they couldn't possibly be real. When they faded into ghostlike images, he shuddered. This was just too weird.

With each change of scenery, they passed through a soft membrane, a dry, gelatin-like substance about ten feet thick that sent a buzzing sensation across Nathan's skin. Although the transparent wall raised a tickle for a few moments, it seemed harmless. During each passage, however, a precipice appeared on the right, and a vague pull forced Nathan to lean to the left to keep from walking over the side and into the dark void. The membrane obviously marked a boundary of some kind—perhaps the wall between different dreams or alternate realities a dreamer could visit. But the dark hole seemed different; something dangerous, something to be avoided.

After a brief walk through a sandy, cactus-filled desert, they penetrated a third membrane, again entering the buffer zone between dreams. Nathan slowed his pace for a moment, allowing his eyes to adjust. Ribbons of light swirled into the void from every direction, as if it were a drain. The pull this time was harder, but not unbearable. Yet Cerulean seemed oblivious to it. A strange sound emanated from the depths, like a song—a soft, familiar song. Nathan craned his neck, listening. Could it be? Yes, it sounded like someone humming "Be Thou My Vision."

"What's that dark place?" he asked.

Cerulean paused and looked toward the abyss. "The void. This world of visions surrounds it. Every dream eventually crumbles and is pulled in there."

"Why is it pulling me? I'm not part of a dream."

Cerulean turned his head abruptly toward Nathan. "The void affects you?"

Nathan gave him a half nod. "Is that bad?"

"I am not sure." Cerulean stared at Nathan for a long moment, then marched on.

Soon, they entered the darkest place yet, a cemetery with old tombstones rising at odd angles from grave plots. Bones littered the weed-infested ground. Gnarled oak trees with hanging moss painted twisted shadows on the path that coursed through the abandoned yard. A large raven perched atop one of the burial markers, staring at Nathan as he passed by.

"Read," it croaked, its red eyes shining. "Read. Read."

Nathan paused and leaned closer. "You mean the tombstone?"

"Read! Read!"

Cerulean grabbed his arm. "It is not wise to heed the words of the dream creatures."

"But if they're not real," Nathan said, "why would it matter?"

Cerulean inhaled deeply, his bright blue eyes sparkling in the candle's glow. "A vision stalker is close. I fear that he has manipulated the environment, and our safety may very well be compromised."

"Just reading the tombstone won't hurt." Nathan took the candle from Cerulean and shuffled to the side of the grave. With the raven still leering at him, he held the flame close to the stone and read, "Here lies Kelly Clark, murdered by Nathan Shepherd and unable to rest in the glare of her killer's light."

"What?" Nathan leaned back. "How could a tombstone know I'm here?"

Cerulean stared at the raven. "Three possibilities. Kelly sees us in her dream, so she created the inscription even as you drew close. Second, a stalker could have manipulated this place, and he is trying to intimidate you to keep you from proceeding. Third, and perhaps the most dangerous of all, is the possibility that you are becoming part of the dreamscape."

"How is that possible?"

"Amber spoke of this when she heard about Jack's entry. If Patar sent Jack here to keep him alive, then he likely expected the poor man to become part of the dream world, a living phantom who wanders in people's nightmares. Jack would be alive, yes, but only Patar would know how to extract him without killing him."

Nathan pointed at himself. "Then can I leave safely? I mean, I'm not becoming part of this place yet, am I?"

Fixing his gaze on Nathan, Cerulean shook his head. "You appear solid, so one of the other two options is more likely. I suspect that a vision stalker is present."

Nathan peered behind the tombstone, but nothing was there. "Who? Mictar?"

"He would be powerful enough." Cerulean took a quick step and grabbed the raven by the throat. It choked out a squawk and flailed its wings under the supplicant's grip, vainly trying to claw his arm. "Where is your master?" he demanded.

"Read!" it croaked again. "Read!"

Cerulean shook its body. "You have a voice. Tell me who sent you."

"Read! Read!" The raven broke free and in a scattering of feathers flew into the darkness above.

As a black pinion floated to the ground, Cerulean took the candle back from Nathan. "Come. We must hurry. The longer we stay here, the greater the danger."

"The raven wanted us to read the inscription again. Maybe there's a new one."

Cerulean held the flame high and wrapped a hand around Nathan's arm. "It is of no consequence. If the message has been written by the stalker, it is likely a lie. If it is a product of Kelly's nightmarish fears, it will only work to heighten your own. And if you are becoming part of this world, deep emotions will only hasten the process."

"Not knowing will drive me crazy." Nathan squinted at the tombstone, but it was now too dark to read. "Taking a second won't hurt."

Cerulean held fast. "The risk is too high. Your unwarranted insistence demonstrates that the effect this place is having on you is escalating rapidly. You are losing your ability to reason."

"But I have to know." As Nathan pulled against Cerulean's grip, the supplicant's blue hair grew fuzzy, like reeds waving under restless waters. "Let me go."

"Nathan!"

The shout sounded like a thunderclap. Nathan spun toward it. Ahead on the path, a man stood with his fists set against his hips, his face bent into a deep scowl.

Nathan blinked. "Is it Mictar?"

"No," Cerulean said, loosening his grip. "It is Patar."

Patar walked three steps closer before halting, the candle-light gleaming on a plastic bag in his right hand. "You should not have come here. It is far too dangerous."

Nathan glanced from Patar to the tombstone, then pointed at the inscription. "I have to know what it says. Kelly might be communicating with me."

"As you can see, Cerulean ..." Patar's voice grew distant, warped, as if he was speaking from the midst of a cave. Nathan could barely make out the words.

"He is already being absorbed." The stalker's slender form now seemed foggy as well, distorted, more like a dream than reality.

Cerulean nodded. "I can see that now. He is showing signs of fading."

"I'm fading?" Nathan pointed at Cerulean, then at Patar. "You two are the ghostly looking ones."

"It's only going to get worse," Patar said. "His mental defenses are withering, and Kelly's nightmare is reaching a climax."

A sudden gust of wind blew away a blanket of clouds. A full

moon, at least five times its usual size, hovered in a purple sky. Its glow illuminated the cemetery, allowing a clearer view of the dozens of tombstones.

"Shall I take him out immediately?" Cerulean asked. "Or should I find Jack first?"

A low rumble sounded at Nathan's side. At the gravesite where the raven once perched, a hand pushed out of the earth, then a second hand and a head. Finally, an entire body, short and feminine, climbed up and shook dirt from her shoulder-length hair. She looked straight ahead and called, "Nathan! Are you here?"

"Kelly?" Nathan stared at her. "It really *is* you!"

Wearing a knee-length nightshirt, she brushed off the soil, revealing letters on the front that read "Sanity Is Overrated." Then, extending her arms, she staggered toward him, feeling for obstacles in her way. "Nathan? Where are you? I hear your voice."

As she drew closer, he stiffened. Kelly had no eyes, only vacant sockets. Could she be the Earth Blue Kelly, somehow resurrected? Or was she Kelly Red, a new victim of Mictar's cruel, electrified hand?

No, Nathan told himself, *she's only part of a dream*. Yet, she looked so real.

Kelly stopped and touched Nathan's cheeks with her icy fingers. "There you are. Why didn't you answer me?" She shivered and rubbed her arms. "I'm cold and scared. Will you get me out of here? I can't see a thing."

Nathan reached for her hand but then jerked his arm back. "You're just a mirage. I can't take you anywhere."

"You are correct." Cerulean lifted his candle higher. "Stay in the light, Nathan. Do not be deceived."

"This is no time for joking around," Kelly said. Bouncing on the toes of her sock-covered feet, she shivered harder. "You can't leave me in this horrible place. It's so cold, so terribly cold.

Please take me home." She reached out and fumbled for him. With missing eyes and a dirty face, she seemed like a pitiful waif as her voice broke into a lament. "Nathan ... please ... I'm scared."

"I'll get you out." He grabbed her hand. "Just hang on."

Her chilled fingers wrapped around his upper arm. She was solid, real, without a hint of fading.

"Oh, thank you." She leaned her head against his shoulder. "I told you never to leave me, not even for a minute. I felt so alone. So scared."

For a moment, dizziness flooded Nathan's mind, but he shook it off. "Just stay with me. Cerulean will get us out of here."

"Nathan!" Cerulean warned again. "If you continue—"

"Let him go for a moment." Patar's voice was fading even further. Turning his attention away from Nathan, Patar poured out the contents of his bag into Cerulean's hand. "When I wrestled with my brother, I recovered these from his energy reserves and was able to reconstitute them. You will find Jack approximately one hundred paces ahead. Restore these and get him and Nathan out of here with all speed."

Nathan stared at Cerulean's transparent palm. Two eyeballs lay there, perfectly formed, with nerves and moist tissue attached. Nathan nearly gagged.

"Have you found your new charge?" Patar asked.

Cerulean gave him a pensive look. "So soon?"

"Have you not been listening? She calls for help from this dream world. If I can hear her, surely you can."

"I have heard the song, but I was unsure of my responsibilities."

Patar laid a hand on Cerulean's shoulder. "You are a supplicant. You chose this duty; you must complete it."

"Then my work with Nathan is finished," Cerulean said. "I will have to find this new gifted one."

Patar gave him a firm nod. "Because Nathan broke the portal mirror, he will not be able to travel to my world to play the violin at Sarah's Womb, at least not right now. You can, however, send him to Earth Yellow to find other options."

"Yes," Cerulean replied. "As we speak, Nathan's mother is playing 'Foundation's Key' to see which mirror is the correct portal. While we were waiting, we decided to try to find Jack, since he entered the dream world from Earth Blue. I was unsure of how the dreamscape would affect Nathan, so this was a test."

"And he failed, just as he did when he allowed his desire for revenge against my brother to outweigh his wisdom. He had the power to escape with the mirror intact."

"Nathan," Kelly said, her fingers growing warmer on his skin. "Don't let him talk about you like that. You did the best you could. You were under a lot of pressure."

"You're right." Nathan stared at Kelly. Even with dirt smeared across her cheeks, black holes where her brown eyes should be, and grungy, tangled hair, she seemed lovelier than ever. "But I really didn't have much of a choice."

"Then don't listen. We'll find our own way out."

"Go now," Patar said, "before that rotting cadaver becomes more real to him than life itself. He will soon bond with it beyond all hope of reason." With that, Patar faded out of sight.

Cerulean put the eyeballs back into the bag and stuffed the top into his waistband. Then, lifting the candle, he pulled Nathan's elbow. "Jack is ahead. Let us get him and flee this place."

Leading Kelly by the arm, Nathan followed Cerulean, now a blue ghost in his sight. "Did you hear that, Kelly? We'll be out of here soon."

"Thank you, Nathan." She staggered along, her empty sockets still wide. "I knew you wouldn't leave me here."

With the moon shining brightly, the going was easier. It took only a few seconds to find Jack sitting on the ground, leaning against a tombstone. He seemed solid, though Cerulean was now as transparent as thinning fog.

Jack looked around with his empty sockets while running his fingers through his thick beard. "Who's there?" he asked.

"He is losing his grip on reality as well," Cerulean said as he crouched next to the tombstone. "I will have to work quickly."

"He looks fine. He's not fading at all." Nathan turned to Kelly. He almost said, "Right, Kelly?" forgetting for a moment that she couldn't see anything.

"Take this." Cerulean handed Nathan the candle. "Watch me through the flame."

"Okay." Feeling dizzy again, Nathan held the flame close to his nose and peered around both sides. Cerulean pulled the eyeballs from the bag. Then, while singing unintelligible words at a high pitch, he laid his palm over Jack's empty sockets and pushed the eyeballs into place.

Nathan stared, trying to focus as blue light seeped around the edges of Cerulean's hand. Strange; the supplicant appeared to have an ability similar to Mictar's, a powerful light that flashed from his palm. Would the mysteries surrounding these citizens of a misty world ever be explained?

With every second Nathan peered through the candle, Cerulean grew more solid while Jack stayed the same. Nathan looked back at Kelly. Her face seemed fuzzier, distant. She angled her head as if listening.

"What's happening?" she asked.

"Everything's okay." As he spoke, her features clarified again. "Cerulean is repairing Jack's eyes. We'll leave in a minute."

Nathan turned back to Cerulean, lowering the candle to see him better. Now ghostly blue again, Cerulean helped Jack to his feet.

"Can you see?" Cerulean asked.

"Very well, thank you." Jack pulled a rumpled fedora from

beneath his jacket and straightened it out. "Everything is clear, except for you."

"Your normal sight will be restored very soon."

"Excellent! Excellent! The end of a nightmare at last!" He put on his hat and turned toward Nathan, his restored eyes glistening. "Nathan! I'm so glad to see you."

"Same here." Nathan gave the candle back to Cerulean and shook Jack's hand with his left, grimacing at the older man's grip. "Now let's all get out of this place. I have to figure out what happened to Kelly and get some eyes for her, too."

"Nathan." Cerulean pushed the candle closer. "You and Jack will come with me. You must leave Kelly behind."

"What?" Nathan shook his head hard. "I can't leave her here."

Kelly's arm locked around his. "No, Nathan! No!"

Cerulean pulled Jack and Nathan together and held the candle's flame near their eyes. His voice mellowed to a soothing chant. "Stare at the flame. It is the light of reality. The images around you are mere phantoms. Bring what is real back into focus, or you will not return to the ones you love." He blew a puff of sweet-smelling air into Nathan's face. "Think of your mother. Listen to her music. It is riding the breeze. She waits for you in the Earth Blue bedroom. You must go back and search for your father. The real Kelly is there as well. We must awaken her from this nightmare so the two of you can go to Earth Yellow and save two world populations from disaster."

The flame's glow spread over Cerulean's face, making his features clearer, almost crisp. He compressed Nathan's chin with his hand, forcing him to keep his stare locked on the flame. "You must let this Kelly go, Nathan. She is not real. Night is over and dawn is breaking."

"No, Nathan!" Kelly's voice spiked into a wail. "You promised to stay with me. This place is cold and dark, and I'm scared."

Ever so gently, Cerulean pulled on Nathan's chin, drawing

him forward, his voice now hypnotizing. "Release her, Nathan. All will be well. You will see the real Kelly in mere moments. We will awaken her, and she will escape this torture."

Heaving and exhaling shallow breaths, Nathan pried Kelly's fingers loose and pulled away.

"Nathan!" she cried. "What are you doing?"

He turned. Kelly, now ghostly and floating backwards, reached for him with open hands. "I'll be alone again. All alone in this cold, dark place."

"I ... I can't leave her," Nathan said. "She's—"

Cerulean twisted him back. His voice sharpened again. "She's ... not ... real!"

His mind now swimming, Nathan repeated the words in a whisper. "She's not real."

Cerulean blew out the candle. As the light faded, Kelly's voice faded with it. "I'm so cold ... so cold."

2

PHOTOGRAPHIC MEMORIES

Light flooded Nathan's vision. He blinked, trying to focus as the Earth Blue bedroom materialized around him. His mother stood near one wall, her violin in playing position, while Amber, the Earth Yellow supplicant, held a small square mirror in front of her. "Foundation's Key" sang from the strings, its simple melody wiping away the remnants of the dark nightmare.

On the floor, Kelly lay on a mattress, shivering. "So cold," she cried out. "So cold."

Nathan dropped to his knees. He grabbed her arm and gave her a strong shake. "Kelly! Wake up! It's just a bad dream."

Her eyes shot open, glassy and wild. "Nathan! Don't leave me!"

"I'm here." He scooped her up and cradled her in his lap. "I won't leave you. I promise."

She wrapped both arms around him. "But you did leave me! I begged you not to, but you left anyway!"

Cerulean, his hair and skin glowing blue, crouched at Kelly's opposite side and spoke to Nathan. "Invaded nightmares are the most vivid of all, and now you understand the danger. When you go to Earth Yellow, it will likely be worse. The nightmare epidemic has proven that the veil between dreams and reality is thinner there, and Mictar will also be watching for you. If you lose your grip on reality, you will fall into his clutches, for he can manipulate the dreams and lead you into a trap."

"But if I think something is real when it's not, how can I ever be sure?"

Cerulean held the extinguished candle in front of Nathan's eyes. "You must focus on the light from the real world. It will keep you anchored."

Nathan set Kelly back on the floor and took her hand, ignoring the pain that shot through his still-injured palm. Kelly's glassy eyes gave evidence of her damaged vision, a souvenir of an encounter with Mictar. A spot of blood on the white fabric of the Newton High School sweatshirt she had borrowed from Kelly Blue's dresser told the tale of another wound she had suffered in the fight. Seeing her so afraid wrenched his heart. "I'd never really leave you in a graveyard, you know."

Tears now drying on her cheeks, she nodded. "I know."

Nathan's mother lowered her violin. "What exactly happened in there?"

After explaining his journey through Kelly's nightmare, with Jack and Cerulean adding a few details he had forgotten, Nathan finished with a sigh. "So that's why Cerulean's worried about what might happen next time."

Amber set the mirror on a pile of matching squares. "We have searched through forty-one mirrors. If we are unable to find one leading to Earth Yellow, then surviving the dream world will be the least of our worries."

"I don't want to drive five hours to the observatory," Nathan said, "not with all the crazy problems going on. Even if we could get gas, who knows what the roads will be like?"

He picked up the mirror with his unbandaged hand, still raw from the burns he'd received sliding down a rope while dangling over the void mysteriously called "Sarah's Womb." After playing the violin strings that had been stretched over the chasm and thrusting Earth Red away from the threat of the merging worlds, he had nearly plunged into the womb. Only Kelly's courageous climb up the rope and her teamwork with

Daryl Blue had saved his life, though in the process Daryl had plunged to her death.

A dragging sound drew Nathan's attention to the bedroom door. Cerulean pulled a wooden chair with a padded seat in from the hallway. "Here, Mrs. Shepherd," he said, pushing the chair close. "It seems likely that your musical search will take a long time."

She gave him a thankful nod.

Amber stooped and picked up the slender candle Cerulean had used during the dream world journey. She walked toward the wall where the mirror squares were once attached, her gait so graceful she seemed to glide. With her long blonde hair draped over her simple yellow dress and her skin shimmering like gold, she looked like a storybook fairy. Sitting on the trunk next to the wall, she said, "I will keep this taper for our journey to Earth Yellow. With all the dark places we are likely to encounter, perhaps even I will need this anchor to reality."

Lifting her head, she gazed upward, her face dreamy and her eyes far away. "I have been so long in my supplicant's dome, I feel lost already. It is as if I am a goldfish released into a massive lake, one still trying to swim in a tight circle. While in prison I could watch and pray for my beloved as I listened to the music of her soul, but here the songs are many, and most are dissonant and troubling. If I do not find my beloved soon, I think I will drown in this sea."

"We'll get back to work on that," Nathan said. "The right mirror has to be around here somewhere."

His mother sat on the chair and laid the violin in her lap. "Do you see anything in that one?"

He turned to the mirror in his hand. The reflection, altered by his mother's performance of "Foundation's Key," showed a terrified boy, maybe five years old, standing with a shivering beagle on a snow-covered sheet of ice in the middle of a raging river.

Nathan shook his head. Another crisis. Should he even tell everyone what was there? With all the terror on Earths Blue and Yellow caused by the approaching collision of the two worlds, they couldn't afford to travel to each place and rescue every endangered person.

He set the mirror back onto the stack of rejects. "Probably another Earth Blue scene."

Kelly pulled another square from the mirrors that hadn't yet been tried. "How many more before you need a break?"

Nathan looked at his mother. She had played "Foundation's Key" more than forty times. He was beginning to regret smashing one of the mirrors in Mictar's face, even if his action was probably the only reason the stalker hadn't shown up at the bedroom door yet. Because that mirror was missing, they weren't able to get the entire mosaic of mirrors operating, forcing them to pry off every square and play the tune for each one in order to find a portal to Earth Yellow. But what was done was done. "Mom? What do you think? Need a rest?"

"Let's make fifty mirrors our goal for now," she said, lifting the violin again. "If they don't show anything we can use, we should try to contact Daryl again."

Kelly sat next to Amber and propped up a mirror. Looking at Nathan, she asked, "If we find the right one, have you decided what to do with the others?"

Nathan shook his head, his eyes focusing on the rejected stack. Assuming Mictar recovered from his wounds, this would be the most likely place for him to show up. Since he now knew that any of the squares a gifted person had used would work for his purposes, he would probably tear the house apart trying to find one. But they certainly couldn't take almost four hundred mirrors with them to Earth Yellow.

Nathan turned back to the mirror in Kelly's hands. As his mother played the key, he watched as the mirror displayed a deserted city scene—closely packed multistory buildings, streetlights illuminating empty sidewalks, and vacant newsstands with magazines and papers rippling in the breeze. A young woman, maybe twenty years old, dressed in a long coat, scarf, and ski cap stood at a corner. As windblown snow buffeted her face, she clasped a bundle close to her chest.

He drew closer to the image. Could that bundle be a baby? Was she waiting for someone? Maybe a bus or a taxi? With the streets so empty and the snow mounting, it looked like she might have to wait for a long time.

Jack leaned over and peered at the mirror with his newly restored eyes. "That's Michigan Avenue in Chicago. I was a cab driver, so I know every corner in the city."

"But which color Earth is it?" Nathan turned toward the window on the far side of the bedroom. Outside, windblown snow raced across the front yard, blending with yellow leaves that had fallen from the now naked cottonwood tree next to the driveway.

Jack pointed at the mirror. "Is there any way we can help this woman?"

"Won't she just go inside if she can't get a ride?" Nathan asked.

"Maybe not." Jack ran the brim of his hat through his hands. "If she could go inside, why would she be standing in the snow with a baby?"

"I don't know, but we have to move on. While we're standing here, Earth Yellow's time is probably zooming by."

"But is there a choice?" Jack's thick eyebrows bent toward his nose. "Is there a way to go there?"

"Well, if we flashed a light, we could travel there." Nathan touched the top of the reject pile. "But any one of these mirrors could lead us to a problem to solve. If we're going to save the entire world, we can't jump through every mirror that shows us a cold woman on the street."

"I suppose not." Jack put his hat on his head. "Can you send me there? I'm not of much use in this world-saving business, but I want to do what I can to help in my little corner."

Kelly touched the glass near the woman's face. "That's strange. I can see her clearly."

"Then it must be Earth Yellow." Nathan eyed the image. The woman was standing still and the snow was whipping across the viewport, making it impossible to figure out whether or not time was flying by. Should they go there? At least they would be on the right Earth, and then Amber could take them to the dream world. Or would it be better to search for a portal in the bedroom or maybe the future site of Earth Yellow's observatory?

Kelly held the mirror closer to her eyes. "She's kind of far away, and there's snow all around, but ..."

"But what?"

She grabbed Nathan's hand, making him wince. "Come with me. I'll need your eyesight."

As she pulled him out of the bedroom and down the hall, Nathan had to jog to keep up. "Where are we going?"

"To my dad's bedroom. I know this house well enough to find it, but I'll need you once we get there."

After turning right and hustling through a second corridor, they entered a spacious bedroom. Still holding the mirror, Kelly slowed and blinked in the dimness. Nathan flipped the wall switch, but the twin ceiling fan lights stayed dark. "Forgot," he said. "Still no power."

Kelly tiptoed around a king-sized bed and stopped in front of a dresser sitting against the far wall. Its attached mirror reflected their shadowy forms and the smaller mirror in Kelly's hands. On top of the dresser, under a jumble of socks and old receipts, was a large leather photo album.

Kelly laid the mirror next to it and lifted the cover. Inside, photos covered the pages, each one neatly inserted in a protective pocket. "I can't see them very well. Can you look for one that shows a woman holding a baby?"

Nathan flipped a couple of pages, then pointed at a photo. "Here's one."

She slid the mirror over the album, stopping it next to the picture. "Does she look like this woman?"

He stared at the two images. The woman in the mirror swayed from side to side much faster than normal, like a movie playing at high speed. With her distance from his viewpoint and blowing snow veiling her body, he couldn't get a good look at her face.

"I'm not sure. I think she resembles—"

"Shh!" Kelly raised a finger to her lips. "Listen!"

Nathan kept quiet. Although he couldn't hear anything, he knew better than to say so. Kelly's gift of interpreting sounds from other worlds was at work.

After several seconds, her finger hovered over the woman's face. "She's singing to the baby. It's real fast, but I can pick it up." Her voice now trembling, Kelly sang the song in a whisper. "Hush little baby, don't say a word. Mama's gonna buy you a mockingbird. And if that mockingbird won't sing, Mama's gonna buy you a ruby ring."

"Ruby ring?" Nathan said. "I thought it was a diamond ring."

"My mother always said *ruby*. I know, because she used to help me babysit."

"Your mother?" Nathan pointed at the photo. "So that's you she's carrying?"

Kelly nodded. "We must be ... I mean, they must be freezing. We have to help them."

"Ahem!"

Nathan looked up. Jack stood at the door. "You had better return to the other room," Jack said. "We have a visitor."

Nathan closed the photo album over the mirror and picked

them up. Then, taking Kelly's hand, he rushed past Jack. When they reached the bedroom, Nathan slowed and peered in. His mother stood with her violin at her side while Cerulean and Amber gazed at a mirror square.

Nathan helped Kelly through the door and gave her the photo album. She opened it and slid out the mirror within.

"What's up, Mom?" Nathan asked.

His mother nodded toward the mirror in Cerulean's grip. "See for yourself."

Cerulean turned the square toward Nathan. A narrow, pale face filled up the entire image—Patar, his eyes glowing red, though a softer hue than usual.

Nathan swallowed. Seeing this vision stalker meant a tongue lashing was probably on the horizon. "I'm here." He cleared his throat. "What do you want?"

"It occurred to me," Patar said, his voice more pleasant than usual, "that my earlier instructions were much too vague. Once you reach Earth Yellow you must find a way to travel back to my world to finish your task." His eyes shifted from side to side, apparently looking at each of the supplicants in turn. "Because of Scarlet's plunge into Sarah's Womb, the portal from your world to mine has closed. The only way to enter my world now is to use the observatory."

Nathan pictured the Earth Yellow observatory mirror, anchored in the foundation at the future site of Interfinity Labs. Nathan knew they'd need more than violins to play "Moonlight Sonata," the song that opened the portal to Patar's home in the misty world. Once in the past, Kelly had persuaded a radio station to play the song, but that wasn't likely to work again. And with Earth Blue in chaos, there was no way they could drive to the observatory here. Still, since Yellow's time was zooming along, things might be a lot different there now. "Any idea how the Interfinity construction is coming along on Earth Yellow?" he asked.

Patar's brow bent down slightly. "I am not omniscient. I suggest that you find out."

"But how? We have a portal, but it leads to downtown Chicago. Can't we try a few more mirrors?"

"No," Kelly said, showing him the mirror. "My mother's walking away. We have to go now!"

Nathan pressed a hand against the side of his head. Once again, the weight of multiple worlds rested on his shoulders, and the wrong decision could mean the deaths of billions. "Okay. Okay. We'll go."

"Do you have a vehicle?" Jack asked. "If so, can you transport with it?"

Nathan looked out the window again. Snow now lay an inch thick on the empty driveway. "No. We left the Toyota at Tony Yellow's house. So even if we went through this mirror, we'd be stuck—"

"Gunther will show up," Kelly said. "I know he will, just like he did at the Burger King when he and Francesca dreamed about us."

Nathan looked at the fierce determination in her eyes. No matter how many times these adventures left her bruised and battered, she was always ready for the next one. "You're probably right." He gave Patar a nod. "We have to go and trust in Gunther and Francesca and their dream prophecies."

Patar's red eyes brightened. "Remember what I told you about how to save the worlds. You have seen it work. Although it is a tragic path, it is the most efficient one."

Nathan sighed. Yes, Scarlet's death did save Earth Red, but the cost was just too high. And what right did Patar have to make that kind of call? He wouldn't have to suffer; those supplicants meant nothing to him. Firming his lips, Nathan shook his head. He couldn't kill Amber and Cerulean, even if their deaths would save countless lives. He had to find another way.

As Patar's image faded, Nathan snatched a cell phone from

his pocket. "Better let Daryl know." He looked at the phone's screen. "No signal and the battery's almost dead."

Kelly tightened her grip on the mirror's edges. "My mother walked out of sight."

Nathan dropped the cell phone, picked a flashlight up from the floor, and aimed it at the mirror. "Everyone on this side. I'm not sure how many it will transport, but we'll soon find out."

While Nathan, his mother, Jack, Amber, and Kelly positioned themselves in front of the mirror held by Kelly's extended arms, Cerulean stepped away. "I can be of no help to you there. I will stay and secure the mirrors." He kissed Amber's cheek. "And then I must search the dream world here. My new beloved calls for me, and I cannot rest until I find her."

"Would I be able to help you?" Jack asked. "Although I had no eyes while I was there, I became well acquainted with the sounds and smells of that world."

Cerulean held out his hand. "Perhaps you would be of service."

As Jack joined the supplicant, Nathan gave them a nod and turned on the flashlight. The beam bounced off the mirror's surface and splashed over their bodies. Shattering into thousands of tiny shards, the room crumbled away, replaced by the city corner they had seen in the mirror. Frigid winds tore into their bodies and snow pelted their faces.

Bouncing on her toes, Kelly rubbed her arms. "Brilliant! We forgot to bring coats."

Nathan untied the sleeves from around his waist and pulled the sweatshirt on over his head. Shivering violently, he scanned the sidewalks. The curtain of falling flakes veiled his view of the nearly vacant block. Tall buildings lined both sides of the street in front of him, and an "L" train rumbled somewhere out of sight, but only a few pedestrians interrupted the sea of white sidewalks and office buildings.

His mother stood to his right, shielding her eyes with one

hand and tucking the violin to her side with the other. Amber, now holding the photo album, stooped and pushed her finger into the six-inch layer of white. As dozens of flakes coated her blonde hair and eyebrows, she looked up at Nathan without a hint of a shiver. "The snow is deep enough," she said. "We could follow her tracks."

A familiar voice made Nathan turn. "Need some coats?"

3

DEFUSING THE BOMB

Nathan grinned. A young woman, her red hair partially covered by a woolen hood, extended an armful of coats, a wide smile on her face.

He puffed her name in a stream of white vapor. "Daryl!"

"In the flesh." She pushed the coats toward Kelly. "Yours is on top, Kelly-kins."

Kelly lifted the coat and slid her arms through the sleeves. "How did you—"

"Easy. You left the coats in the observatory. I brought them. You know what I always say." She used her fingers to spell out letters in sign language.

Nathan strung them together. "Be prepared?"

"Hey!" Daryl said. "Look who knows sign language!"

"You always say, 'Be prepared'?" Kelly asked.

"Well, lately, anyway." She peeled off the second coat and gave it to Nathan's mother. "This was Daryl Blue's. I think it'll fit you."

Nathan took the last coat and passed it to Amber, but she pushed it back. "I am not cold."

He gazed into her bright eyes. Her body, now glowing with a pale golden aura, shifted back and forth as if swaying with an inaudible tune, her bare feet rising to tiptoes and then falling with each cycle. She smiled. "Are you perplexed, Nathan?"

"I guess so." He pushed his arms through the coat sleeves. "I'm wondering how you stay warm."

"Now that I am in this world, I can hear the music in the air, and it has eased my troubled mind. Once you learn to dance with the heavenly sounds, the corruption of the elements will no longer affect you." She touched his cheek with her warm fingers. "This will be a new journey for you, one that cannot be explained here and now."

"Right," Kelly said. "We need to find my Earth Yellow mother. She was here a few seconds ago."

Daryl looked at her wristwatch. "More like seven minutes ago. Gunther and I picked her up while we were looking for you guys."

"Did Gunther have a dream?" Nathan asked as he zipped up the coat.

"Yep. He and Francesca locked in on you popping into this world right at this location. He picked me up at the observatory yesterday, which was about an hour ago, Earth Blue time."

"Why did you decide to make the jump?"

She held up a finger. "One, I was on generator power at the observatory, so the equipment couldn't run much longer, and two"—she lifted another finger—"I found out Earth Red's in a heap of trouble, so I came here to see what I could do about it."

"Earth Red? I thought we pushed them away from interfinity."

"Well ... sort of. You see—"

A gunning engine sounded from behind her. As Daryl turned, Nathan looked over her shoulder. A van marked "Stoneman Enterprises" wheeled around a corner, slipping and sliding through the snow. As soon as it straightened, Gunther came into view through the windshield, his face taut.

When the van pulled up to the walkway, Nathan opened the side door, revealing a woman seated on the rear bench holding a bundle in her arms. With shoulder-length brown hair and matching brown eyes, she could have passed for Kelly's older sister. "Mrs. Clark?" he asked. "Molly Clark?"

Molly tucked the blanket around her baby and scooted away from the cold air. "I am." An Irish accent flavored her words. "It seems that every stranger in town knows my name."

"Hop in," Gunther said, leaning toward the back from the driver's seat. "Let's get moving before the zone police find us."

Nathan helped his mother step up into the van. As she slid close to Molly, she asked, "The zone police?"

Gunther pointed at himself with his thumb. "I'm a marked man. They're cracking down on us travelers."

"As well they should," Molly said, now sitting next to the window. "You people get us all in trouble."

Gunther gave her a thin smile. "And *out* of trouble, it seems."

Nathan reached for Amber's hand, but she drew it back. She leaned toward the van and peered inside, angling her head as she scanned the interior.

"It's safe," he said. "It's nothing like your prison dome."

"I have seen such machines in my visions, but I never imagined I would ride in one." She took his hand, stepped up to the bench, and settled next to Nathan's mother.

Nathan stepped close to Daryl and whispered, "You can ride shotgun, and I'll sit with Kelly in the cargo area. I don't want to mention Kelly's name in front of Molly for obvious reasons."

"Gotcha, boss!" Daryl jumped into her seat. "But I wish I *had* a shotgun. That could come in handy."

With an eye on her Earth Yellow mother, Kelly hopped up and squeezed into the back. Nathan joined her, whispering, "Is that baby you?"

Nodding, she pushed aside an empty Ritz Crackers box and sat cross-legged on the flat carpet. "Ask her why she's by herself. It's important."

As Gunther began driving away, Nathan cleared his throat. "Uh ... Molly. We were wondering why you were standing out in the snow. Was someone supposed to pick you up?"

As she turned toward him, a worried look crossed her face,

and her Irish accent thickened. "My husband, Tony. We just returned from Europe, and he dropped me off at Neiman Marcus to shop while he picked up a shipment he sent from Scotland. The store closed because of the snowstorm, so I had to watch for him from the sidewalk. I couldn't very well look for other shelter, because he wouldn't be able to find me. I had to keep my baby warm somehow, so when Gunther drove by with Tony's old girlfriend, I decided to ride around with them until Tony came back."

"His old girlfriend?" Daryl let out a huff. "When pigs fly to Pluto."

"Tony is a fine man," Molly said, her voice sharpening, "and since he calls you his former flame, it seems that pigs have sprouted wings."

Daryl swung toward Molly, her red hair flying. "Speaking of pigs—"

"Cool it!" Nathan barked. "Let's just concentrate on finding Tony."

Crossing her arms, Daryl glared straight ahead, muttering something unintelligible.

Kelly reached up and touched Molly's shoulder. "Was the shipment a bunch of mirror squares?"

"What?" Molly looked back at her. "How could you know that?"

"It's a long story, but when we find Tony, I'll try to explain. He's at a sports bar just a couple of blocks away."

"A sports bar?" Molly asked. "He wouldn't—"

"He would. Trust me. You'll see." Kelly pointed at a Ford pickup in the distance. "I don't know the name of the bar, but I think it's just past that truck."

Gunther hit the accelerator. "We'll be there in a second."

As the van slipped across the snowy pavement, Kelly whispered to Nathan, "My parents have argued about this incident ever since I can remember."

"A turning point in their marriage?"

"Big time." She fastened the top button on her coat and rose to her knees. "Let's see if we can defuse this bomb before it explodes."

"What are you going to do?" Nathan asked.

"Find Tony and come up with a story that'll get him off the hook."

"You mean, tell a lie?"

"If I have to." She scooted toward the front, her whisper now harsh. "I'll do anything to keep them loving each other."

"But maybe we can—"

"Nathan." The soft, melodic voice came from the seat in front of them. "I sense disharmony."

Nathan looked up. His mother and Amber had both turned his way. Her brow wrinkling, Amber continued in a low tone. "Emotional turmoil creates dissonance just as surely as a discordant measure interrupts the flow of a musical masterpiece."

He bit his lip. Amber was every bit as insightful as Scarlet had been. He wouldn't be able to hide even the smallest secret from her.

"We're here," Gunther announced. The van slid to a stop behind the pickup, a beige Ford F-150.

Molly squinted at it. "That *is* our truck."

"Could it be stuck in the snow?" Kelly asked as she squeezed between the seat and the side of the van. "Maybe Tony's just trying to get help somewhere." She hopped out of the van and high stepped toward the pickup.

"Everyone wait here," Nathan said. "I'll be back in a minute." Shuffling his feet to clear a path, he followed Kelly to the truck. After brushing snow from the small window on the side of the truck's cap, he peered inside. Several boxes lay on the bed with "Glasgow, Scotland" imprinted with bold red letters.

He turned to Kelly. "The mirrors."

"Right." She nodded toward the bar, a small establishment less than half a block away. "He's got to be inside."

A slamming door made them turn. Amber stood on the sidewalk and scanned the area, her eyes narrowing. Hundreds of snowflakes swirled around her head as if attracted to her aura. Her graceful sway now at rest, she shivered, and her voice trembled. "There is much turmoil in the air. The sensation of coldness has penetrated my shield."

"Then maybe you should get back in the van," Nathan said.

She shook her head, making the snowflakes fly. "Earth Yellow's song has drifted away. I must find it again."

"Who am I to argue with a supplicant?" He took her by the arm. "Let's get you inside before you freeze."

He led Amber and Kelly past the bar's outside seating area. Bordered in front by a wooden rail with varnished support slats, it held five snow-covered tables, but no chairs or stools were in sight.

At the entrance, Nathan stomped his feet to shake off the snow before opening the door. A wave of television noise and rumbling conversation flowed from within, followed by the stench of beer and cigar smoke.

Amber wrinkled her nose. "Is this a latrine? It smells of human waste."

"It's called a sports bar." Nathan waved them inside and closed the door. "But you're right. It stinks in here."

"This is a new experience." She looked all around, her eyes unblinking in the smoke-filled room. "I don't think my beloved has ever been to a place like this."

"If you mean Francesca Yellow, you're probably right." Nathan scanned the area, letting his gaze rush past ten or so unfamiliar faces, mostly male, until he spotted Tony sitting on a stool with his back to the bar, his long legs reaching the floor. Clutching a sweating beer bottle, Tony watched a television mounted on a side wall. A cheer erupted from the speaker, and Tony's bellow followed.

"All right! Three pointer!"

Nathan strode toward him, waving a hand. "Tony! It's me, Nathan."

Tony swiveled his way, and a smile spread across his face. "Future Boy! Glad to see you again." He took a swig from his bottle. "I'd offer you a beer, but you don't look old enough to drink."

"I'm not." As Kelly and Amber joined him, Nathan pointed over his shoulder with his thumb. "We picked up your wife. She was standing out in the snow."

Tony jumped down from the stool. "In the snow!"

"Yeah. She was—"

A roar broke out from several of the men. A few pointed at a screen on the opposite side of the room while one raised both fists into the air.

Nathan winced at the sound. "What are they so excited about? Haven't they already dreamed about who was going to win?"

"Things have changed." Tony guided Nathan toward the exit while Amber and Kelly followed. "Did I ever mention Flash, a friend of mine?"

"Yeah." Nathan paused at the door. "You said I looked like him."

"Well, he's got some kind of spiritual connection going on. You know, spooky stuff like in the movies. Anyway, he figured out how to stop the next-day dreaming, and now only travelers get a hint of what's going on, and they're not always right. It's helped a lot. Things are getting back to normal."

The door burst open, and Daryl bustled in, shaking snow out of her hair. "The ice planet Hoth's got nothing on this place."

"Something wrong?" Kelly asked.

Daryl gestured toward the door with her thumb. "Molly's

getting all worked up about Tony leaving her out in the cold, and baby Kelly's got a good temper tantrum going so Molly's in no mood to be mollified."

Tony pointed at her. "Mollify Molly. That's a good one."

"Since I'm the 'former flame,'" Daryl said, giving Tony an icy stare, "I took the brunt of her wrath."

He shrugged. "She loves to shop, so I decided to give her some time while I caught part of the game."

"Well," Daryl continued, "to quote Mad Molly"—she pinched her voice into a scratchy, witchlike tone—"'I can't believe he would leave me with Kelly for so long! He knows I can't handle her when she gets like this.'"

Tony scowled, his cheeks turning red. He grabbed a coat from a nearby table and shoved his arms through the sleeves. "I'll talk to her."

He jerked open the door and stomped down the stairs to the snowy sidewalk. The snowfall had eased up, leaving only a few straggling snowflakes swirling here and there.

Nathan followed close behind, motioning for the others to keep up. No matter what happened with Tony and Molly, they had to hurry. Two worlds needed saving, and the zone police, whatever they were, might find them at any minute.

Amber rushed ahead and grasped Tony's arm. "There is disharmony in your spirit," she said as she shivered in the cold breeze. "Wait for the music to balance before you speak."

Tony stared at her, his eyes bulging. "Who's the glowing girl?" he asked, looking back at Nathan. "One of your friends from the future?"

"Not exactly. She's—"

"She's right." Kelly stepped forward and nodded toward the van parked only a dozen or so paces away. "Molly's probably in no mood to hear how you wanted to let her shop. All she knows is that she was trapped in a snowstorm with a crying baby while you were at a bar watching basketball."

Tony eyed the van. "So what do I tell her?"

Kelly looked at Nathan, Daryl, and Amber, then gazed into Tony's eyes. "Tell her you're sorry. Tell her you won't let it happen again." With snowflakes gathering on her eyelashes, tears began streaming down her cheeks as she continued in a trembling voice. "Tell her it was a big mistake and that you love her with all your heart, that you'll never let sports come between you and her ever again, and that you'll help her learn to deal with a crying little girl who needs both her mother and her father very, very much."

Tony raised his brow, his eyes darting from Kelly to Amber to Nathan, then back to Kelly again. "I can do that."

Amber caressed Tony's shoulder. "Dance with her music, and she will be able to hear yours. Only then can harmony overcome discord."

"Dance with her?" Tony looked at Amber's trembling hand for a moment, then sighed. "I think I know what you mean."

"Tell you what," Nathan said. "Why don't you and Molly ride in your truck and follow us to the Interfinity Labs observatory? When we get there I'll explain everything about us coming from the future. And I'll tell you more about those mirrors in the back of your truck."

Tony glanced at the pickup. "You seem to know about everything, don't you?"

"Being from the future has its advantages."

Tony touched a cell phone on his belt. "Can Flash get in on this? He's in town, and he's been talking about this stuff for weeks."

"Sure. Call him and ask him to meet us at Interfinity Labs with Francesca. I'm sure he can find it."

"Interfinity Labs. Gotcha."

Nathan pointed at Tony's phone. "Can I get your number in case I need to call you?"

"Sure thing." Tony pulled a wallet from his back pocket and

fished out a business card. "It says 'Office Phone,' but that's my cell."

"Thanks."

"Can I see that?" Daryl asked.

"The card?" Nathan gave it to her. "Sure."

Daryl glanced at the information and handed it back to him. "I like to memorize numbers."

"That's all the time you needed?"

"Sure." She gave him a wink. "And I love pi. I have it memorized to a thousand places."

"I think I'll stick to cherry pie." Nathan stuffed the card into his pocket. "Stay close, Tony. It could be tough to follow in this weather."

"Not a problem. I have four-wheel drive." Tony strode to the van and opened the side door. He helped Molly step down to the sidewalk, careful to keep one of his large hands under baby Kelly. Arching over Molly and whispering into her ear, he guided her across the slippery sidewalk. Her face, tight and tense at first, relaxed as they approached the truck.

Nathan opened the van's front door for Daryl, then stood by the back with his hand out for Kelly. "Let's get going. It sounds like my Earth Yellow father's been busy keeping this world from going crazy, but we still have a lot to do."

"I will go with Tony and Molly," Amber said, touching Nathan's arm. "Their music is not yet fully in harmony."

Nathan shrugged. "Okay. It looked like there was room in the front for three."

Amber flashed a smile. "The closer she sits to him, the better for the blending of their music."

Once everyone was seated—Daryl in front and Nathan's mother, Nathan, and Kelly in the back—Gunther shifted into gear and drove away, keeping his eye on the rearview mirror. "Tony's right behind us, and he's already on his cell phone."

"Perfect," Nathan said. "Now we can talk about what's going on."

His mother touched his knee. "I heard Tony mention Flash. That's your father ... I mean ... well, you know what I mean."

"I know. We're hoping he'll come to the observatory. Apparently he's put a stop to the next-day dreaming, at least for a lot of people, so he must have a handle on what's going on." Nathan looked at Gunther. "Tony says pretty much only travelers have dreams now. I guess we should be grateful you're one of them."

"I'm just glad the weather kept the zone police from hunting us down." Gunther turned onto a narrow back road and sped up, taking advantage of the lack of traffic as a strangely warm sun broke through the clouds. "They caught me once and did some tests to determine that I'm a traveler." He tapped the back of his skull. "They implanted this tracking device, and if I go outside of my zone it sounds an alarm somewhere. If that happens, these police dressed in army fatigues swoop in like a SWAT team in camo. If they catch a wayward traveler, they have the authority to shoot him on the spot, but usually they just use torture to get him in line. First, they zap you with these sonic rods, then they—"

"Sonic rods?" Nathan spread his hands two feet apart. "Are they this long, as thick as a policeman's nightstick, and make a sound that'll split your skull?"

"That's them. How did you know?"

Nathan arched his back, recalling the pain he'd once received from a paralyzing rod. "I got zapped by one."

"Hurts like crazy, doesn't it? Anyway, if you're a traveler who hasn't been implanted, they fingerprint you, register you as a traveler, and send you to a deprogramming camp where they do the surgery. And it's a particularly nasty deal. The chip is booby-trapped with a tiny bomb. If I got my own surgeon to take it out, it could go off, and my brains would be scrambled eggs."

"Whoa!" Nathan said. "That's awful!"

"Yeah, not so good for travelers, but everyone else is doing a lot better. Solomon and Francesca worked with the two Dr. Simons to cook up this megacool way to stop the dreams, and just about everyone is participating. People are clueless about the existence of other worlds, but since they're tired of knowing the future, and since it keeps Mictar from sneaking in and dream-snatching their souls, they're going along with Solomon's plan.

"So now Zelda's getting desperate. She had enough entrenched influence to hang on to her power, but she's losing her grip. Her henchmen aren't so quick to obey her commands, and even travelers like me are getting bolder. Without Mictar literally scaring people to death, she'll be history in no time."

"Don't be surprised if Mictar makes a comeback," Nathan said. "He had a little run-in with a mirror, so that might have kept him away for a while."

"I heard about that. Nice going. I wouldn't mind taking a mirror to that creep myself." Gunther glanced over his shoulder and gestured at a duffle bag lying on the floor. "By the way, I thought you guys might be hungry, so I brought some crackers and stuff. Help yourselves."

Nathan rummaged through the bag and passed around the food. As he handed Daryl an apple, he asked, "So what's going on back home?"

Daryl planted an elbow on her armrest. "Before I lost contact with Dr. Gordon, he said news reports were buzzing about sound waves getting bent out of shape. It started with mid-range musical notes. If someone played a middle C on a piano, it didn't sound right, like the frequency got warped in the air. Then it spread to all sorts of sounds, and finally it killed analog radio and TV broadcasts. At least that's what Dr. Gordon thinks, since he couldn't get any reception."

"And then you got cut off from him."

"Yep. Just before it happened, I asked Dr. Gordon to call my father to let him know I'm all right, but I'm not sure he understood. Even his voice sounded weird, like he was doing whale-speak—you know, long, moaning notes, like Dory when she talked to the whale in *Finding Nemo*. I suggested that he switch to digital encoding, but I don't think he heard me."

"So Earth Red people probably can't talk to each other."

"That's my take, unless they all learn whale-speak."

Nathan blew out a sigh. It was like the Tower of Babel all over again. The world would be in chaos soon, if it wasn't already.

He turned toward Kelly, but she showed no sign of concern. Her mind seemed far away, and a sweet smile made her face seem to glow. He smiled back. No doubt defusing the bomb, as she had put it, gave her reason to celebrate. Maybe Kelly Yellow would have a better life than she'd had.

After they drove out of the city and onto a narrow country lane, Gunther glanced back and forth between the mirror and the road. "We've got trouble."

4

TO DANCE OR DIE

Daryl turned around and looked out the back window. "Zone police?"

"Looks like we picked up two of them," Gunther said.

Nathan swiveled in his seat. A pair of red cars with gold racing stripes and flashing lights roared up from behind, splashing through the fast-melting snow. One blared a horn as it passed Tony's pickup and pulled within a few feet of Gunther's bumper.

"What're you going to do?" Nathan asked.

Gunther pressed the gas pedal, making his engine whine. "I can't outrun them, not in this hay baler, but I'm not about to get shot or stunned by those sonic rods." He nodded toward the back. "Open the hatch. I have a surprise for them."

While Nathan climbed toward the rear, Gunther continued. "Daryl, look under your seat and get the first-aid kit."

Daryl bent over. "For what? To bandage your brain when it explodes?"

Nathan opened the rear hatch, swinging it out and up, and hustled back to his seat.

"It's a fake kit," Gunther said. "I keep a gun inside."

"You're going to shoot them from the driver's seat?" Daryl slid out a white metal box, withdrew a short, fat-barreled pistol, and squinted at it doubtfully. "You'd be better off with a good blaster at your side, kid."

Gunther took it from her. "It's a sound-wave gun Solomon and I invented. It neutralizes a sonic rod, but since there are two zone cops, I can't stop them both if they use different frequencies."

Nathan looked back again. One of the police cars shifted to the left lane and eased closer, its lights flashing and siren blaring as it pulled up to their side. The other car drew so close behind the van, the driver's gaunt face and pale complexion became clear.

"It's a stalker!" He glanced at the car to their side. That driver and a man in the passenger seat also looked just like stalkers from the misty world.

The window of the car to their left zipped down. The passenger, his lips thin and firm, pointed a sonic rod at Gunther. A blue light flashed on at the tip, and an ear-piercing shriek ripped across the rushing air and into the van.

Gunther cringed. Keeping one hand on the wheel, he pointed his gun at the pale-faced officer and pulled the trigger. A loud bass tone roared from the barrel. As it melded with the sonic rod's wall of sound, the combined noise shook the van, rattling the frame, but the painful shock waves no longer scrambled their brains.

Another shriek blasted through the open hatch, higher-pitched and louder. Nathan clapped his hands over his ears. His mother and Kelly did the same, while Gunther kept his gun trained on the first officer, his jaw trembling as he grunted through his words. "Have to slow down before this tin can breaks into pieces!"

"Want me to close the hatch?" Nathan asked.

"Not yet. I might have to aim back and forth between these two and hope for the best."

The van slowed to thirty miles per hour. Tony's truck and the two stalker vehicles matched its pace, maintaining their positions at the side and rear.

"Call Amber!" Kelly shouted. "Maybe she can neutralize the other rod!"

Daryl reached over and unclipped the phone from Gunther's belt while Nathan fumbled in his pocket for Tony's business card. "Don't bother," she said. "I know it."

With the van shaking so hard his teeth ached, Nathan watched Daryl punch the numbers in from memory. With her own teeth clenched, she held the phone to her ear and waited. Nathan looked back again. Tony had pulled his pickup alongside the squad car trailing Gunther's van, and all three front-seat passengers came into clear view. Amber's expression was serene, but Molly and Tony both looked tense as Tony pressed the phone against his cheek.

"Tony!" Daryl shouted. "Ask Amber if she can cancel the other rod."

Lowering the phone for a moment, Tony turned to Molly and Amber, moving his lips while keeping a tight grip on the wheel. Two seconds later, Amber's head emerged from the passenger window, her bright yellow hair whipping in the wind.

"She has to do what?" Daryl yelled. "You've got to be kidding!"

"What?" Nathan asked.

Daryl pulled the phone away from her ear and looked back. "Sounds like she's going to do an Indiana Jones!"

Nathan's mother and Kelly crawled into the cargo area with Nathan and stared at the pickup. Amber, the sleeves of her dress beating against her arms, climbed out the window. She sat on the frame for a moment, then stretched her arms over the roof and grasped the back edge. She pushed up to her feet, and, with the grace and power of an Olympic gymnast, swung her legs to the top of the bed cover. The officer, still aiming his sonic rod at the van, stared at her, his eyes wide.

Now standing, Amber raised her hands. As her hair blew across her face, she took in a breath and sang a note as low and loud as a ship's foghorn. Like a battering ram, her song plunged into the rod's wall of sound, counteracting the horrible noise.

The officer withdrew his sonic rod and extended a pistol, pointing it at Amber. His hand shaking, he fired a shot. With a deft turn, Amber angled her body to the side, dodging the bullet.

Nathan grabbed the cell phone. "Tony! Back off! The stalker's shooting at Amber!"

"And leave you to face the zone police?" Tony shouted. "No way! Besides, she's got it under control."

"Yeah, but—"

"Duck!" Tony pushed Molly's head down. The gun fired again. The window on Tony's side shattered, sending glass flying. The stalker shifted his aim toward the van and shot a third time.

"Arrgh!" Nathan's mother dropped to her back, clutching her wrist. Blood poured from her left palm and streamed down her arm.

"Mom!" Nathan threw himself down beside her.

"Mrs. Shepherd!" Daryl called from the front. "Are you all right?"

Grimacing, Nathan's mother pressed her fingers against a tear in the side of her hand and called out, "It's just a flesh wound."

"This is no time to do a Monty Python routine!" Daryl searched the area around her seat. "Do we have a real first-aid kit anywhere?"

While Daryl searched frantically, Nathan glanced at the scene behind him. The stalker aimed the gun again, this time at Tony. Amber set one foot on the truck's side wall and leaped for the police car. She seemed to float across the gap, her dress fanning out as she stretched toward the roof. Landing feet first, she spun 180 degrees on her toes, then slipped and fell to her belly, latching on to the window frame just in time to keep from sliding off the passenger side. While holding the frame with one hand, she grabbed the stalker's wrist with the other. His fingers straightened into rigid lines, and the gun clattered to the road.

The car decelerated and dropped back. Still keeping his sonic gun trained on the other officer, Gunther slowed to stay close.

As Amber rose to her feet, she jerked the stalker out through the window and planted the tall, thin man upright on the roof. The driverless car rolled on, swaying from side to side, but not enough to knock the glowing supplicant off her feet. She radiated bright yellow streams of light as the stalker dropped to his knees and folded his hands as if begging.

Gunther eased the van to a stop, allowing the trailing car to press against his bumper until it stopped as well. The other police car roared away.

Amber set a palm on top of her captive's white hair. As she drilled her stare directly into his eyes, she sang a high-pitched note. His jaw dropped open. His eyes bulged. Then his cheeks sank and his body withered, his shirt slipping off his shoulders as he seemed to age at high speed.

Nathan got up and leaned out the back hatch. "Amber! No!"

She turned toward Nathan, her eyes ablaze in yellow. The stalker heaved in rapid, shallow breaths, spitting out short, pathetic vowel sounds.

"Spare me, O mighty supplicant," Kelly translated as she leaned out with Nathan. "Forgive me of my many transgressions against you."

Amber moved her hand from his head, sweeping a shower of white hair to the roof of the car. Now smiling, she reached for his hand and sang a burst of notes.

"Will you dance with me?" Kelly said, again translating. "I will provide the music."

With his hands still folded and his chest heaving, the stalker forced out a halting lament. Kelly gave each note its meaning the moment it passed his lips.

"I beg you, holy one. Spare me, and I will fight against my brethren." His eyes wide within his sunken face, his voice shook wildly. "But I cannot dance with you. One such as I could never be your partner in dance."

She gazed down at him, love bathing her expression as she crooned a musical reply.

This time Kelly swallowed hard before she translated. "You have always had the ability to dance with me, and I will gladly be your partner, but if you refuse, I will have to kill you."

The stalker closed his eyes and wailed. Again, Amber responded, this time with a lengthy reply. Nathan looked to Kelly for the meaning, but she just shook her head, tears glistening in her eyes.

Amber laid her hand on the stalker's head again and reprised her song. His limbs stiffened. His clothes dropped away; lines now etched his skin, making a patchwork of decaying flesh until it flaked away from his skeleton-like body. Soon, he crumbled into a heap of dust.

As a breeze carried the dust away, Amber let her shoulders sag. She watched the pile dwindle for a moment before walking down the windshield and jumping to the pavement.

Kelly clutched Nathan's hand. "What ..." She swallowed hard again. "What *is* she?"

"I wish I knew," Nathan replied, keeping his voice low. "We saw that the stalkers feared the supplicants. Now we know why."

Daryl let out a long whistle. "I'll tell you one thing. If Amber asks me to dance, I'll be ready to rumba."

Amber walked toward the truck, head down, a tear tracking down her cheek. Inside, Molly rolled up the window and punched the door lock, her eyes wide with alarm. Amber halted.

Tony's voice pierced the silence. Nathan lifted the cell phone to his ear, keeping his stare on Amber. "Sorry, Tony. I couldn't hear you. What did you say?"

"Molly's scared to death." His voice was low and shaky. "Can Amber ride with you?"

Nathan waved at her. "Hop in the van," he said, speaking through the open hatch. "There's plenty of room."

Kelly opened the side door. "I'll get Molly calmed down. I know what usually worked with my mother." She jumped out and hurried toward the truck, pointing at the van as she passed by Amber. With a smile and a wink, Kelly said, "Keep an eye on Nathan for me while I'm gone."

The shining supplicant nodded and shuffled toward the door.

Nathan helped his mother up and guided her to the bench seat. "How's your hand?"

After sliding all the way to the side window, she peeled her bloody fingers away from her ripped hand. The pressure had temporarily closed a gash an inch or two below her little finger, but blood still trickled. "It's not too bad, but it looks like neither one of us will be able to play for a while."

Nathan tried to rip his sweatshirt sleeve, but it was too strong. "Got a knife, Gunther?"

"Yep. It ain't much, but it's sharp."

A small pocketknife landed in Nathan's lap. While he sliced his sleeve, Amber climbed into the van, her blonde hair in a frenzy. Nathan slid closer to his mother to make room. What should he say to Amber? What *could* he say? Sure, that stalker was out to get them, but did she have to kill him? And he even begged for mercy before she disintegrated his body.

As she settled onto the seat, he cleared his throat. "Uh ... I see why those other two stalkers took off like that."

She turned toward him. The fire in her eyes had vanished. "Yes." Her voice was little more than a whisper. "They were surely frightened."

After Nathan cut a wide strip from his sleeve and wrapped his mother's hand, Gunther put the van into gear and eased ahead, his acceleration slow. He and Daryl kept their gazes forward, saying nothing.

Nathan's mother broke the silence. "I don't understand. Why did you insist that he dance with you?"

Amber looked at the truck behind them. "Did the interpreter not tell you? I told the stalker, though he already knew. I explained my actions for your benefit."

"I guess she thought it wasn't important," Nathan said.

"Not important?" Amber glanced back again, then took Nathan's hand. "The explanation is vital, especially for Kelly's sake. You see, the three Earths once danced together in a cosmic waltz, in perfect balance and harmony. When dissonance shattered the harmonic structure, the worlds bent away from the dance and into a collision course. Playing the violin in Sarah's Womb will restore the balance, but since you were unable to finish the song, only one world broke free from the converging path. But Earth Red now has no dance partner. It spins alone and is suffering, because it cannot comprehend the music."

"What exactly is Sarah's Womb?" Nathan asked. "And what does spinning alone do to Earth Red?"

She formed her hand into a loose fist and slowly expanded her fingers. "Sarah is the great emptiness, the void that pushes the worlds apart, like a barren womb that is filled with heartache."

"So is it a buffer?" Daryl asked. "Like insulation?"

"In a manner of speaking. Yet she offers more than insulation. Just as when the biblical Sarah's womb was filled with a child of promise, when the cosmic Sarah is filled with perfect song, she gives birth to harmony that pushes the worlds into their proper paths, the paths they must follow to stay away from destruction."

"If it's song Sarah wants," Nathan's mother said, "why did Scarlet's sacrifice make any difference at all?"

"We supplicants represent the elements that make up perfect music. Although we all have the gift of song, Cerulean is the master of musical notes, Scarlet is the mistress of words, the lyrics of the psalms, and I"—Amber set a finger on her chest—"I am the mistress of dance. When Scarlet fell into the void, Sarah was filled with only part of what makes for perfect song. Perhaps Earth Red is safe from interfinity's reach, but with no dance partner she labors in toil."

Daryl slid to the edge of her seat. "So that must be why everyone is messed up on Earth Red. You know how dreams kind of fool you sometimes? You think you're awake, but you're not quite sure?"

"Yeah," Nathan said. "It's only when you're really awake that you know for sure that you aren't dreaming."

"Exactly. But Dr. Gordon says on Earth Red, they're *never* sure, even when they're awake. When they get out of bed, it feels like they woke up from a dream inside a dream, and they're still dreaming, or maybe they just had a dream inside a dream inside a dream. Dr. Gordon says it nearly drives you crazy, and you're afraid to really go to sleep, because it feels like you might drop into a lower level of sleep, and you'll have to add another awakening to get to full wakefulness." She set a finger near her temple and drew fast circles. "They're all going nuts."

"Their world needs to dance," Amber said. "It restores balance and brings light to darkness. If that stalker had agreed to dance with me, he would have come into harmony with my purpose."

As Nathan looked out the rear hatch, the image of the pleading stalker came back to his mind. "But he said he couldn't. He seemed to think he wasn't worthy."

She nodded sadly. "That is the way of the faithless. Whenever someone dances with another, he is saying that he agrees with every aspect of his partner's purpose—the partner's beliefs and the principles by which he or she lives. When dancing, the partners move with each other step by step, symbolizing that they will never stray from one another in thought, word, or deed, not even for a moment.

"Most of the stalkers have no faith that such a perfect dance is even possible, and they think that anyone who would even try to dance with a supplicant will be accursed. Yet they do not realize that a supplicant's song provides the music that guides every step, empowering them to perform the very dance they fear."

Nathan looked at his mother and Daryl in turn. Each one stared at him, as if waiting for him to ask more questions. Yet, there really was only one more question on his mind. "How much of that explanation did Kelly hear?"

"I had only a little time to explain, but she heard that dance is the symbol of submitting to the greater purpose, a humbling of ourselves in order to move in step with the greater music."

"So do both dancers humble themselves?" Nathan asked.

Amber gazed at him, her eyes bright, though she spoke in a somber tone. "If the music is greater than that of both partners, each one gives up his own path to follow the music's universal call."

Nathan gave her a nod, but he was glad when the cell phone in his lap chimed, giving him an excuse to turn away from those eyes. He handed it to Gunther and settled back in his seat.

"Hello," Gunther said. "Yeah, Tony. I think there's a station in a couple miles. We can stop."

Nathan leaned toward his mother. Heat from Amber's body radiated into his, sending mixed sensations; both the soothing warmth of a protective friend and the chilling ice of the unknown. He glanced at her out of the corner of his eye. She stared straight ahead, her lovely face still exuding a golden glow. As he let his gaze linger on her gently curving throat, a placid hum emanated from within her, a melody that was all too familiar — "Foundation's Key," the piece he had tried to play on the strings that spanned Sarah's Womb. The tune fit her perfectly — simple, yet powerful ... lovely, yet frightening.

Yes, this woman was a mystery, a deep, dark mystery.

When they stopped for gas, Kelly hurried to the van and opened the door. "Amber," she said, "would you be willing to switch again? Molly wants you to ride with her now. She's sorry for being so scared."

Amber's smile seemed to melt her somber mood away. "Very well. I will be glad to."

As soon as Amber climbed out, Kelly jumped in and scooted close to Nathan. "This is all so cool," she said, keeping her voice low. "Tony and Molly are like lovebirds right now. He's sweet talking her, and she's eating it up."

"Yeah," Nathan said, "that *is* cool."

Letting out a sigh, she slid her hand into his, intertwined their fingers, and leaned against his shoulder. He tensed his muscles and glanced at his mother, but she just smiled and took his other hand, weaving her fingers into his in similar fashion.

Nathan sighed, content. There was no doubt about it. Dancing in harmony was very cool.

After a moment or two, a pang of doubt pierced his reverie. As if following the path of a sweeping flood, Francesca Yellow's voice pushed into his mind, the last words she spoke before returning to her world. *Just be sure to tell Kelly why Nathan Shepherd is who he is. Remember, your talents are a gift, not a birthright.*

Soon, her voice passed away in ever quieter echoes. The scent of roses pushed into his nostrils, and a bittersweet film coated his tongue, a sign that Scarlet's presence had again emerged. From where, he had no clue. But no doubt her eloquent words would follow.

Seconds later, a melody drifted across his mind as if played on the strings of a vibrant violin. Scarlet's voice, soft as a whisper at first, rose to join the song, rising and falling with the cadence of each lilting phrase.

So now I leave a gift sublime,
The poet's flair for words and rhyme;
A smell, a taste, you'll know I'm near;
Unbidden words will soon appear.

And then another gift I'll bring
To add to hymns your heart will sing;
For songs of love deserve reply,
A dance that lasts until you die.

A day will come when love mature
Will take the hand of one made pure
In everlasting song and dance,
A knight, a lady, sweet romance.

The words seemed to hang in the air. Nathan breathed in the song, freshening the flowery aroma. Kelly had sung that poem while they returned from Sarah's Womb, just moments after he had thrown Scarlet's dead body into the pit. Now it revived the painful truth that so much still separated Kelly from him ... too much.

He glanced at her. What had she thought of the words while she sang them? She must have known what the everlasting dance implied, but did she understand all that Amber had explained? Or did she know only what dance symbolized, that as they listened to the music from on high, they had to play in harmony, each with a unique instrument, guided by the conductor's baton as they submitted to a holy score?

And now she had taken his hand. What did that gesture mean to her? Did she want to dance with him? If so, what would it mean to her? Was she hoping to join him in everything he held dear? Even his faith?

He closed his eyes. It wasn't the right time to ask questions. She had offered a touch of friendship, so he just had to relax and enjoy it. The time to talk it all out would surely come later.

A gentle squeeze tightened his fingers from Kelly's side. He opened his eyes, meeting her piercing gaze.

"Is something wrong?" she asked.

Her voice was like a haunting melody—reaching, probing. Her gift had already interpreted a thousand silent messages, and now she sought out one he had hidden for far too long, though he couldn't explain why.

"Yeah," he finally replied. "Something's wrong."

She tilted her head, her eyebrows lifting. "Well, what is it?"

"Ask me later." He settled back in his seat again and closed his eyes. He had to escape her penetrating stare. "When we're alone."

She slipped her fingers away from his. "I'll wait." Her voice dropped to a whisper. "As long as it takes."

Gunther maintained a steady speed and frequently checked his rearview mirror, apparently watching Tony's progress and keeping watch for anyone else who might be following. After that brush with the zone police, there was no telling when or if the two stalkers in the first car might pick up their trail again, maybe with reinforcements.

After sporadic conversation about recent events, including Mictar's Lucifer machine and how he would probably get it re-energized, they pulled into the parking lot of the observatory.

Nathan gazed out the window. As expected, it looked exactly like the observatories on Earths Red and Blue, including bronze block letters on the front brick wall that spelled out "Interfinity Labs." The company apparently never took the name StarCast as it had on Red and Blue. Since Simon Yellow already knew what the observatory would become and how to contact Blue and Red, he probably persuaded the Dr. Gordon of this world to bypass the original moniker.

Gunther pulled into a space in the first row of the nearly empty lot, and Tony parked his pickup alongside. Daryl jumped out first, followed by Kelly, Nathan, and his mother. They hurried around the van and joined Amber and Gunther, who were watching Molly gently lift baby Kelly from her place in the backseat.

Now wearing a gray sweater over her yellow dress, Amber leaned close to Nathan. "Tony allowed me to use his outer garment, but I have no need of it. Harmony has been restored."

"I heard. That's great news." Nathan looked up. With the sun shining through scattered clouds, the temperature had climbed quite a bit. The sky looked strange, more purple than blue, and hints of the atmospheric holes he had seen on Earth Blue speckled the canopy.

Kelly strode toward Molly. "May I hold her?" she asked, extending her arms.

"She's almost asleep." Molly passed her bundle to Kelly. "I gave her a bottle in the car, then Tony sang a few selections from an Italian opera. She seemed to like it."

As soon as Molly let go of her baby, she reached for Tony. The two clasped hands and gazed at each other lovingly. "He has a soothing voice, you know."

Kelly nodded, tears welling in her eyes. "I remember. I mean, I could tell." She pushed the baby's blanket to the side and stared, mesmerized.

Nathan sidled up to Kelly and looked at the drowsy little girl in her arms. With delicate pink skin, dainty eyelids, and a button nose, she seemed like a tiny angel, as vulnerable as she was beautiful. He let his gaze wander to Kelly's face and combed across her features—the same nose, to be sure, but her skin had changed, tougher now with peach tones instead of pink. Still, the vulnerability remained, a girl wracked with pain—pain that her own life couldn't reflect the joy of the life she had arranged for the duplicate angel in her arms.

A tear streamed down Kelly's cheek, then another. Soon, she began weeping, her head bobbing as she clutched baby Kelly to her chest.

Nathan reached out a hand, but his mother spoke first. "Kelly? Are you all right?"

Tears still flowing, Kelly glanced at Nathan, but only for a second. She looked at his mother and nodded. "Can we talk?"

"Of course."

Kelly sniffed and wiped a tear on her shoulder. "Let me collect myself first."

"Whenever you're ready."

Tony pulled a collapsible pink stroller from the back of his pickup and unfolded it. "Time for baby Kelly to test out her new wheels."

As Kelly laid the baby into the stroller, she looked up at Molly, her voice strained. "Why did you choose the name Kelly?"

"Well, Tony wanted a boy, and I wanted a girl, so we settled on a good Irish name that would work for either one."

Kelly buckled the baby in place. As she pulled away, she locked gazes with the infant. The pair of small orbs shifted to follow her twin's face, every movement seeming to bring awe and wonder to the tiny girl's mind.

Kelly took Nathan's mother's hand, and as the two strolled to another part of the parking lot a new sound rode across the air — a car motor, chugging as if missing a spark plug.

Nathan turned toward the lot's entrance. A sky blue Volkswagen Beetle lumbered in, a young man at the wheel. As he parked next to the truck, the woman in the passenger's seat came into view: Francesca.

Amber squeezed Nathan's arm. "My beloved!"

She stepped toward the car, but Nathan grabbed her hand and pulled her back. "She's never met you, has she?" he asked.

Amber looked at him, her brow wrinkling. "We have met in her dreams, but she will likely not remember."

"Then maybe it's better to wait a minute. You don't want to startle her." Just as Nathan released her hand, a nervous shiver buzzed along his skin. The driver had to be Solomon Shepherd, the Earth Yellow version of his father. Meeting him would be so strange ... maybe too strange.

5

SOLOMON YELLOW

Solomon, who appeared to be in his early twenties, helped Francesca out of the car and nodded at Nathan, as if to say, "I'll talk to you in a minute." He then folded down the front seat and lifted a baby from an infant carrier in the back.

After settling the baby in Francesca's arms, he strode toward Nathan, a big smile on his face. "You must be Nathan, my Earth Red son."

Nathan cleared his throat and extended his hand. "Yes, sir. I mean, yeah. That's me."

"Glad to meet you." Solomon shook Nathan's hand firmly. "We have a lot to talk about."

"We sure do." Nathan stared into Solomon's deep brown eyes, the same eyes that had watched over him for sixteen years. Or were they? Did those eyes reflect the wisdom that sixteen more years of life as a father would bring?

"Would you like to meet your twin?" Solomon asked, pointing over his shoulder with his thumb.

Nathan shoved his hands into his pockets. Solomon's voice and tone matched his father's exactly. "Yeah," Nathan said, shrugging his shoulders. "Sure."

"Only for a moment, though." Solomon's brow creased slightly. "We have a considerable amount of work to accomplish. As soon as I heard about your arrival, I arranged for the others to meet us here. We've been waiting for Tony to bring the mirrors from Scotland, so now we can carry out our tests."

Francesca joined them, carrying the blanket-wrapped baby in her arms. "Hello, Nathan," she said. "It's so good to see you again."

"Yeah." Nathan tried to hide a nervous swallow. With her raven locks flowing in the cold breeze and her smile as vibrant as it had been when he met her as a precocious ten-year-old, she was as beautiful as ever. Yet now, dressed in a long trench coat with the collar pulled high, she looked like a wife and mother, a flower in full blossom. "It's good to see you, too."

She placed the baby into his arms, helping him make a safe cradle. "I suppose you don't have to guess what we named him."

Nathan pushed the corner of the blanket out of the way, revealing little Nathan's face. With wisps of blondish hair protruding from the edges of a blue cap, thin lips pursing into a lax pucker, and a tiny nose wrinkling as he nestled into his protector's arms, this little one was as familiar as Nathan's own reflection, the living image of dozens of photos that adorned an album his mother always kept on her dresser.

Francesca touched a slight dimple in the baby's chin and grinned. "He looks just like you, Nathan."

Nathan's cheeks warmed. She was right, almost embarrassingly so. Would this child do everything he, himself, had done? Even the stupid things? "Yeah. I can see that. At least, I remember the pictures."

The baby squirmed, then whimpered. Nathan handed him back to Francesca. "When he turns six, he might give you a hard time about violin lessons, but don't listen to him."

As she laid the baby in a stroller, she winked. "Don't worry, son. I won't."

Gunther slapped the side of his van. "I'd better get going before the zone police track me down again."

"Where will you go?" Nathan asked.

He shrugged. "Anywhere but here. Maybe I'll find a shady spot to sleep." He jumped into the driver's seat and started the engine. "Just call if you need me." After giving everyone a wave, he drove out of the lot.

Solomon nodded at Tony. "Did you bring one of the mirrors?"

"Got it right here," Tony said, lifting a Wilson sports bag. "The others are locked in the back of my truck."

Nathan looked at the far side of the parking lot. His mother and Kelly were now walking back, still hand in hand. "I guess we'd better get going," he said. "It might take a while if we have to figure out the security codes."

"No need for codes." Solomon led the way, walking at a quick pace. "I called ahead. Both Dr. Simons are waiting for us, so the security doors should be deactivated."

Nathan looked back. His mother and Kelly were now jogging to catch up. "How long have you been working with the Simons?"

"For a while." Solomon opened the front glass door and held it, waiting for Kelly and Nathan's mother to arrive. For a moment he fell silent, and Nathan watched Solomon's eyes take in Francesca Red as she approached. He wondered what it would be like to meet your spouse from the future. He half expected them to start a conversation, but they only nodded at each other as Francesca and Kelly passed through the open door and into the spacious lobby.

Solomon cleared his throat and turned his attention back to Nathan. "We have been analyzing all the data, and we came up with a theory that might explain what's happening, but we need the supplicant to do something for us before we can test it."

While the others made their way inside, Nathan scanned the lobby, a room he had not yet visited. Polished terrazzo floors returned a skewed reflection of his body, and a huge crystal chandelier dangled about ten feet overhead. Earth-toned panels covered every wall, with photos of the observatory's groundbreaking ceremony hanging at precise intervals, their wooden frames matching the panels perfectly. He tried to make out the faces of the people in the gatherings, but they were too far away. "What about Gordon Yellow?" he asked. "Is he around to help?"

Again Solomon led the way, this time along a corridor to the right, another unfamiliar area. "Since Dr. Gordon is the founder of Interfinity Labs, he is here, but we haven't entrusted him with all we know." He stopped in front of an elevator, much bigger than the one in the secure area, and pushed the call button. "Since Gordon Blue chose the path of greed, we can't be sure Gordon Yellow wouldn't do the same. I'm afraid he has a poor temper at times, so I decided to watch him for a while."

A humming sound emanated from behind the double doors. Nathan eyed Kelly. Her firm chin revealed that her thoughts matched his own. Solomon was right. They couldn't risk Gordon Yellow teaming up with Mictar. The combination had proved fatal for Nathan and Kelly on Earth Blue, and the image of the vacant eye sockets in their limp bodies still seared his mind. This time, Gordon's unholy alliance with that vision stalker could mean the deaths of countless millions.

When everyone had piled into the roomy elevator car—Nathan and Kelly Red scrunching into one corner; Molly and Francesca Yellow pushing their strollers into the opposite corner, followed closely by Francesca Red, who couldn't seem to take her eyes off baby Nathan; and Daryl and Amber crowding the middle—Solomon squeezed in and pushed the floor button. "Although this observatory will seem familiar," he continued, raising his voice to compete with the elevator's humming motor, "the two Simons have worked with Gordon Yellow to make some important enhancements that will come into play very soon."

The elevator slowed to a halt, and the doors slid open, revealing a hallway. To their left, another door stood open, the tourist entrance to the telescope room. Directly in front of them on the opposite wall, two restrooms flanked a water fountain.

Tony pointed at the men's room. "Mind if I go? I only had one beer, but that ride was enough to scare the—"

"Tony!" Molly scolded. "Not in front of the baby!"

"Oh, yeah. Right." He smiled sheepishly. "I forgot."

Solomon nodded at the door. "It would be a good idea for everyone to go. We have no way to know when our next opportunity will be. But let's hurry—interfinity won't wait for us."

Walking into the restroom behind Solomon, Nathan kept his eyes averted. He went through the motions at the farthest urinal while trying his best to be nonchalant and quiet. For some reason, being too familiar with this young version of his father seemed inappropriate, like he was prying into his father's past without permission.

After washing up, he hurried back to the hallway. Daryl had already returned, rubbing her hands against her sweatshirt. "No towels. The others are using TP, but that just seems wrong. That's reserved for ... uh ... other body parts."

When everyone had returned, Solomon led the way to the tourist entrance, marching well ahead. He peered through the doorway before waving for the others. "It looks like everything is ready."

Nathan glanced at Kelly and tried to transmit the mental question, *Ready for what?* With one eye narrowing as they neared the door, she seemed to have the same question.

As Nathan entered, light from the corridor faded. The telescope room was illuminated only by a candelabrum that sat on the floor near the telescope at the center. Flickering candlelight made the chamber seem like an underground cavern or a vestibule in an ancient castle—dark, cool, and mysterious.

He passed by a piano and hard-shell cases for cellos, at least three violins, and a viola. Apparently, they had been experimenting with various instruments.

With the mirrored ceiling reflecting only the flickering flames of six candlewicks, and the mounted telescope barely visible in the dancing orange glow, the place seemed an odd mix of medieval and modern, as if a caravan of mystified travelers had just strolled into King Arthur's court.

Nathan looked again. Something strange in the mirror caught his attention. The candles stopped flickering. His fellow travelers slowed to a halt, and every sound, even the quiet buzz of nearby computers, fell to silence. A sense of heaviness entered his mind—grave and foreboding.

Someone new appeared on the reflective ceiling; a tall, pale man with white hair, walking through the doorway they had just entered.

Nathan shifted his gaze down and looked at the door. As expected, Patar came into view. He weaved around Tony and Molly, his scowl not quite as deep as usual. "You don't seem surprised to see me, Son of Solomon."

"Not really. When everyone stops moving, I kind of guess you're around somewhere."

With a hint of mirth in his expression, Patar drew within a few feet and stopped. "I come only when you need a gentle push in the right direction."

"A gentle push?" Nathan rolled his eyes. "I'd hate to see one of your forceful shoves."

Patar's white eyebrows bent down. "If you continue ignoring my counsel, you might very well get the opportunity."

"But you said we had to go to the observatory to get to the misty world," Nathan said, spreading out his arms. "That's where we are."

"True, but the scientists here will not offer to send you to play the violin at Sarah's Womb. They have other plans, and they will reveal only what they want you to know."

"But what choice do I have? I can't tell them what to do with their own equipment."

"No, but you also do not have to follow their instructions. It is clear that you are mesmerized by Solomon Yellow's presence.

He is not your father, so do not allow him to tell you what to do. It is crucial that you follow my counsel instead." Patar folded his hands behind his back and strolled past Solomon, looking at his rigid face for a moment before circling back to the piano. He set his fingers on the keys, played a scale effortlessly, and turned to Nathan with a haughty air. "The fools know so little about real music. They have no idea that passion must enhance precision to open the portals."

Nathan pondered the strange words. "Why don't you just tell them what to do instead of freezing everyone and giving me orders?"

He played an irritating set of chords. "One of them has a mind to kill my people. His hatred for my race is so intense, trying to persuade him to be rational would be impossible."

"Okay," Nathan said. "I'll just have to take your word on that."

"These self-proclaimed scientists," Patar continued, "plan to transport you to the world of dreams, which fits well with my plan, because once you are there you may do as I tell you. You must find Cerulean's new charge and give to her the Earth Blue mirror you brought. In the gifted one's hands, Cerulean will be able to use it to send you where you need to go."

Nathan looked at Kelly, frozen in mid step only a couple of paces behind him. She carried the photo album she had picked up in her parents' bedroom, and the edge of the Earth Blue mirror once again protruded from the top.

"Who is Cerulean's new charge?" Nathan asked. "And will I be able to find her in the dream world?"

"I have not yet learned who she is, and we are not even sure that she is a she. We only know that a high voice calls for help from the dream world, so it could very well be a male child. In any case, Cerulean seeks for her there. If you find her, she could lead you to her real-world form, and you could give her the mirror."

"And if I don't find her, then what?"

Patar began another stroll, this time focusing on Amber. With her arms stiff and her glow dissipated, she looked like a normal girl. As he circled her, his eyes glistened and his lips softened; he looked like an old, sad grandfather. "In the dream world, there is a way to enter Sarah's Womb, though the violin is not within reach from that entry point."

Nathan kept his stare locked on Patar. Whatever he had in mind, it couldn't be good. Over and over, Patar had said to kill the supplicants, so his plans probably included taking that drastic action once they arrived.

"Look for a flaw in the wall of the dream world's central core," Patar continued. "It will take some effort, but Amber should be able to open it for you. Then ..." From behind, he grasped Amber's neck and lightly dragged his pointed nails across her throat. "You must slay this supplicant and cast her inside."

"Coward!" Nathan took a hard step toward him. "I've seen how powerful she is. You wouldn't dare talk about killing her if she wasn't paralyzed."

"Oh, how little you know." Frowning, he stepped away from Amber. "If she knew there was no other way to save the worlds, she would gladly give her life. This is the lesson that you cannot seem to grasp—true sacrifice, a love that allows no obstacle to prevent its fulfillment, whether in deed or in word."

"I know more about that than you think," Nathan said, but the words seemed to wither in the air. Did he really know what he was talking about? Had he really done everything he could in sacrifice?

He gazed into Amber's beautiful gold eyes. Even if he hadn't done all he was supposed to do, he could never kill this amazing girl. It was time to change the subject. "What about Mictar? Is he still alive? Do I have to watch out for him?"

"Oh, he is very much alive, and he is still quite able to kill all your friends." Patar reached out and touched Nathan's forehead with his finger, as if anointing him. "But you have no reason to fear him yourself. Just leave him to me. After what he did to Abodah, either I or one of our children must see that justice is carried out."

A whispered voice came from behind Patar. "Nathan?"

The stalker spun and backed out of Nathan's way, a slight tremble in his legs.

Amber blinked and moved her limbs stiffly. "There is a strange power here," she said. "I have not felt it in a very long time." After blinking again, she stared at Patar. "What are you doing here? Has the time to dance arrived so soon?"

Patar tightened his jaw, squeezing his words into tense bullets. "No, it is not the time. I did not intend for you to see me yet."

"When the time comes, will you be ready to dance with me?" She spread out her arms, now loose and graceful. "I will provide the music."

Patar dipped his head low. "As long as my brother lives, I cannot dance with you. No harmony can be realized until justice is served."

"You have spoken well." Amber's golden glow returned, casting her once again in a brilliant aura. "As always, there is no deception in your speech. Although I am not your supplicant, I will pray for your grieving heart."

He gave her a brief bow. "I am grateful for your kindness."

Amber's eyebrow arched up. "Perhaps when we meet again, harmony will have been restored, and the music in the air will guide your feet into the liberating dance."

"Perhaps." Patar bowed again, backed away three steps, and vanished in a column of mist.

Everyone in the room instantly continued moving. Kelly bumped into Nathan, nearly dropping the photo album. "Whoa!" she said as she repositioned her load. "Your brake lights must be out."

Nathan steadied her. "Sorry. We had another Patar event."

"We did?" She looked around, her eyes wide. "What did he want?"

"Same as usual." He glanced at Amber, who was now walking close to Francesca Yellow. "Need I say more?"

Kelly shook her head. "That creep needs a new song."

A shadow passed through the candelabrum's glow, short and hurried. Dr. Simon's voice penetrated the silence, its familiar British flavor sounding strangely appropriate. "Another intersection will come around in moments. An especially strong dream is within reach." Simon Blue's bespectacled face and nearly bald head appeared as he drew near. "We should prepare everyone immediately."

"Shouldn't we take the time to explain what we've learned?" Solomon asked.

"That can wait. This is only an experimental journey to see if we can monitor their activity and use the findings to calibrate the dream viewer. It should be short-lived, and we can explain when they return. We might not get another intersection for hours."

Solomon pressed his lips together and nodded. "I understand."

"Have you asked the supplicant about penetrating the veil?" Dr. Simon stared at Amber, fidgeting.

"We thought we would wait until the last moment to introduce the gifted one to her supplicant." Solomon took Francesca Yellow's hand. "It could be quite a shock."

"True enough." Simon glanced back into the darkness. "And have you told your wife who else is here?"

"Not yet." Solomon heaved a sigh. "I hope you're right about this. I'm uncomfortable with keeping secrets from her."

Francesca looked up at him, her expression curious and perhaps a little stung. "Secrets? What secrets?"

"You'll find out in a minute."

Nathan gazed at Francesca. The little girl he had known had changed. She was still sweet and lovely, but her face gave away a good deal of pain. Had married life dimmed her bright, precocious aspect?

"I expect that your decision will pay dividends," Simon Blue continued. "The emotional upheaval from both meetings will serve our purposes."

Solomon nodded toward the outer wall. "Turn on the engine. I'll make the introductions."

Dr. Simon waved toward the perimeter and called, "Begin the sequence."

Instantly, violin music poured from somewhere in the darkness—sweet, vibrant, and alive with joy. Nathan searched for the source of the lovely sound—Vivaldi's "Spring," one half of the arrangement he and his mother had performed so many times before. As he mentally played his part, his wounded fingers flexing slightly with each note, another man walked slowly into view, an older gentleman with wispy gray hair, large ears, and a kind, wrinkled face. With a violin tucked under his chin, he smiled as he stroked the strings with fervor.

Nathan smiled. It was Dr. Nikolai Malenkov, Francesca's adoptive father.

"Daddy!" Francesca leaped ahead, but Solomon held her back.

"I'm sorry, dearest one," he said, "but you must not approach him now."

Francesca pulled away. "Why? I haven't seen him in months."

"We are identifying your emotional energy signatures so the receivers can track you and Amber while you're in the dream world."

A new voice called from the outer wall. "Reception is excellent. The emotion waves match the predicted amplitude and frequency."

"Are you capturing the energy?" Solomon called. He turned

and addressed the others. "That's Dr. Gordon of Earth Yellow. I will explain in a moment."

"Yes," Dr. Gordon replied. "Now we need the counterbalance."

As the violin played on, Solomon reached for Amber's hand. "Francesca, I would like to introduce you to Amber, your supplicant, whom you have met in many lonely dreams."

Francesca turned toward Amber. "But I have never met—" Her eyes suddenly grew wide. As Amber's golden glow strengthened, Francesca stepped closer, her chin trembling. "I ... I *do* know you."

Amber raised a hand and touched Francesca's cheek, then crooned, her voice soft and lovely. "My beloved, I have guided you through troubled waters, both in dreams and in reality. To finally touch you and feel your love is my dream come true."

"I know." Francesca's voice quavered. "Why didn't I remember you until now?"

Amber brushed a tear from Francesca's cheek. "At the dawn of every day, you remembered my face, my song, my love, but the troubles of the waking hours would always push me into the periphery, a realm in your mind that you would revisit when you swept away the cares of the day and retired into slumber."

Francesca heaved a short breath. "I called you"—she licked her lips, her voice faltering—"I called you Sarah, my shepherdess."

"You heard that name whispered on the winds, for Sarah is the shepherd of the three worlds. She guides them in the cosmic dance."

"Wave forms are balancing," Dr. Gordon called. "We are nearing perfect harmony."

Solomon touched Amber's shoulder. "Will you open the dream gate for us?"

Her glow now pulsing, Amber glanced around the room. "For how many? I have never taken more than one."

Solomon reached for the candelabrum and pulled out one

of the long, slender tapers. "We need six, including you." He handed her the candle and reached for another.

"How do you know so much about this?" Francesca asked as he gave her the second candle.

Solomon withdrew a small notebook from his back pocket. "You talk in your sleep." He opened it toward the back and squinted at a page. "Now comes the dance, correct?"

Clutching the candle close to her chest, Amber looked at Francesca hopefully. "Do you remember the steps, my beloved?"

Francesca glanced at Solomon, then back at Amber. "The circle waltz?"

"Yes!" Amber's fingers tightened around her candle as she lifted to tiptoes. "I'm so glad you remembered!"

Francesca gave her a hesitating nod. "I think I can do it."

Amber turned to Solomon. "The music is not complete. We need the accompanying part."

Dr. Simon Yellow appeared from the dimness, extending a violin and bow. "It was exactly where you said it would be, Solomon."

Solomon gave Nathan a candle, then nodded toward Francesca Red. "Will you accompany Nikolai?" he asked.

She took the violin. "I can if I must."

"Is something wrong?" Solomon asked.

She raised her left hand, showing him her lacerated palm.

"Ouch. Okay, not a problem. My Francesca recorded every possible combination of interdimensional travel pieces, including each part of the duet. It's on Simon Blue's iPod."

"I'll play it through the speakers." Simon Yellow turned and hustled away.

"Amber," Solomon said, "will you be able to hear the music from the dream world?"

She nodded. "My sense of hearing works in both places simultaneously."

"Good." Solomon gave the final candle to Daryl. "As long

as the dream world is in sync with this one, Dr. Malenkov will continue playing. When he stops, it will be your signal to return. If we wait too long, it could be very difficult to come back. And, less importantly, our data could be ruined and the experiment would fail."

"I understand," Amber said. "Our purpose is not to find Solomon Red during this journey but to gather data."

Nathan counted the candles. One very important person wasn't carrying one. "Since my mother's not playing the violin, can't she come with us?"

"I suppose she can," Solomon said, extending the final candle toward her. "I had thought Gunther would come, but she can be number six."

"It would be better if she did not," Amber said. "There is an old song we supplicants know that says if two people from different worlds see each other in the dreamscape, Sarah's walls would be breached."

Nathan looked at her. "You mean the barrier between the dream realms?"

"Yes. The result would likely be catastrophic."

"Would it be like interfinity in the world of dreams?"

"Much worse, Nathan." Amber's lips turned downward. "Although it is only a theory we supplicants devised based on our understanding of energy fields, we believe Sarah's Womb would rupture, and the dream worlds would become barren and fly apart, possibly causing the real worlds to collapse as well. In trying to save the universe, we could become the cause of its complete destruction."

6

FELICITY

Nathan took a deep breath. "Well, I'm ready, if everyone else is."

"Good," Solomon said. "You have to enter the dream world as soon as possible, but you don't have to stay long this time. Once we have the data for calibration, we can send you on a longer journey to find your father."

Nathan gazed into Solomon Yellow's eyes. It seemed strange that he knew so much about events on Earths Red and Blue, but with Gunther and the two Simons getting him up to speed, it made sense. "Does that mean you aren't coming?" Nathan asked.

Solomon looked at the candle. As the flame on the wick burned higher, the yellow glow washed over his tense features. "I wasn't expecting to go. I have to consult with the others as the data stream comes in." He gave a nervous laugh. "Besides, you heard what Amber said. Suppose we run into Solomon Red. We wouldn't want to breach Sarah's walls, would we?"

Nathan took a step closer to Solomon Yellow and studied his expression. This man who looked so much like his father now seemed very different. His father would never seem so relieved to send his wife on a dangerous journey in his place. He would want to dive right in—boldly, bravely. He was a man so con-sumed with his mission that he often didn't consider himself at all, sometimes to his own detriment.

Setting his bandaged hand on Solomon's shoulder, Nathan tried to add just an edge of sarcasm to his voice. "It'll be hard, but I'm sure Amber will get us through okay. She's a brave girl."

Solomon didn't seem to notice. "Who will go in Gunther's place?" he asked, lifting his candle. "The group will need a bass voice."

"We have to sing?" Nathan felt a knot forming in his throat. "I'm a violinist, not a singer."

"Maybe you'll have to sing. Maybe you won't." Solomon handed Nathan the notebook. "Read about it here."

"I'll go." Tony stepped forward and took the last candle. As he caressed it, he nudged Solomon's ribs with an elbow. "Hey, Flash. Remember how all us guys used to serenade the girls back at the dorms? I sang the bass part with you. We weren't half bad."

Solomon laughed. "You're right. We were one hundred percent bad."

Dr. Gordon's voice broke through the violin music. "We're in perfect balance. I'm not sure how long it will last."

Solomon waved his hands. "Everyone who has a candle, make a circle around Amber and Francesca." He then kissed Francesca tenderly. "Don't worry about little Nathan. I'll take good care of him."

"I'm sure of that." She shed her trench coat, revealing a bright white blouse and a skirt that fell to her ankles. White and yellow daisies decorated the blue material, a pattern so lovely she seemed surrounded by a heavenly garden. Yet, with a cell phone clipped to her waistband, she looked like a high-tech flower girl. "And don't worry about me," she said. "I will be well cared for."

He stared at her for a moment, shifting his weight from one foot to the other. "Oh, yes. I'm sure you will."

While Nathan and the others gathered, Amber and Francesca stood face-to-face, about three feet apart, holding their candles at chest level. With the undulating flames flickering in their faces, their gazes locked. A light flashed in Amber's eyes, then in Francesca's, as if one pair of orbs had set the other aflame. Twin beams emerged, thin shafts of light that met at the center and blended, brightening as they touched. Then, as the violins played a crescendo, Amber swayed to her left, dipping first before rising again. Francesca matched with a sway to her right.

As Amber shifted from side to side, her every move reflected by her beloved, she opened her mouth and tilted her head up. Vowel sounds began to pour forth, warbling and echoing in the vast chamber.

Nathan's throat tightened. This had to be the most beautiful song ever sung. Yet, it was more than song; it was passion—pure emotion wrapped in a melody, an expression of love so untainted, it was as if Amber poured out her life energy, bleeding and dying for her beloved Francesca.

A hint of roses freshened the air—Scarlet's presence. Surely this was her song as well, an expression of love he never really understood until now. He could see the love of a supplicant in Amber's eyes, in the passion of her dance. Did Scarlet love him this much? Surely she did. Time and again she poured out her light to guide his way, turned danger from his path, and finally, she died to save his mother and had ultimately saved him as well.

Kelly slid her hand into his but said nothing. Still, her touch seemed to change Amber's song. The vowel sounds transformed into words, clear and resounding. Had Kelly's touch created this magic, or had Scarlet offered again the gift of lyrics?

My love is pure, my love is wild;
It longs to dance with heaven's child.
O let the music flow within,
The song of love that purges sin.

Amber joined her free hand with Francesca's, palm to palm, and they intertwined their fingers as they swayed on.

To dance with me is life from death;
To dance with me is reborn breath;
To join our hands, to meld as one,
Reflects our merging with the Son.

To supplicate is but a sign,
A portrait of your savior's mind.
His love for you, his gift to share,
Compassion bleeds in souls stripped bare.

Forgiveness flows in hearts of praise,
In eyes that choose the forward gaze.
Let partners lose what love has burned,
For love sets fire to pages turned.

So dance with me, forget the past,
Re-pour the mold, the die is cast;
The music burns the settled dross;
Our dance restores the deepest loss.

As the song began again, Nathan drank in the words once more, and this time he sang along. Kelly, too, joined in, as did Tony and Daryl. Somehow everyone in the circle knew the lyrics, though no one had ever taught them the song.

As pure ecstasy danced before his eyes, questions still nagged at his mind. What could the song and swaying dance mean? When Cerulean opened the dream gate in Earth Blue, he sang a song, and they stepped through a black hole that floated above Kelly's sleeping body. Now, however, no one slept, and this supplicant had her beloved in her presence. If Cerulean had been paired with Nathan Blue, would they have danced to open a path to the dream world? Or was Amber different somehow?

Nathan glanced at Kelly. Surely she heard every word. Did

she understand what Amber meant by merging with the Son? Could she comprehend what it meant to forget the past and burn the dross? Yet, some of the poem remained a mystery. What did "Eyes that choose the forward gaze" mean? And "Let partners lose what love has burned, for love sets fire to pages turned" was as cryptic as the untranslated vowel sounds.

With candles in hand, and their fingertips touching, the two dancers twirled, rising to tiptoes in time with the song's easy rhythm. As if brushed by loving hands, their hair flowed around them, black and gold fanning out with each graceful turn.

Nathan stared in awe. The image of a much younger Francesca came to mind. He had played "Brahms' Lullaby" while she swayed in similar fashion, a pixie ballerina in canvas shoes—a miniature model of the beautiful lady who now glided along the floor like a raven-haired angel. Maybe even back then she had danced with Amber in her dreams, storing these steps in the recesses of her mind.

Soon, their surroundings brightened. Above them, sunlight shone though a veil of clouds, making their candles seem feeble by comparison. A cold breeze whipped across their clothes, but it didn't affect the flames at all.

The music faded, and the song died away. As the last syllables tripped off Nathan's lips, he relaxed his muscles. For some reason, as beautiful as it had been, he was glad it had ended.

Tony patted his trousers pocket. "I have matches. Should we blow out the candles and light them later if we need them?"

Her smile unabated, Amber ceased her dance and released Francesca's hand. "We must keep the candles burning. Their light is the only connection we have to the real world. Nothing from the dream world will affect the flames, but we could extinguish them ourselves if we tried."

The golden glow in her eyes dimmed, and her voice lowered. "As you interact with the dreamscape, keep the flame close at hand. It is your anchor. The images here are figments—fabricated manifestations that display the fears of the faithless as well as the hopes of those who eagerly await the dawn. Whether for good or evil, they will draw you in. They will reach for your hearts, even reading your thoughts to see by what means they might capture your compassion." She gazed into each pair of eyes, her voice growing even more somber. "If you give in to their siren call, you could be trapped here forever."

Nathan stared at his candle's flame, conical and unwavering, a steady beacon, like a lighthouse signaling safe haven. If not for Cerulean, he would still be trapped in the world of dreams.

With the flame's image firmly seated in his mind, Nathan scanned the area, a playground in the middle of a park. Two swing sets, one with a tire swing, lined the right side. Sliced and shredded, the tire wobbled, dangling under rusted chains. Three broken seats hung by frayed ropes in the other set.

On the left side of the park, a wooden carousel spun lazily in the stiffening wind. Skeleton oaks stood here and there, the low-hanging branches dipping toward small tombstones that dotted a meadow of lush green grass.

Nathan shuddered. This wasn't a playground at all. It was a portrait of perdition—a child's worst nightmare. "I don't see anyone. Is there a way to find out whose dream this is?"

"Very odd." Amber looked through the candle's flame, blinking as she turned in a full circle. "This is not one of the usual blended dreams. It seems that at least two minds have created this children's cemetery and playground, and its borders are indistinct." She lowered the candle. "A new breed of blended dreams could be a very dangerous place."

Daryl hugged herself and shivered. "Well, if *you* think it's dangerous, then I'm ready to push the panic button."

"What do you think?" Kelly asked, touching Amber's hand. "Should we turn back?"

"Well, I think—"

"No." Nathan searched again for any sign of life. But even

if he did see someone, how could he tell if he or she might be Cerulean's gifted ward? "We're here for an important reason, so we should stick it out. Besides, I don't see anything to be scared of yet."

"Nathan is correct." Amber's smile wilted, and her eyes grew dim. "I, too, am a sojourner in the world of dreams. I always learn something new, so this revelation of a blended dream is not shocking ... Unsettling, to be sure, but not shocking." She lifted her candle. "As long as we hold to our anchors, we will be safe."

"What are you doing here?" a gruff voice called.

Nathan pivoted toward the sound. At a nearby sandbox, a small boy pushed a plastic shovel into the dark sand. Dressed in a miniature business suit, complete with a button-down shirt and a tie, he seemed half man and half child. He poured the scoop into a black bucket and glared at them, his short, curly black hair tossed by a foul-smelling breeze.

Setting a finger to her lips, Amber whispered, "Just you and me, Nathan. The others should wait here. We want to avoid too much sensory input."

Walking a little ahead of Nathan, Amber stepped into the sand with her bare feet and sat on the corner board of the sandbox. "What is your name, little boy?"

He scowled at her. "Who wants to know?"

"My name is Amber." She reached out to pat his hand, but he jerked it back. "Do you mind if I ask you some questions?" she asked.

Still scowling, the boy raised a pair of fingers. "You already asked two. How many more questions do you have?"

As Nathan edged closer, a stench drifted into his nostrils. He knelt and pinched the brown sand. He raised the sample to his nose. Dried manure? Surely this boy couldn't be the new gifted one, could he?

Amber laughed gently. "A few more questions. I will not weary you."

"Then out with them." The boy pushed the shovel in for another scoop. "I'm busy."

"I can see that." She touched a finger to her chin. "Again, what is your name?"

He kept his eyes down and answered with a sharp, "Frederick."

"May I call you Fred, or perhaps Freddy?"

His scowl deepened with each punctuated word. "My name is *Frederick*."

"Very well, Frederick. Have you seen a man you don't recognize, tall and broad shouldered?" She pointed at Nathan. "He looks like this young man, only older, with thicker arms."

Frederick glared at Nathan, patting down the manure in his bucket with hefty slaps. "Ask the others. No one ever stops to play with me, so I wouldn't know."

Amber cast a glance at Nathan, then turned back to Frederick. "Where may I find these others?"

He flipped over his bucket and pulled it up, leaving behind a castle of packed manure. "Hard to say." Keeping his head low, he gave his shoulders a casual shrug, though he glanced at her every few seconds. "Stick around. They'll come by eventually. They always do."

"From which direction?" Amber asked. "The little tombstones?"

He squinted at her. "What tombstones?"

For a moment Amber just stared at him, but she soon gave him a knowing nod. "I see."

"I thought you said no one plays with you," Nathan said. "What do the others do when they see you?"

Frederick lifted his head, but this time his expression softened. "They spit on me."

"Spit on you? Why?"

"I can't understand it." Frederick reached into a back pocket and pulled out a fat wallet. "No matter how much money I offer, no one will be my friend."

"Money cannot purchase friends," Amber said. "Only sycophants and flatterers would respond to such a call."

He scooped another shovelful of manure and muttered, "Another do-gooder."

Amber rose. "I have no further questions."

Nathan helped her step out of the sandbox, whispering, "What's the deal with the tombstones?"

"It's the blended dream. I believe Frederick is one of the sleepers, but the tombstones are not part of his dream. Someone else has conjured the cemetery."

"But no one else is around. Could he or she—"

Kelly's voice stretched out in the breeze. "Naaa-than. You'd better come and see this."

Nathan spun around. Backing toward him, the four others stared at a group of tombstones, six or seven ashen pillars arrayed in a broken circle. Gray mist rose from each, human-shaped, though warped and stunted.

Kelly clutched his arm. "What are they?"

As the mists gathered into small, deformed bodies, Daryl gulped. "Dead children?"

"Well," Frederick said with a snort, "they might remind you of children, but I'd keep my distance if I were you."

The bodies congealed, clarifying their features. A boy, his body bent and his limbs crooked, stood in front of the largest tombstone. Gathering around him in a semicircle, several others solidified—a girl, tall and slender, with deep cuts marring the underside of her forearms; another girl, this one gripping a crutch on one side that supported her one-legged frame; two other boys, apparently twins, each with pale skin and barely a wisp of hair blown about by the breeze; and two other girls in the back, one with a tattered shawl over her head and shoulders that covered a ratty mop of gray hair, and the other with a long scar that ran across the bridge of her nose. Wearing dark glasses and carrying a walking stick, she grabbed the fringe of the shawl of the girl next to her and shivered.

Nathan's throat tightened. These children were handicapped; they were—

"They're zombies," Daryl whispered. "Somebody's dreaming about zombies."

"Stay behind me." Tony spread out his arms. "If they're just kids, maybe I can scare them off."

Frederick snorted again. "Good luck."

A smile spread across the face of the lead boy. Circling around Tony, he limped toward Nathan, his arms flopping at his sides. "Excuse me, good sir. Would you please help us?"

Nathan glanced at Kelly and Amber, then at Frederick, who stood in his sandbox, gripping his shovel and pail as if they were weapons.

"Help you?" Nathan replied. "What do you need?"

The girl with the slashed arms joined them, wringing her hands. "Tell him nothing, Thibault," she said with a heavy Irish accent. "He is one of the ghosts."

Thibault nodded. "He's a ghost, all right, but he looks like the man who saved us from the pale one. What was his name?"

"He did not say," the girl said. "He was a snob, to be sure."

"Liar!" The girl with dark glasses hobbled forward, tapping her walking stick on the ground. She stopped in front of Nathan, sniffing the air through her blood-tinged nostrils. "Your voice carries Solomon's melody, and you bear his scent as well."

"Solomon?" Nathan reached for the girl but hesitated. "Do you know where he is?"

The girl, barefoot and smiling, groped for his hand and, finding it, latched on. "I am Felicity. Come with me. I will help you find Solomon."

"Nathan." Amber's call bore a warning tone. "She is a phantasm, a figment who will vanish with the dawn. Do not be taken in. Focus on the light of reality."

He lifted his candle and looked at Amber through the flame. Already she seemed less solid than before. "But maybe she's seen my father in her dreams. Shouldn't we at least find out what she knows?"

Frederick pointed at Felicity. "Don't trust her. She's the worst of all, a beggar with the bite of a serpent."

"Oh, Freddy," Thibault said, limping toward him, "you are such a pathetic soul."

Frederick stepped back into the sandbox, tightening his grip on his shovel. "Don't you dare!"

"Or else, what?" Thibault set a foot in the manure. "You should be used to this by now." The boy spat, sending a dark wad, black and bloody, shooting from his lips. It landed on Frederick's hair and spread across his scalp like reddish-black tar.

While Felicity hung on to Nathan's hand, the other children joined Thibault, spitting viciously. Wads of various colors flew toward Frederick. He flung his pail and shovel at them, then covered his head with his arms. "Get away, you monsters!" he cried pitifully. "Get away!"

"Leave him alone!" Nathan shouted. He took a step forward, but Amber pulled him back.

"Do not let his cries sway your resolve. You must stay anchored with me."

Nathan stared at Amber's glowing eyes. They passed back and forth between a pair of blurry orbs and her normal, crystal clear gems. "This feeling," he said, now wobbling in place. "It's ... it's something I can't seem to control."

"Your instincts are strong." Amber pushed his wrist, lifting his candle closer to his eyes. "You have been taught to help the suffering and the downtrodden, but you must realize that Frederick is a victim of his own fears. He is punishing himself."

With Felicity still quietly clutching his hand, Nathan looked back at the others. Kelly's mouth hung partially open, apparently in a hypnotic state, but she seemed far more solid than Amber.

As the cries grew louder, Nathan cringed. Tony, now fading into a ghostly blur, walked closer. He grasped Nathan from behind and propped him up. "Shake it off. The kid's a creep, some kind of money-obsessed adult who never grew up. He's not worth it."

Amber caressed Nathan's cheek. "On the contrary, my kindhearted friend, Frederick is worth your sympathy. But have no fear. He will likely wake up soon, and his demons will crumble to ashes."

Felicity tugged on Nathan's hand. "I'm real."

He looked down at her. With dark glasses covering her girlish face, and a cane propped against her narrow chest, she seemed so vulnerable, so lost and helpless. Was she the one he was looking for? But if she was just part of a dream, she couldn't really be Cerulean's new charge.

"You'll stay with me, right?" She sniffed, and her voice rattled. "Please don't go away like all the others."

"Don't listen to her, Nathan!" Amber's voice seemed distant, foreign. "She has seized your heart and will soon wring it like a sponge!"

Holding the candle with a shaking hand, Nathan concentrated on the flame. He had to fight this pull. All his life his father had taught him to be strong, to stay in control of his emotions, but his father had also taught him compassion, that every suffering person was worth sacrificing for—even wretched, overgrown children like the little brat in the manure pile, and especially a little blind girl who begged for rescue from a lonely cemetery.

Suddenly, Frederick screamed. Nathan jerked around but stayed put. The dark sand under the dreaming boy crumbled away, and he and Thibault fell into the void. Air swept into the hole, creating a cyclone that slurped the surroundings into its swirling grip. The swing sets tore from their moorings and flew toward them.

"Hit the deck!" Tony yelled.

Everyone dropped to the ground. Nathan pulled Felicity into his arms and crouched over her, still holding his candle as its undisturbed flame stood tall in the center of his vision.

As debris flew overhead, Daryl called out, "Shades of *Twister*!"

An oak tree flew past, then the carousel and several tombstones. One by one, five other children fell into the sweeping wind and disappeared in the dark vortex.

The vacuum jerked Felicity from underneath Nathan and dragged her toward the void. She fought back, sliding as she dug in with her toes. She reached toward Nathan with spindly arms and bony fingers. "Help me!"

Nathan lunged and grabbed her arm with his bandaged hand. "Hang on! I've got you!"

"Beware!" Amber shouted from her knees. "You can go with her, but I do not know how to bring you back. It is far too dangerous."

"But she knows where my father is!" Nathan looked into the pitiful girl's eyes. The wind had torn her dark glasses away, revealing vacant sockets. He swallowed a hard lump. Was she one of Mictar's victims?

Kelly crawled toward him, ducking her head to avoid flying branches. "She's just a dream, Nathan!" She held her candle close to his. Both flames burned steadily in the violent gale. "You have to let her go!"

Ripping pain shot up his arm and into his spine. "If she was just Frederick's dream," he grunted, "she wouldn't have known my father's name!"

Amber shouted again. "She probably knows something, but if

she is one of the dreamers, I cannot explain why the dreamscape is crumbling. Maybe she, too, is waking up. If so, she will be whole in mere moments, and her fears will vanish."

Nathan gritted his teeth. He had to hold on. He just had to. If Felicity was lucid enough to know his father's name, she had to be thinking clearly.

He looked back at the others. Tony clutched a metal rod protruding from the ground while holding Francesca in his arms. "Get a grip!" he shouted. "Your father wouldn't want you to take the risk!"

"To save the world?" Nathan strained to push out each word. "Maybe he would!"

Nathan, Kelly, and Daryl slid closer to the roaring black tornado. Felicity hung sideways, her feet pointing toward the cyclone and her long dress flapping. "Save yourself!" she called. "Let me go!"

Nathan's hand cramped. He couldn't hold on much longer. "Can you take me to my father?" he yelled.

After hesitating for a second, she closed her sockets and cried out, "I'm not sure! But I have met him!" Her voice seemed to pass through Nathan's body and into his ears. "If you come with me" — her sockets opened again, revealing a glimmer of light within — "I'll explain everything there."

Nathan rose to his feet, and, pulling Felicity against his chest, let his body slide toward the void.

Kelly grabbed a fistful of his sleeve and jerked him back. Her eyes flashing, she roared into his ear. "Listen to me! If you can't fight this dream world, you'll never find your father." She pried his bandaged hand away from Felicity's arm and pushed him toward Tony. The release made her stumble backwards and she fell into the rushing wind.

"Kelly!" Nathan lunged for her, but Tony held him back. As if swimming in a whirlpool, she fought against the cyclone, but it soon sucked her and Felicity into the black hole along with the remains of the dreamscape. Seconds later, everything vanished.

7

PASSION AND PAIN

With only their candles lighting the area, Nathan fell to his seat. He couldn't say a word. He could barely breathe. What had Kelly done? Why had she let herself be taken? Would she be safe? How would he ever find her again?

He scanned the area—dim, cool, and vague. No sign of anything except his fellow travelers.

A few paces away, Amber stood near Francesca, touching her arm as if checking for injury.

Daryl shook her head and pushed up to her hands and knees. "I think I just did the twist with the Tasmanian Devil!"

Tony set a hand under Nathan's elbow and helped him rise. "You okay?"

"I think so." Nathan blinked, trying to focus. His cheeks flamed. His stomach churned. Kelly had sacrificed herself once again, making sure he didn't get sucked into that sandbox. Pivoting toward Amber, he spread out his arms. "Will she be all right?"

"I cannot be certain." Amber glided toward him through the dimness, the glow of her candle lighting her way. "Dreams always end," she said, her voice calm and soothing, "but I have never followed one into the mind of its creator."

"So Kelly's trapped in Frederick's mind?" Nathan asked. "How could that be?"

Amber shook her head. "I suspect that Felicity was the second dreamer, and Kelly went with her, but I know not where.

Felicity was a strange phenomenon. We supplicants can easily discern the vague profile that the phantoms carry, but Felicity never displayed it."

Francesca took Amber's hand. "I noticed, too. She didn't fade at all."

"Then perhaps she has taken Kelly to a place of safety. She indicated that Nathan could travel with her to find his father, so we have to trust that all is well."

Nathan gritted his teeth. Yes, he had to trust—otherwise he'd go crazy. Maybe the Simons and Gordon would know where Kelly went.

"So where are we now?" Daryl asked. "Someone else's dream?"

"No, but we are still in Earth Yellow's dream world." Amber swept her arm across the darkness. "It is an infinite universe with infinite horizons, and it abounds with countless visions of the night. If we were to walk in most directions, we would soon come upon another dream, but, for now, we are in an area void of the imaginations of mankind."

"Most directions?" Francesca said. "Not all?"

"No, not all. One direction will take you to the barrier that separates the dream world from Sarah's Womb. It is difficult to see it when you are actually within a dream, unless you know what you are looking for."

Daryl's gaze drifted across the expanse. "It's like being on the holodeck in *Star Trek*."

"So what do we do?" Nathan asked. "Now we have two people to look for." He almost said "three people," but with Kelly missing, searching for the new gifted one didn't seem so important, no matter what Patar thought. They would have to find another way to the misty world.

"We have no choice but to return to the observatory." Amber tilted her head as if listening to something in the air. "The music is dying away, so I have to take us back."

A few seconds later, the darkness faded. Light filtered in, brighter with each passing second. Soon, the telescope room came into view, still dim and now without the sounds of two violins.

"They're here," someone called.

"I see only five." The second voice was closer, deeper.

Nathan searched for the source. Solomon Yellow stood next to Francesca Red, his finger lifted in a counting pose. "Kelly is missing."

"Nathan!" his mother called. "Where is she?"

Lights flashed on from the perimeter of the circular room. Nathan narrowed his eyes as he shuffled toward her, his legs weak and wobbly. "I don't know." He took in a deep breath before continuing. "She got sucked into a dark hole with a girl named Felicity, and I couldn't follow her."

"That's terrible!" Francesca Red looked at Solomon. "Is there a way to find her?"

"Maybe." Solomon picked up the empty candelabrum and reached for Nathan's candle. "Does she still have her light?"

Nathan gave him the candle, still burning and now about three-quarters its original size. "I'm pretty sure she does."

Solomon blew out the flame and showed Nathan the lower end. Something circular and dark was stuck to the bottom, like a thumbtack driven into the wax.

"A transmitter." Solomon dug his fingernails around the circle and plucked it out. "As long as she hangs on to the candle, Dr. Gordon should be able to track her movements."

"I have a signal," Dr. Gordon called. "It's weak, but it's definitely hers."

Solomon turned toward him. "Can you locate what realm she's in?"

"The computer says the echo signature isn't like any we've encountered, so I can't determine its origin. But she seems to be moving, so I assume she is alive and well."

A cold sweat dampened Nathan's shirt as relief swept through his mind. "So if you can't find her using the tracking device, can we go back and look for her?"

"That depends." Solomon laid an arm over Nathan's shoulders and led him toward a row of desks that abutted an outer wall. "Amber is capable of taking you back to the dream world, but even she would have no idea where in the dreamscape you would go."

Nathan looked at Amber, raising his eyebrows in a questioning way.

"He is right," she said. "If I am physically with a dreamer, I can easily find his or her dream, but if we jump in from a random place, we are more likely to enter a gap than anyone's dream. It would be like jumping into the ocean, hoping to find a specific fish."

"So," Solomon continued, "it would be better to try to find the fish using its tracking device. And now that we're not detecting any nearby dreams, Amber's entry would likely be in one of the gaps she mentioned. We could wait for another dream to come close enough for the computers to pick it up, but unlike planetary orbits, intersections can't be predicted. But be patient. I think we will be able to show you a new searching option in a minute."

Nathan nodded. He didn't really have much choice but to follow along. Now that Kelly was gone, their plans seemed to be falling apart. How could they get to the misty world without the Earth Blue mirror she'd been holding? That realm and its healing violin seemed farther away than ever.

Nathan and Solomon stopped near a desk where Dr. Simon Blue sat in a rolling swivel chair. Next to him, Simon Yellow sat facing an adjacent desk, while a man who looked like a younger, heftier version of Dr. Gordon attended a computer screen on a third desk.

Simon Blue spun toward Nathan and gave him a wide smile.

"Upon meeting Dr. Gordon of this world, my counterpart and I were able to combine his technological knowledge with our experience studying the various cross-dimensional phenomena. We have also been in contact with the Earth Red Dr. Gordon through a digital channel that gives us clear transmission, and he added to our understanding, enabling us to deduce how everything works."

"Is Gordon Red okay?" Nathan asked. "Does he know how Clara's doing?"

"They're both doing well, considering the circumstances there. Clara wanted to join us, but we had to decline. We have been able to receive inanimate objects from Earth Red using the digital channels, but transporting humans is far too risky."

Gordon Yellow pushed back, rose to his feet, and rolled his chair toward Francesca Red. "Please. Rest."

The two Simons followed suit, offering their chairs to Francesca Yellow and Molly.

Dr. Malenkov strolled into the area, his violin now tucked at his side. "If you no longer need me," he said, "I should go."

Francesca Yellow ran to him and gave him a hug. "Is Mother well?"

"She has fallen ill." He pushed her back gently and offered a weak smile. "I trust that God will heal her, but even if he chooses not to do so, she will merely fly to his arms and be healed there."

"I will pray for her." Francesca kissed his cheek. "And I'll come to be with her as soon as I can."

His smile withered. "I will tell her. She has longed to see you again."

Nathan laid a hand on his back. "I'll pray for her, too."

"Thank you. The fervent prayers of a righteous man availeth much." He turned and shuffled to the tourist entry, looking older than ever.

"Well," Solomon Yellow said, clapping his hands. "Shall we get on with it?"

Nathan tried to keep from scowling. Didn't Solomon Yellow have any sympathy? This version of his father was getting worse all the time.

Dr. Gordon handed Solomon a page of printed data. "The experiment worked perfectly. We captured the energy flow and imported its fingerprint. If we assume that the other dream worlds have the same format, we can shift our instruments to read and reproduce them, perhaps even in a holographic image."

"Then our theory is correct?" Solomon asked.

Dr. Gordon pointed at him. "It was *your* theory. Let's give credit where credit is due."

"What theory?" Nathan asked. "And what does this have to do with finding Kelly? We can't stand around and pat each other on the back while she's stuck somewhere in the great beyond. And we still have to stop interfinity."

Dr. Gordon eyed Nathan for a moment, his expression making him appear a bit annoyed, then returned his gaze to Solomon. "It will take a few minutes to align the telescopes and search for the signals. Perhaps you should take that time to explain the situation to Nathan."

"Very well. I will start at the beginning." Solomon reached for an iPod on Simon Blue's desk and extended it to Nathan, letting the ear buds dangle. "Here is the key, perhaps literally in one sense of the word."

"I've seen it before," Nathan said. "It holds the music that opens dimensional portals."

"True, but we added a very important piece that has a different function. Have a listen." While Solomon slid his finger along the iPod's wheel, Nathan caught the ear buds and inserted them. Within seconds, a violin played the simple melody of "Foundation's Key", but it was more than a rote recital. The violin sang with majestic fervor, a brilliant rendition that only one person in the world could have created.

Nathan looked at his mother. Obviously, she couldn't have recorded it. She had been with him or in Mictar's clutches the entire time. As the exquisite music continued, he turned to Francesca Yellow, now holding hands with Solomon. She gave Nathan a timid smile.

Returning the smile, Nathan nodded. Of course. That Francesca could play like this. No doubt about it.

Solomon turned off the iPod and retrieved the ear buds. "After many nights of experimenting, we learned that Francesca's playing of that piece protects sleepers from dreaming about the future and blocks Mictar from entering their dreams. We think it somehow interferes with the open channels that the wounds created. How does it work?" He shrugged. "I don't know."

"So what did you do?" Nathan asked. "Distribute it on the Internet?"

"It's nineteen ninety three. The Internet isn't nearly as wide-spread as it is in your world, and the circumstances we've lived with have delayed its progress, so we sold the recording the old-fashioned way — in Wal-Mart."

"So are the worlds still running in parallel? I mean, with all the disturbances we've caused, I guess nothing is really predict-able, is it?"

Simon Blue took the iPod and laid it back on his desk. "You are correct. In fact, accurate next-day dreaming would likely have ceased on its own. Fortunately, when Solomon invented the cure, it was still a huge concern, so we sold hundreds of millions of copies and made a fortune."

Nathan tried to hide a frown. Was this all a moneymaking venture? It couldn't be. The man who eventually became his father couldn't be just a greedy profiteer. Yet Gordon Blue was obviously in it for the money, even though Gordon Red wasn't, so maybe ...

Solomon laughed. "And nearly every penny went to finance this observatory." He patted Nathan on the back. "Did you see that jalopy I was driving? You'd think I'd keep a few dollars to get a better car."

"Yeah. I saw it." Nathan lowered his head. Better to withhold judgment about Solomon. He obviously wasn't a perfect gentleman, but he had some good qualities.

Simon Blue spread out his arms. "And as you will soon see, it is a vastly improved observatory from the ones you knew on the other Earths."

Nathan looked around. So far it didn't seem much different. In fact, the laptop computers were bulkier, obviously an older technology, and the smaller screens forced them to feed the video signal to large stand-alone monitors. Those looked pretty sharp, though they were an old style, not the flat screens that would come out in a few years.

"Now here's an interesting invention." Simon Blue opened a drawer and pulled out a device that looked like a walkie-talkie with a video screen. "We call this an interworld audio receiver and transmitter unit. It's so new, even Dr. Gordon on Earth Red doesn't have one yet. The only three in existence are here in our lab."

"An interworld what?" Nathan asked.

"Interworld audio receiver and transmitter unit." He set it in Nathan's hand. "Just call it IWART. That should be easy enough."

Nathan suppressed a grin. That was really an awful moniker, but he was right. It would be easy to remember. "What's it do?"

Simon Blue touched a round plastic knob at the center of the IWART's front casing. "This switch has three settings, one for each of the three Earths. For example, if you use the Earth

Yellow device while you're here and turn the switch to the Earth Blue setting, you will be able to talk to someone holding the Earth Blue device while he is in that world, regardless of the difference in time passage. First, you press the talk button." He pointed at a black button on the side. "Then you say something and let the button go. It transmits the sentence or paragraph or whatever in its entirety, allowing the receiver to play it at a normal rate. The only drawback, of course, would be for the person on the faster world. It would seem to him that the person on the slower world is taking forever to record his reply."

· "Sure," Nathan said. "That makes sense."

Simon pointed at one of the computers on the desk. "We have the same technology in our transmissions between the laboratories, but this allows someone to be mobile; that is, he would be able to use it outside of the lab. You would still, however, have to be stationary for it to make cross-dimensional contact. It doesn't work while you're moving, but since it also has a built-in GPS receiver, it might come in quite handy for many applications, don't you think?"

"Definitely." Nathan eyed the switch on the IWART. The three settings were labeled "Yellow", "Blue", and "Red". "What happens if the Earth Yellow device is set to the Earth Yellow position?"

"It contacts us here in the observatory, and, as you might expect, the Earth Red device's Red setting would contact Earth Red headquarters, and so on. We will be sending the IWARTs to those worlds soon. But now we must turn to other matters." Simon Blue nodded at Dr. Gordon. "Is the Scotland mirror locked in place?"

"It is. I can show them the local energy emission first. Perhaps by the time they synchronize, we can look deeper." Dr. Gordon leaned over his laptop and tapped a few keys, then turned toward the center of the room and pointed upward. "As you watch, I'll explain what you're seeing."

Nathan looked at the ceiling. As he expected, a curved reflection of everyone in the room looked back, their heads tilted. Soon, the mirror darkened, and pinpoints of white light dotted the purple canopy—stars twinkling in the night sky. Then, the darkness in a third of the mirror broke apart and scattered, like oil droplets on water. They changed into oddly shaped globules of various colors, much like the patterns at the other observatories—shapes that represented the noise gathered from space by the radio telescope. It seemed that a wedge of dark pie had been removed, revealing part of a circle covered with crawling, multicolored worms.

"Instead of one radio telescope," Dr. Gordon explained, "we have three. With the wounds in the cosmic fabric, we can hone in on the sounds from each universe and compare them to see how they function as a tri-universe whole. What you are seeing is the noise generated here in Earth Yellow. As you might expect, it has the strongest signal. The computer will lock on the closest dream and interpret its sound emission. Then we should be able to see a visual representation. All the light energy we collect is now sent through the mirror Tony brought from Scotland, and we believe that is the key to viewing the dream world. This should allow us to visually search the three realms safely. And I hope we will eventually learn how to open a portal to the stalkers' world. From what I have learned, eliminating those creatures would help our cause greatly."

"Can you play the transmissions out loud?" Nathan asked. "I'd like to hear them."

"Very well, but it will be severely garbled until we translate it."

"I'd like to give it a shot, if you don't mind." As Nathan continued to stare at the scene above, static began buzzing from hidden speakers. He concentrated on the noise, trying to pick it apart and decipher the tune as he had once before.

Francesca Yellow scooted toward him. "You don't have to tax your brain, Nathan. The computer can do it."

"I need to get better at this. Without Kelly around, I might need it." He closed his eyes and imagined a blank musical staff floating in front of him while a mental vision of himself held a violin. As he caught each note from within the static, his imagined self played it. A black spider formed on his strings and flew to the staff. After a few seconds and many more notes, a page of music filled his mind.

During his previous try, he had a real violin and played the piece out loud. This time he wanted to do it all in his head and really get the hang of interpretation, something his mother was able to do without any effort. If he was gifted, too, he should be able to learn this skill.

When his mental picture played the first measure, he hummed along. The static began to clear. Just like last time, his physical ears heard what his brain composed.

Dr. Gordon's voice broke through. "Shall I begin the translation? Nothing will happen without the appropriate music."

"No!" Francesca said sharply. "Let Nathan do it. He must do it."

Someone shushed her, and then static blended with the music. His eyes still closed, Nathan concentrated. He had to get it back.

Soon, the melody flowed once again, and it took only seconds to recognize it—"Be Thou My Vision"—the same piece that had cleared the air during Daryl Blue's nightmare. Yet, this didn't sound like a choir of angelic singers. It was more like a duet—a violin and a piano, beautiful in passion and haunting as each piano note echoed in perfect precision with the violin's long strokes.

Someone slipped a violin and bow into Nathan's hands. "Now play it, son. Play it with all your heart."

He recognized his mother's voice. "But my hands, they're—"

"Play it anyway!" Her voice sharpened. "Let the pain flow. Without pain there is no passion."

Nathan rubbed his fingertip across the violin's smooth wood grain. It felt good ... very good. Maybe his mother was right. Maybe he could still play. "Okay. I'll try."

Keeping his eyes closed, he raised the bow to the strings. His mother's voice smoothed to a poetic cadence. "Only sacrifice draws a holy flow from within, and only a bleeding soul can reach down deep enough to find the blazing fire—the God-given inferno that purges every particle of dross that spoils the master's silver."

Cringing at the pain, Nathan pressed down on the finger-board and pushed the bow across the strings. A note screeched through the air, worse than nails on a chalkboard.

He lifted the bow. "I can't. My hands hurt too much."

"Consider them healed," she said. "Imagine yourself playing with soft, supple, perfect hands. Let the pain melt away."

Nathan focused his mental image. As his mother probably suspected, the teenager in his mind had bandaged hands. He forced the imaginary Nathan to strip off the wrappings, but the hands were still raw and oozing blood. He couldn't make the redness go away.

Again he pushed against the strings, and again a horrid screech erupted. Pain ripped from the tips of his fingers to his shoulders.

"Let's just do it with the computer," he said, lowering the violin. "I just wanted to see if I could translate the noise."

"Nathan." His mother's voice was still calm, yet forceful, "I have told you a hundred times that you have more talent than I do, yet you have not reached into your soul to grasp it. You have to roll away the stone that's keeping that talent from rising into your heart and into your hands." She pressed a fist against her chest. "If you don't let God play through you, your music won't come from a heart of pure passion. It will be nothing more than a mechanical recital of rigid notes on a page."

Nathan touched his own chest with the butt end of the bow. "But there isn't a stone in the way. There isn't anything blocking my passion."

His mother's brow eased upward. "Isn't there?"

"No." He lifted his bandaged hand. "This isn't pretend. We're dealing with reality."

"I see." She took the bow and pointed it at the violin. "I will need that, please."

As the static continued, Nathan laid the violin in her extended palm. His makeshift bandage had loosened, exposing her bloody gash. "Mom. Your hand. There's no reason to—"

"I told you I'd show you some of my old spunk," she said as she set the bow over the strings. "You might want to take notes."

Grimacing as she pressed down on the fingerboard, Francesca played the last few notes of the song, apparently matching what she heard in the static. Although she began with a slight hint of flatness, the melody soon sharpened to the proper pitch. As she glided into the first phrase, cringing with every note, the tune's lyrics came to Nathan's mind, as if bidden to rise by the matchless virtuoso.

Be thou my vision, O Lord of my heart;
Naught be all else to me, save that thou art.
Thou my best thought, by day or by night,
Waking or sleeping, thy presence my light.

She took a breath and looked up at the ceiling, tears flowing. Then, raising the bow again, she played the same notes, this time even more beautifully than before. Every push and pull of the bow brought an anguished frown and the weakest of grunts, but she played on, sweating, crying, and—Nathan looked at the hand running up and down the fingerboard—and bleeding.

A trickle of blood dripped and streamed down the finger-board. Francesca Shepherd seemed to pay no mind. Playing on and on, she had lost all awareness of her surroundings. Only the slightest bend in her brow gave any indication that pain still shot through her fingers. She was a woman in love, but Solomon Shepherd was not the man on her mind.

As the tune began again, the words to the second verse flowed through Nathan's soul, each one echoing from ear to ear as they faded.

> Be thou my wisdom, and thou my true word;
> I ever with thee, and thou with me, Lord;
> Thou my great father, I thy true son;
> Thou in me dwelling, and I with thee one.

He looked up. The globules in the curved mirror had already burst open, and the colors had merged into a scene within the pie-slice wedge, blurry but discernable. Little Francesca Shepherd stood in her old bedroom, no more than ten years old, playing her violin in front of a music stand.

Nathan gaped at the sight. How could this be? Gordon had said they would pick up the strongest signal, but his mother wasn't dreaming. He looked back at her face—eyes closed, breathing steady, body moving in a flowing rhythm.

Or was she?

In the scene above, little Francesca stopped playing and crawled under her bed. As if followed by a movie camera, she appeared in the dim shadow of her bed's frame, her eyes peering under a frilly dust ruffle at shoes rushing past her hiding place. Then, closing her eyes, she folded her hands into a praying clench and moved her lips rapidly.

Francesca's violin played on. Nathan glanced at his mother out of the corner of his eye. Deep lines creased her brow. Blood dripped from her hand to the floor. More words arose in his mind, now fainter, more desperate.

Be thou my battle shield, sword for the fight;
Be thou my dignity, thou my delight;
Thou my soul's shelter, thou my high tower:
Raise thou me heavenward, O power of my power.

Little Francesca crawled out from under the bed. Kneeling by her mother's body, she wept pitifully, rocking back and forth in time with her sobs. Soon, a large hand came into view. Francesca took it, rose to her feet, and walked away with Nikolai Malenkov, hand in hand, into a dense fog.

The scene shifted suddenly. Now in the backseat of an old car, she gazed out the window, watching her home shrink in the distance. As she held a stuffed bear in her arms, tears streamed down her cheeks.

The lyrics marched on.

Riches I heed not, nor man's empty praise,
Thou mine inheritance, now and always:
Thou and thou only, first in my heart,
High king of heaven, my treasure thou art.

The scene shifted again. Francesca, now a young woman, walked down the center aisle at a church. Dressed in silky white and her raven hair decorated with tiny white flowers, she glided like an angel, her bridal veil unable to hide her brilliant smile. Nikolai, dressed in a black tuxedo, walked at her side, his smile nearly as wide as hers, though a tear sparkled on his cheek.

A tall, broad-shouldered gentleman, also dressed in white, waited at the front. His smile, muted and trembling, communicated much more than joy. It shouted, "I can't believe the amazing blessing that walks my way."

When they reached him, Nikolai laid her hand in the groom's and seated himself in the front pew. Then an organ blended with the violin, also playing the wondrous hymn.

Now breathless, Nathan again looked at his mother. Her

bleeding had eased. The lines in her forehead had disappeared. Her eyes still closed, a gentle smile graced her lips — soft, pain-free, content.

As her playing slowed, the notes lengthened, growing stronger, deeper, richer. Majestic lyrics broke into Nathan's mind like a flood.

> *High king of heaven, my victory won,*
> *May I reach heaven's joys, O bright heaven's sun!*
> *Heart of my own heart, whatever befall,*
> *Still be my vision, O ruler of all.*

The final note rose from the strings — stretched out and fading to a whisper. Francesca withdrew the violin and dipped her head low, letting her black hair drape the front of her shirt. After taking a deep breath, she looked at Nathan and gave him the violin and bow. Her smile was weak and sad, but she said nothing.

Nathan held the bow and violin. He couldn't say anything either. There was nothing to be said. She had once again proven that something was wrong inside him. If he really did have her talent, he hadn't yet dug deep enough to let it flow. Somehow, he had to find a way. The fates of three worlds might well be hanging in the balance.

8

THE NIGHTMARE HOLOGRAM

"That was remarkable!" Dr. Gordon called. "I'm learning something new with every experiment."

Solomon turned his way. "What happened?"

"Francesca generated her own sphere. Her thoughts penetrated the dream world, and the Earth Yellow telescope picked it up." Dr. Gordon tapped away at his keyboard. "I am adjusting the fields to plunge deeper into the dreamscape."

"And what of the other Earths?" Solomon asked.

"Francesca's energy surge allowed me to refine the calibrations. I'm pretty sure we can bring the other two in clearly. I'll let the computer generate the music for each world, but I'll keep the volume down. With three different tunes playing simultaneously, it wouldn't be pleasing to our ears."

Nathan looked up again. His mother's wedding scene had darkened, while two other slices transformed into the usual chaotic colors. At the center, however, where the three wedges met, a circular portion stayed dark, taking up about a tenth of the entire screen. With a black hole in the middle, the curved viewing area now looked more like a doughnut than a pie.

After several seconds, all three wedges began to clarify. At the upper right, the section his mother had filled earlier with her daytime dream, a snow scene took shape—the same city block where they had picked up Molly and later found Tony. With deepening drifts covering parked cars and sidewalks, no pedestrians braved the cascading sea of falling flakes.

Nathan cocked his head and whispered to his mother. "Since someone's dreaming this, that's not the real weather. The snow stopped quite a while ago."

"But who is the dreamer?" she asked.

"Good question." Nathan tilted his head back. Watching the huge screen directly overhead made his neck ache and dizzied his brain.

In the upper-left section, another picture took shape, dotted with static, like a TV broadcast from far away. Weather-beaten tombstones rose at crooked angles from a weed-infested lawn. Storm clouds boiled in the sky. Jagged bolts of green lightning crashed to the ground, raising sparks and igniting fires that sent purple smoke and yellow embers into the swirling breeze. Again, no one was in sight.

"Another cemetery?" Nathan glanced at his mother to his right, then at Daryl to his left. "Why is it always a cemetery?"

Daryl shivered. "Reminds me of *The Omen*. If I see triple sixes on the screen, I'm out of here."

Finally, on the lower third, at least from Nathan's awkward angle, an even fuzzier scene came into view—the New York City skyline on a clear, sunny day. Standing tall in the midst of their lesser neighbors, the two World Trade Center towers reflected the morning sun. Nathan eyed the buildings. Why would they still be there? They collapsed years ago.

The scene switched to an airplane cockpit. The pilot, sweating profusely, spoke into a microphone attached to his headphones, but no sound came out. A man of Middle Eastern descent stooped at the pilot's side and pushed a blade against his throat.

"That's my daddy!" Daryl cried. "The pilot's my daddy!"

Tony put a hand on her shoulder. "It's okay. It's just a dream."

"Oh, yeah." She sniffed and wiped her fist under her nose. "Now I remember. He's talked about this dream. He's the pilot of a jet that crashes into one of the towers. He says he always hopes he can stop the tragedy, but—"

The hijacker jerked the pilot from the seat, leaving a trail of blood. With the limp body at his side, he took the controls. Through the windshield, the tower drew closer and closer at tremendous speed. Then flames blasted across the screen. Glass, furniture, body parts, and streams of fire flew everywhere.

Daryl covered her eyes. "I can't look! I can't look!"

Nathan cringed but kept watching. What would happen next? Surely this was the end of the dream. Would everything get sucked into a void as it had done at the playground?

A crack formed at the top of the section, tearing open the boundary between the dream and the ceiling's central black circle, the doughnut hole Nathan had labeled in his mind. Darkness blew into the fiery carnage, swirling as it slurped everything in sight. Within seconds, the scene vanished, and only a sea of blackness appeared in the section.

Nathan looked at the computer desks. Dr. Gordon and the two Simons alternately watched the ceiling and their monitors.

"Can someone give me an explanation?" Nathan called. "What's going on up there?"

"Yeah," Daryl said. "This is like *The Twilight Zone* meets *The X-Files* meets *Night of the Living Dead*."

Simon Yellow pointed at the snow scene. "That's the dream world here. Someone has likely fallen asleep recently and is remembering the snowstorm, but he or she has exaggerated its ferocity." He shifted his finger to the cemetery. "That is the Earth Blue dream world. It seems clear that a dreamer has imagined quite a terrible graveyard nightmare. Perhaps soon we will see that person appear." He walked closer to the center of the room and nodded toward the final section. "That was a dream in Earth Red. Apparently our telescope found Daryl's father and showed us his dream."

He looked at Daryl, half closing one eye. "From what you said, I gathered that this disaster is one in your history, but no one has told me about it yet."

"Nine-eleven," Nathan said. "Terrorists flew airliners into the World Trade Center towers on September eleventh, two thousand and one."

Daryl smacked her palms together. "Knocked 'em both flat. My dad's been obsessed with it ever since. He never made it as a pilot for the big airliners, and he dreams about what he would've done if he'd been there."

Simon Yellow looked at Simon Blue but said nothing, though his brow was bent, making his owl-like glasses slip down his nose.

Nathan eased back a step. The tension was thick. Since the two Simons had been working together to prevent Earth Yellow disasters, apparently Simon of the Blue world had been giving his Yellow counterpart a history lesson, a morbid laundry list of the calamities that were going to befall the people of Earth Yellow. Apparently, Simon Blue hadn't mentioned "nine-eleven," but that was still several years away, and with all the differences now between the worlds, the terrorists' plot might not come about at all.

He stepped closer to the computer screen and eyed the unintelligible digits filling several windows. "So how did we happen to dial in Daryl's father?"

"We're picking up the strongest signals," Dr. Gordon said. "My counterpart on Earth Red told me that Daryl's father is waiting for her at the observatory in that world. Perhaps he has been there a long time and has fallen asleep under the mirror. It could have magnified his dream signal."

Nathan nodded. The same thing had happened to Daryl Blue. She dreamed in the Earth Blue observatory, and he and Kelly had walked through her nightmare until Cerulean rescued her from it. "Are there any more clues to where Kelly's signal is coming from?"

"It is somewhat stronger," Dr. Gordon said, "but we still have no way to determine its source. There just isn't anything else comparable."

Simon Blue raised a finger. "Shall we show the new arrivals the hologram imaging?"

Dr. Gordon studied his screen for a moment. "Since we have good data in all three realms, I don't see why not."

"If this works," Solomon said, "we can begin our search for Solomon Red immediately. We already have my energy signature in the computer, so we just have to find an exact copy somewhere in the dream worlds. He may well provide the final pieces to the interfinity puzzle."

Using his touchpad, Dr. Gordon adjusted a slider on his screen. "As of this morning, we were able to display the real world images in the hologram, but the new mirror should give us an unfragmented representation of the dream worlds."

At the center of the room, something clicked underneath the telescope, and a humming sound emanated from the floor. The telescope descended on a circular platform, and a metal plate slid from the adjoining floor panel to cover the hole.

Above, dozens of beams of light shot out from all around. Nathan searched for the source, but the lasers, or whatever they were, stayed hidden behind a narrow shelf that encircled the observatory where the base of the dome met the walls.

The beams converged just above where the telescope had stood. Fog swirled in the midst of a wide cylinder of multicolored light, rising from near the floor to about twelve feet in the air.

"Synchronizing the beams," Dr. Gordon announced in a mechanical voice. "Visual clarification commencing."

The fog evaporated, leaving behind recognizable shapes within the cylinder, the same trio of scenes that had been displayed on the ceiling, but now upright and in 3-D.

Sliding closer, Nathan gawked at the hologram. In the section nearest him, a knee-high tombstone stood near the edge of the cylinder, though the surrounding light made it look like a ghost, too vaporous to be seen clearly.

"Reducing background radiant energy," Dr. Gordon said, his voice now shaking with emotion. "In a few seconds we'll see the results of all our efforts."

The laser beams diminished somewhat but stayed visible. The cylinder of light, however, faded away, leaving only the holographic images within. Now the tombstone became clear. Staying outside the original cylinder's perimeter, Nathan stooped near the marker and read the engraving.

Here lies Felicity, an ugly blind girl.
Born — No one knows
Died — No one cares
Doomed to rot in this dark hole for all eternity.

Another hard lump grew in his throat. This had to be Felicity's dream. Whoever she was, she must be able to generate powerful signals. But where was she now? Might she appear in this dream and bring Kelly along?

A shadow rushed away from the tombstone, then darted back. Nathan squinted but was unable to see into the dimness well enough to sort out the competing shades of darkness. The shy ghost would stay hidden, at least for now.

"Ladies and gentlemen," Dr. Gordon said as he rose and walked toward the hologram, "welcome to a dream come true."

Solomon joined Nathan near the grave marker and whispered, "Almost literally a dream come true, don't you think?"

"Yeah." Nathan shivered. The cadence and quality of Solomon's voice matched his father's exactly. "I think the graveyard is Felicity's dream, and Kelly went to wherever she went. Should I tell Dr. Gordon, or just play it cool and check it out on my own?"

"Let's keep it to ourselves for now," Solomon said. "I think he will tell us what to do in just a minute."

While the others gathered around, Nathan drank in the details. Several other tombstones had appeared, each with etchings too small to be read. He strained his eyes. Could he get closer? Was it safe to lean in or even walk in?

Dr. Gordon walked over and pushed his hand into the hologram field. Like electrified ripples on a pond, the boundary shimmered with warped light waves, but it seemed to offer no resistance. "As you can see," he said, "I can interrupt the flow without disturbing the image. You can literally walk through this dream without harming it or yourself."

Nathan pushed a hand through. Although a slight tingling sensation crawled along his skin at the entry point, it didn't hurt at all. "All right if I go in and look around?"

"I was hoping someone would." Dr. Gordon withdrew a pair of eyeglasses from his shirt pocket. "These lenses are similar to the one inside your father's camera. You see, we had already conducted experiments that helped us look at the dream hologram, but because of the danger in trying to get an Earth Blue mirror and because the Earth Yellow mirror was inaccessible until now, we had to use fragments from the shattered Earth Red mirror that Simon Blue recovered from the funeral site.

"The images we created were just as fragmented as the glass, and without the calibration we just gained from your travel to the dream world, much of our data was suspect. Yet, we did learn that dream images are skewed in both space and time. Because of these distortions, we were rarely able to figure out what was happening. Dreams might move at ten times normal speed or appear warped. We were unable to sort them out."

Nathan nodded toward the graveyard. "Yeah. I noticed something moving in there. It was too quick to see."

"That's why you need these." Dr. Gordon slid the glasses over Nathan's eyes. "Now when you walk inside the hologram you will see a much clearer picture, as if you were actually within the dream world."

Nathan took off the glasses and looked at one of the ear-pieces. "I felt something cold."

Dr. Gordon touched a tiny metallic plate showing through the plastic. "You're feeling two amplification devices, one for each ear. Although the mirror transmits sound, the signal is too weak for our instruments to detect outside the hologram. These will amplify the signal, allowing you to listen to the dream, just as if you were actually there."

"But without the danger," Solomon added. "You will be invisible to anyone in the dream world."

Nathan put the glasses back on and rubbed an earpiece. "What does Kelly's signal sound like?"

"That device picks up dream sounds," Dr. Gordon said. "Her candle's signal can be detected only by the radio telescopes. We will continue to monitor it and let you know if we can pinpoint its source."

Nathan let out a sigh. "Okay. What should I do? Just walk around in there?"

"Yes. Go from one Earth to the other and study every feature. When you come out, you can report your findings. In the meantime, we will search for your father's signature."

"Will do." Nathan took a deep breath and marched straight into the hologram. For a moment, the ripples of light blinded him, but once he stepped fully within the perimeter, his vision returned. Now surrounded by the graveyard scene, he studied the area. Several paces away to his front and to each side, the scene blurred, as if a wall of fog blocked his view. Could these fogbanks be boundaries to the next world's dream?

Standing still for a moment, he listened. The only noise his earpieces transmitted sounded like the whooshing of a breeze, evidenced by the occasional wisp of fog that blew slowly past.

He turned to his left and walked parallel to the outer

boundary. Lifting his legs high, he stepped over crawling vines and weeds, then dodged a tombstone that stood in his way. Stopping for a moment, he tried to lay his hand on its rough concrete top, but his fingers passed into the stone. With his elbow on one side of the marker and his bandaged hand on the other, it looked like a mummy had punched through it.

He straightened and pressed on. Obviously, it wouldn't hurt to pass right through these markers, but it seemed sacrilegious somehow, so he continued to leave space between himself and each grave while he searched for the fleeting shadow, or least footprints in the moist grass and mud.

As he walked, he glanced from time to time at the others. Several looked back at him, slightly hazy but still recognizable. Daryl stared with her jaw hanging open. Tony and Molly held hands, both watching in awe.

The only others in sight were Dr. Gordon and the two Dr. Simons. All three beamed, obviously proud of their incredible feat. And why not? They had figured out how to display dreams in virtual reality, presenting mental images from three different worlds. But could they use it to locate his father? Was this venture really the key to stopping interfinity? And if so, wouldn't he have to hurry and get the job done?

Something moved—a shadow, small and quick, but not as fast as before. Nathan held his breath. Slowly turning, he searched for the little ghost. The image was eerily like Francesca's appearance in the Wal-Mart, an out-of-place specter, lost and scared. Yet this one seemed taller and a little slower.

Ahead and to his left something behind a tombstone flapped slowly in the breeze. He skulked toward it, approaching from the back. Even though the "ghost" on the other side likely couldn't see or hear him, it still seemed wrong to rush ahead.

As he rounded the tombstone, the sky suddenly darkened. Something sat on the gravesite's bare earth, leaning against the marker, but now the figure was shrouded in shadows. Rain began to fall, penny-sized drops that raised noisy splashes around Nathan's shoes.

He stooped, trying to get a closer look at the huddled shape. Lightning flashed. The sudden light revealed a shivering girl, a split-second image, yet one that stayed emblazoned in his mind's eye. Wearing dark glasses, the girl clutched her tattered sweater and walking stick close with long, skinny fingers. Thunder boomed an echo, making her shake even harder.

Nathan sighed. It was Felicity, living through another graveyard nightmare, worse than the one she had conjured in the midst of Frederick's playground.

Lightning streaked across the sky, illuminating her again, this time for several seconds. With stringy hair plastered to her face, and ratty clothes sticking to her trembling body, she seemed more pitiful than ever. Her head leaned just below the words "Here lies Felicity, an ugly blind girl."

Nathan looked back at the tombstone near the edge of the hologram, the first one he had seen. Did they all bear the same inscription?

He curled his fingers into a painful clench. Part of him wanted to scream, "Where's Kelly? What did you do to her?" But that would be stupid. The poor girl was suffering. She was the victim of fear and loneliness, dreaming the darkness in her mind.

Nathan stepped back, and his throat began to tighten. What could he do to help? Even if he offered his sweatshirt, she wouldn't be able to feel its warmth. His words of comfort would fall on deaf ears. All he could do was watch her suffer and hope that she would soon wake up from the nightmares that plagued her mind.

He looked up into the rainy sky and breathed a quick prayer. The words of the ancient song again flowed through his thoughts: *"Waking or sleeping, thy presence my light."*

Leaning over, he kissed Felicity's forehead, though it felt like kissing air. It was time to move on. Interfinity wouldn't wait.

Still walking parallel to the cylinder's outer boundary, Nathan stepped through the fog, blinding his eyes for a moment. When he blinked away the flash, the Chicago snow scene came into view. Although nearby objects, such as a fire hydrant next to his shoe, were clear, distant objects, especially tall ones, seemed indistinct. Maybe they stood outside the dreamer's thought range or were veiled by the wind-driven snow. He half expected to feel a chill from the breeze, but the temperature and air movement stayed the same—a bit cold, but not nearly blizzardlike. Of course, the whooshing sound continued to rush into his ears, louder now as the snowstorm raged.

He marched on, this time plowing right through the snow drifts that piled against cars and vans on otherwise deserted city streets. Since his legs left the drifts undisturbed, any telltale footprints from dream-world inhabitants would be easy to spot, but none appeared. Whoever was dreaming this scene hadn't bothered to include any living creatures—no people, no dogs, not even a shivering bird to mar the pristine layers of white.

He paused at a street sign and read the labels—"Michigan Avenue" and "Chicago Avenue." To the right, a department store stood without a hint of customers, barely visible as it rose into the hazy borders. To the left, Neiman Marcus stood equally empty, even blurrier in the distance. This was definitely the same area where Gunther had picked them up. Could Gunther be the dreamer? He had driven a long way, so he might have stopped somewhere close by to take a nap.

Nathan looked up at the falling snow, each flake just a tiny dot of white—there was no sign of crystalline uniqueness, making them more like Styrofoam particles than true snow. With nebulous boundaries all around, he felt like a human ornament in a recently shaken snow globe.

Again he strode ahead until he reached another dividing

wall of fog. This time he paused and pictured the entire cylinder in his mind. If he continued going in the same direction, he would pass into the Earth Red dream world, but that dream had ended, so he wouldn't do any good in there. Then he would complete a full circle, but with the huge expanse of the dream world left to search, what good was this doing?

Amber had said this was a limitless realm, but he could only see a few dreams. Still, maybe somehow his presence could draw the dreamers he loved. Maybe they would be attracted to his emotional energy. It wasn't much of a hope, but it was better than nothing.

Yet neither a footprint nor a wandering ghost would whisper a clue to either Kelly's or his father's location. It all seemed so futile.

He turned ninety degrees to the right and looked at the center of the hologram, dark and foreboding. Could that be the central core Patar had mentioned? If he went into it, could the hologram show him what was inside Sarah's Womb? When it was on the ceiling, that portion had been the doughnut's center hole, the mystery spot that hadn't yet revealed any secrets; maybe the telescopes hadn't penetrated it and couldn't display its contents.

A gnarled oak stood near the barrier. With bent, twisted branches and long vines hanging from top to bottom, it looked like one of the trees Cerulean had said to avoid. Nathan walked up to it and studied its tough, ridged bark. Harmless as it was in its hologram form, it gave him a shiver all the same.

Gritting his teeth, Nathan plunged through the dark barrier and into the center of the hologram. For a moment, only blackness greeted his eyes, then a flicker of light, like a firefly that glowed red for a brief second, then another light glowed blue, hovering at eye level not more than two steps away. He blinked and looked for the lights again, but they were gone.

After a quick shudder, he pressed on and exited the blackness, expecting to enter the darkness of the Earth Red dream world, but something appeared. A piano sat on a hardwood floor, a Model B Victorian like the one in Kelly's living room. Other furnishings faded in and out of the scene—a chandelier dangling low directly over the piano bench; portraits on the wall of people with contorted faces, some looking as if they had eaten sour pickles; and a basketball hoop, complete with a backboard and net hanging from a pole that suspended the orange metal rim within free-throw distance of whoever might play the piano's keys.

Atop the piano sat dozens of glass figurines, each one a little girl in a different pose. Some were dressed in feminine dresses and gowns, while others donned athletic gear—everything from a racing swimsuit to football pads and helmet to basketball shorts and a tank top.

Beyond the piano, Tony and Molly stood at the hologram's boundary, peering in. Nathan followed their line of sight. To his left only an arm's reach away, a little girl, maybe nine years old, stood glaring at the piano, her brown ponytail protruding from the back of a baseball cap.

He swallowed. Could it be? It had to be—Kelly Clark as a young girl.

9

KELLY'S SONG

Nathan scanned the room, hoping to pick up some clue that might reveal where Kelly was sleeping. When nothing jumped out at him, he turned his eyes back to her young, dream self.

She slid onto the bench and turned up the keyboard cover, exposing a set of warped, stained keys, very different from the keys on the real piano back at her Iowa farmhouse. With a slap, she opened a music book poised above the keys and let out a huff.

Nathan couldn't suppress a grin. That huff was definitely Kelly's. He had heard it plenty of times before.

Squaring her shoulders, she set her fingers on the keys and looked up at the chandelier. It hung so low, the bottoms of the prismatic crystals nearly brushed the top of her cap as they swayed ever so slightly.

Beings of light, colorful and sparkling, began to dance around her head like wingless fairies in long dresses. Representing every color of the rainbow, each pint-sized pixie shook a tiny conductor's baton at Kelly and shouted chipmunklike commands that were too squeaky to understand.

Nathan knelt at Kelly's side and gazed into her eyes—the same walnut-brown eyes the real Kelly had. He shifted his gaze to the pixies and studied their tiny faces. Each one looked like Molly, stern and demanding as they shook their toothpick batons, almost comical in their exaggerated expressions. Each wore a low-cut dress, far too revealing.

He averted his eyes. Could that be the dress Kelly wore for Steven, the one her mother borrowed to attract a partner in adultery? The same dress Kelly, overwhelmed by shame, later ceremonially burned?

Questions about Kelly's past drilled into his mind. Why was she so ashamed? What did she do? How far did she go?

Nathan clutched a handful of his shirt and squeezed. It must have been too far ... just too far. After all he had been taught about remaining pure and someday marrying someone equally pure, how could he ever hope for a relationship with this girl? She was a strong, brave, and loyal warrior, but ...

He shook his head. Could it ever happen? Did she even want a relationship with him? Was singing "Amazing Grace" while plunging in a doomed airplane evidence of a cleansed soul?

He let out a silent sigh. He hoped so. He really, really hoped so.

Returning his gaze to little Kelly, he again watched her eyes. They seemed so innocent, reflecting the days before she had to face the trials of adolescence, the days when childhood fun held sway over fashion, popularity, and boys.

Flashing an impish grin, Kelly batted the pixies away. A basketball appeared in her hands, and she shot it toward the hoop. It banged against the backboard, swished through the net, and bounced on the piano top, bowling over the collection of figurines as it dribbled back into her hands.

The pixies returned, buzzing around her head like a swarm of angry hornets. Kelly sighed and tossed away the basketball. It bounced once and disappeared.

After giving the pixies an angry scowl, Kelly played, expertly running her fingers through a scale. Then, after finishing a second warm-up drill, she flipped through an old music book, its pages more like ancient parchment than the thin paper in modern varieties. She looked at the musical score and played with a lovely touch, lifting her fingers and hands in slow, graceful arches.

The notes passed through the transmitters and into his ears, familiar notes that pieced together a haunting tune. Nathan looked at the music book in front of her. The title, written in bold black script, seemed to float above the page — "Amazing Grace." Now, as he looked back at her lovely little hands, the music synced with her strokes, each finger fall recreating one of the most heartfelt songs in human history.

Barely able to breathe, he looked into her eyes. How could she know to play the song he was thinking about? Could her gift of interpretation reach into his mind from so far away, even in a dream?

Kelly swayed in time with the song, and her lips seemed to move, but only slightly, as if she were singing in her mind but not letting the words come out. She now seemed older, maybe twelve or thirteen. Her baseball cap was gone, and she wore a long skirt and a button-up blouse that revealed her blossoming femininity. The pixies had vanished, and new figurines appeared on the piano; young men dressed in white tuxedos, one for every Kelly figurine.

As if getting ready to dance, they paired up, and when their hands touched, each Kelly transformed. The old clothes burned away, revealing a long, lacy gown every bit as white as her partner's tuxedo. Then they danced, a waltz of sorts, though slower, moodier, and more contemplative.

Nathan leaned close to Kelly but heard nothing. The dream was slowly becoming a nightmare, at least for him. Why wouldn't the amplification device pick up the sound? Was Kelly not dreaming the music? Although the visual quality of this hologram was as perfect as real life, the missing dimension of sound made it feel like a true nightmare — surreal, out of sync, haunted. He squinted to read her lips, but she formed words that seemed unfamiliar, certainly not the lyrics of the famous hymn.

He looked back at the page. Again, words floated above the ragged parchment. They pulsed with each press of her finger, as if energized by the music. With tears flowing down her cheeks, Kelly played on. Now dressed in the blood-stained safari outfit she had worn when they first traveled to Earth Yellow, she seemed sixteen again. Even the cut on her head returned, oozing a dark red stream.

Kelly began to sing, her voice sweet, yet tortured, and dirge-like in cadence.

Amazing grace is lost for me,
A harlot soiled and stained.
A wretch I am, a wretch I'll be,
Till love unlocks my chains.

As the notes echoed in Nathan's mind, the figurines danced on. Each young man drew an image of Kelly closer and waltzed with more energy. Nathan eyed the male faces, perfect reproductions of his own.

Kelly continued her song, her voice still wracked with pain.

Could Nathan ever dance with one
So foul, unclean, a liar?
Will grace he plays on strings of ice
Be wrought in hands of fire?

Kelly's clothes ignited. Fire swept across her sleeves and down her legs, raising showers of sparks as it consumed the bloodstains. As every dark thread sizzled away, spots of white appeared. Soon, a radiant gown covered her body, its long sleeves running to the heels of her hands, the hem brushing her ankles. Now, with her eyes sparkling, she played on, her voice louder, less tortured, yet filled with plaintive passion as she stretched out the final words.

The girl I was is crucified,
Impaled by God's dear Lamb.
Can Nathan purge the girl I was
And love the girl I am?

Trembling, Nathan backed away. Thousands of thoughts flooded his mind, battling each other until no single thought made sense. What could all this mean? Kelly had to be dreaming this, but where was she? How could his thoughts and feelings make their way into her mind?

He swallowed hard and tried to slow his breathing, but the thoughts continued to storm. What about those lyrics? So beautiful and heartfelt! Yet, did they reflect a current reality? Or was she reaching out for a hope that glimmered in the distance?

He leaped out of the hologram, the barrier's splash of light again blinding him for a moment, a blindness that seemed to last longer than the previous episode. His eyes burned, yet not as if they had been scorched from the outside. The heat seemed to come from within, more like the scalding touch of ice than fire.

As he rubbed his eyes, Solomon braced his shoulder. "That dream really shook you up, didn't it?"

"Yeah." His eyes now clear, Nathan looked again at the dream. As it slowly faded away, Kelly seemed to stare at him directly, her eyes still sparkling.

He mumbled, "Those eyes . . . they're clear. And she's dreaming in Earth Red."

"What?" Solomon asked.

Nathan wagged his head and looked again. The Earth Red section was now dark. "How long was I in the hologram?" he asked. "I . . . I kind of lost my head in there."

Solomon glanced at his wristwatch. "Not long, maybe two minutes."

"Two minutes?" Nathan stole a glance at Solomon's watch. "It seemed more like ten."

"Your mind adjusted to the time shift. The events in the dreams moved so quickly we couldn't tell what was going on, so I waited for you here while the others looked around." He nodded toward the Earth Yellow sector where Daryl stood with Tony, Molly, Amber, and Francesca. Snow continued to fall within the hologram, though the white blanket seemed no deeper than before.

Nathan pointed at the Earth Red sector. "It had to be Kelly's dream. Since she's the interpreter, her signal is probably strong."

"That was my thinking as well." Solomon turned toward the central core of the hologram and shouted, "Dr. Gordon! Any word on Kelly's signal?"

"It's stronger," came the echoing reply. "We're still hunting it down."

Nathan pointed at the hologram. "Since Kelly's dreaming there, doesn't it mean she's in Earth Red?"

"Not necessarily. Apparently Felicity is able to dream in both the Yellow and Blue sectors, so the wounds must be allowing passage. Maybe someone in another world can dream in Earth Red."

Nathan pinched Solomon's sleeve and pulled him closer. "Can Dr. Gordon send me to Earth Red? The least I can do is look for her. It's better than staring at dreams—"

"Hey!" Daryl yelled. "You'd better get a look at this!"

Nathan looked her way. "What is it?"

"See for yourself!" Daryl waved an arm. "Hurry!"

Nathan ran to Daryl and squeezed between her and Amber as they watched the Chicago snow scene from the edge of the hologram.

Inside, a tall, lanky man stalked through the blanketed street, a white ponytail swinging behind him. Nearly as pale as the snow, he peeked into each car he passed, his eyes narrowing with every search. A red scar etched his cheek from ear to chin, stitched but still oozing blood.

Nathan whispered, "Mictar!"

"Yes." Amber's whisper sounded like a calm wind. "The stalkers heal quickly when they feed on life energy. I fear that he has murdered again."

"Any idea what he's doing?" Nathan asked.

"If I am reading his eyes correctly, he is looking for the dreamer." Amber's voice turned melancholy. "He seeks to murder the dreamer's vision of himself. He has the power to reach through to the dreamer's mind and deliver a mortal shock. Once he finds the dreamer, rarely does he fail to kill."

While Tony, Molly, and Solomon gathered around, Nathan kept his stare riveted on the stalker. With a bare hand, Mictar brushed snow away from a pickup truck's windshield. Obviously he had physically entered the dream world. Even his breath raised clouds of white vapor that were quickly swept away by the wind.

"Can he hear us?" Daryl whispered. "I mean, is he dangerous?"

Solomon stepped close and peered into the dream. "He's dangerous, all right. Just not to us. What we're seeing is like a satellite broadcast of a movie. He has no idea we're watching."

Daryl shuddered. "That might be, but if we could switch it to *Pride and Prejudice*, maybe I won't hurl my breakfast."

"Then I'd hurl mine," Nathan said. "That movie is so—"

"Look!" Daryl pointed at the hologram.

Mictar yanked open a taxicab door, grabbed a man's arm, and dragged him out onto the sidewalk, knocking a hat from his head in the process. He pushed his victim face-first into a snow drift and stepped on his neck. As snow swirled, Mictar appeared to be shouting something, but no sound came out.

"It's Jack!" Nathan leaped into the hologram and knelt at Jack's side. Now aided by the transmitters, Nathan picked up the dream's sounds.

Jack grunted and cried out, but Mictar just laughed and twisted his heel into Jack's neck.

"No more playing with supplicants for you," Mictar said. "If you'll tell me where to find the gifted girl, I'll let you live."

From his hands and knees, Nathan shouted, "Can we stop Mictar from killing him?"

Amber strode into the hologram, carrying a lit candle. Standing toe to toe with Mictar, she stared at him through the flame. As her glow strengthened into a blinding aura, a deep frown marred her features. "This is not a portal. I could enter the dream world, but I have no way of knowing if I will be able to find this particular dream."

Laughing again, Mictar leaned over and laid a hand over Jack's eyes.

"We have to do something!" Nathan yelled, rising to his feet. "Mictar will kill him!"

Solomon ran into the scene, shouting toward the computer desk. "Dr. Gordon, did you test the transport?"

"I didn't have the mirror." Dr. Gordon's voice sounded distant, warped. "It was impossible to conduct a test."

Sparks flew from the sides of Mictar's hands. Jack's body jerked, his arms and legs flailing.

"Do you think it would work?" Solomon yelled.

"So far every prediction has proven true, but transporting someone to the dream world is beyond the scope of predictable science."

Nathan grabbed Solomon's arm. "I'll go. Send me."

"You cannot defeat him," Amber said. "I will go."

Solomon shook his head. "We can't risk either of you. We have to—"

Another figure rushed into view—also tall, lanky, and pale. With a series of gruff pushes, he shoved everyone else out of the hologram, making Nathan and Solomon stumble backwards and knocking Amber to the floor. "Send me," he shouted. "You can risk my life."

Nathan righted himself and reached for Amber's hand, but she had crawled back to the edge of the hologram, the candle still in her hand. "Patar," Nathan said, "I thought you said I was supposed to—"

"Never mind!" Patar stood behind Mictar and looked toward the computer desk. "I demand that you send me immediately."

"A few seconds," Dr. Gordon yelled. "I have to check the—"

"Now!" Patar screamed. "We have no seconds to spare!"

Light flashed all around Patar, veiling the scene. The dream then returned with Patar still behind his brother, puffs of white blowing from the mouths of both stalkers.

Nathan and the others walked to the very edge of the hologram and looked on. Patar grabbed Mictar's ponytail and jerked him backwards. Mictar flew away from Jack, fell into a drift at the edge of the sidewalk, and banged his head against a snow-covered car.

While Patar helped Jack to his feet, Mictar opened his mouth and spewed a jagged black bolt. Arching his body over Jack, Patar ducked and launched his own barrage of dark lightning.

Mictar threw himself to the sidewalk. Patar's blast splashed against the car, sending the snow scattering in a mix of black and white droplets.

"I'd better listen," Nathan said, straightening his glasses. "They might say something important." He stepped back into the hologram and stood a few feet away from the struggle.

Patar propped Jack up, then barked at Mictar. "Leave now before this dream dissolves. When I awaken this human, you will be left without a light."

Mictar sneered. "I know how to negotiate the dreamless gaps."

"The rifts are many. It is now hazardous to stalk the dreamscape."

Mictar pointed a long finger at him. "You feign concern, dear brother, but I know you all too well. One of the gifted humans hides here, and you are protecting her. You are playing the weakened mother bird and keeping me from locating my prize."

"Weakened mother bird?" Patar seemed ready to laugh. "Your metaphor eludes me."

"You are holding back. Using darkness against me instead of reversing my own energy is not your usual way. You are trying to keep me here."

Patar heaved a sigh. "A darkened heart has no ability to understand nobility."

"Ah, yes, this from the one who would have the boy slay the supplicants." Mictar spat on the snow-covered sidewalk. "Such nobility is simply beyond my grasp."

"I have no need to explain myself to you!" Patar pointed a rigid finger of his own. "Be gone!"

"Tell me where to find a mirror used by one of the gifted, and I will gladly go."

With blinding snow swirling around him, Patar folded his arms. "The gateways to Cerulean are out of your reach." Patar lowered his head and muttered, "No thanks to the gifted ones who should have secured them."

Nathan shoulders slumped. Patar's quiet words were obviously meant for him. Cerulean had said he would take care of the mirrors, but he might not have known enough about the real worlds to find a good hiding place.

"So be it," Mictar said, walking away and looking back with a scowl. "I will leave you and your nobility to die with the rodents you seem to admire."

Patar laid a hand over Jack's eyes and spoke with a gentle voice. "Awake now, my friend. I heard your murmurings."

"Yes ... I was tired. Had to sleep."

"How is it that you are dreaming in the Earth Yellow realm? Have you and Cerulean left the Earth Blue dream world?"

"Cerulean found a wound and thought it best for me to sleep near it, hoping I'd search in other dream realms while I rested. It seems that the rift led me here."

"I see," Patar said. "Is your real self with Cerulean now?"

"I assume so. He was at my side when I went to sleep. He hoped to search here as well."

"You must arouse him immediately and send him to the dreams of his new charge."

"Where"—Jack squirmed in Patar's grip—"where should he go?"

"Cerulean knows that she dreams in Earth Blue, and I have seen her there, but that is not where she sleeps. If he goes to find her physical body, he will not be able to return." Patar pulled his hand away from Jack's eyes. They were whole, glowing like two phosphorescent marbles.

"I don't understand."

"Cerulean will. Tell him that Mictar is on the prowl and has grown strong again. He must find the gifted one before Mictar does."

Nathan looked up, searching for the ponytailed stalker. In the distance, at the boundary of the hologram's central black section, Mictar stopped and stared at the dark wall. As if ripping a flaw in the fabric, he opened it with both hands and slid inside. The gap then sealed itself, hiding the stalker from view.

Fixing his stare on the dark wall, Nathan remembered the Earth Blue dream world, where he and Cerulean had passed from dream to dream through a series of membranes. Each passage revealed a dark hole on one side. Was that void represented here by the hologram's dark core?

Nathan stepped out of the hologram and rejoined the others. "Mictar's still on the move, but I have no idea where he went."

Solomon gave him a somber nod. "And we don't know where Amber went either."

"She's gone?" Nathan looked in every direction. "Where did you see her last?"

"When Patar knocked her out of the hologram." Solomon stooped at the spot where Amber had been crouching. "I saw her right here, but after that I was paying so much attention to the fight, I didn't keep an eye on her."

"Could she have transported with Patar?"

"I suppose so, but I never saw her in there."

"I'll go take a look." Nathan walked back into the snow scene and headed straight for the dark center, passing by Patar and Jack without a pause.

When he came within a few paces of the central core's wall, the entire city scene darkened. The dream was coming to an end. Only the old tree was still easily visible, standing like an ancient sentry just a step or two from the wall.

A movement to his right caught Nathan's eye. Amber skulked out from behind a car and, giving the tree a wide berth, came to a halt in front of the barrier, her candle raising a steady spherical glow on the black surface. Although her dress flapped violently, the flame stayed steady. Apparently unaware of Nathan's presence, she ran searching fingers along the wall.

A few seconds later, she pushed through a vertical flaw, covering her hand up to the heel. The material appeared to be similar to rubber from a tire, somewhat pliable but still tough. She set her candle down, then pulled with both hands to separate the two flaps, straining as if trying to open a stubborn pair of jaws.

Finally, she created a narrow slit and stepped into it, leaving half her body barely visible in the candle's light. Keeping one arm and a leg in the opening, she lunged for something in the darkness outside her candle's faint glow, caught it in one hand, and reeled it toward herself as if she were pulling a rope.

She reached to the ground and picked up her candle. After looking around once more at the darkened Earth Yellow dream world, she whispered, "Nathan, I hope you are still listening. Although the reasons are a mystery to me, I believe the cosmic wounds have allowed the vision stalker to use Sarah's Womb as a portal to go from one dream world to another. If so, I will learn his secrets and perhaps use them to locate your father and Kelly. When I do, I will try to find a way to contact you. I am very concerned about Mictar's new discovery. It could well mean that your loved ones are in great danger, so I have to follow him." Her eyes shining with a light of their own, and the wind, fiercer than ever, blowing her hair into the void, she let out a sigh. "Please tell Francesca that I love her, and I hope to be able to supplicate for her through the mirrors of the Yellow world."

Straining again, she pushed farther into the slit. With a final grunt, she popped through and disappeared from sight.

Nathan turned, searching for Patar and Jack in the darkness, but they were gone. Unlike the other dreams he'd experienced where everything had been sucked away in a cyclone, this one just faded into nothingness. Could it be a difference of perspective? Maybe if he had actually been there, the swirling windstorm would have been easy to see.

Now that this sector of the hologram had no dream to display, the observatory again filled his vision, and the echoing noises pounded into his ears.

"We lost the signal," Dr. Gordon called. "I will have to search for another dream in that realm."

With the dream gone, the futility of his position flooded Nathan's mind. In reality, they had done nothing, nothing at all. They had simply sat in the bleachers watching dreams come and go, hoping that one would reveal what they were searching for.

It was worse than looking for a needle in a haystack; it was looking for a tiny impulse in an ocean of overstimulated neurons.

He hurried back to Solomon and jerked off the glasses. "We can't just stand around here and watch nightmares all day! I've had enough of singing and dancing and roaming through dream worlds. My father is missing, Kelly got slurped into a manure-filled sandbox, and we're just standing around here waiting for a computer to locate a signal when we're not even sure Kelly's holding the candle!" He pushed Solomon's chest. "Send me into the dream world. I have to look for Kelly and my father!"

"But that's exactly what we're doing." Solomon pointed at the floor. "Searching from here is safe."

"Safe?" Clenching his fist again, Nathan tilted his head up and looked Solomon in the eye. Every feature was so much like his father's—the eyes, the chin, the confident jaw. Yet, something was so different. He pointed at the graveyard. "My father would've risked his life to help that little blind girl, even if it meant getting sucked into that cyclone. My father would've moved heaven and earth to find me or Mom or Kelly! Instead, we're sitting on our hands while the world is about to end. It's just plain stupid!"

Solomon laid a hand on Nathan's shoulder. "What's the bottom line, Nathan? What do you want to do?"

Nathan shrugged away his hand. "I'm going in there. Maybe Felicity doesn't know what happened to Kelly, but it's a good place to start. And I don't know if we can believe that she knows where my father is, but it's worth a try." He strode toward the graveyard and stood at the edge of the hologram, crossing his arms over his chest. "Tell Dr. Gordon to play the music and flash the lights. I'm going in!"

10

THE SUPPLICANT'S CALL

Solomon gave Nathan a stern look, but it quickly eased. "Okay. I'll make it happen." He strode to the computer desk where Gordon and the two Simons watched their screens. "Get ready to make the jump," he called back.

"Wait!" Daryl sprinted around the hologram and grabbed Nathan's arm. "You ain't jumping to light speed without me, buster." She pointed at herself with her thumb. "You need a cool-headed thinker, and I'm your girl."

"And I'm going, too." Nathan's mother walked toward him with the violin and bow. "My husband is in that dream world somewhere, so I'm going in, and I'm not coming back without him. Besides, who else will play when you need music?"

Nathan touched his reflection on the violin's smooth surface. "You showed me how to play through pain. I'm sure I can do it. But I'll be glad to have you along anyway." He looked into her wise, piercing eyes. Did she know why he really needed her? To help him play the great violin if they ever found it? In any case, he would tell her soon.

The others began gathering around, but Nathan raised a hand. "Look, I know you're all willing to come with me, but you can't." He pointed at Tony, Molly, and Francesca Yellow in turn. "Stay here and raise those babies. They need you. And hide all the mirrors. Mictar's sure to come looking for them eventually."

He stepped closer to Francesca Yellow. Smiling, he took her hand. "Amber gave me a message. She wants you to know that she loves you, and she'll try to supplicate for you through the mirrors."

Francesca wiped a tear from her eye. "Little Nathan and I will be watching for her." She leaned close and kissed his cheek, whispering, "And I will pray for you and Kelly with all my heart."

Nathan shivered at the touch. Even though he loved this girl like a sister, this was no time to get sentimental. He just breathed a heartfelt, "Thank you."

He gestured for everyone to draw close and peered over Tony's shoulder to get a look at Solomon and the three scientists. They were busy on the computer, apparently preparing for the next cross-dimensional leap.

With Francesca, Tony, Molly, Daryl, and his mother huddling around, Nathan lowered his voice. "Listen. No offense to anyone, but you guys are the only people on Earth Yellow I trust. Can you keep a secret?"

Tony glanced at Solomon. "Even from Flash?"

"Yeah. Even from Flash."

"Sure. I guess so." Tony smiled and pointed at Nathan. "You're Future Boy, so you know more about this stuff than I do."

"Thanks." Nathan almost added that he wasn't sure what he knew anymore, but he thought better of it.

Francesca fidgeted, then took in a deep breath before whispering, "Nathan, Solomon is my husband. I know you've been my friend for a longer time, but I made a vow. I can't keep secrets from him."

Nathan pressed his lips together. She was right. Asking her to go against her word was a terrible idea. "Then tell him if you have to. I know I can trust your wisdom." He looked at Tony again. "Do you remember how to use Daryl's transmitter?"

"The one that talks to the future? Sure. I have it all figured out."

"Then get a message to Dr. Gordon Red for me."

Daryl pulled on Nathan's sleeve, her whisper a little louder than the others'. "We didn't test it after Earth Red pulled away. I'm not sure he'll be able to contact—"

"We have to try it." Nathan raised a finger. "There's one thing I never figured out: that plastic card I took from the shotgun guy, the one with all the letters and numbers on it. It has to be important."

"Where is it?" Tony asked.

"I left it on the computer desk in the Earth Blue observatory, so Gordon will have to—"

"It's not there," Daryl said. "Gordon Red wanted to see it, so Daryl Blue loaded up the interdimensional fax machine and shot it over to him."

Nathan gave her a thumbs-up. "Even better. Tell him to send it over to this observatory so you guys can transport it to me in the Earth Blue dream world."

"And use channel three," Daryl added, showing Tony three fingers. "That'll send a digitally encoded message straight to Dr. Gordon's computer. With all the whale-speak going on there, I doubt that anything else will work."

Tony spread out one of his huge hands. "But it's five hours to Newton. By the time I get there, this cemetery dream will be history. How can anyone find Nathan to give him the card when it gets here?"

"Okay, okay." Spreading out her hands, Daryl heaved a sigh. "I'll take care of it."

"What do you mean?" Nathan asked.

She flicked her thumb toward the computers. "I watched El Gordo work the gizmos. Tony and I will figure out how to get everyone to scoot so we can do the transmissions right here, and maybe I can get the card to you before that dream ends."

"Thanks, Daryl." Nathan gave her a light pat on her back. "I know you wanted to come. I appreciate it."

"Not so fast, Tin Man. If you had a heart, you'd remember that I've already spent too much time in this world." She poked his chest with her finger. "You're not leaving me here again. I'm going to find you and hand deliver the card."

Nathan suppressed a laugh. "You're amazing, Daryl, you know that?

With a wink and a grin, Daryl tossed her hair back. "As a matter of fact, I do. It's obvious you need me around."

Returning the grin, Nathan looped his arm around his mother's. "I guess we're off to see the wizard without the scarecrow."

"Scarecrow?" Daryl shook a finger at him. "Listen, Twister Boy, if you're looking to wrestle with another tornado, I'll be glad to—"

"Time to go!" Nathan pulled his mother into the hologram. After the initial flash of light, he put the glasses on. Again, everything slowed to a normal pace—the rain, the windblown fog, and the swaying trees. He turned and looked back. "I hope to see all of you soon," he called, waving.

Their replies sounded muffled and warped, and their waves seemed slow. Music filled the air, something mournful he couldn't identify. "Do you know what that song is?" he asked. He leaned close to his mother so she could hear through the transmitters.

After a few seconds, her head bobbed up and down with the tune. "Speed it up in your mind, Nathan. You'll figure it out."

He concentrated on the notes, trying to push them together, but he didn't have much time. The flash sending them to the dream world could come at any moment.

He nudged her side. "Give me a break, Mom. What is it?"

Smiling, she whispered, " 'Danse Macabre.' "

Nathan shuddered. "The Dance of Death" was the same

piece he had played when boarding Flight 191 in Chicago. At this slow pace, it was creepier than ever.

While waiting for the flash, Nathan glanced around, looking for any sign of Felicity. In the midst of a shroud of fog and windswept rain, her shadow arose in front of the tombstone where he had seen her before. She staggered backwards, her face and form becoming clear. With her mouth agape and her arms trembling, she seemed petrified of something, but in her blindness how could she see any danger?

Nathan followed the direction her face pointed. At the wall that led to the hologram's inner core, a hand protruded from a gap—a long, pale hand. Then, a body emerged along with a familiar face and white ponytail, but it looked like he was having trouble pushing all the way through.

"Now!" Nathan yelled. "Send us now!"

Lightning flashed. Thunder boomed. Nathan sucked in another breath to yell again, but the air felt cold and wet in his lungs. Raindrops pelted his hair, matting his bangs to his forehead, and mist coated his glasses.

His mother pushed the violin under her sweater. "Looks like we made it."

"Stay there!" Nathan yanked off the glasses, ran to Felicity, and took her hand. "It's me, Nathan. Are you okay?"

"I smell death." She pointed straight ahead with her walking stick, her voice thin and frail. "Among the tombstones, I always smell death, but now it's stronger than ever. He has finally come to take me away."

"Not if I can help it." Nathan stepped between her and Mictar. The stalker shook his leg, trying to free it from the dark wall.

"He's stuck," Nathan said. "Let's get out of here before he gets loose."

She resisted his pull. "No need. I smell my new friend. He will protect me."

"You're dreaming. The only real things here are me, my mother, and a crazy murderer named Mictar, and we don't want to mess with him." He scooped her up into his arms and hurried back to his mother.

"Did he see you?" she asked.

"Hard to say." He nodded toward a cluster of gnarled trees. "Let's find a place to hide."

Still carrying Felicity, Nathan half-ran to the biggest of the trees, a thick leafless oak so bent it looked like an old, arthritis-stricken man covering his moss-covered head with his crooked arms. They huddled behind the trunk, stooping as they watched.

Mictar finally freed himself from the dream boundary. With rain plastering his ponytail against the back of his shirt, he raised his hands and sang out a pair of vowels that sounded like a long E and a short A.

A puff of gray smoke arose from his palms, cloaking them for a moment. When the air around him cleared, a black violin and white bow lay in his hands. He lifted the violin to his chin and pulled the bow across the strings. A high note sang out, warbling with a songbirdlike vibrato.

"I hear the song," Felicity said, her voice quiet and mysterious. "Death is calling me."

Nathan clamped a hand over her mouth and whispered, "When death calls, don't pick up the phone."

Playing more vibrating notes, Mictar walked along a path through the graveyard, looking at both sides of each tombstone as he passed by. Suddenly, he stopped and sniffed the air, turning as he took in long drafts.

Nathan pushed everyone lower, but he didn't dare utter a word. If that stalker smelled fear, staying quiet might not do any good, but why give him any more clues than he already had?

Another sniff sounded, this one coming from under Nathan's

protective arm. Felicity whispered through Nathan's fingers, "I smell the clutching wood."

The tree's trunk let out a long creaking sound, and the branches sagged lower, obviously saturated and heavy. If much more rain fell, this might not be a safe place to hide.

Mictar looked their way, his nostrils flared. Shuffling closer, he played three short notes as if calling out, "Where are you?"

Nathan clamped down tighter on Felicity's mouth. Why was Mictar hesitating? He had to know they were nearby. Why hadn't he rushed ahead to find them?

The rain stopped suddenly, and as the clouds raced away, a strange glow shone in the distance. Mictar halted and tilted his head up. Nathan, too, looked skyward. The canopy above had turned from gray to purple, with hints of azure and blue spreading from treetop to treetop, but no sun appeared. The light seemed to be coming from over the horizon, as if dawn was about to break, but the sky was brightening too quickly—far too quickly.

Mictar pointed the bow at their hiding place. "I smell your presence, Nathan and Francesca Shepherd. The aroma of the gifted ones is one you cannot hide."

Felicity struggled, but Nathan kept her locked down. "Since you're staying put, Mictar, I don't think we're the only ones who reek. I can see the yellow stripe down your back from here."

"Oh, yes, the heroic barb, the comical insult to buttress your sagging courage." Mictar propped his bow against his shoulder and laughed. "But I must give you credit: you really are good at comic relief, flinging taunts from behind a spider tree."

Nathan looked up at the branches. Although the rain had ended, the branches continued to sag as if reaching down. Felicity's words came back to his mind. *I smell the clutching wood.*

A knobby-fingered hand reached down and grabbed Nathan's arm. He jerked away and pulled his mother and Felicity back just in time to avoid two other wooden claws, but as he hurried backwards, he tripped over a root and fell on his rear.

Mictar laughed again. "Watching a clown perform his arts is truly entertaining."

Nathan jumped to his feet and wiped mud from his back-side. Felicity groped for him. "Death is near. I hear him, smell him, feel his presence."

Grabbing her wrist, Nathan pulled her to his side, while his mother picked up a hefty branch and wielded it like a club.

"Why were you hunting for Felicity?" Nathan asked. "She's just a dream."

"What do you take me for, a fool? I keep my own counsel." Mictar took a step toward them, but stopped. A new voice, powerful and deep, sang from over a hill in the distance, send-ing beautiful vowel sounds across the cemetery.

Felicity whispered, "Mictar seeks a gateway to the mind of the new gifted one, the sleeper, the dreamer, my beloved."

As the blue light brightened near the hilltop, Mictar backed away, crouching like a wary cat.

Backing away at the same pace, Nathan caressed Felicity's arm. "Did you just interpret that song?"

"Yes," she replied. "He called me his beloved. I must go to him."

A head appeared at the hilltop, then the body of a young man came into sight as he walked to the crest. An aura of blue light surrounded him, and its glow spread throughout the grave-yard. With his silky blue shirt and dark blue hair flowing in the breeze, he seemed more unearthly than ever. Jack walked a step behind, threading his hat through nervous fingers.

Nathan stopped and bent close to Felicity. "His name is Cerulean. And another friend is with him, a guy named Jack. They'll keep death from finding you."

Mictar squared his shoulders and glared at Cerulean. "Since

your doom is certain, cursed supplicant, coming to the grave-yard is most appropriate."

As Cerulean approached, tombstones crumbled, weeds shriveled, and lush grass grew in their places. Flowers sprouted near Mictar's feet, yellow, orange, and purple blossoms bursting forth with radiant petals. Flashing a brilliant smile, Cerulean spoke, this time with words instead of vowel sounds. "Grave-yards become gardens, darkness becomes daylight, and daisies decorate the feet of death."

The stalker leaped to a bare spot in the path and kept his icy glare trained on the supplicant. "Poetry won't save you from your fate."

Cerulean's glow diminished, but his eyes stayed as bright as his smile. "Sacrifice appears as a curse to those of limited perception. To the beneficiary, it is life itself. To the provider, it is the path to enlightenment and the end of all fear, for perfect love casts out all fear."

"Trite moralisms nauseate me. You sound like my fool of a brother."

Slowing his pace, Cerulean pointed at himself. "That is because he has listened to my song, to Amber's song, and to Scarlet's song. He has learned the meaning of sacrifice."

"Bah! Fodder for girlish romance." While keeping his stare locked on Cerulean, Mictar pointed at Nathan. "Did you know that Patar has more than once insisted that this boy kill you along with your color-coded sisters? Did you know that this boy and his mother are the reason Scarlet lies dead in Sarah's Womb, never to return to your loving embrace?"

Cerulean glanced at Nathan, his smile wilting ever so slightly. He halted and folded his hands at his waist. "All three of us have asked for the cup of death to pass by, but if the master of the table pours it into my goblet, I will drink it to the very last drop."

Mictar sneered and waved his hand. "You can stay at the

side of this ugly little blind girl forever, but you can't stop me. With Scarlet's corpse now rotting in the abyss, you will never be able to protect all three of the gifted Earth Red dwellers. I will eventually find one unguarded, and when I do, the Lucifer machine will again be fueled."

With Jack standing at his side, Cerulean stretched out his hand and called with a deep, commanding voice. "Felicity, my beloved, come to me!"

Felicity pulled against Nathan's grip. "I have to go to him."

"But Mictar's in the way, the guy you call 'Death.'"

She took off her glasses and looked up at him with her vacant sockets. "We all have to suffer the presence of death to enter the arms of our supplicant, but death is merely an odor. It comes and it goes, like breath in our nostrils, and after it passes by, only the fragrance of life remains."

Nathan stared at her, slowly releasing his grip. How could a blind girl who has seen only darkness, who has suffered through countless nights of fear, speak so beautifully?

As Felicity pulled away, Nathan's mother touched his arm. "Dreams often give us eloquence, Nathan, for God pours wisdom into the dreams of men."

Looking at his mother, Nathan shivered. "Did you read my mind?"

"In a way." She smiled and held his gaze for a long moment. "It's as if your thoughts are spoken through your eyes."

Nathan had to look away. He reached out and took Felicity's hand again. "I'll lead you to him."

Cerulean shook his head. "Let her go, Nathan. Her fears are many, and she cannot overcome them if you guide her." Again extending a hand of invitation, he called out, "Felicity, come to me. I will lead you across the shadow of death with song."

Clutching her walking stick, she tapped the ground in front of her, now without her dark glasses. Cerulean stood about a hundred feet down the path. As Felicity drew closer, he crouched and held both hands out as if waiting for a baby to approach with her first toddling steps.

Mictar stood between them, closer to Cerulean than to Felicity, no more than sixty feet away from the supplicant. The stalker glanced back and forth between the two, looking frightened and confused. Obviously, he didn't dare confront Cerulean, but he didn't seem to want to leave. Every time he looked at Felicity, his eyes took on a hungry look, even though the little blind girl had no eyes for him to take.

Cerulean sang new vowels, each one sounding like a daddy's comforting lullaby. Felicity echoed the translations. Her voice, strong yet tremulous, carried to Nathan's ears.

You need no crutch, no hand to hold.
My voice is all you need.
So cast away your fears and cares
And harken unto me.

Felicity threw her walking stick to the side and, extending both hands in front of her, walked forward.

The smell of death grows strong and foul.
It permeates the air.
It threatens those who fear the dark;
It kills when souls despair.

As she neared Mictar, Felicity slowed. Cerulean raised his voice, his passion rising with every note.

But neither height nor depth nor darkest pits
Will separate us hence;
The healing one will find you soon
And mend the cosmic fence.

Felicity came within reach of Mictar, her arms still extended and fingers groping, and her feet within inches of the stalker's long, spindly shadow. Mictar lifted his violin to his chin, its black wood a stark contrast to his pale face. He played a loud note that muffled Cerulean's voice. Then, sawing across the strings, he created a scratching, buzzing noise that barely resembled music at all.

As Mictar stepped back toward Nathan, the path ahead of Felicity collapsed. A deep crevice stretched at least fifty feet from side to side. With earth still crumbling away, the edge crawled to within inches of her feet.

Nathan jumped ahead. "Felicity! Stop! There's a—"

"No!" Again Cerulean held up his hand. "Do not add to her fears!"

Felicity halted at the very edge and stretched out her fingers. "Is it safe to walk?"

"No!" Mictar said as he lowered the violin. "If you take one step you will fall into endless depths, and you will never be in your supplicant's arms."

"He lies," Cerulean countered. "Run to me. This is your dream. You can do whatever your faith allows. No valley will swallow you as long as you believe."

Mictar raised his violin again. While Felicity paused, every limb shaking, Nathan whispered to his mother, "It's time to replace that musical hack. Play something. Anything. As long as it's melodic and loud."

She lifted the violin and played the opening measure of *Finlandia*. Nathan lunged toward Mictar. Like an out-of-control linebacker, he rammed into the stalker's lanky body and bulldozed him into the ground. He jerked the violin away and jumped to his feet, careful to avoid Mictar's deadly hands.

Standing over Mictar with the violin raised, Nathan growled, "Remember the last time I clubbed you with one of these? If you move or make a sound, you'll get an encore performance."

"Fool!" Mictar sang out a shrill note. A streak of blackness shot from his mouth and splashed across Nathan's chest, sending him flying into a backwards somersault. He slid on his back, and the violin's strings banged against the turf, sending out a violent stream of twanging notes.

As he righted himself, Felicity spun toward him. "Nathan?"

The ground shook in time with the echoing call of Mictar's violin. The edge of the crevice gave way. Felicity toppled into the void and disappeared. Her screams, loud and heart-wrenching, faded away. Still clutching his hat, Jack jumped in after her.

"Nathan!" Cerulean shouted. "Take off your sweatshirt! Francesca! Keep playing!" In a flash of blue light, he dove into the growing chasm.

Nathan looked down at his chest. A mass of blackness stretched like wiggling fingers toward his face. Dropping the violin, he grabbed the back of his sweatshirt and peeled it over his head, careful to keep his face out of whatever that black stuff was.

His mother ran to his side, then resumed her playing as she stared at Mictar. She had switched to "Danse Macabre," and the notes seemed to fly toward the stalker in long ribbons of white.

Mictar scrambled to his feet and grabbed some of the ribbons out of the air. He threw the handful to the ground and stomped on them with his boot. "I may not be able to overpower both of you while you play," he said as he swatted down more of the ribbons, "but I have another victim in mind."

He picked up his violin and strode back to the dream world's core. He clawed at the dark barrier, searching, groping. Finally, it gave way. He ripped open a gap and squeezed through, disappearing as the wall sealed behind him.

Heaving a long breath, Nathan's mother lowered her violin. "At least we know how to defend ourselves against him."

"Yeah, but Kelly doesn't, and I'm sure she's his prime target."

WHEN COURAGE IS BORN

Nathan walked to the chasm and looked down. There was no sign of Felicity or anyone else; only darkness spread out below. As he shuffled back to his mother, he spread out his arms. "Now what?"

"What choice do we have?" she asked. "We can't go anywhere, can we?"

"So we just stand around and wait for Cerulean to show up? Hope that Felicity is with him so we can look for Dad?"

"Patience, son." She pointed her bow at him. "Since your father's not here, I think it's time for a mother-and-son chat."

"What do you mean?"

"You lost control with Mictar and distracted Felicity. Remember the proverb? *A fool always loses his temper, but a wise man holds it back.*"

"I remember." Letting out a sigh, he looked around the deserted cemetery. Another proverb entered his mind, his father's favorite. *Do not be afraid of sudden fear nor of the onslaught of the wicked when it comes; for the Lord will be your confidence and will keep your foot from being caught.*

And his father faced every danger with squared shoulders and a firm jaw. "Maybe you can help me figure out Solomon Yellow. In comparison to Dad, he seemed ... well ..."

"Yellow?" she offered.

Nathan laughed. "I didn't want to say it. It sounds too corny."

She sat on the ground and patted a spot next to her. "There's a story I don't think you've ever heard."

"Sure. As long as we have to wait, why not?" Bracing his body, he lowered himself, favoring his bandaged hand. "I wonder how long this dream will last. When I fall inside a dream, it usually means I'm about to wake up."

"That's happened to me, too." She set the violin in her lap. "If this dream ends, what will happen to us?"

"I'm not real sure. Some dreams get swept up in a storm, while others just fade away. But I think it'll just get dark and we'll be in a gap between dreams." He looked around at the former cemetery. It was already too dark to see the newly sprouted flowers.

"Darkness is fine," she said. "I used to tell you stories in the dark quite often. Do you remember?"

"Yeah. I finally made you stop when I was about eight. I said I was too old for bedtime stories."

She reached over and touched his knee lovingly. "Are you too old now?"

"Too old?" He shook his head. "I think maybe I'm finally old enough to start again."

"Well, this is a story about courage." She looked at her wounded hand. Blood still oozed into her palm. "Your father learned courage when he and I were courting. You see, we met when I first started playing for the CSO. During my premiere performance as concertmaster, I played the Tchaikovsky concerto, and your father was in the first row. Back then, he was a college student, but he was interning for the summer at an applied sciences company in Chicago. That's where he learned a lot of what he knows about physics and light bending and creating illusions, but I never understood enough to make sense of it."

Nathan stared at her. This *was* a story he hadn't heard. "How old were you then?"

"I was all of twenty-one years old, not much more than a girl, really."

Nathan reached for his discarded sweatshirt and ripped a piece from the sleeve he had cut earlier. Whatever the black stuff was, it had disappeared. "So, when Francesca Yellow married," he said, tying the fresh bandage around her hand, "she was a lot younger."

She smiled as she watched him work. "Yes, and that's why I'm telling you the story. You see, after that performance, your father waited for me at the door, even though I had taken a long time to come out because of a reception in my honor. Apparently, he was mesmerized by my performance and wanted an autograph, so he paced around the area until after midnight. Unfortunately, a group of four other men also seemed overly interested in seeing me. As soon as I stepped out the door, three of them brandished handguns while a fourth opened a cello case and pulled out a shotgun."

"A shotgun," Nathan repeated. "Double barreled?"

"Yes. As a matter of fact, it was."

"Did the guy have a gray beard?"

"He had a beard, but it wasn't gray." She squinted at him, darkness now shadowing her features. "Why?"

"Just thinking. Go on."

"Well, at first your father—"

"No! Wait!" Nathan felt for the violin in her lap and picked it up. "Play it, and show me."

"What do you mean?"

Nathan tried to see her facial expression, but it was too dark. Still, her inquisitive motherly stare came through in his mind. "We're in the dream world," he explained. "Show me, like you did when you played the scenes of you growing up and getting married."

"Can we do that from inside the dream world?"

"There's no dream going on right now. And I have a hunch

about those gunmen. I want to see what one of them looked like." He found her wrist and set the violin in her arms. "It won't hurt to try."

She laughed under her breath. "It certainly *will* hurt, but I'll do it."

"Oh, yeah," Nathan said, grimacing. He reached to take the violin back, but grasped empty air.

"Just watch and pay attention," she said. "I don't want to do this more than once." She paused for a few seconds, the sound of her tuning the violin breaking the silence, then her words blended in, spiced with a doubtful tone. "If it works at all."

She began humming the opening of the Tchaikovsky piece, the orchestra's introductory measures, then, after a short pause, she played.

Nathan leaned close. The vibrant tones sounded more beautiful than ever. Somehow the darkness enhanced the music, allowing only his mother's song to penetrate his mind. In a way, he felt like Felicity—his eyesight impotent, but his other senses acute. He breathed in deeply. Each note had a smell, even a taste, as the music-saturated air rushed into his nostrils and then out his mouth, passing over his tongue with a sweet caress.

The sensation reminded him of Scarlet. Her eloquence hadn't emerged in a while. Had he lost touch with her spirit? Would it ever come back? Nathan let out a sigh and concentrated on the music again. This was no time for mooning over his lost friend.

Soon, a dim light illuminated the area—a lamp perched high above a street about twenty paces away. It shone on a set of four wood-and-glass doors that led into a brick building, and lights attached to the façade on both sides of the doors cast their glow on the wide walkway in front.

Nathan rose to his feet. He stood across the street from

Orchestra Hall, deep enough in the shadows to escape notice if someone in the dream world should walk by.

A raven-haired young woman stepped out of the hall. Dressed in a flowing black gown, she smiled at an older woman, also dressed in black, who walked at her side.

"That's Mom," Nathan whispered to himself. Staying low, he hurried across the dark pavement and ducked behind a car parked at the curb. Now that he had stepped fully inside the dream, the sounds of his mother's violin faded away, replaced by the voices of young Francesca and her companion.

"Tchaikovsky himself would have asked for your autograph," the older woman said. "It was superb. Magnificent."

Francesca blushed and touched the woman's hand. "Clara, you're too kind, but I'm thankful for your encouragement. I was so nervous I almost got sick right on the conductor, and now I don't remember a single note I played."

Nathan tried to slow his heartbeat. His mother had just exited the orchestra hall with Clara, his tutor, not too long before he was born. This was way too strange.

A man walked out of the shadows holding an open book and a pen. "Excuse me, Miss Malenkov. May I have your autograph?"

Francesca stepped back, her eyebrows raised. "Oh!... Well, yes, of course."

Francesca held the pen while looking at the man's beaming face. "And to whom shall I sign it?"

"Solomon." His voice trembled, but he quickly brought it under control. "Solomon Shepherd."

Francesca smiled. "I like that name. It carries a pleasant melody."

"I know this young man quite well." Winking, Clara shook a finger at him. "Do you often wait two hours after orchestra performances to get autographs?"

"Uh ... no." Solomon shifted his weight from side to side.

"This was my first time here, and I was so transfixed by Miss Malenkov's performance, I just had to meet her."

"Well, she really needs her rest." Clara hooked Francesca's arm. "We have to —"

"Oh, Clara." Francesca's eyes sparkled as she gave Solomon his autograph book. "It's all right. I can sleep in —"

Four men jumped out of a car parked in front of the one Nathan hid behind. Three ran toward the door, handguns drawn, while the fourth, a bearded man, lagged behind, carrying a cello case.

Clara pulled Solomon in front of her and Francesca. "I hope you don't mind being a shield."

"Shut up, lady," one of the men said, "and step away from Malenkov."

Clara wrapped an arm around Francesca and pulled her close. "Or you'll what?"

The bearded man withdrew a shotgun from the cello case and aimed it at Solomon and the two ladies. "Or we'll have to drag more corpses away than we counted on."

Solomon leaped for the shotgun and wrestled it away. One of the men shot him in the chest. As Solomon backpedaled, he returned fire, blowing away his attacker with one barrel and two more with the other. With blood soaking his shirt and suit jacket, he glared at the fake cellist. "Drop to the ground," he said, breathing heavily, "before I kill you, too."

The man laughed and dug into his pocket. "You might need some of these," he said, displaying a handful of shells.

"Not when I have a club." Solomon reared back and bashed the man's arm with the shotgun, knocking him down. Then, gasping and gurgling, Solomon wobbled back and forth before toppling to the concrete. The attacker scrambled along the sidewalk toward the gun, but a high-heeled shoe stomped on his wrist.

"That's far enough, cello boy!" Clara said, aiming a handgun at his head.

As a siren wailed, the man looked at her with menacing eyes. "I have friends in high places. I will be back to kill the gifted one."

Nathan crept closer to get a better look. There was no doubt about it. The guy with the shotgun was the same gunman who had chased Clara and him through the streets of Chicago and then stalked Kelly and him in the observatory. His beard was dark back then, but it was definitely the same guy.

Francesca cradled Solomon, crying and mopping his brow as they whispered to each other. Nathan tried to listen, but two police officers ran onto the scene, one barking into a radio about needing an ambulance while the other shouted commands.

His heart again beating wildly, Nathan backed away to the street and then completely out of the dream. With the glow of the streetlight guiding his way, he found his mother, still playing her part of the Tchaikovsky concerto.

She opened one eye and smiled. Then, easing through a final note, she let out a long sigh. "The bullet missed his heart, but there was quite a bit of damage. He almost died from loss of blood. He was in the hospital for over a month."

With the light from the street beginning to fade, Nathan sat down and tried to calm his heart. "I saw you whispering, but I couldn't hear what you said."

She gave a gentle laugh. "I'll never forget his words. He said, 'It will never hurt worse than it does now.' So I asked him what he meant, and he said, 'Protecting you. I took a bullet for you. I will gladly take another.'"

She drew a fist to her mouth, covering her trembling lips. "He told me later that what he did was really an instinctive jump, but since then he's never let fear stop him from doing anything. It's as if he faced death and stared it down."

Nathan touched her arm and replied in a near whisper. "And

Solomon Yellow never had a chance to do that. That's why he's so different."

She nodded, took a deep breath, and composed herself. "I assume Francesca Yellow is not yet concertmaster of the CSO, so I wonder how they met."

"I guess Kelly and I talked her into marrying him," Nathan said. "Since she spent so much time in the other Earths, she missed some years on Yellow and lost ground. She was kind of hesitant, because she was so young, but they managed to get together."

She stroked her violin with tender hands. "Well, as long as they married and had a baby they named Nathan, I assume it will all work out."

"But that Nathan won't learn what I learned from Dad. Solomon Yellow won't be able to teach him to stare down death." He touched his chest. "I learned not to let fear stop me from doing anything."

She lifted her eyebrows. "Oh, is that so?"

"Well ..." He let his hand drop. He was no match for his mother's skeptical stare. "I think it's so."

With only the slightest of glows still radiating from the dream, she was barely visible as she wiggled her fingers across imaginary piano keys. "It moved by very quickly, but I recognized what Kelly played in her dream. I know what you fear."

Nathan's heart thumped faster again. "Are you saying I'm scared to talk to her?"

A knowing smile stretched her lips. "She's dying for you to talk to her, Nathan. Begging. Praying. Pleading. But she won't ask you herself. You have to be the one to reach out to her."

"She keeps saying she'll wait for me, as long as it takes. I thought maybe she wanted, you know, to be my girlfriend or something." He pointed at himself. "I mean, I'm only sixteen. I don't want to go there yet."

"I don't think she wants to go there yet, either. I'm not

sure she ever wants to go there. She's not hoping to marry you someday."

"So what *does* she want? Just for me to talk to her?"

She nodded. "That's all. Love that doesn't demand something in return. No one has ever loved her that way before, and she sees it in you. She doesn't want a boyfriend. She just wants to know that her past is erased in your mind."

"But I thought I was supposed to tell her about my faith in God. Her song made it sound like she already believes. Maybe I don't need to say anything."

She took his hand and massaged his thumb. "She's trying her hardest to believe, but she won't truly understand forgiveness until you show it to her. She can't believe God would really forgive her for what she's done."

"But what did she do? I mean ..." He hesitated, wondering if he should go on. "Do you even know?"

"Yes, Nathan. She told me." Three deep lines creased her brow. "It was hard to understand everything, because she was crying so much, but she told me."

"So, what did she ..." Nathan hesitated again. Did he really want to ask what she had done? Did he really want to know? After a second or two, he took in a deep breath and said, "Was it really all that terrible?"

Her voice cracked. "Yes. Yes, Nathan. It was."

Nathan swallowed. Tears welled and trickled down his cheeks. "So what do I do?"

As she folded his hand into hers, her voice spiked with passion. "Forgive her, Nathan. Forgive her with all your heart. She's already heard about faith from a hundred TV sermons, but she has never seen the real, vibrant, down-to-earth forgiving heart of Jesus lived out in reality, certainly not in her father or in her mother." Now weeping, she lifted his hand and laid it on his chest. "She needs to know that this brave-hearted young knight will treat her like the fair maiden she so longs to be, no matter what she's done to soil that label." She loosened his bandage and unwound it until his bloody wound lay exposed. "She has crucified herself a thousand times for her sins. It's time for you to put an end to her suffering."

Nathan stared at his hand, barely visible in the waning light. A tear fell from his mother's eye and landed on his palm. As it trickled into the wound, the salt stung, but he didn't flinch. Somehow the pain felt right.

He rolled his hand into a fist, letting the pain increase. It was about time he took the brunt of the pain. So far, Kelly had risked her life time and again for his sake, and all he had given her in return was halfhearted acceptance. She longed to be loved by someone she perceived to be pure, but he had put up a barrier—a brick wall that said purity, once lost, could never be regained. But it was just a smoke screen, a smoke screen to hide his fear.

He rose and groped for his mother's hand, now invisible in the darkness. "We have to go."

She grabbed his wrist and let him pull her up. "Where?"

"Anywhere but here. We can't keep waiting for Cerulean. If I'm going to take a bullet for Kelly, I have to find her first. This time, I'm not going to let her down."

A new voice made them both turn. "Man, Nathan, that was beautiful."

He squinted in the darkness. "Daryl? Is that you?"

A beam of light flashed on, illuminating Daryl Red's face. "Present and accounted for. I got here just in time. That cool shoot-em-up dream was ending."

"Is that a flashlight in your hand?"

"Of course. I'm scared stiff of the dark, remember?" She guided the beam toward a canvas bag draped over her shoulder. "And I have fresh Energizer bunnies in there along with three candles and matches, so we're good to go."

"Did you get the card?"

"Yeppers." She put it in his hand. "And something else."

The sound of paper wrinkling rose from somewhere underneath the flashlight's beam. "Remember that report folder you picked up in the conference room back what seems like a thousand years ago?"

"Yeah. I never got to look at it."

"Gordon Red did." Daryl handed him a piece of paper, now unfolded. "Actually, he was supposed to be at the meeting but had to skip it because he was chasing hot-rod Nathan down the highway. So he read through the report, and apparently someone put a new page in there he didn't know about, but it was just a bunch of numbers. He went through all the offices and dug up the other copies, and one had remnants of a torn-out page exactly where this page was, but there weren't any other pages missing."

"So the report I picked up and one other report had this page." He guided Daryl's flashlight toward the wrinkled paper. Several lines of neatly handwritten numbers covered the top half. "Think it's a code?"

Daryl shrugged. "What else could it be?"

"Did Gordon Red try to decipher it?"

"Yep, but it's a brain-buster. He didn't have time to send it to any cryptology experts."

Nathan's mother peered at the numbers. "So were there two conspirators on Interfinity's board of directors?"

"Probably," Nathan said. "This thing goes a lot deeper than I ever thought. I got a good look at the shotgun guy in your dream. He's the same one who tried to kill Clara and Kelly and me. I guess he's been hunting 'gifted ones' for a long time."

His mother shook her head. "I didn't keep track of him. He was in jail during my CSO career, but after I started traveling with your father, I never heard about him again."

"So he got out." Nathan lifted the plastic card into the light. "But he's definitely dead now."

"But which one is dead?" Daryl asked. "Bearded Guy Red or Bearded Guy Blue?"

"I'm not sure." Nathan shrugged. "I can't keep everything straight in my mind."

"Yeah. You need a scorecard to keep up with all the players."

Nathan's mother ran her finger along the card's numbers. "And did he work for Mictar?"

Nathan shook his head. "He wanted me to destroy the mirrors so Mictar couldn't use them. For some reason, he was trying to kill Francesca Yellow before Nathan Yellow was born. I'm guessing that we gifted ones somehow energize the mirrors, and this guy and whoever he works with wanted to stop us to keep interfinity from coming. He just played along with Mictar to get to us."

"Well," Daryl said, "while you two gifted gabbers try to figure it all out, I have something else to show you from my goody bag." She lifted an iPod into the beam. "Of course I'll return it to Dr. Simon when I'm finished, but I figured we could put it to better use while he's playing with his hologram."

"That's great!" Nathan took the iPod and showed it to his mother. "This has all the musical pieces that set the mirror up for transport. With this and your violin we can …" He let his words drift away.

"What's wrong?" she asked.

"We don't have a mirror."

"Au contraire, mon ami." Daryl slid a mirror square up from her bag, then lowered it again. "While Tony was unloading the mirrors to hide them, I grabbed a couple out of the stack. I gave one to Francesca Yellow and kept one for us. I was thinking maybe we could use it to contact Amber, and maybe Francesca could, you know, do the supplicating thing with Amber. And I also brought the Earth Blue one in the photo album. Obviously someone we won't mention, but his initials are *NS*, left it behind."

Nathan clapped her on the back. "Great thinking, Daryl!"

"Like I said, you need a clear thinker." She tapped her head with a finger. "I'm all brains and no brawn, so I'd better put what I've got to work." She pinched his shirt and drew him closer. "Francesca said to tell you she's praying you'll find your father soon. I mean, she was really insistent."

"Thanks," Nathan said. "Me, too." He pulled the Earth Yellow mirror from the bag and looked at its reflective surface. "Since Amber's not my supplicant, I wonder how I can use this to call her."

Daryl shrugged. "Music? A flash of light? Dance a jig? The rules of this game aren't exactly the easiest to follow."

Nathan allowed a weak smile to break through. "I can't keep up either, but I hope I don't have to dance. Mom made me take lessons, but I never liked it."

"So what do we do?" his mother asked. "Go back to the observatory and jump into the yellow section of the hologram?"

"Can't," Daryl said. "El Gordo ranted about entering some kind of eclipse phase that would make creating the hologram impossible for the next few hours, so I hopped in just before it happened."

Nathan held the iPod near the flashlight beam and dialed through the selections. "Let's see if there are any dream-jumping options."

"If you mean from one dream world to another, don't waste your time. Simon and Simon said they have no clue what music will open dream portals. But I brought it anyway, 'cause I figured we might need it if we make it back to the real world."

"*If* we make it?" Nathan looked at Daryl's mirthful, yet frightened eyes. She was searching for a confidence boost. "We *are* going to make it," he said firmly. "I don't know how yet, but we're going to find my father and Kelly, and we're going to save the world."

"Hey, that works for me, but tell it to interfinity. Dr. Gordon's radio telescopes can track the meshing of the three worlds, and it's getting real bad again. He showed me a map and a computer projection of how long it will take before everything collapses." She held up a pair of fingers. "Two days, Nathan. Unless we can stop the bleeding, that's all we have."

12

WITHIN SARAH'S WOMB

"Two Earth Yellow days?" Nathan asked.

Daryl nodded. "At least that's what the computer says."

"Then we'd better figure out how to use the mirror to get to Earth Yellow. Finding my father is still priority one."

Nathan's mother pressed the violin under her chin. "I'll try 'Foundation's Key.' That seems to unlock a lot of puzzles. At least it might let us see something we need to know."

He pointed the mirror at his mother. "Do you remember all of it?"

"I played it about fifty times back on Earth Blue. I'd better know it." After quickly tuning the violin again, she began playing.

Nathan shifted his body, using one hand to point the mirror at himself, Daryl, and his mother. In the flashlight's narrow beam, only his mother's face and hands showed in the mirror's image. Her left hand, still wrapped in a strip of Nathan's sweatshirt, trembled.

The reflection darkened for a moment before glowing with a soft yellow light. Amber's face appeared against a background of darkness. Deep lines ran across her forehead as she spoke in a whisper. "I am nearby. Come to the dark wall. Find a wound and rip it open. I cannot locate one from the inside."

She looked from side to side as if watching for approaching danger. Her voice lowered even further. "I have seen Mictar lurking, so we must be quiet. I will tell you much more when you let me out. But, whatever you do, do not point the light at the mirror. If you transport to this place, we will lose our opportunity to create a path between the Earth Blue and Earth Yellow dream worlds."

Daryl flicked off the light and handed it to Nathan. "Okay. It's dark now. Better talk me through this."

"It's okay. We can still use the light. We'll just hide the mirror for a while." Nathan looked again at the supplicant. "Amber, we're going to put the mirror in Daryl's bag while we look for the barrier. We'll be with you soon."

After securing the mirror, Nathan guessed where the barrier ought to be, aimed the flashlight, and pushed the switch. Like a wide laser, the beam shot through the darkness and cast a circle on a wall of blackness.

"Coolness," Daryl whispered. "Clear sailing."

Nathan waved the beam from side to side. "As long as we don't walk near any of those hungry trees. Cerulean told me they're fixtures in the dream world, one of the few realities we have to deal with."

"And a dangerous one," his mother added. "One of them tried to grab us."

Daryl covered her head with an arm. "Got it. Avoid carnivorous trees."

"Okay," Nathan whispered. "Stay close." Setting out at a slow pace, he followed the beam's path, keeping his arms tucked against his body. He tried to imagine the trees in the cemetery. But which ones were part of the dream, and which ones were still there, ready to grab lost wanderers with their powerful wooden hands? Every few seconds, he made a quick global scan with the light, but nothing came into view.

When they reached the wall, Nathan reached out and touched it with a finger. As expected, it felt tough and hard, like a rubber tire. "Pull Amber out of the bag and keep her up to date. Just don't point her this way."

"Will do, Captain." She withdrew the mirror from the bag and, keeping the mirror's back toward the barrier, spoke in a barely audible whisper. "Hey, Amber. We're at the wall looking for a flaw. Update in a minute."

Guiding the beam slowly from left to right, Nathan and his mother studied the smooth black surface. "See anything?" he asked.

His mother leaned close and squinted. "Only tiny cracks."

"Let's try this." He dug his nails into one of the longer cracks, but it wouldn't expand, not even a millimeter. Stepping back, he studied the wall. The cosmic wounds had apparently weakened the structure, so what would weaken it further? What special powers allowed a supplicant and a vision stalker to break through?

As he thought, the image of Scarlet came to mind. Surely his supplicant could have pierced the wall—but how? With every second her lovely face hovered in his mind's eye, the fragrance of roses strengthened in his nostrils, and a bittersweet film grew on his tongue. A jumble of words flew around in his mind, like pinballs in an over-juiced arcade machine. Finally, when the sensation became overwhelming, he took in a deep breath and let it out slowly. "A song. We need a song."

His mother showed him the violin. "What do you want me to play?"

"'Foundation's Key.' I'll sing the lyrics."

"It has lyrics?"

"Not yet, but it will soon."

She lifted the bow to the strings. "I'll start whenever you do."

"Okay." He concentrated on the flying words. Some seemed brighter than others, almost on fire with red light. Maybe if he sang them out from brightest to dimmest, the phrases would make some sense. He took another deep breath and began.

A wall divides and sets apart
Our bodies, minds, and souls;
It stymies all embracing arms,
Exacting heartache tolls.

The walls we build are merely smoke,
Forgiveness trapped inside;
Release the love, the spirit's wind,
And sweep away your pride.

One breath for me, your supplicant,
One breath for hearts in need;
One breath for you, beloved son,
In threes we gladly bleed.

Nathan sang out the last words in a long, labored breath. His mother lowered the bow and massaged his shoulder. "Scarlet?" she asked.

He nodded but said nothing.

"I thought so. Your voice seemed touched by heaven."

"So, Elvis," Daryl said, "did your song open a hole?"

"It's not the song; it's the breath." Nathan gave his mother the flashlight, then set his mouth over the crack and blew. Wind poured out, growing hotter and hotter, almost scalding his lips. As the fragrance-saturated air met the wall, the cracks seemed to glow cherry red.

Daryl lifted the mirror and talked into it. "Hey, Amber. Stand by. I think we're about to break through."

"Shine a light through the breach," Amber said. "I will look for it."

Nathan took in another breath and blew again. The fissure widened, making a slight crackling noise, like dry leaves burning.

His mother aimed the flashlight at the rift. "Keep it up, son. Maybe the third one will make it weak enough to tear."

Feeling dizzy now, Nathan inhaled as deeply as he could and pushed the air out slowly, pursing his lips to focus the flow on the growing crack. Now hotter than ever, the flow dried out the inside of his mouth and stung the tender skin.

With a final push, he emptied his lungs and staggered back. Daryl caught him and propped him up, laughing. "The big bad wolf's hyperventilating!"

Nathan shook the mental cobwebs away and lunged back to the wall. Using both hands, he thrust his fingers into the glowing crack. The touch burned his raw skin, but he just gritted his teeth and pushed deeper.

As if groaning in pain, the wall creaked and popped. The breach widened to three or four inches and deepened to almost a foot. Soon, a cooling wind rushed by Nathan's hands and into the inner core. With his mouth still in pain, he rasped, "I think we broke through."

His mother pointed the flashlight beam into the hole. "Keep pulling. Maybe Amber can work from that side."

"I'll help!" Daryl set her bag and the mirror down and pulled one side while Nathan pulled the other. As the hole widened, rushing air whistled past.

After a few seconds, a small voice broke through, strained, as if battling the wind. "Nathan? It's Amber. Can you hear me?"

Nathan called back, "I can hear you! Can you see us?"

"Grab this!" Something that looked like a rope protruded from the hole.

"Mom," he said, still pulling with both hands. "Can you get it?"

She tucked the flashlight under her arm and wrapped her hands around the thick line. "Got it!"

Amber's hands pushed through, reeling out the rope. "No, Nathan. *You* take the vine and tie it to one of the spider trees. I will keep the hole open."

"The vine?"

"Yes. It's from a living tree in the Earth Yellow dream world." Grunting, she pushed an arm against each side of the hole. "Go now. I have it."

Nathan eased his hands out and took the vine. It vibrated in his grip, wiggling to get free. "Daryl, stay here and help Amber if she needs it. Mom and I are going to look for the tree."

"Watch out," Daryl said. "That thing's bite is probably worse than its bark."

"You'll be okay without the flashlight?"

"Get going," Daryl said, lifting her bag. "I'll fire up a candle."

While his mother guided their steps with the beam, Nathan pulled the vine, walking a step or two behind her. Obviously alive and aware, the fibrous line curled around his wrist and jerked back, but not with enough force to slow his progress. "I think the tree's at about eleven o'clock," he said. "Just a hair to your left."

After a few seconds, the beam swept across the familiar silhouette of a bent oak. It appeared to jerk at the passage of light, as if awakened.

"Better slow down," Nathan said. "You keep out of its reach while I do the tying." He bent forward and lugged the vine toward the tree. How long was this thing? He had already pulled it at least sixty feet.

Now within reach of the twisted oak, Nathan paused and looked up at its leafless branches. Slowly, they bent toward him, reaching with their knobby-fingered twigs.

Dashing ahead, he ducked under the branches and leaned against the trunk. He passed the vine halfway around, but it stopped. He pulled, but he couldn't gain another inch. "Amber!" he called. "I need more slack!"

"I have no more, Nathan." Her distant voice sounded strained. "The vine is tight."

The branches arched toward him, closer and closer. Following the flashlight's beam, he looked up into the tree's skeleton. A nest of looping vines sagged from nearly every limb.

A wooden claw snatched at his shirt but missed. Still holding Amber's vine, Nathan leaped straight up and grabbed a vine from the spider tree. Now hanging two feet off the ground, he looped one vine into the other, then dropped, pulling the end of Amber's vine with him. After yanking it tight, he began fashioning a knot. Again the branches drew closer.

"Watch behind you, Nathan!"

Nathan cringed. He couldn't look. He had to finish the knot. A sharp claw dug into his back, and a knife-edged finger slid around his arm. Ignoring the pain, he jerked the knot tight and jumped, but the claw pulled him back and lifted him off the ground.

"Nathan!" His mother shone the beam on his chest. "Fight!"

He thrashed and kicked, but to no avail. Another set of wooden fingers caught his legs and squeezed them together, immobilizing them. Tiny threads shot out from pores in the wood and arced over his limbs, like webbing over a captured fly.

Nathan's mother ran to the trunk, clambered up the lower limbs, and banged the flashlight against the branches. "Let go of him!"

"Mom! No! It's too dangerous. I'll get out some—" The claw tightened, squeezing his breath away.

"Daryl!" his mother screamed. "Help!"

"Coming!" A stream of light signaled Daryl's approach, and her voice grew louder with each word. "I have something that'll teach that pile of kindling a lesson."

Holding the candle high, she touched the flame to the lowest branch. The tree shuddered. Its limbs popped and crackled. It jerked the branch away from the fire, but Daryl stalked closer to the trunk, keeping the candle lifted. "Let him go, or you'll be ashes!"

"Daryl!" Nathan called. "If you set it on fire, we'll get—"

"This rotting hunk of driftwood"—she touched the trunk with the flame—"just needs a little persuasion."

A branch swiped at her, scratching her head. Wincing, she caught the branch and set the flame against a wooden finger. "Eat fire, you Treebeard wannabe!"

Several branches swung wildly, loosening the web. Nathan kicked free and jumped to the ground. As his mother climbed down, he checked the knot: still tight.

"Let's go!" he shouted.

Daryl let the branch snap back. Nathan grabbed his mother's hand, and the three ran to the barrier, following the taut vine, now illuminated by the jiggling flashlight beam.

They found Amber still holding the gap open with both arms. "Come through," she called, grunting. "Bring your candles."

Daryl piled the flashlight, the violin and bow, and the mirror into her bag but kept the candle in her grasp.

While Amber shifted to one side of the hole and tugged with both hands, Nathan held the other. Although the earlier adrenaline rush had made him forget about his injured palms, now they really ached. He couldn't keep his grip on the wall for very long.

His mother pushed into the narrow opening, but with the two flaps pressing against her body, she had to wiggle to make any headway. As soon as she popped through, Daryl climbed in feet first. Bracing her back against one side and her feet against the other, she made a bridge of sorts that opened a gap underneath. "I can hold it," she said, extending the bag to Nathan. "Take this and crawl under me."

Nathan grabbed the bag, ducked under Daryl's legs, and crawled through. When he came out on the other side, he reached for the ground but found only air.

"Grab the vine." His mother hoisted him up by his elbow.

Groping with his fingers, he found the vine and hung on.

Seemingly suspended in midair, Daryl's bag floated freely at his side.

Daryl reached the candle to Nathan. "I'm coming through!" With a kick and a push, she rolled out and grabbed his leg while hanging on to the candle. "This is so cool! We're astronauts!"

Amber released the barrier. It snapped closed, the two sides merging until the gap disappeared. The vine, now locked in place, quivered but held firm.

"Where are we?" Nathan asked.

As Amber plucked a lit candle out of the air, its glow illuminated her tired face. "We are somewhere in the midst of Sarah's Womb, the center of the three Earths. It acts as a barrier for the dream realms as well as the worlds that dwell in what you call reality." She wrapped her fingers around the vine. "I have joined Blue and Yellow, so we can travel between them whenever we wish."

Nathan ran a finger along the vine. "I guess no one ever came up with this idea before."

"I am certain it was impossible before. The exterior of the core was impenetrable, but when the celestial wounds began to appear, so did the cracks that allowed passage from the outside to the inside. Yet I found no way to pass through from the inside to the outside."

"So how big is this place?"

"Infinite in depth, as far as I can tell, but its breadth is only a stone's throw."

Nathan fanned the air. "Why does it have oxygen and no gravity?"

"I am not sure, but I have heard from the stalkers that Sarah's Womb has everything necessary for sustaining life. As to our weightlessness, I was surprised, too. This is a new experience for me."

"Gravity might exist," Daryl said, "but who can say what's physical or metaphysical in a dream world? What has mass and what doesn't? Everything could be so perfectly balanced, no force overpowers any other force."

"Come." Amber pulled herself along the vine, drawing her body away from the barrier. "We must search for your father."

Nathan followed, Daryl's candle in one hand and the bag hanging by a strap over his shoulder. His mother and Daryl trailed close behind. With no sound but their breathing, the dark chamber felt empty, as vast as space itself. The two candles cast oddly different glows. Amber's shone bright and undisturbed, while Nathan's flickered as he pulled his body through the black air.

In less than a minute, Amber stopped and pressed her hand against a new boundary. "This is the wall separating us from the Earth Yellow dream world. Since the vine keeps the hole partially open, we can escape."

Nathan gave her a nod of approval. Using the only permanent object in the dream world to keep the barrier open was brilliant. He pushed two fingers between the vine and wall, then, hanging on to the vine, he pulled to the side as hard as he could. Without anything to press his feet against, the job seemed impossible, but as he clenched tightly to the vine, the gap slowly widened. The coarse wood scratched his wounded hand unmercifully, but it couldn't be helped. He had to get the hole open.

When it stretched far enough, Daryl and Amber pitched in. Soon, Daryl was once again making a bridge within the hole. Nathan's mother and Amber went through first. Then Daryl gave him a nod. "Last call, Captain. You're not going down with this ship."

"Just a second." Nathan looked at his hand, bleeding once again. Wiping it on his shirt would have to do, unless ... He looked at the barrier wall. Why not? It would be germ-free, wouldn't it? He reached to the side of the hole and smeared blood on the black wall, but instead of making an indistinct smudge, he drew a small heart.

Pulling back, he looked at the heart. What did it mean? Love was the reason his hands bled—love for his parents, love for Scarlet, and love for ... Yes. Definitely. Love for Kelly.

Giving Daryl a wink, he crawled under her legs. "Captain to the bridge. Give me another inch of clearance if you can."

Daryl grunted. "I'll try. Good thing you're the skinnier version of Captain Kirk, or you'd never make it."

Once through the barrier, they found themselves in a dimly lit bedroom. The vine, still as rigid as a tightrope, ran out a partially open window. A cool breeze wafted in, fresh and moist. Outside, the vine was attached to a spider tree standing a few feet from the exterior wall. One of its outstretched branches bent with the breeze, and a leafless twig tapped against the pane.

At the opposite side of the room, a child, curled in the fetal position, slept in a bed against a wall near the exit door. Sitting on the mattress next to him, a woman played a violin, gently coaxing the beginning notes of "Brahms' Lullaby." With her back turned, her face wasn't visible, but long black tresses draping her flannel pajamas and her brilliant music gave her away.

Nathan tugged his mother's sleeve. "Look," he whispered. "It's you."

She pointed at the sleeping child. "And that must be you in bed."

He set the bag down and surveyed the scene. No one in this realm would be dreaming this. Nathan Yellow wasn't that old, so neither Francesca Yellow nor Solomon Yellow would know about Francesca Red's habit of playing that tune as a bedtime lullaby.

Nathan pulled his three companions together and whispered, "This has to be my father's dream."

"Then where is he?" Daryl asked.

"Let's find out." Nathan's mother pulled the violin and bow from the bag and played along, embellishing the piece with a few intermixed scales.

Letting out a gasp, the other Francesca stopped abruptly, stood, and spun toward them. With her eyes wide, she simply stared, letting her violin dangle limply.

Nathan's mouth went dry. She looked exactly like his mother, only ten years younger.

"Do not be frightened," Amber said, gliding closer. "I am—" She halted and gazed into the dream-world Francesca's eyes. After a few seconds, she turned to Nathan. "The dreamer is not using this woman as his viewpoint person. Her eyes do not carry the vision of a living spirit."

"What are you talking about?" The dream-world Francesca asked, pointing her bow at no one in particular. "Of course I have a living spirit."

Nathan gazed at this younger version of his mother. She did look kind of vacant. "If my father is the dreamer, how is he seeing this bedroom?" he asked.

"He must have created this scene in his mind and then departed," Amber said, "but since he is manipulating this figment's actions, he must hear us. I suspect, however, that he doesn't see us, or this Francesca would have noticed that her virtual twin stands before her." She touched the dream-world Francesca's elbow. "Would you please call your husband?"

"I will, indeed." Francesca marched to the bedroom door, pushing past the vine as if it were a normal fixture in every child's bedroom. "Solomon!" she called. "We have company. Their voices are familiar, but I don't recognize them."

Nathan shuddered. This was all just too creepy for words. And now who was going to walk through that door. His father? A dream representation of him?

While they waited, Amber pointed at the bag still hanging

from Nathan's shoulder. "Francesca. Daryl. Please light a candle. We must be sure to stay in touch with reality."

Daryl reached into the bag and pulled out two candles. She touched the wicks to Amber's, then passed one of the candles to Nathan's mother.

A man appeared at the door, tall, broad shouldered, and dressed in dark blue sweats. Nathan took a step back. His mother gasped, trembling as she whispered, "Solomon?"

At first, Solomon squinted, closing one eye more than the other. Then, as a flicker of light danced in his eyes, the dream-world Francesca faded to a wisp along with the bed and the sleeping child. His lips quivered, and his voice shook. "Francesca?" He swallowed hard. "Is that you, my darling?"

She stared at him through her candle's light, trembling so hard, the flame shook wildly. "Amber?" she called pitifully. "Is he real or a dream?"

Amber gazed at him through her own flame. "He has not faded yet in my sight, but a powerful mind creates stronger images in this world. At the very least, he is the dreamer's vision of himself, so in one sense, he is real. Solomon, your husband, speaks through this man."

"Of course I'm real," Solomon said, marching straight to Francesca. He set his hands on her shoulders. "Don't you recognize me?"

"I ... I mean, you look like ..." Her legs buckled, but he propped her up. "You were wearing Solomon Blue's khakis and a ... and a polo shirt and trench coat."

Solomon looked down at his clothes. "After all I've been through, I had to change clothes. I found these in a drawer, and they fit."

"But this is a dream world," Nathan said, keeping Solomon within the light of his candle. "Any clothes you find here aren't real."

"They're real enough. They fit, and they cover me." He

pulled Nathan into a three-person hug. "Son! It's so good to see you again. Why are you both acting—" His eyebrows shot up, and he pulled back. "Oh! Did Mictar tell you I was dead?"

Nathan cleared his throat. "Not dead ... uh ... Dad. We're just not sure if you're real or an image in your own dream."

Solomon locked wrists with Nathan. "Does that feel like an image? Can a dream embrace you like I just did?"

"Well," Nathan said. "Yeah, I think it can—in the dream world, that is." He raised the candle again, but his father showed no signs of fading.

Daryl pushed the two apart. "Look. It's time to use a little logic. Someone's dreaming up this place." She pointed at Solomon. "If it's not you, then who is it?"

He looked at her and blinked rapidly. "I'm not dreaming. I know I'm in a dream world. I figured that out when I fought Mictar, but I'm fully awake."

Nathan's mother held up her candle. "He's starting to fade."

"Indeed," Amber said. "He is losing hold of his dream."

Trembling, Nathan trained his gaze on his father, looking at him directly through the flame. Every detail stayed clear—his noble brow, his firm chin, his sparkling eyes. "Are you sure? I don't see any fading."

Daryl held up her candle. "He's a ghost, Nathan. Better get a grip. We all see it."

Solomon pulled Nathan close. "Do you remember what I told you about having a minority opinion?"

"Yeah." Nathan let his head rest on his father's shoulder. His embrace felt good. "Strength doesn't lie in numbers. Strength lies in standing up for the truth, even if you're alone in your opinion."

"Nathan," his mother called. "Come back to us! You're fading, too!"

Dizzy now, Nathan looked at her. Her outline blurred, and

her voice sounded distant. "No, Mom. You're the one who's fad-ing. You'd better look through your candle."

"Time for drastic action," Daryl said. She reared back and slapped Nathan's father in the face. "Wake up, Mr. Shepherd!" she shouted. "You're dreaming, and your family needs you!"

Solomon jerked away. Staggering, he braced his hand against a wall. The bedroom darkened. The wall disappeared. He fell to the floor, touching his wounded cheek. "I thought I had found you," he murmured. "I really thought I had found you."

Nathan knelt at his father's side and scowled at Daryl. "Why did you hit him? He was just—"

"Can it, Nathan." Still looking like a ghost, Daryl opened the window a notch wider and let in the cool breeze. She joined them on the floor and patted Solomon's other cheek. "Mr. Shepherd, wake up. You're almost there."

The room darkened further. Three candles burned steadily while Nathan's flickered in the breeze. He pushed a hand under his father's shoulder. "Dad, get up. We have to find Kelly and save the worlds."

As he lifted, the weight evaporated. His father's body crumbled and vanished.

Gasping for breath, Nathan leaped to his feet and backed away from Daryl. "What happened to him?"

She snatched the candle from him. "I'm so stupid! I lit this one while in the dream world." She blew it out and touched her flame to the wick. After sparking for a second, the new flame grew high and bright. "Now take this," she said, sliding the candle into Nathan's hand. "Look at it until you can see us better."

Nathan gave his head a hard shake and stared at the flame, watching the others as they gathered into a cluster. Their num-ber split to six for a moment before congealing back to three.

"The guiding light must originate where truth is born," Amber said. "Concentrating on the false light in this world surely made it worse for Nathan. It is no wonder he lost his bearings."

Daryl nudged the bag on the floor with her foot. "My bad. But what do we do now? Where's the real Solomon Shepherd?"

The newly lit candle shone in Amber's eyes. "I have no experience with dreams that come from the dream world itself, but I assume he is close by."

"If the dream is gone," Nathan's mother said, "he must be awake."

Daryl pointed at her. "Right, but he still wouldn't know we're here. He probably thought it was all a dream."

"Solomon! Can you hear me? It's Francesca!"

"Mr. Shepherd!" Daryl shouted. "This is Daryl. You don't know me, but that's okay. When you do, you'll like me."

Stumbling toward them on wobbly legs, Nathan pointed at his mother's violin, still in her grip. "Call him with that. If this place is anything like it was where I first found you, your music will travel farther than our voices will."

"Good idea." She raised the violin and played a rousing rendition of "The Star Spangled Banner." The strings sang out as clear as any bell, though in the emptiness, nothing echoed at all.

After several seconds, she stopped. Nathan held his breath, straining his ears. Now that his vision had cleared, his hearing also seemed more acute.

"Not a sound," Daryl said. "But if you're right about voices, maybe he's trying to answer, and we can't hear him."

"I have an idea." Amber turned toward the spider tree, letting her candle illuminate the branches. She angled her head directly toward its trunk and sang a high note. A lovely echo replied and drifted into the darkness.

She then pointed her body toward the barrier leading to Sarah's Womb and sang out again. No sound rebounded from the dark wall. "I will sing in all directions," she said, shifting a few degrees to her right. "If anyone hears the slightest echo, stop me. That will indicate a true physical presence, perhaps Solomon Shepherd."

"Or another spider tree," Nathan said, "but it'll be worth the effort if we eventually find him."

Amber slowly pivoted, repeating her note every few degrees. Nathan stepped away a few paces, hoping to hear something besides her voice. His mother walked in the opposite direction until only her candle gave any indication she was there. Daryl cupped her hands around her ears, turning in sync with Amber.

After a few seconds, Daryl spoke up. "Wait! I heard something."

Amber stopped and pointed. "That way?"

"I think so. It was really soft, though, so I'm not sure."

Holding her candle high, Amber strode forward, singing out once more. After a minute or so, she stopped, turned a few degrees, and sang a short note. They waited. A few seconds later, a weak echo sounded.

"I heard it again!" Daryl said.

Amber pointed. "That way!" She ran straight ahead, her dress flying as her heels kicked the hem. The other three hustled behind her. The dream world's air rushed past, but the candle flames they held before their eyes stayed steady.

Soon, Amber stopped and sang out. This time the echo sounded loud and clear. She glided forward, extending her candle. "Solomon?" she called. "Are you here?"

"Honey?" Nathan's mother hurried ahead, then slowed. "Can you hear me?"

Nathan caught up and walked at her side. With both candles raised high, the darkness seemed to fly away.

A low, creaking noise sounded from above. Nathan jerked his mother backwards. A big claw swiped by, barely missing them.

Heaving a sigh, Nathan looked at his mother. Her chin quivered, and every line in her face turned downward.

Daryl stamped her foot. "Cursed spider trees!" She stalked toward it, lifting her candle close to the lowest branches. "This'll teach you to pretend to be a human!" She stepped back, still holding her flame high.

"What's wrong?" Nathan asked.

"Spider's got a fly. A big one."

Nathan edged closer, watching the creaking branches for any sign of attack. As he joined his light with Daryl's, a web-covered shape appeared in the branches. The spider tree had caught a victim, a human one.

13

SOLOMON SHEPHERD

Nathan dropped the bag and pushed his candle into Daryl's hand. "Hold this!" With a flying leap, he vaulted to the first limb and scrambled out to the branch that held the webbed captive. As it sagged under their combined weight, Nathan reached for the closest extremity. A claw stabbed at him, driving a sharp finger into his side. He batted it away, but the motion sent him sliding down the branch. Summoning all his strength, he lunged forward. Grabbing the captive in his arms, he dropped through two sets of thin branches, landing feet first and rolling to the ground with his load.

He jumped up and dragged the web-covered mass to a safe distance. His mother, Daryl, and Amber rushed to his side, holding their candles close. He found a mouth—a man's mouth—the only part of the body exposed to the air. Using both hands, he ripped the hole wider. The strings were sticky and tough, but Nathan tore through them like a maniac.

"Shades of Frodo," Daryl whispered. "He's been Shelobbed."

After just a few seconds, Nathan had cleared the stuff from the man's face. Although he appeared gaunt and pale, his familiar jaw and cheekbones revealed his identity.

"It's Dad!" Nathan shouted.

His mother cleared away a few loose strings from her husband's mouth. "Solomon, can you hear us?"

He blinked, then opened his eyes wide. He pursed his lips to speak, but only a rasping whisper came forth. "Francesca?"

"Yes! Yes!" She ripped away a chunk of webbing from the top of his head. "Hurry, everyone!" she said, laughing. "It's him! It's Solomon!"

While the others stripped away the cocoon, Amber set her candle close to Solomon's eyes. "Have you kept your focus on the living world, dear Solomon?"

"I had no light to guide me ..." His voice still carried a sandpaper grittiness. "But Scarlet gave me ... gave me a song. Whenever I felt like I was losing touch, I sang it."

Amber brushed dark bangs from his brow. "How did you become a victim of the spider tree?"

As Nathan pulled a sticky strip from his arms, Solomon winced. "While searching for a way out of this place, I walked into a cemetery. A girl, a blind girl, called for help from the branches of this tree. Half her body was already covered with the web. I climbed up to free her, but while I was working, the tree caught me. Of course, I couldn't jump down until she was free, but by the time I pulled the last binding strands from her, the tree had already bound me so tightly, I couldn't free myself. Then, a strange wind pulled the girl into a cyclonic swirl and dragged her away."

"Was her name Felicity?" Nathan asked.

"Yes." His eyes shifted toward him. "How did you know?"

"We've met." Nathan smiled at his mother and tore a long strip from his father's thigh.

His mother simply glowed. Her smile, her eyes, even her skin seemed to radiate their own light. "Cerulean's taking care of Felicity, my love. Don't worry."

"But if we're in a dream world, aren't you just part of another dream?" Solomon coughed and spat out a thread. "I have walked through many dreams, some better than others, but I must say this is the best one of all."

Amber pushed the candle closer, cupping her hand underneath to catch the dripping wax. "Solomon, look through the flame. Sing Scarlet's song. Soon, you will know the truth."

Solomon blinked again. As his rapid breaths disturbed the flame, he crossed his eyes to concentrate.

"Dad," Nathan said, sliding a hand under his father's back, "it might help if you sit up."

After rising to a sitting position, Solomon kept his focus on the candle and began humming, following the tune of "Be Thou My Vision."

"Nathan. Daryl." Francesca Shepherd picked up her violin. "You two finish. I'm going to play for my husband."

Now that his upper body was free, he stretched out his arms, cleared his throat, and sang in a raspy bass, still watching the flame.

Be thou my vision, O Lord of my mind.
Lead me through darkness when these eyes are blind.
Thou my bright candle, and thou my true light.
Guide me to morning and through the dark night.

Francesca lengthened the final note, letting it slowly fade. Solomon blinked again and looked at her, his eyes now glistening with tears. He reached for her hand. She took it. Then, he pulled her into his lap, laughing as he wrapped her up in his strong embrace. "Francesca, my darling! It's you! It's really you!"

After a tender kiss, he looked up at Nathan with a grin. "You rascal! Did you drag your mother all the way to this dream world to find me?"

"Did you think I'd ever stop looking for you?" Nathan slid his bloody hand into his father's palm. "I'd do anything to get my father back."

Solomon stared at Nathan's wounds, then curled his fingers and kissed the back of his hand. "Son, I am the proudest father in any world. You are a true blessing to me."

Daryl sniffed. "You three stop it, or I'm going to bawl for sure."

"We'll stop," Solomon said, pushing Francesca to the side. "We have too much work to do."

Nathan pulled his father to his feet. His hand smarted, but it felt good to watch the real Solomon Shepherd rise to his full stature.

"So," Solomon said, brushing strings from his khakis. "I'll give you a quick update on what I know, and then you can tell me what you've learned."

Nathan couldn't stop smiling, even though his cheeks ached. "Sounds perfect."

"But we should try to find our way out of here while we talk." Solomon nodded at the glowing supplicant. "Amber, it's good to see you again."

She curtsied. "It is my pleasure. The days have been long since our previous encounter."

"Can you get us out of this dream world?" Solomon asked.

"I can, but we have another soul we must find here. Kelly of Earth Red is lost somewhere within this realm."

"Oh, yes. Tony's daughter. What happened?"

Nathan piped up. "We were in a dream here in Earth Yellow, and she got sucked into a cyclone thing with Felicity. We haven't seen her since, except in a dream."

"Interesting. It seems that this Felicity, blind though she is, has a habit of getting folks into trouble."

Francesca touched Solomon's hand. "Honey, Nathan and Kelly grew really close during their search for us. They're ... well, let's say they're like brother and sister now."

Solomon looked at Nathan, his brow bent. "I'm sorry for my lack of sympathy. I didn't know."

"It's okay." Nathan shifted his feet on the dark floor. "After I saw her in the dream, it made me realize she's alive somewhere. So I wasn't so worried anymore. We just need to find her."

"I have watched many dreams disappear, and, as you mentioned, they often get swept into a cyclone that funnels into a hole of some kind. But if dreams go back into the minds of dreamers, where could Kelly have gone?"

"This sounds like a job for the logic queen," Daryl said. "Look, dreams are color-coded, right? Red people dream in the red zone, Yellow in yellow, and Blue in blue, but this Felicity chick showed up in both the yellow and the blue dream worlds. And now Kelly's showing up in Earth Red, so I'm guessing they're both snoozing where there's access to all three. And there's only one logical place for that."

"Sarah's Womb?" Nathan asked.

"Bingo! Time to search through infinite darkness with a flashlight, a few candles, and nothing to walk on." She picked up the bag and hu..g it from her shoulder. "Sounds like we'd better get started."

Touching his father's arm, Nathan stared into the darkness. "Amber stretched a vine from a spider tree to Sarah's Womb, so all we have to do is find the tree again."

"Right," Daryl said. "And then we follow the yellow brick, uh, vine, I guess."

Solomon narrowed his eyes as he surveyed the area. "Sounds like a good plan. Maybe we can figure out a way to get to the violin that spans the top of the Womb. If we can play it, we might be able to buy a little more time."

"We'll need it," Nathan said. "According to Gordon Yellow we only have two of their days before interfinity hits."

Solomon looked at Amber and bowed his head. "Does our supplicant know the way to the tree?"

"I do. If you will please follow." Amber lifted her candle and glided ahead as if floating above the dark floor.

As they walked, the entire area brightened. The sun appeared overhead in the midst of a cloudless, deep-blue sky. The black ground brightened to a lush green lawn. Warm, pleasant

air blew gently all around, and an amusement park materialized, filled with the typical attractions—a merry-go-round, a
Ferris wheel, various thrill rides, and carnival barkers yelling
from game booths. Dozens of adults and children milled about,
some munching cotton candy, others standing in line for the
rides. One male teenager, short and bespectacled and carrying a
slide rule, seemed different from the rest. Dressed in throwback
schoolboy knickers and a button-down shirt, he stood rather
stiffly and looked at the other children, but he didn't take part
in the fun.

Nathan called ahead to Amber. "Can you tell whose dream
this is? The guy with the slide rule?"

"I think so, but it is another blended dream. If you look carefully, you will see that there are tombstones scattered among
the amusements."

Nathan scanned the littered fairgrounds. Next to a trash can
spilling over with popcorn boxes, soft drink bottles, and hypo-
dermic needles, a small tombstone leaned at a slight angle.

"Felicity again?" he asked. "Is she around somewhere?"

"I think that's likely."

Nathan gave the boy another quick glance. He looked very
familiar, like a younger version of Dr. Simon. Could Simon Yellow be taking a nap? Could this be his dream?

As a hand slid into his, a feminine voice sounded at his side.
"I thought I smelled the aroma of courage."

Tapping her walking stick, Felicity faced straight ahead, dark
glasses no longer masking her vacant eye sockets. "May I walk
with you a while?" she asked. "I was getting pushed around in
the crowds."

Nathan held his candle toward her and stopped. "Of course
you can, but I'd like to ask you a few questions, if you don't
mind."

A pleasant smile eased across her face, revealing white, yet
crooked teeth. "Of course. I will answer what I can."

As the others gathered around, Nathan looked into her sockets. A tiny spark of blue light pulsed deep within. "When I first saw you, you were sucked into a sandbox by a swirling wind, and Kelly, a friend of mine, went with you. Have you noticed her presence around you anywhere?"

She shook her head. "I knew she was with me in the wind, but when it settled, I was alone in my usual nightmare."

"When you're alone, what's around you? Can you hear anything? Smell anything?"

"It's cool and dry and dark. Until recently I heard and smelled nothing. But during the most recent nightmare, I finally smelled something." She paused, then whispered, "Blood."

"Blood?" Nathan repeated. "Are you sure?"

"I know the odor well. I have smelled my own."

"So, what do you do when you're in that place?"

"In my nightmare?" She shrugged. "Nothing. Nothing at all. I can't walk, so it's worse than just being blind. I just wait until I wake up, then I try to find someone friendly to talk to."

"So you think you're awake now?" Nathan asked.

"Of course I'm awake." Her smile seemed to add a new light to the dream world. "I'm talking to you, aren't I?"

"Nathan," Solomon said. "We need to press on. Let her tag along, and we'll see what we can do to help her when we get each other up to speed."

Felicity stopped and tugged on Nathan's hand. "I smell him again."

"Who?" Nathan asked.

"Death."

Nathan drilled his stare into the crowd, but with so many people flitting about from place to place, Mictar could be hiding anywhere. "How far away is he?"

"Close," she said. "But not real close. I will tell you if he comes closer."

Daryl touched Felicity's head. "Cool. A stalker alarm. She'll come in handy."

As Nathan turned to Amber, her glow brightened. With eyes narrowed and piercing, she seemed ready for battle. He gave her a nod, knowing that all was well. Mictar wouldn't dare approach while she was on guard. "Okay, Amber," he said. "We're ready."

Glancing both ways, Amber pressed through the crowd. Following less than a step behind, Solomon spoke loudly enough for all to hear. "Nathan, I'm not sure how much you've learned about the three worlds and the dream worlds. They are actually all in the same planes of existence, but invisible to each other. Where we stand right now is level ground somewhere in Earth Yellow. And it sounds like you know about Sarah's Womb. It's visible in the dream world, but not in the awakened realm."

They passed a barker who invited them to throw rings over the heads of live ducks that swam in a small pond, but the rings were no bigger than doughnuts, and the ducks were the size of geese. A wayward ring rolled their way. When Francesca picked it up and tossed it toward the pond, one of the ducks grabbed it and swallowed it whole.

"Since I've been here," Solomon continued, "I have been able to tell how people are reacting to the cosmic wounds by how nightmarish their dreams are. I get the impression that perceptions on Earth Yellow are much better now."

Nathan dodged a small boy and then another who chased after the first. "They are better. Your counterpart invented a way for people to dream peacefully."

"Is that so?" Solomon rubbed his chin stubble. "I hope that was the right decision. Sometimes it's better to face reality, even if it's frightening. I know how hard it can be, but if people would learn to overcome their fears, they would be able to move mountains."

"Can't argue with that," Nathan said. "It's worked for me."

As soon as the words spilled from his lips, he lowered his head. Sure, he had faced many fears, but he hadn't faced them all. With a silent sigh, he looked at his wounded hand. It was a good time to change the subject.

"Hold up a minute." Nathan reached into his pocket and withdrew the card and the report page. "Check these out. I took the card from a guy who tried to kill me. He had connections with a group that wanted to protect the Quattro secrets. The paper was in an Interfinity Labs report I picked up in their conference room."

Solomon took the paper and tried to focus on it in the bright sunshine. "It's hard to read."

"I see the vine," Amber said.

The wind kicked up. Clouds rolled in and blocked the sun, sending baseball-sized raindrops splattering to the grass. One hit Nathan's head and splashed all around. It felt cold and wet, but it didn't soak in. Somehow his clothes stayed completely dry.

The people scattered, vanishing as they ran. The breeze swirled into a cyclone that wrapped around Felicity and began pulling her body. "Help me, Nathan! I don't want to go back to my nightmare!"

Nathan held on with his pain-wrenched hand. "Felicity! Keep listening and sniffing. I want to find you in your nightmare, but I need more clues."

With a sudden gust, Felicity jerked out of his grip. Her body spinning wildly, she plunged into a grave and disappeared. A small tombstone, etched with letters too small to read, crumbled and melted away in the torrential downpour.

The cyclone slurped the rain and clouds and everything else in sight. Then, like a high-speed corkscrew, it drilled into the ground and vanished.

Silence fell and with it a cold chill. Nathan shivered. That girl needed help, but how could he find her in a completely dark, infinitely deep place?

Amber lifted her candle, revealing a nearby tree. "The barrier is very close, only a few paces away."

Solomon drew close to Amber's candle. "Let me read this before we go on." As his eyes darted back and forth, he nodded. "Hmm. I know about these people. They call themselves Sarah's Covenant, a cult of sorts. They're the ones who infiltrated Interfinity's technology, inciting Dr. Gordon to get in touch with Dr. Simon and me. While Simon worked with Gordon to install security features, he became engrossed in the communications with the other worlds, while I used the mirror technology and a bit of undercover work to track down the cult. I snooped around their headquarters and found a transport room that sent me to a world inhabited by white-haired men and women who made up the worst choir any world has ever known."

Nathan laughed. "You're not kidding. I've heard them."

"Well, you'll have to tell me about that experience. In any case, while I was there, I met Patar, one of the white-haired men, a vision stalker, as he called himself. He was quite sober, and truly frustrating, but he also seemed very wise. After telling me about Mictar's plot to steal a Quattro mirror and to kill all the gifted ones, he explained the cosmic environment—the three Earths, the dream worlds, and Sarah's Womb—and allowed me to speak to the supplicants. Cerulean, since he watched over Nathan Blue, alerted me to the deaths of Solomon and Francesca Blue. Scarlet thought that Francesca and I should switch places with them in order to put Mictar off our trail."

"So that's why so many of them called me 'Son of Solomon.' They already knew you."

"It's also why Dr. Gordon and company decided to label the three Earths by their colors. I suggested it, though I didn't tell him all the reasons. I wasn't sure whom to trust, so Dr. Simon and I arranged our deaths. You were supposed to come with us, but it didn't work out the way we had hoped, so your mother and I hid my camera and her violin in the trunk in order to give you clues to what happened to us. We knew between you and Clara, you'd eventually figure it all out."

"But it was Kelly who helped the most. She has a gift, too. She can get messages from musical notes."

"Yes," Francesca said. "Scarlet told us God would lead you to an interpreter. And now, it seems, we must ask him to lead us to her again."

"So"—Nathan nodded at the page—"do you know what it means?"

Solomon pointed at the numbers and letters. "These represent GPS coordinates that give the locations of the latest foundation points of Sarah's Womb in the real worlds. The cult members guard those spots, because they are the most vulnerable places in the cosmos. If Mictar found them, he could place a stalker at each location, and if they sang their foul songs, with the weaknesses already in place, they could rip the cosmic fabric to shreds."

"Then why print them on a piece of paper that someone like me can pick up?" Nathan asked. "That's not secure."

"It's secure enough. First, you would have to know you're looking for GPS coordinates. Second, they only *represent* the coordinates. They're musical codes, and only an interpreter can decode the music." He pointed at the first line. "Each symbol is a musical note, zero through eleven in a middle C chromatic circle. It's base twelve, so *A* represents the number ten, and *B* represents the number eleven. As you can see, there are three lines, one for each Earth."

"Can I take a look?" Daryl asked.

Solomon handed her the sheet. "Sure."

While Daryl studied the numbers, Nathan looked at his father. "Do you know where those places are?"

"I had a few ideas and visited some possible sites. I even conducted experiments, asking your mother to play her violin at those spots. But if we were off even by a fraction of a minute on those coordinates ..." He shrugged. "A miss is as good as a mile."

"That makes sense, but how can so few notes do the job?" Nathan asked. "I mean, how does the interpreter figure out that they're coordinate numbers instead of a message in words?"

"That's where the other codes come in." He took the card from him and ran a finger along the embossed symbols on the front. "It's a setup string of notes. An interpreter listens to this and it shifts her brain to a kind of numerical listening mode. This code never changes, but the cosmic shifts can cause Sarah's Womb's location to shift with reference to our worlds, so the cult updates their members with the new coordinates. That's why the updated numbers were in that report."

"It's been a while since I picked it up. Maybe the numbers have changed again."

"It's possible, but this is all we have to work with." Solomon squinted at the card. "Strange, though. There's room for another line of code, but it's blank. I'm not sure what to make of that."

Daryl folded the sheet of paper. "No obvious pattern. I'm stumped."

"We'll just have to wait, I guess." Nathan took the page and the card and pushed them into his back pocket. "Right now we need to find Kelly."

"Look," Francesca said, tilting her head upward.

Dim light filtered in from above, illuminating the area. Tombstones materialized in a weed-infested lawn, and a crescent moon appeared in the purple sky.

"Is Felicity dreaming again?" Nathan asked. "Cemeteries seem to be her trademark."

A new voice floated in from the darkness. "Someone say my name?" Feminine and frail, the voice was beautifully familiar.

"Kelly-kins!" Daryl shouted.

Kelly stepped into the glow of four uplifted candles, squinting at the light. "I guess it's about time I showed up, isn't it?"

With her arms spread wide, Daryl lunged ahead and embraced her. "You're a sight for sore eyes."

Kelly patted Daryl's back and smiled, but she looked worn out. "Yeah. You, too."

Nathan squirmed. It would feel so good to leap ahead and hug Kelly, but maybe she wasn't real, and he would be fooled yet again. He held up his candle and looked at her through its flame. She looked solid, but it was still too early to tell for sure. "Where's your candle?"

She nodded toward the barrier. "I lost it in there when I stretched that stupid hole open. Good thing the vine was there, or I never would've found a way out."

Nathan stared at her weary face and frame. She looked so sad, so lost.

Taking in a deep breath, she smiled and extended her arms. "Nathan?"

He gulped. The sight of Kelly's open arms made his heart ache. But if he gave in to his impulses and embraced another dream image, especially this one, he'd lose his mind completely. Trembling, he turned to the others. "Amber? Is she real?"

Extending her candle, Amber walked up to Kelly and looked her in the eye. "Too early to be certain. I see a spark of life, but she could be a figment of her own dream. Also, with this dreamscape, whoever Felicity really is might well be dreaming that she is now Kelly."

"Why?" Nathan asked. "Because she knows I'm looking for Kelly?"

Amber gave him a sad sort of smile. "Discerning the reason for dreams is something I learned to leave to the prophets."

"What are you talking about?" Kelly cried, spreading out her arms. "Look at me! Of course I'm real!"

"Every dreamer thinks she's awake, Kelly-kins." Daryl pulled away and nudged Nathan. "We need some kind of test to prove it. If this is Kelly's dream, we would need a question only the awake Kelly would know."

"What?" Kelly crossed her arms tightly. "How could you possibly ask me something my sleeping self wouldn't know?"

"What difference does it make?" Francesca asked. "If we take her with us, and she's not real, she'll just vanish, right?"

"And then we'll have to come back and hunt for Kelly again. We can't waste time." Nathan looked around at each face. With furrowed brows and narrowed eyes, everyone seemed stumped, even his father. How could they come up with a question that would work? The sleeping Kelly would know everything, except ... He snapped his fingers. "I've got it."

Kelly tapped her foot, her arms still crossed. Although she sniffed back a sob, she seemed to be getting angrier by the minute. "Go ahead," she grumbled. "Ask me your question."

Nathan pointed at the vine's exit point. "If you really opened that hole, then you might have seen something I left on the inside wall."

Kelly held up her hand. A heart-shaped bloodstain covered her palm. "It was still wet." She crossed her arms again. "I was hoping it was for me."

His heart ready to explode, Nathan rushed to her and wrapped her in his arms, careful to keep the candle flame away from her clothes. She, however, kept her arms locked tightly against her chest. "I'm sorry, Kelly, but if you only knew. I've been fooled by so many dreams. I even saw you playing piano, and I wanted to hug you, but I knew it was a dream that time, because these pixie things were flying all around."

Her arms loosened, but her voice sounded aloof. "They looked like my mother."

"They did, and her dress was kind of ... well ..."

One hand slid around his back. "That was my dress, the one I told you about. I wore it too many times."

"That's history. You burned it. It's gone forever."

"What else did you see?" she asked.

"I saw you play the piano, and . . . I heard your song."

Now both arms slid around his torso. "All of it?"

Nathan took a deep breath. Her embrace felt warm and wonderful, but this couldn't go on. He pulled back and held her hand. "Look, we'll have to talk about your song later. We have three worlds to save."

Closing her eyes tightly, she nodded. Her voice cracked, almost squeaking. "Whatever you say, Nathan."

After a few seconds of silence, Daryl clapped her hands. "So, now that we're deep in the heart of Awkward City, let's figure out how to escape."

14

MICTAR RETURNS

Nathan swallowed the most painful lump in history. He needed to talk it out with Kelly, but there wasn't enough time. "So, Dad, you have a plan?"

"We have two choices. Either get to the top of Sarah's Womb and play the violin strings, or get to the GPS coordinates on each Earth and play the music that will heal the wounds from there."

"What music? 'Foundation's Key'?"

"Exactly. I'm glad you figured that out."

Nathan gave him a doubtful look. "And coordinate them from three places at once? How can we do that? We're running out of time."

"You're right. We should go with the Sarah option."

Daryl shivered. "With all those stalkers around? I kicked a few of their butts into the hole, but it won't be easy to sneak up on them again."

A new voice broke in. "Are you forgetting the third option?"

Nathan clenched his fist. He didn't have to look for the source. It was definitely Patar.

The tall, gaunt man walked into view and stepped close to Nathan, towering over him. "Must I remind you again?"

Solomon stepped between them and shoved Patar backwards. "Have you been telling my son to kill the supplicants? Didn't I tell you that wasn't an option?"

Patar scowled and pointed at Nathan. "Your own wife lives because your son killed Scarlet and cast her into the womb. He slowed interfinity's progress, thereby giving billions of souls another chance. Has he not told you of his heroic deed?"

Solomon's eyes shifted toward Nathan, but only for a split second. "I will tell you again, we will save the worlds with the musical harmony that God has ordered in the cosmos, the breath of God as my wife calls it, not by shedding innocent blood."

A thin smile spread across Patar's face. "Sometimes, Solomon Shepherd, the willing sacrifice of an innocent lamb is the only way to save the world. The true breath of God has already proven that."

"I can't argue with that." Solomon took in a slow breath, then let it out, shaking his head. "You heard our plans. If you have something to add, then let's hear it. Otherwise, I think you should just move along."

"Since Mictar is busying himself with trying to find this girl," Patar said, nodding toward Kelly, "I can provide a safe path to the great violin, but only if she stays away. Mictar has tasted her life force, and now that she has escaped from the Womb, he will track her down."

Solomon looked at Kelly, then at Nathan. The perplexity in his face spoke volumes.

"You and Mom should go," Nathan said. "Daryl and Kelly and I will figure out the GPS coordinates and get that started. If you can buy us some time by playing the violin, maybe we can get it done."

"I will take you three back to the observatory," Amber added. "From there you can transport to any real world. Once you locate the proper foundation point, perhaps my beloved will play at the Earth Yellow site."

Solomon looked at his wife. "Do you think we can play it?"

She nodded. "We really need a bow, but pizzicato will have to do."

"Maybe it'll be enough to give Nathan time." Solomon stuffed his hands into his pockets, turning his head slowly and pausing as he looked at each of his fellow dream-world travelers. "Okay. We'll go."

"Remember," Patar said, pointing at Kelly, "do not doubt my prophecy. Mictar is a dream stalker. If you sleep, you open a door by which he may find you."

Nathan clenched his fist again. He wanted to say, "And he'll be sorry," but he just couldn't spit it out. Finally, he heaved a sigh and said, "We'll try to be ready for him."

"So be it." Patar leaned close to Amber as if to whisper, but his voice stayed loud enough for everyone to hear. "I will show the observatory personnel how to open their mirror to my world, and when I go, I likely will not see you again until this crisis is over, and perhaps not even then."

She nodded. "I understand." A hint of a tear welled in her eye. "I am ready to give my life if need be, but I prefer to stay and help my beloved."

"Of course you do. We shall see what transpires."

Amber's chin quivered. "I had no opportunity to say good-bye to Abodah. I am very sorry for your loss."

"I am grateful for your compassion," Patar said, patting her shoulder. "Her sacrifice will not go unnoticed by the one who watches every fallen sparrow."

Amber turned and abruptly strode into the darkness, lifting her candle once again. "Come," she called. "Our entry point into the observatory is this way."

"Wait just a second!" Nathan called. "I have to say good-bye."

Amber waited, firming her lips as if holding back her emotions.

While still holding a candle, Nathan hugged his mother.

"This time," he whispered, "I'm going to roll away that stone. Nothing will stop the flow."

She shook as she returned the embrace. "I have seen your gift from afar. I hope I get to see it played out, face-to-face."

"Someday, even if it's in heaven, you will." Nathan pulled back and strode into his father's waiting arms. "Dad," Nathan said, gripping his father's wrist. "I ..." He bit his lip hard. There was no way he could say what was on his mind without losing control, so he just blurted it out. "I love you, Dad. I'm so proud to be your son. Thank you for teaching me courage and—" He glanced at Kelly but couldn't keep his gaze on her for more than a split second. "And love. I think I know what I have to do to complete your training." He nodded at his mother. "Mom can fill you in."

With that, he turned and caught up with Amber, looking back to make sure Daryl and Kelly followed. "So how do we get out?" he asked.

"As you might have guessed, we will also get out through a dream." After a minute or so, she stopped and looked around. "Yes, this is the place."

When Kelly and Daryl joined them, Amber pulled the mirror from Daryl's bag and laid her palm on the surface. Within seconds, her soft glow strengthened into a brilliant aura. "Francesca, my beloved, are you watching?"

A face appeared under Amber's hand. She slid fingers away, revealing a bleary-eyed Francesca Yellow. "I'm here. Do you need me to do something?"

Amber's aura dimmed to normal. "Are you still in the observatory?"

"Yes. Solomon and Tony set up a cot and a mirror stand in one of the offices."

"Can you go to sleep?" Amber asked. "I need to follow your dream path as a way of escape from here."

"Sure. Nathan's napping, so I was about to join him."

"Put the mirror somewhere that will allow me to see you while you sleep."

The four gathered around to watch the scene in the mirror. The heels of Francesca's hands pressed against the sides of their view, then her face bobbed up and down for a moment as she walked the mirror square to another location. Soon, the image settled. A baby, wrapped in a blanket, slept on the floor next to a low cot. Francesca, wearing loose gray sweats, slid into a sleeping bag that lay on the cot. "Can you see me all right?"

"Quite well," Amber said.

"It's kind of hard to go to sleep on demand, but I'll do my best."

"Just close your eyes. I will sing a lullaby. It will calm your mind."

When Francesca's eyes fluttered closed, Amber began a song in a lovely alto, her voice silky and pure.

A gentle wind, a tumbling brook,
A kiss good night, a well-read book,
The blessings of love coming down from above
Are found in simple places,
In places of the heart.

A crackling log, the smell of life,
A candle's flame, a loving wife.
The finest treasures are never measured
By monetary rules,
The treasures of the heart.

After a few seconds, the mirror emitted an aura of its own, a yellow glow that surrounded the square. It grew at a rapid rate, enveloping Amber and then the others. Soon, it took over the environment, illuminating the expanse with a fuzzy yellow that quickly morphed into lights on a ceiling, walls and hangings on the sides, and a carpeted floor beneath their feet.

Immediately in front of Amber, Francesca slept on a cot with the edge of her sleeping bag tucked under her chin. Next to her on the floor, little Nathan lay curled in his blanket.

Nathan looked at the mirror. Their surroundings had become an exact copy of Francesca's office area. She was dreaming about the room she was sleeping in.

Amber handed Kelly her candle, then, still holding the mirror, she sat on the cot and rubbed Francesca's back. "Can you hear me, my beloved?"

Francesca squirmed and let out a "Hmmm," while in the mirror, she stayed still and quiet.

"Arise, my love." Amber prodded her shoulder. "We must join you in the waking world."

Francesca sat up and blinked. Then, as if counting, she nodded at each person in turn before breaking into a wide smile. "You found Kelly!"

"We did, and Solomon, too, but he and his Francesca have embarked on a different journey." Amber rose from the cot. "Now, wrap your mind around us and awaken. Although you are very weary, you must arouse yourself and take us out of this world of dreams."

While Francesca slid out of the sleeping bag, Nathan kept an eye on the mirror. A shadow crossed the sleeping woman's form, growing bigger and darker. "What's that?" Nathan whispered to Kelly.

Kelly grabbed his arm. "I don't know, but I don't like it."

The image now showed a lean pale hand reaching for the baby.

"Amber," Nathan said sharply. "Wake her up! Quick!"

"My beloved!" Amber cried, turning the mirror toward Francesca. "Awaken! Now! Expand your thoughts and wrap us into your dream."

Francesca's eyes shot open. Jumping to her feet, she spread out her arms. "Come close, everyone!"

Nathan, Kelly, Daryl, and Amber hustled into a tight group, holding candles at their chests. The little Nathan in the dream world faded away, as did the cot and the walls.

Francesca clutched her eyes shut and screamed, "I'm trying to wake up! I have to save my baby!"

Nathan angled his head toward the mirror in Amber's grip. The pale hand now covered the little boy's eyes, and light began to surround the attacker's fingers.

"Why aren't I waking up?" Francesca stamped her foot. "My baby needs me!"

"Okay," Daryl said. "I guess I have to."

Francesca jumped. "Ouch! Who pinched me?"

A strong gust of wind swirled around their huddle. Wrapping them up in a cyclonic funnel, the wind pulled them toward the mirror. Francesca slid into the reflection first, followed by Daryl, then Kelly.

Nathan resisted the pull, more out of instinct than fear.

"Allow it to take you," Amber shouted through the rush. "I must be last!"

Nathan let his muscles go lax. As he stretched toward the mirror, everything warped. The funnel's suction pulled his breath away. Now that his body had been fully taken, he tensed his muscles again. He had to be ready for a fight.

One second later, all was clear. Francesca held the baby in her arms and rocked back and forth. Although he whimpered, he seemed fine.

Grunts and screams erupted from behind. Nathan pivoted. Kelly and Daryl were sprawled over Mictar, beating him with their fists. A black violin lay on the floor at the stalker's side.

Just as Nathan cocked his arms and made ready to pounce, Mictar flung Daryl away, sending her tumbling across the carpet. She rolled against a wall and sat up, stunned but breathing.

"Stay back!" Mictar shouted, clutching Kelly around her waist and pinning her arms. "Or I will kill her."

Nathan threw down his candle and ground in its wick. He had to think fast. He couldn't just wait. That would be the worst option.

A bright glow made him turn. Amber appeared at his side, still holding the mirror.

Dangling Kelly like a rag doll, Mictar leaped to his feet, his eyes wide. "Beware, supplicant. You know I will not hesitate to take this wench's life energy."

Amber's eyes flashed like two suns. "And I will dissolve your bones into dust. Now that I have you in my sight, you cannot hide from me."

Kelly twisted and rammed her knee into Mictar's groin, but without even a wince he jerked her around and again wrapped his arm around her waist, squeezing so tightly, her eyes bulged. "If you allow me to escape, I will release her unharmed."

Nathan looked for a weapon but saw only a stapler on a nearby desk. "Why should we trust a liar?" he said. "Once you're free, you'll just kill her."

"Then it seems we're at an impasse once again." A crooked grin bent the scar on Mictar's face. "You won the previous battle. What will you do now?"

Amber touched Nathan's elbow. "Just say the word, and I will kill that monster, and we will have no obstacles to saving the worlds. You, your mother, and my beloved will play the musical key at Sarah's foundation points. If Kelly dies, she will be honored on the three Earths for a thousand years."

Mictar loosened his grip on Kelly, allowing her to breathe. "Is that your choice? Shall I take this harlot's eyes and do battle with the supplicant?"

Panting for breath, Kelly choked out, "It's okay, Nathan. Let him take me." She pulled one arm free and showed him her hand. A heart-shaped smear still covered her palm.

Nathan's legs quaked. He knew what the heart meant. It was her way of saying "I love you."

With tears flowing freely, she used that hand to blow him a kiss. "Now go save the world."

"So," Mictar said as he squeezed Kelly harder and moved his long fingers toward her eyes, "will you trust me to leave and release her, or shall I kill her now?" His eyebrows lifted. "Or do you have another offer?"

Nathan leaned closer and studied the stalker's face. What did he have in mind? Was there really another option? Kelly's head drooped, her hair dangling. Had she fainted? Could she breathe?

Finally, he extended his wounded hand. "Take me hostage instead."

"What?" Mictar half closed an eye, but he seemed more delighted than curious. "Why you?"

"I'm a gifted one, too. With Kelly, you get only what you left behind. With me, you get a full dose of life energy."

"Nathan." Amber pulled on his sleeve and whispered, "Without you, we won't have a third violinist."

He showed Amber his bleeding palm, keeping his voice as low as possible. "I can't play anyway. Maybe you can sing the key."

"I do not know if Sarah will respond. I am not one of the gifted."

"Then set up a keyboard at the spot. Kelly can play it."

Kelly didn't even flinch at the sound of her name. She looked more like a rag doll than ever.

Nathan took a step closer, again extending his hand. "So, what do you say? Will you let her go and take me hostage? I give my word that I won't try to escape."

"So, allow me to understand you correctly." Mictar loosened his grip on Kelly. Her body stayed slack, but she seemed to be breathing. "Are you saying you trust me to let you live once I escape?"

Nathan spoke through clenched teeth. "I trust you less than I trust the Devil himself, but at least Kelly will survive."

"Wait!" Daryl said as she struggled to her feet. "Let me tag along. I'll be kind of like insurance. You know, if Mictar doesn't keep his word, I can ... uh ... drag Nathan's body away."

Nathan grimaced. That wasn't very good insurance, but it was better than nothing. "How about it, Mictar? Can she follow?"

Mictar pointed at Amber. "As long as the supplicant stays here."

Amber sat on the cot, her eyes now glistening. "I will stay with Kelly and my beloved. We must plan the world's escape from interfinity. Without Nathan."

"Very well." Mictar threw Kelly to the floor, picked up his violin and bow, and grabbed Nathan's wrist. "Come, fool."

Amber rushed to Kelly, sat at her side, and gathered her limp body into her arms. "She is alive, Nathan. I will care for her."

Daryl touched Amber's shoulder as she passed by. "I know I'm not your beloved," Daryl said, "but I'd appreciate a big helping of supplication. I have no idea what I'm doing."

As Mictar led Nathan toward the office door, Nathan looked back. His eyes blurred by tears, he could barely see Kelly nestled in Amber's arms. Now that he would probably die at the hands of this monster, maybe he would never get to tell her what he had to say. The simple message ached to get out, but he never had the courage to release it. Somehow, he had to let her know. "Amber, please tell Kelly—"

"No more chatter!" Mictar jerked open the door and pulled Nathan into a curved hallway. His voice lowered to a whispered growl. "I don't want to alert the fools in the observatory."

Daryl slid through the half-closed door and pressed her body against the wall, several steps away from the stalker.

"You two lead the way," Mictar said. "I want to keep my eye on you." He raised a hand, showing Nathan a flash of light in his palm. "If you want that girl to live, I advise you to put aside all thoughts of escaping."

After quickly scanning his surroundings, Nathan recognized their location: the security corridor on the floor below the telescope room. The smaller elevator was probably a dozen paces in one direction, while the exit door lay about thirty paces in the other. "Which way?"

Mictar pointed toward the exit. "Do you know where the back door is?"

"Yeah. If it's like the ones on the other Earths."

"Good. Move along."

Nathan looked at Daryl. Her eyes blazed with fear. Somehow he had to make sure she'd survive, but how? Obviously, the closer to Amber they stayed, the better her chances. "If you want to kill me," he said, "why not do it inside? At least it's heated in here."

"I want it cold. You will see why in a moment."

While Nathan and Daryl walked three or four steps in front of Mictar, Daryl formed signals, keeping her hands close to her waist. She spelled out, "Any ideas?"

He signaled back, "Not yet."

Ever so slowly, she pulled out her shirttail, exposing a mirror at her waist.

As he watched, Nathan kept his head as still as possible. Which mirror was it? The one Amber had?

Daryl spelled out "Blue" and re-tucked her shirt.

Nathan pushed open the security door that led to the main hallway and held it for Daryl. As she exited, Mictar grabbed Nathan's shirt collar. Then, when all three had come out into the corridor, he let Nathan go and returned to his position a few steps behind.

Nathan shrugged out the tightness in his clothes and continued toward the back door. He glanced at Daryl's shirt. Could that mirror help? Since Cerulean wasn't his supplicant, would he respond to their call?

When they reached the exit, Nathan pushed it open. Again, Mictar hung on to Nathan's shirt while Daryl walked outside.

As soon as Nathan stepped out into the cold breeze, he shivered and slowed his pace. "How far do you want to go? This is as good a place as any to commit a murder."

"I fully intend to kill you, but that was not my reason for coming out here." Mictar used his fistful of Nathan's shirt to jerk him closer, but instead of placing his lethal hands over Nathan's eyes, he dug into Nathan's back pocket.

"Ah! Here they are." He threw Nathan to the ground and displayed the card and folded page. "I learned about these co-ordinates when I tortured one of the cult members, but it was not until I overheard your conversation with your father that I learned where to find them and how to use the codes."

As Daryl helped him to his feet, Nathan glared at the stalker. Did he know only an interpreter could understand the codes? If he had been eavesdropping, wouldn't he have heard that he needed one? Did that mean he would still go after Kelly?

Mictar held the card toward the fading sunlight. "The cultist told me the truth. The cold weather has revealed more codes."

He flipped it around to show them. Nathan and Daryl squinted at it. A new line of symbols had appeared near the bottom edge.

Carefully folding the paper around the card, Mictar smiled at Nathan, a truly horrible sight. "I must thank you for coming along so easily. Although I yearn for the girl's energy, this revelation is far more important. Now, which of you should I kill to satisfy my hunger? I am unlikely to be able to hold you both."

Easing back a step, Nathan hid his fingers behind his back and spelled out, "Run."

Daryl set a fist on her hip. "So, Mictar, how are you going to use it? Even if you figure out what the codes mean, I'll bet you don't even know 'Foundation's Key.'"

Nathan whisper-shouted, trying not to move his lips. "Quiet!"

"Do you think me a fool?" Mictar waved his violin. "Of course I can play that infernal piece, but I will not be baited into it. I see through your ploy."

"Chicken?" Daryl pushed her thumbs under her armpits, flapped her elbows, and made a horrible clucking noise.

Nathan shouted through clenched teeth. "Daryl! Cut it out!"

"You fool! You will be my sustenance." With a grunt, Mictar reared back and thrust his hand forward, as if throwing a boulder.

Just as a black jagged streak shot from his palm, Daryl jerked out the mirror and deflected the bolt right back at him. It splashed against his shoulder, spreading dark liquid across his chest and arm.

Spewing a barrage of raging sounds, he hurled streak after streak, aiming low and high. Daryl blocked the first two, but the third struck her knee.

Nathan dropped to the ground and swept his leg through Mictar's, toppling him to the gravelly surface. With a quick thrust, Nathan leaped to his feet to attack again with his fist, but the stalker reached out a long arm and grabbed his ankle.

Stumbling, Nathan fell face first, scraping his cheek and nose on the sharp pebbles. He cringed at the pain, but only for a second. Flipping over, he kicked and punched but struck only air.

As he climbed to his feet, he searched for Mictar. Just a few feet away, Kelly knelt on the stalker's back, yanking his ponytail. Growling, she clawed at his eyes from behind. "I'll give you a taste of your own medicine."

Nathan leaped toward them, but the sight of Mictar's black stuff made him stop short. It had already spread over half of the stalker's torso and was now creeping around toward Kelly.

He snatched her arm and pulled her off Mictar's body. As he

backed away with her, he found Daryl, standing as if stunned. Her own black splotch crawled up and down her jeans.

"That stuff will kill you!" he yelled.

She shook the cobwebs away. "Enough said." She set down the mirror, kicked off her shoes, and pushed down her jeans, revealing long thermal underwear covered with smiling cartoon bunnies. She then dropped to her seat and began kicking off each pant leg. "How about giving me a hand?"

Kelly pulled the cuffs and slung the jeans away. Setting her hands on her hips, she grinned. "Well, look who came prepared."

"Yep." Daryl's cheeks flushed. "My mother always told me to wear clean underwear. You never know when you might have to show someone your bunnies."

After helping her get up, Nathan looked at Mictar. Now almost completely black, the stalker picked up his violin, struggled to his feet, and shuffled away, slumped and wobbling. "I have the codes, Shepherd," he said weakly. "I will win this war."

Nathan searched for a weapon. Should he finish that monster off? Should he risk getting any of that black gunk on himself?

"C'mon," Daryl said as she scooped up her shoes. "Let's get out of the cold."

Keeping his stare fixed on Mictar as he slinked away, Nathan felt for the mirror and picked it up. It was better not to focus on Daryl. Her thermal underwear covered her modestly enough, but he wasn't sure he could keep from laughing. "You're right. Let's go."

He offered Kelly his elbow. As she curled her arm around his, he looked her in the eye. "Thanks. You saved me again."

Kelly gave him a tired smile. "Amber said you saved me first."

"Well . . ." He paused, searching for the right words. "You're worth it."

Her bottom lip trembled. She seemed ready to say something, but Daryl barked, "Cut the schmaltz! I'm freezing!"

While Daryl hopped on her socked feet, pulling up one foot at a time to slip on her sneakers, Nathan hustled to the door and pulled the handle. It wouldn't budge. "It's locked!"

Daryl moaned. "Are you telling me I have to parade around to the front of the building in my long johns?"

Nathan punched a couple of strings of numbers into the nearby pad, but the lock didn't make a sound. "I don't think we have a choice."

She stooped and tied a shoe. "Well, I'm not exactly a modest maiden, but ..." She looked up, tugging the material on her leg. "Why didn't I wear my camo thermals? At least I wouldn't look like a girly girl."

Suppressing a grin, Nathan held out his hand. "C'mon. If we hurry, we'll be back inside in no time."

After pulling upright, Daryl glanced at Kelly, then, smiling, kissed Nathan on the cheek. "Thanks for rescuing me."

Warmth surged through his ears. "No problem. I just wish we could've hung on to the codes."

"Oh, we have the codes." Daryl began marching toward the side of the building. "The problem is that he has them, too."

Nathan and Kelly caught up and matched Daryl's quick pace stride for stride. "What do you mean?"

Daryl tapped the side of her head. "I memorized them, both the card and the page."

"You did?" Kelly said. "That's amazing!"

"Yeah." Daryl tossed her head back in mock conceit. "I *am* pretty amazing."

Pushing up a slight incline, the trio followed a gravel-covered path that led around the observatory's circular building. A few seconds later, they approached a footbridge that spanned a deep ditch leading to a pipeline protruding from the lab's basement. As they crossed it, a memory flowed into Nathan's mind—driving a Camry across this bridge in another world while Kelly literally rode shotgun.

He smiled at her. She smiled back. Obviously they were on the same wavelength. As they continued walking, he looked at her out of the corner of his eye. The shoulder of her sweatshirt again showed a dark splotch, blood from her wound. And with her eyes sure to go bad again when, or if, they ever returned home, she had suffered much more than he had. His hands would heal, but would she ever get her eyesight back?

She looked at him. "What are you thinking?"

"You don't know?"

"I'm not a mind reader," she said.

"Could've fooled me. You're always probing my brain."

"Not really. If I could always read your mind, I wouldn't have so many questions."

"Questions?" He arched his brow. "Like what?"

"Questions I really can't ask. I mean ..." She shook her head and looked away. "I'm sorry. I can't explain right now."

Firming his lips, he nodded. "I think I understand. Maybe I can answer the questions without being asked."

She looked at him hopefully. "When?"

"Soon." With another nod, he added, "As soon as possible."

VIEW OF A KILLING

When they neared a tall tree, stripped of leaves for the winter, Nathan ran ahead and crouched behind its forked trunk, peering through the gap. With the parking lot and the lab's front portico in view at the bottom of a grassy slope, he scanned the path leading to the entry. He caught a glimpse of Gunther's van as it zoomed from the lot. Then, back at the building, someone hurried out the door holding a cell phone to his ear.

As the girls joined him, Nathan whispered, "Is that who I think it is?"

Daryl pressed close to his side and squinted. "Solomon Yellow?"

"That's what I thought. Maybe he's running to his car to get first aid or something."

"Not for me," Kelly said as she huddled with them. "I just fainted because I couldn't breathe. I was okay after that."

"How about the others?" he asked. "Did you see them?"

She nodded. "Tony showed up with Molly, and they took Francesca and the babies out. They said it was getting too dangerous for the little ones."

"So," Nathan said, "they must have called Gunther to come and get them. I just saw them leave."

"Tony seemed real nervous. He said something about Flash staying behind to help with the equipment, and he looked really annoyed."

Nathan rolled his eyes. Solomon Red wouldn't leave Francesca under such dangerous conditions, especially in a room by herself where Mictar could attack her in her sleep. This version of Flash was getting on his nerves.

He laid a hand on each girl's shoulder. "Come on. Let's try to catch him before he gets out of the parking lot. We'll find out what's going on."

"The way I'm dressed?" Daryl shook her head. "No way, buster. I only show my long johns to close friends."

Nathan looked at her, trying to keep his focus on her green eyes and frazzled red hair. He couldn't leave her by herself or even with Kelly, not with Mictar possibly looking for someone to reenergize him. He stole a quick glance at her long johns. He wanted to match her quips but everything he came up with was just too lame. Finally, he huffed, a little harder than he intended. "Okay, we'll wait till he's gone."

As they continued watching, Solomon jumped into his old Volkswagen, started its noisy engine, and puttered out of the parking lot. With a screech of the tires, he buzzed away.

"Coast is clear," Nathan said.

They hurried down the slope and stopped on a walkway that ran under a portico from the parking lot to the front door. Nathan listened to the Volkswagen's motor fade in the distance. Apparently, Solomon Yellow hadn't seen them.

As a cold breeze buffeted their bodies, Daryl bounced in place. "Let's go! I'm freezing my bunnies off!"

Still carrying the mirror, Nathan jogged to the front door and held it open for the girls.

Once inside the warm lobby, Daryl stopped, her teeth chattering. "So, after Tony and company left, where did Amber go?"

"I don't know," Kelly said. "She told me to stay in that room, then she took off."

Nathan raised a finger. "I say we visit the telescope room.

That was the center of activity. Whatever happened, happened there."

After a final shiver, Daryl narrowed her eyes. "Yeah. Come to think of it, isn't it strange that none of those brave men charged outside to help us?"

"Good point. Courage is kind of hard to find in these parts."

"Don't dis Tony," Kelly said. "He was probably torn between protecting us and protecting those babies."

"Another good point." Nathan nodded toward a stairway. "The telescope room, but quietly."

Daryl shivered again. "As they say in *Star Wars*, 'I have a bad feeling about this.'"

Nathan tucked the mirror under his arm and led the way up three flights of stairs. When they reached a closed door at the landing, he peeked out the small, eye-level window. "No one in sight," he whispered.

As he slowly opened the door, it let out a slight squeak. He cringed, but he couldn't stop now. He pushed himself through the expanding gap, then waited for Daryl and Kelly to squeeze through.

He looked down the curved corridor. The entry to the telescope room wasn't in sight, but it had to be only twenty or so steps away. He handed Kelly the mirror and used sign language again to spell out "Watch from door. Wait for signal."

He waited for their nods, then skulked toward the door, glad to see it come into sight after only a few steps. He glanced back to check on Kelly and Daryl. They tiptoed behind him without a sound.

When he reached the door, he turned the knob and peeked in through the smallest of cracks. Inside, the lights had been dimmed, so opening the door any further would brighten the inner room, giving away his presence.

Daryl ran to a bank of switches and turned off the hallway lights. When she returned, she whispered in his ear, so close, her breath moistened his skin. "Don't leave us here long. Remember my phobia."

He grasped her hand and pulled it into Kelly's. He signed "Trust me" in her palm but, in the darkness, he couldn't tell if she understood.

Again pulling the door just enough to slide through, Nathan squeezed into the room. Ahead, the floor was clear; the big telescope was still in its hideaway under the floor.

Walking on the balls of his feet, he headed straight for the computer desk where a solitary man sat staring at a screen. Shorter than most men and wearing ovular glasses, he looked like one of the Dr. Simons, probably the younger of the two.

Nathan crept closer, watching for any sign that Dr. Simon had seen him. It would be perfect if he could just read the screen, figure out what was going on, and then get out without anyone knowing he had been there. But would he show up in the screen's reflection? Would Simon notice?

Holding his breath, he took a step, but his shoe slid in something wet. He lifted his foot, eased to a crouch, and touched the dark puddle. Pulling his finger close, he studied the splotch on his finger. Could it be blood?

Jumping up, he lunged toward Dr. Simon and grabbed his chair. The scientist's glasses slid down his nose, revealing a bullet hole between his closed eyes. The desk lamp highlighted his face, pale and unmoving.

Nathan swallowed hard and began to shake. He backed away and looked from side to side. Who could have done this? Was he still around? And where were the others—Simon Blue and Gordon Yellow? Were they safe?

Again he gazed at the limp body, now a perforated shell. Simon Yellow had devoted his career to stopping catastrophes in his world, saving the lives of people who had perished on Earths Red and Blue, and now he had been repaid with a bullet.

Nathan averted his eyes. He couldn't stand to look at that

face any longer. With nausea churning his stomach, he might vomit at any second.

He turned toward the door. He couldn't call Kelly and Daryl. Without knowing who might be watching from the darkness, it was too dangerous. But who would figure out what happened? Maybe Daryl could check all the computer settings and see what was going on when—

"Hello?"

He jerked toward the voice. It came from the computer.

Still queasy, he tiptoed around the puddle and searched for a microphone, but none of the dozens of pieces of equipment resembled one. Clearing his throat as quietly as possible, he whispered, "Someone call me?"

No one answered. The computer's hard disk whirred, and several meter readings, both numerical and graphical, pulsed with constant change. As he leaned closer to try again, a speaker let out a sputter, then a voice.

"This is Dr. Gordon of Earth Red. Is that you, Nathan?" A quiet static interrupted the transmission but quickly died away. The voice seemed mechanical, but it still sounded like Dr. Gordon.

"Yes. This is Nathan Red. Your speech is normal speed. Are the two worlds traveling through time at the same rate now?"

Again, a long pause ensued. As he waited, he drummed his fingers quietly on the desk. Finally, after almost a minute, the speakers came alive again.

"No. The computers are buffering our transmissions and re-playing them at the right speeds. Since I'm much slower, you have to wait to hear me, so after this I will make my communications as short as possible, perhaps even terse."

Nathan scanned the readouts on the computer screen until he found a loudness meter, a vertical line that bounced slightly with the fluctuations in static. Above the meter, a graphical switch was set to digital instead of analog. "Dr. Gordon, Simon

Yellow has been shot. He's dead. Were you listening in? Do you know who did this or where he went? Do you know where the other Simon is, or the other Gordon?"

Making sure to avoid looking at Simon Yellow, Nathan sat on the desk and watched the meter rise and fall. When it stopped moving, a horizontal white bar appeared beside it and quickly filled with blue from left to right, obviously the translation procedure Dr. Simon had mentioned earlier when talking about the IWART devices.

When the blue struck the right-hand side of the bar, it disappeared, and the speakers clicked on. "I heard male voices, then a female voice, then a gunshot. Silence after that."

"Solomon Yellow left in a hurry," Nathan said, "but he didn't have a gun, at least not one I could see."

The voice meter rose and fell several times, then the buffer bar reappeared, filling with blue a little faster this time.

"You think your father's double is a murderer?" Dr. Gordon asked. "That doesn't seem likely."

"Your double helped Mictar kill quite a few people, didn't he?"

This time, the delay was much shorter.

"Touché."

Nathan shook his head. This conversation was taking too long, and they really weren't getting anywhere. "I'll be back in a minute. I have to do something." Avoiding a direct look at the body, Nathan crossed Dr. Simon's arms over his chest and rolled him and his chair near the wall. He found a panel of switches and turned them on, flooding the room with light. Daryl and Kelly hustled in, Kelly with the mirror in hand.

"Someone murdered Simon Yellow," Nathan said.

Kelly covered her mouth. "That's awful!"

"Ewww!" Daryl lifted her foot, grimacing at the blood dripping from her shoe. "A messy murder, too."

"Yeah. I pushed his body out of the way, 'cause it's really

gruesome. Dr. Gordon's on the audio link, but he doesn't know who did it or who went where, so I thought maybe Daryl could check the computer to see if she can find some kind of log."

"I'm on it." Daryl rolled up another chair and pecked at the keyboard. "Dr. Gordon? You listening?"

After a few seconds, his mechanically altered voice snapped on. "I am here, Daryl."

She huffed. "Stupid translator. He sounds more like R2-D2 than Dr. Gordon." As she slid her finger across the touchpad, she scanned the screen. "Would the data log be in the system maintenance directory?"

The voice meter lifted again. After a few seconds, Daryl clicked on something with her mouse, apparently halting Dr. Gordon's transmission. "Never mind," she said, "I found it." Her eyes shifted back and forth for a few seconds. "It's too complicated. I'm going to run the stream through demo mode and see what happened."

"What's demo mode?" Nathan asked.

Her fingers flew along the keys. "If the recorders captured all the images, the system will use the mirror to display everything that took place here, and the monitor will show me every command that anyone entered through the computer. But since it's demo mode, it won't actually create portals or zap anyone to another world."

After tapping a final key, she slid her finger down the touchpad, dimming the overhead lights. She rolled the chair back from the desk until she could easily look back and forth between the screen and the ceiling. "Okay, let's see what she does."

The mirror above flashed once, darkened for a few seconds, then displayed the telescope room. Dr. Gordon Yellow and one of the Simons stood next to the computer while the other Simon sat in one of the rolling chairs with his elbow on the desk. Gordon seemed to be shouting, apparently angry, while

Solomon stood with his arms crossed, staring at him with a stern expression.

"Can you turn on sound?" Nathan asked. "Looks like an argument."

"Let's see. It's a little different here." Daryl searched the screen, moving her finger around on the touchpad. "What's this gizmo?"

As soon as she tapped on the pad, the mirror flashed again. The hologram lights shot multicolored beams into the room, but this time, instead of focusing on a central cylinder, they covered one end of the floor to the other. Images appeared—Simon Yellow sitting in his chair, Gordon Yellow and Simon Blue standing next to Solomon Yellow. All four seemed to be physically present in the room, though Simon Yellow's chair fizzled in and out, proving that the computers had limited their reproductions to the main players' immediate surroundings.

Nathan passed his hand through Solomon Yellow's body. He was nothing more than a realistic ghost.

"Got the sound," Daryl said. "Here goes."

The speakers erupted with Dr. Gordon's shouted voice. "So you just sent them without consulting me? I wanted to see that place, maybe even go there. At least give me the secret to why 'The Moonlight Sonata' doesn't work, even on the piano."

Solomon tightened his crossed arms. "Patar's instructions were clear. Only he and the Red Shepherds were allowed to go, and no one may follow."

"He's a stalker!" Dr. Gordon's face blazed scarlet. "Those fiends have been terrorizing our world for years, and now we have a chance to strike. Next you'll be siding with Mictar himself!"

"I am no ally of Mictar." Solomon's jaw quivered, but he kept his cool. "Patar told me his evil twin is near. We'd do better to stop fighting and get ready."

"Ready?" Gordon slid out a desk drawer and withdrew a

revolver. "I have this ready for any stalker." He paused and glared at Solomon. "Or any stalker's friend."

Simon Blue touched Gordon's shoulder. "Please, if you will just—"

With a quick elbow thrust, Gordon knocked Simon Blue to the floor. "I am finished with you so-called scientists who want to sit around and wait for your salvation concert to begin." As his finger slid over the trigger, his face flushed again. "Interfinity will collapse the cosmos in days, not weeks or months. If you'd just tell me how to open the portal, we could send the Navy Seals into the stalkers' world and clear them out. We can't hope that three musicians will somehow enchant the powers that be by sawing their fiddles at random points that we don't even know yet."

"They're not random," Solomon said, his voice sharp. "They're the foundation points, the anchor loci that brace the triad structure."

"That's irrelevant." Dr. Gordon pulled the gun's hammer back and pressed the barrel against Solomon's forehead. "I want the musical key to their world, and I want it now."

A slight tremor shook Solomon's legs. Keeping his head perfectly still, he swallowed. "If you murder me, you'll never get it."

"True enough." Dr. Gordon turned and aimed the gun at Simon Yellow. "First him, then the other Simon."

Simon Yellow grabbed his chair arms and shook violently.

"I find it quite rational," Dr. Gordon continued, "even virtuous, to sacrifice a couple of hesitant scientists in order to save billions of innocent lives."

"I am on your side," Simon Yellow said. "I just want to save lives."

"And we will." Dr. Gordon pushed the barrel against the bridge of Simon's nose, bending his glasses. "What do you say, Solomon Shepherd?"

Solomon uncrossed his arms. "Look, if I give you the right music ..." As his voice trailed off, his gaze wandered toward the far side of the room.

"What?" Dr. Gordon looked all around. "What's wrong?"

"We have company." Solomon folded his hands behind his back. "Very important company."

Amber's image walked into the room. She glided toward Dr. Gordon, her hand raised and her voice thundering with authority. "Put down your weapon!"

Dr. Gordon staggered backwards. The gun fired. Simon Yellow flailed and spun toward the desk, then slumped back. Simon Blue pushed Dr. Gordon to the floor, kicked the gun away, and ran toward the exit. His image disappeared in the darkness.

As Dr. Gordon crawled toward the gun, Solomon grabbed a cell phone from his belt and hurried away, shouting into the mouthpiece, "Francesca! Where are you?" He, too, vanished.

Nathan balled his fists. The coward! He didn't stop to check on Simon Yellow. He didn't try to get the gun. He didn't even stay to protect Amber.

Just before Dr. Gordon's fingers reached the gun's butt, Amber picked it up. She swung out the cylinder and spilled the bullets into her hand. Then, without another word, she turned and walked away, dropping a bullet behind her.

Dr. Gordon climbed to his feet and shook his fist. "I know who you really are!" he screamed, pushing back his hair. "You're one of the stalkers! The apple doesn't fall far from the tree, and your fruit is just as rotten as your father's!"

After taking a few deep breaths, Gordon staggered over to Simon Yellow and checked his pulse. He patted the corpse's hand and quietly said, "I am truly sorry. I know you had our best interests in mind, and I never intended to shoot you. It was only a ploy."

With that, he sighed and stalked away. Soon, all was quiet.

Daryl studied the data. "Looks like there's not much else until we show up."

Nathan shuddered. His mouth was so dry he could barely talk. "If everything's in the log file, why didn't Dr. Gordon play it back and find out how my parents transported?"

"He couldn't." Daryl nodded at the screen. "I started from the beginning. Everything before that's been erased."

Kelly bent over Daryl's shoulder and looked on. "So Solomon Yellow covered Patar's tracks."

"Pretty much." Daryl turned off the hologram. "But we have an auxiliary backup."

"A hidden log file?" Nathan asked.

"No." Giving him a wink, Daryl touched one of the computer speakers. "A hidden eavesdropper. Dr. Gordon was probably listening in."

"Oh, yeah. Can you get him on the ceiling?"

"I'll see." She pulled the keyboard close and squinted at the monitor. "I haven't done this in digital mode before."

While Daryl worked on the computer, Kelly lifted herself onto the edge of the desk, her shoulders low. "Too many delays. At this rate, we'll never get to the foundation points in time."

"Right," Nathan said, "and we still have to translate the code."

Kelly pressed her finger against the desk's surface. "Translate it here? Even though Mictar might be lurking? And what about Gordon Yellow? We don't know where he went."

"I think we're as safe here as anywhere else." He leaned over the desk and spoke to the computer. "Dr. Gordon, we're going to try to get you on our ceiling mirror. In the meantime, do you know what's up with the music they played to transport Patar and my parents to the stalkers' world? Was it 'The Moonlight Sonata'?"

After the usual delay, Dr. Gordon replied. "Yes. I'm quite certain I heard it. Someone played it exquisitely on the piano."

"You mean it wasn't Francesca's violin from the iPod?"

Nathan drummed his fingers again, this time more loudly. He glanced at Kelly and Daryl. Both girls rolled their eyes, apparently sharing his frustration.

Finally, the speakers came on. "I couldn't tell from here. All I know is that I have never heard it played with greater passion."

Nathan glanced at the piano near the wall and imagined Patar sitting at the bench, playing the keys with his long, narrow fingers. From what he could tell, Dr. Gordon had tried to play 'The Moonlight Sonata,' but, being a violist, he probably wasn't adept enough on the piano to perform it with the passion Patar had mentioned earlier, back when they first entered the telescope room.

"I think I found the converter," Daryl said. "Ready to see Gordon?"

Nathan shook his head. "Better not bother. It's just too slow."

Dr. Gordon's voice broke through again. "Daryl, your father asked me to send his love. He's not here right now, but he will return soon."

"Soon?" Daryl's ears turned redder than her hair, and her voice cracked. "That might not be soon here."

"No," Dr. Gordon said.

Pulling in her lip, Daryl nodded slowly. "I haven't seen him in years." She opened her mouth as if to continue, then lifted her fist and bit it.

Kelly rubbed her back. "Don't worry. This'll be over before too much longer."

Daryl buried her face in her hands, nodding as she wept.

"What's next?" Kelly asked.

Nathan raised a pair of fingers. "Two options. We can either check on my parents in the misty world, or we can figure out the foundation points from the card and that report page."

Kelly raised her hand. "I vote for figuring out the points.

Even if we call up that world, we'll probably just see the long hall and a lot of fog."

"I can monitor the interfinity forecast," Daryl said, wiping her reddened eyes. "If your parents pull it off, I'll be able to tell."

"That's true." Nathan nodded toward the piano. "Could you play the sonata if you had to, Kelly?"

"It's been a long time, but I should be able to remember some of it. Whenever my parents had a fight, I'd sit down and play the first movement over and over."

Daryl tapped at the keyboard. "If you give me the symbol correspondence, I'll translate the codes into notes—that is, if I remember them."

"*If* you remember them?"

She turned and winked. "Just kidding. I remember."

"Okay, let's try to get this done quickly." Nathan looked at the screen. Daryl had already typed several strings of base twelve numbers into a word processor. He pointed at a zero, the first character. "Those should all be middle C."

"Right." She switched to the computer's music generator program and entered the note. "I knew that one."

He moved his finger from the zero to a numeral one farther down the line, then to a two, and so on as he spoke. "Then it goes C-sharp, D, D-sharp, E, F, F-sharp, G, G-sharp, A, A-sharp, and B."

"Okay. Makes sense." Daryl continued typing, her gaze locked on the screen. "Just tell the interpreter to get ready. I'll play a violin synthesizer over the speakers in a few seconds; first the notes from the card, then from the report."

"Great." Nathan peered at the doorway. No sign of Mictar or Gordon Yellow yet.

Daryl turned, narrowing one eye. "Whole notes, you think?"

"Probably. Where will the music play? From the desktop speakers or from the wall units?"

"I'll pipe it to the big ones. If El Gordo comes back, this might be our only shot."

Nathan walked Kelly to the center of the room, guiding her with a gentle hand on her back. "Ready to give it a try?"

"Sure. Uh ... what exactly am I doing?"

He set his hands on her forearms and looked into her eyes. "Just concentrate on the music and use your gift, just like when you could pick words out of music when the stalkers' choir sang. This time, it might not be words, so just say whatever comes to you, and we'll record it."

"Right," Daryl called. "I'll be the transcriptionist."

Kelly closed her eyes. "Okay. Ready when you are."

"One minute!" Daryl said, raising a finger. "Last line."

As the keys continued to click, Nathan looked back and forth between the two amazing young ladies, both exercising their extraordinary talents. Daryl, a spunky techno-wizard who always seemed to dance to an offbeat rhythm, and Kelly, a pensive, quiet artist. With her eyes closed and her head tilted slightly upward, she seemed to be in prayer, ready to communicate with the music—the breath of God, as his mother called it.

Nathan pushed a hand into his pocket, again feeling the sting in his palm. If only he, too, could dig deep into his soul to unearth his gift. Now with his hand so maimed, it might be weeks before that could happen, but he didn't have weeks. The time was drawing near when he would have to try.

He searched the room again, his gaze lingering at the tourist door, then at the small elevator on the opposite side. Still no sign of Mictar or Gordon Yellow.

"Here we go!" Daryl struck a key that echoed in the huge room. Notes played from hidden speakers; a violin, mechanical at best.

Nathan grimaced at the poor quality. It sounded like his own playing when he was about six years old. Would it be good enough to transmit the codes properly to their interpreter?

For a few seconds, Kelly said nothing. Her brow wrinkled, but she showed no other reaction.

Nathan identified some of the notes and translated them to numbers in his mind. The early codes were designed to program Kelly's mind, preparing her for the coordinates, so her silence made sense. But would it work? Could this impossibly strange code really provide three obscure pinpoints on a world map?

Finally, Kelly took in a deep breath and spoke, loud and clear, each word separated from the next by a pause as if guided by a rhythm. "Red ... north ... five ... one ... five ... zero ... zero ... west ... zero ... one ... four ... six ... yellow ... north ... two ... seven ... one ... seven ... four ... east ... seven ... eight ... zero ... four ... two ... blue ... north ... four ... two ... four ... four ... four ... west ... eight ... eight ... eight ... eight."

With a click, the music ended. Opening her eyes, Kelly blew out a long sigh. "And one more eight."

"That's five eights in a row," Daryl said. "Are you sure?"

"That's what I heard. It sounded kind of strange to me, too."

Nathan walked with Kelly back to the desk. "Do those look like GPS coordinates?"

"You tell me." Daryl rolled away from the desk and nodded at the screen. "I'm not a travel geek like you."

He pointed at the first number. "If they're all three decimal places, then that one could be fifty-one-point-five degrees north of the equator, and zero-point-one-four-six west of the prime meridian."

"Got it." Daryl rolled back to the desk. "I'll put in the decimal points for all three worlds."

"Does that computer have a way to look up GPS coordinates?"

"It's easy at home," Daryl said, "but I don't think Google Maps was around sixteen years ago."

Nathan nodded toward the ceiling. "Can you send them to Dr. Gordon? Maybe he can find them."

"Good idea." Daryl typed madly for a moment, then turned back to Nathan. "Let's hope they still have Internet there."

"Right. And even if they do, it could be a long wait."

Kelly walked across the room, scanning the floor in front of her. "In the meantime, I'll look for that bullet Amber dropped."

Nathan hustled to join her. "What are you thinking? She left a trail?"

"Exactly." Holding her hair back as she looked down, she took slow baby steps. After a few minutes, she pointed. "There it is!"

Nathan stooped and picked up the brass-colored bullet. "She was heading for the smaller elevator."

"Think we'll find another one where she got off?"

"That's my guess."

"Incoming email!" Daryl called.

Nathan pushed the bullet into his pocket and hurried back. "Did he find the locations?"

"Yeah. Kind of strange, that's for sure." She read the message out loud. "The Earth Yellow point is on the front walkway to the Taj Mahal. Blue is very near the radio telescope site on that world, which should be only a few miles away from where you're standing now, if you were on Earth Blue, that is, and Red is the back lawn at Buckingham Palace."

"Buckingham Palace? That was one of the photos we developed back when—"

"I know," Kelly said. "So was the Taj Mahal."

"My father said he experimented at some sites. He must have been real close when he went to London. He just didn't have the exact coordinates."

"So what now, boss?" Daryl asked. "Are you heading home for a world-saving performance at the palace?"

"Eventually, but since this is the fastest-moving world, we'd better coordinate from here. We have to get Francesca Yellow to India. She'll be our Earth Yellow player. I guess we should call Tony, since she took off with him."

"And your mom has to go to a telescope site?" Kelly shook her head. "That could be dangerous, especially if they have to be there at night while you're ready to play in London in the daytime."

"Good point, except that in the three worlds, we can't count on the time zone differences to work the way we expect. Maybe if she and Dad did a good job in Sarah's Womb, we'll have some extra time, and we can work it so that we're all in daylight."

"I'll check the collision status." Daryl's fingers went into action once again. A graphical representation of the three worlds appeared on the screen, each one moving along a color-coded line. Earth Red had pulled well in front of Earth Blue, and Earth Yellow seemed to be catching up with both at a rapid pace.

"That's the relative time speed," Daryl said. "Now I'll switch it to a multidimensional view."

The graph warped, gaining depth and shading. Now the three planets traveled on curved lines, two of which merged at the far right side of the screen.

Daryl pressed her finger on the intersecting point. "That's the big kabloowie for this world and Earth Blue. Interfinity is about five days away."

"Five is better than two." Nathan bent closer to the screen. "Mom and Dad probably did the best they could. At least they bought a little more time."

"I can run the simulator through the projected path. It'll give us a graphical representation of what will happen."

"Sure. If it's quick. We need to get going."

"Right. Old Scarface still wants Kelly's eyes." Daryl tapped a few keys and pressed her finger near the center of the monitor. "That's the impact point, an hour or so less than five days from now. Although the movement on the horizontal scale is based on Earth Yellow time, the distances between the spheres aren't based on time differences. What you're seeing is a representation of metaphysical proximity, so the collision doesn't mean their calendar dates have come together."

Three rotating spheres drifted toward Daryl's finger, each one seeming to float on an undulating surface. The sphere farthest away in the screen's perspective, shaded blue, and the closest sphere, shaded yellow, pulled ahead of the third Earth. They arced toward each other and melded together directly in front of Earth Red, then disintegrated into a scattering of green pixels that slowly expanded from the collision point. Earth Red continued on its course and passed through the debris.

Daryl lowered her finger. "I suppose that splash at the end is just animation. I don't think anyone really knows what will happen to the planets once they collide."

"Earth Red passed right through the collision point," Nathan said. "Does that mean it's not out of the woods? If the combined worlds somehow survive, won't Earth Red just plow right into them?"

Daryl shrugged. "Could be. It's just a simulator. I've never seen a three-world metaphysical collision before, so I can't help you there."

"Whatever happens, we have less than five Earth Yellow days to stop it, so the first priority is to contact the players."

"Think your parents will come back here?" Kelly asked.

"Maybe, if they're able. But we can't wait around. We have too much to do, like hopping a flight to England and hoping we can get there in time."

Daryl opened the drawer containing the IWART devices and picked up one of two lying inside. "If you're going to play a concerto, you'll need these to conduct your orchestra."

Nathan took it from her and clipped it on his belt. "One's missing."

"I'll bet Solomon Yellow took it for Francesca," Kelly said. "I noticed he had two devices hanging from his belt."

Daryl grabbed the last IWART. "After I send you and Kelly home, I'll wait here for your parents and zap them over to Earth Blue. Then I'll see if I can find Amber. I think she still has the Earth Yellow mirror, so she can contact Francesca Yellow."

"If Francesca took hers along," Nathan added. He glanced at the office chair deep in the shadows. "What do we do about Simon Yellow's body?"

Daryl looked in that direction. "If I get in touch with Solomon, I'll ask what to do. It's not that I'm unsympathetic or anything, but the farther away I stay from dead bodies, the better I like it."

"So you don't mind waiting here?" Kelly asked. "I mean, you were stuck in this world for so long before."

Daryl pressed her hand against her chest. "Hey, I'm as altruistic as the next girl, but we haven't proven that a digital transport to Earth Red won't fry your circuits, if you know what I mean. If it works, I'll be right behind you."

"Well, if it doesn't work," Nathan said, "our gooses are as good as cooked anyway."

Kelly jogged over to the musical instrument area and returned with a violin and bow. "How's this one?"

Nathan took them and held the violin close to his ear as he plucked each string. "Needs tuning, but it sounds pretty good."

Kelly glanced at the overhead mirror. "No time like the present." She hooked her arm through Nathan's and led him to the center of the room. "We'll either fly together or fry together."

"That's not exactly comforting."

Kelly swatted him playfully on the shoulder. "Buck up, young man! Where's that motorcycle-racing bravado when we need it?"

Heat raced into Nathan's ears. She was right. His bravado had leaked out at the sight of Simon Yellow's corpse. The reality of death had drained every drop of moxie. He had to generate more confidence, at least visibly. He raised the bow and waved it back and forth as if conducting an orchestra. "Don't worry about a thing, Kelly. This is going to be a command performance. Just take a seat and enjoy the show."

RETURNING TO RED

Daryl set her fingers on the computer's keyboard again. "I'm dialing in Earth Red. Say your prayers."

Nathan tried to laugh at her quip, but his lungs seemed to freeze. Above, the ceiling mirror brightened to a Red copy of their own room, displaying Dr. Gordon and at least two other people in the shadows—it was too late to try to guess who they were. Lights flashed on. Wide beams shot down from somewhere above, making a laser cage around them.

As they had experienced several times before, the scene in the mirror melted and descended as if ready to swallow their bodies. But this time, the lights collapsed around him, sending a buzzing shock through his body. His teeth clenched. His fingers strangled the violin's neck, and his arm locked so tightly with Kelly's it felt like their bones were cracking. He looked at her. Her eyes were closed, and her head rocked back and forth, sending her hair into a static-driven frenzy.

The Earth Red observatory took shape slowly ... too slowly. Pain shot through his body from head to toe and hand to hand. His heart fluttered. His vision dimmed. He couldn't take it for another second. He'd pass out for sure.

Two figures ran close, too fuzzy to make out. Then something hit them from the side, knocking them both down. He sprawled over Kelly, stunned. She moaned under his weight, lying on her belly with arms and legs splayed.

Strong arms lifted Nathan to his feet. He wobbled, blinking as he tried to focus on the blurry faces staring at him.

"Are you all right?" a woman asked.

"I'm not sure. I think so." He stared at the violin, still wrapped tightly in his fingers. Whoever that was sounded very familiar.

"Well, you'd better be all right, hotshot. I hear we have to hop a flight to London."

He blinked and looked at the tall, gray-haired woman. With bent brow and taut cheeks, she looked as stern as ever. "Clara?"

"Oh, well!" A wide smile cracked her harsh façade. "I'm glad you still know me."

Nathan shook his head hard and looked again. This time, everything clarified—his tutor, the telescope room, the fact that three other people were standing nearby. "What happened?"

"You and Kelly looked like you were trapped in an electrical field, so I tackled you." She brushed her hands together. "Not bad for an old lady, huh?"

He let out a laugh, but it hurt his chest muscles. "You should have been a linebacker." He turned in a slow circle. "Where's Kelly?"

"I've got her." Dr. Gordon walked Kelly to him. With her hair thrown every which way and her legs wobbling, she looked as dazed as he felt.

"You okay?" he asked.

She pushed her hair out of her eyes, now glassy and bloodshot. "I think so, but I'm almost blind again."

Nathan took her hand. Her fingers quivered. Since her vision had been restored for what seemed like several hours, it had to be a huge letdown to lose it again. As he took in a deep breath, the odor of burnt clothes and hair assaulted his nose. Kelly's hair looked scorched on the ends, so his own probably looked just as bad. He ran his thumb across her palm, and she gave him a weak smile.

Now that his brain seemed to function normally again, memories of their mission flooded his mind. "Okay, that wasn't the best cross-dimensional jump in history, but we survived. We have to get going." He turned to Dr. Gordon, who now stood next to a man Nathan didn't recognize. Both were looking at a cell phone with a full keypad in Dr. Gordon's hand.

"Did you check flights to London?" Nathan asked.

"We were just doing that." Dr. Gordon showed him the phone's screen. "Nothing is available. Our communications here have been inoperable for quite a while, so all flights have been cancelled."

"Oh, yeah. The whale-speak."

Dr. Gordon drew his head back. "Whale-speak?"

"Daryl's term for how you talked. But you sound fine now."

"I see. Yes, whale-speak would be a good description, but everything snapped back into place only moments ago. Analog communications are again operational. That's why we decided to look into the airline schedule, but it's doubtful that they will return to normal capacity anytime soon."

Nathan ran a thumb along one of the violin strings. His parents' success on the huge violin must have restored Earth Red's communications, but how long would it take to get flights back on line? Several days? Maybe several Earth Yellow weeks or months? That wouldn't work at all. "So if all analog communications are on track," he said, "can you get Daryl over here?"

"I just checked to see what she was doing." Dr. Gordon nodded toward the ceiling, which showed the empty Earth Yellow telescope room. "She's not in the Earth Yellow lab, but I sent her an email letting her know that we can switch back to analog. The transport should be much safer now."

"She must still be looking for Amber," Kelly said, watching the image above.

Nathan glanced at her as her eyes moved from left to right, scanning the mirror. As usual, she could see Earth Yellow, even from other worlds.

"Nathan," Dr. Gordon said, "have you met Daryl's father?"

"I don't think so." He extended his hand. "Nathan Shepherd."

"Victor Markey." He reached past Nathan's hand and patted his shoulder. "No sense inflicting more pain, son."

Dr. Gordon pushed his cell phone into his pocket. "Victor has a plan that I think is worthy of consideration."

"You mean you know how we can get to London?" Nathan asked.

Victor pointed at a lapel pin, a set of wings. "I don't know if Daryl told you or not, but I'm a pilot, and I know how to fly the big jets."

"But where can you get one?"

"Well, considering all the problems with the schedule, there are plenty sitting on the ground at O'Hare. Some are probably fueled and ready to go."

Nathan furrowed his brow. "You want to steal a jet?"

"Not steal. Borrow. I think the airline company would beg us to take one if they knew what was going on."

"Yeah. I can't argue with that. But what about security? Even with no flights, O'Hare's got to be battened down. We'd never even get to sniff jet fuel, much less climb aboard and take off."

Victor offered a knowing smile. "I flew in to a small airport in the suburbs. The security people know me, so getting through won't be a problem. We'll fly from there to Chicago. With no air traffic, landing will be a breeze. Then just stick with me. I called someone I know with the Feds. He'll take care of the rest."

Nathan looked Victor over. Being on the runway in the private plane would give them access to the big jets without having to go through security. But could this guy pull it off? Daryl said that he had lost his nerve after his brother died. He'd have to get some of it back to make this work. "So, when do we leave?"

"As soon as our airport transportation arrives," Victor said. He withdrew a cell phone from his pocket, flipped it open, and scrolled through his directory. "I asked Kelly's father if he knew anyone in this area who had a vehicle that might not raise suspicion if we stowed away inside, like a florist's delivery truck." He pushed a button and held the phone against his ear. "Yeah, Tony. Did you get hold of him? . . . Great." Victor looked at his watch. "Did you give him my number? . . . Super." The phone beeped. "Wait. That must be him now. Call you later."

Victor looked at his phone, pushed a button, and again put it to his ear. "This is Victor Markey . . . Yeah. We're ready . . . A van? What color? . . . Okay. Drive around back. We'll meet you there." He slapped the phone closed. "Okay. Everything's set. Let's get this show on the road."

Clara pulled a wallet from her purse. "I withdrew some money from your trust fund and put it in this. If we ever find your parents, we'll just—"

"My parents?" Nathan almost choked on his words. "No one told you?"

"Told me what?"

Barely able to contain his excitement, he took in a deep breath and spoke rapid-fire. "We found them. Dad and Mom are alive. I thought Daryl might've told you about Mom, because that was a while ago, but we just found Dad recently. He was trapped in a cocoon in a spider tree, so we had to tear him out of it. And Mom was all but dead, so Scarlet gave her life energy—"

A light flashed at the center of the room, interrupting Nathan's report. A female human figure appeared with a bag dangling from her shoulder. Now wearing baggy jeans over her bunny thermals, Daryl shook out her red locks and grinned at Nathan and Kelly. "Good thing analog's working again. I saw what happened to you two." She pulled a cell phone out of her pocket and turned it on. "Anyone got the time? It might take a few minutes for this to sync up."

Dr. Gordon checked his watch. "Four eighteen in the afternoon."

"Daryl?" Victor's eyes lit up. "Is that you?"

Daryl gasped. Her mouth fell open, and she swallowed hard. "Yeah," she said, pushing back her hair. "Do I look that much older?"

"Yes. I mean, no. I mean ..." He drew close and squinted at her. "What happened?"

"Oh, Daddy!" She leaped and threw her arms around his neck. "I missed you and Mom so much!"

Victor returned the hug, laughing. "You've only been gone a few days. Science camp was a lot longer than that."

"I was gone for years!" she cried, pulling back. "Earth Yellow moves a lot faster than—"

"Better explain later," Nathan said. "We'll have time on the way to the airport."

"We're all flying to London?" Daryl asked as she looked in her bag. "And I didn't bring a power converter."

"Yeah, we're all going, but first we're flying from a smaller airport to O'Hare. I'll tell you all about it in a minute."

"I'll stay here in case we need some kind of cross-dimensional transport," Dr. Gordon said. "Anyone else?"

Clara nodded. "I'm going to London. My knowledge of the city will likely come in handy."

Victor and Clara led the way out the tourist entry door, and Nathan guided Kelly by the hand. Daryl followed, carrying her bag. "I have the Earth Blue mirror, candles, and batteries for your IWART," Daryl said. "Remember what Simon told us? That thing has GPS mapping built in. We could have looked up the points on that instead of emailing Dr. Gordon. Anyway, I played with it and figured out how it works before I gave it to your father. So he and your mom headed to Earth Blue fully equipped, including a new violin."

"Did you find Amber?" Kelly asked as they piled into the elevator.

"I followed her bullet trail out to the parking lot. She had the hood up on Tony's truck trying to hotwire it. She was so determined to find Francesca Yellow, I think she almost figured it out. So I just went back inside, used an office phone, and called Gunther. Good thing I memorized his number, too. Anyway, they all came back and picked her up, so Amber's going to help Francesca and Solomon Yellow at their foundation point." She pulled up her oversized jeans and tightened an extension cord she had threaded through the loops. "Thank goodness for Gunther. That guy's like a Boy Scout—always prepared. He packed an extra pair of jeans along with all that food. Boy, was I glad. I was tired of showing my bunnies to everyone."

"So they're on their way to India now?" Nathan asked. "Flights are still running there?"

"Yep. I gave them the coordinates. They know what to do, but they'll be there long before we get to London."

As soon as the elevator door opened, Nathan helped Kelly out. With the violin in one hand and her hand in the other, he hustled down the hall. Although she winced with every few steps and favored her wounded shoulder, she didn't let it slow her down. She was definitely in warrior mode.

When they arrived at the rear entry door, he stopped and peeked through the embedded window. An old white van had backed up to the steps, and one of its rusted double doors was open, as if welcoming them aboard.

"That must be our ride," Nathan said as the other three caught up.

Victor opened the door. "I'll speak to him." He walked up to the driver's side window and spoke to the owner of a burly arm resting on the frame. After a moment of conversation, Victor waved for them to get in.

Nathan helped Kelly into the back, a cargo area with an old carpet covering the floor. Shelves on the side panels sat empty except for a few old newspaper pages, folded or wadded into balls. After Daryl jumped in, Victor followed, while Clara hurried around to the passenger side, sat up front with the driver, and ducked out of sight.

As soon as everyone had settled, the driver started the engine and looked back. "Hey, kid," he bellowed. "I see you survived. That witness-protection program must've worked out okay."

Nathan looked at the man. Even with the graying hair sticking out from under his Chicago Bears cap, it didn't take long to figure out who he was. "Gunther?"

He shifted the van into gear and drove away from the building. "I don't remember telling you my first name, but that'll do."

"But how did you get in touch with Tony?"

Gunther took off his cap and scratched his head through his thinning hair. "On one of my deliveries to the Newton Wal-Mart, I started wondering what happened to you. I remembered the house you went to, so I stopped by and asked the guy who lives there. He told me a pretty wild story. I'm still not sure how much I believe, but I gave him my card, and today he called me saying he needed a driver, someone who had a delivery truck. I was in the area, so I asked if this old van would do. I used to haul newspapers in it years ago. It's old, but it runs."

Nathan picked up one of the newspaper pages and read the date: July 29, 1978. "Nothing wrong with this van at all," he said, smiling. "Nothing at all."

"Well, I hear you're in need of speed, so I'll do the best I can."

Once they had traveled well away from the observatory, Clara sat up in her seat, while Nathan and Kelly stretched out as much as they could, and Daryl fell asleep against her father's shoulder.

Nathan pulled the IWART from his belt, switched it to Earth Blue, and pushed the talk button. "Anyone there? Dad? Mom?"

He released the button. No one answered.

"Maybe it's the metal in the van," Kelly said.

"No. I just remembered. We have to be stationary." He called toward the front. "Gunther, can you find a safe place to stop, just for a minute?"

"No problem. There's a stop sign ahead, and no one's around."

As soon as the van halted, Nathan turned the dial to Earth Yellow and tried again. "Francesca?" After waiting a few seconds, he whispered, "Solomon?"

A buzz sounded, then a quiet female voice came through. "Nathan?"

He pressed the button. "Francesca, I'm just checking on you. Are you in India?"

"Yes, we're at a hotel. I thought I'd try calling you in the morning."

"How's the delay? Do you have to wait very long?"

"Oh, sorry. I fell asleep again. What did you say?"

He held the unit close to his lips, hesitating a moment before pressing the button again. "I guess the delay's pretty bad. We're just leaving for London, so you'll have to wait a while."

"I understand. We're prepared. My father ... Nikolai, I mean, came with us, so he'll watch little Nathan. But it has already been a day and a half since we left. Time is running out."

"We'll get there as fast as we can. Don't worry about answering. I'll give you an update soon."

After reclipping the IWART, he turned to the front. Gunther propped his arm on the seat and nodded in Nathan's direction. "Ready to go?"

"Yeah. Let's hurry."

While they rattled along, Nathan explained everything he could remember from their adventures. Although Clara asked a hundred questions, and Victor added several more, Gunther never said a word. He laughed from time to time when Nathan described Gunther Yellow's roles, especially when he took out the murderer in Francesca's room and wielded a tire iron when he thought Nathan was a kidnapper.

Nathan had barely finished his story when they pulled into the nearly empty airport parking lot. Daryl woke up and rubbed her eyes, while her father opened the rear door and helped her and Kelly get out.

"I'll drive around until I see a plane take off," Gunther said. "You have my number if you need me."

Nathan reached over the back of the seat and shook Gunther's hand. Although the muscular driver's grip hurt like crazy, it was worth it. "Thanks for everything," Nathan said. "Both for what you did in this world and in the other one."

Gunther smiled. "My pleasure. If it wasn't for all the crazy stuff going on, I wouldn't have believed a word of it. But it actually all kind of makes sense."

Again leading Kelly by the hand, Nathan followed Victor into the terminal building, while Clara and Daryl tagged along behind. Victor spoke to a uniformed man, who let them pass, and soon they were walking out to a small Cessna parked inside a hangar.

"My brother's old hangar," Victor explained. "That's why I use this airport. He rented it until he died, and I just kept up the payments. He was my best friend, so it's sort of a sacred place for me. I can almost feel his presence when I'm here."

"Daddy!" Daryl leaped into his arms. "Didn't Nathan tell that part of the story?"

"What part?" he asked, leaning back to look at her face.

"On Earth Yellow I saved Uncle Harry's life!"

Victor's mouth dropped open, but he quickly closed it and cleared his throat. "You saved his life? How?"

Daryl grinned and pointed at the plane. "Let's get airborne, and I'll tell you all about it."

"Okay," Nathan said. "I'm going to check up on the other worlds while you get the plane ready." He grabbed the IWART again and pressed the button. "Francesca, we're at an airport, and we'll be heading toward London soon. Just checking on your time status there."

Francesca Yellow's sweet voice, now more lively, erupted from the unit. "Hello, Nathan. It's nearly noon the same day."

"Okay. That's pretty fast, but not too bad. Any sign of Mictar?"

"No, but we brought Amber with us, so he isn't likely to come by when she's around."

"Amber? How did you get her through security?"

"We're living in the days before your nine-eleven, so it wasn't too hard. Solomon was able to get a passport with a girl's photo that looks similar to her, so we managed."

"Perfect," Nathan said. "That should help."

"I'll try calling you this evening to let you know where we are on the timeline."

"Cool. Thanks." He switched to Earth Blue. "Dad? You there?"

After a few seconds of silence, a crackling sound burst through the speakers, then a voice. "Yes, son. Thank God you made it safely to Earth Red."

"How's Mom?"

"She's fine. We managed to play a few notes, but the Womb shook so hard, we couldn't continue. At least twenty stalkers showed up, and Patar helped us escape through a hidden door in the wall."

"A hidden door?" Nathan glanced at Kelly and Daryl. Daryl

rolled her eyes, while Kelly just stared blankly. "I wish I had known about that."

"Patar isn't one to dispense much information. Anyway, we went back to Earth Yellow, and Daryl gave us the GPS coordinates and the IWART. Before she sent us off to Earth Blue, she showed me the collision simulator. It appears we had some success with the violin, but those few days might not be enough."

"Tell me about it. We're leaving now for O'Hare. I'll check in again when we get there."

"Very good, son. We're camping out in some woods close to the telescope site. If need be, we can be at the exact spot in less than a minute."

"Sounds like a plan." After Nathan clipped the unit back on his hip, he helped Kelly climb the airstair and showed her to a comfortable seat just behind the pilot's. He slid in next to her while Clara sat across the aisle.

Daryl jumped into the copilot's seat and grabbed the yoke. "Let's get moving!"

"Patience," Victor said as he grabbed a headset. "You know the drill."

She gave him a mock glare. "I thought you said this thing was fast!"

Victor slid on the headset and gave her a stern look in return. "Traveling through hyperspace ain't like dusting crops, boy!"

While everyone laughed and Daryl and her father continued to volley *Star Wars* quotes, they pulled out of the hangar and onto the short runway. Soon they took off, climbing at a steep angle. When they leveled out, Nathan tried the IWART again, but, as expected, it didn't work. He wouldn't be able to give or get updates until they reached O'Hare.

After a short flight, they landed on a much longer and wider airstrip. Victor guided the plane toward one of the terminals where at least fifteen airliners sat ready to load at jetways. A few others were parked nearby. Not a soul stirred—no mechanics, no food service personnel, no baggage handlers.

They stopped near one of the larger jets, which sat by itself well away from the terminal. As Victor walked down the aisle toward the back, hunched over to keep from hitting the ceiling, he said, "Be ready to go as soon as I give the word. We will be dealing with men who will be in no mood for anything but quick obedience." He pulled a garment bag from a shallow closet and withdrew a hat and dark jacket. When he had put them on, completing his sharp pilot's uniform, he opened the back door and descended the airstair.

Daryl climbed out of her seat and joined the others in the back. "Good time to check on the others," she said, pointing at the IWART.

"Gotcha." Nathan set the unit to Earth Blue and pressed the talk button. "Dad? You got your ears on?"

"Right here, wild man."

"Any problems?"

"No. Just waiting for you. We had some concerns that Mictar might be around, but the cavalry showed up. Cerulean's standing by in case Mr. Ponytail rears his ugly head."

"Yeah. I know what you mean." Nathan released the button, but as a new thought burst into his mind, he pressed it again. "Did Cerulean mention Felicity? Did he find her?"

"He was just starting the story when you called. I'll have to buzz you back when we know more."

"Sounds good, but we might be in a rush real soon."

"Roger that. We'll worry about Felicity later."

"Right. Say hi to Mom for me. I'll check on the other Francesca now." Nathan switched to Earth Yellow. "Francesca? Are you there?"

"Yes, Nathan. It's evening now of the same day. Solomon and I are having dinner at a restaurant in Agra."

"Have you gone to the Taj Mahal yet? You know, to check on the coordinates?"

"We found the precise location. If the coordinates haven't shifted, we shouldn't have any trouble."

"Yeah. If there's been any shift, this could all be for nothing." After taking a deep breath, he continued. "I won't be able to call you till I get to London, so ..." He looked around at the three beautiful ladies, both young and old, staring at him. "So pray for us. We're going to need it."

"I will, Nathan." She paused. Then, her voice filled with emotion, she added, "With all my heart."

Nathan pressed his lips together. If he tried to say another word, he would squeak like a mouse. He re-clipped the IWART and reached a hand to Kelly and another to Daryl. Then Clara joined in, completing a circle, with Kelly and Clara in their seats and Daryl and Nathan stooping in the aisle. "Things could get hairy from here on out," he said. "The lives of billions of people are at stake, we have no idea if this plan will even work, and with those cultists probably guarding the spot and with Mictar around, our chances of survival are pretty much zero. So I just wanted to let you three know ..."

His throat tightened as he looked at the teary eyes all around. "I just wanted to let you know that I love you all. Each one of you has saved my life more than once, even at the risk of your own. And now I'm asking you to risk your lives again. We don't have a supplicant watching over us this time. Amber is with Francesca, Cerulean is with my parents, and Scarlet"—he swallowed down the growing lump—"Scarlet is dead. But we're not on our own."

Nathan rocked forward off his haunches and lowered to his knees. "I haven't done this nearly enough, especially with anyone else around, but I think it's about time I did."

Staying completely silent, Daryl knelt with him, while Kelly and Clara stayed in their seats with their heads bowed. Nathan licked his lips, tasting again the bittersweet film on his tongue and smelling the delicate scent of roses. Was Scarlet around after all? Would she help him say the right words, the words he so desperately needed to say?

A tune drifted through his mind, a light, sing-song melody from his childhood, though he couldn't remember its name. Words attached themselves to the notes, creating a hymn of sorts. As it grew fuller and stronger in his heart, it seemed to well up into his throat. He had to sing it.

Beginning with a trembling voice that sounded somewhat like his own, yet altered into something more beautiful, he sang.

> O Father in heaven, so holy and true,
> Defender of pilgrims who cry out to you.
> O Jesus, my supplicant, holy and wise,
> Who guides our next footstep, our hands, and our eyes.

The scent grew stronger with every phrase, its taste more biting, yet still sweet and lovely.

> O Spirit indwelling, my comfort, my friend,
> We beg for the words that break through and transcend.
> Receive our low groanings, our pleas, and our prayers.
> Protect us, defend us, remove all our cares.

In his mind, a low gong sounded, as if announcing a tragedy—a death before its time, a funeral, the sadness of lost loved ones.

> We hear the sad toll of the bells in the tower
> For widows, for orphans, to fear and to cower.
> It rides on the wind, and it calls from the sky,
> "Bewail and despair, for you all will soon die."

He clenched Kelly's hand, then Daryl's, his passion rising with his pain.

Restrain the foul stalkers and silence the bell,
And cast all the demons and killers to hell.
Prepare us to battle the dissonant choir
With music that heals us with water and fire.

When the song ended, he took in a deep breath and added, "Amen."

"Amen," they all echoed.

He looked again at their tear-streaked faces. "Are you ready?"

"Ready!" Daryl put her hand in the middle of their circle. Clara laid hers over it, then Kelly added hers, and finally Nathan covered them all with his still-bloody hand.

Daryl shouted, "Let's do this gig!"

VISIONS OF SCARLET

Nathan laughed, feeling lighter than he had in days. As he stood and helped them rise, he nodded toward the back exit. "Let's gather over there. We want to be ready."

Less than a minute later, Victor bounded into the plane. His face grim, he waved toward the airstair. "This has gotten a lot more complicated. We'd better get moving."

Nathan led the way, his violin in hand. When he reached the bottom, he looked ahead. About fifty paces away, four men stood next to a larger airstair that led up to a passenger jet entry door. Dour expressions complemented the dark suits and open jackets that revealed shoulder holsters. One of men, a guy with a headset over his short gray hair, broke rank and marched their way.

After helping the ladies off the plane, Victor came up behind Nathan and whispered, "His name is Barker. Just stay cool. It's all under control. I told him what he needs to know, but nothing more."

As he approached, Barker spoke quietly into the headset's microphone, then pointed at Nathan while looking at Victor. "Is he the one?"

Victor nodded. "He is."

Barker shifted his finger to the three ladies. "We don't need them. Only the violinist."

Nathan jerked his head toward Victor, using his eyes to shout his disapproval. There was no way he could do this without them, especially Kelly. Who could tell whether or not he would need her gift?

"They come together or not at all," Victor said. "I don't think their extra weight will bother our transport."

Barker frowned but said no more. He turned and waved for them to follow, talking into his microphone as he marched.

Victor waved rapidly, whispering, "Go! I'll be right behind you."

Nathan followed Barker, again leading the way. When Barker reached the other three men, he stopped and pulled a small plastic box from his pocket. "One of you has dog breath. Take a mint." He tipped a small piece of orange candy into each waiting palm, then strode on.

As Nathan passed by the other three men, he tried to read their faces, but they wouldn't make eye contact. The short-haired and clean-shaven men looked more like marine sergeants than FBI types, ready to chew him up and spit him out.

Nathan averted his eyes and walked on. No use losing his nerve looking at these guys.

After climbing the steep stairway and entering the empty airplane, Barker stepped into the cockpit and grabbed a clipboard and its attached pen. While he jotted down something on the top page, Nathan guided the others inside. "Just sit anywhere?" he asked.

Barker replied with a grunt, sat in the copilot's seat, and stared straight ahead.

When Victor climbed aboard, he gave Nathan a nod and whispered, "First row will be fine." Then, without another word, he entered the cockpit and closed the door.

Nathan turned toward the front of the plane and sat in the left-hand aisle seat, while Daryl took the window seat and Kelly the middle. Clara sat across the aisle and whispered, "Maybe you should practice something. This is all for nothing if you can't play your instrument."

With the violin and bow in his lap; he stared at the palm of his bow hand, still swollen and oozing blood, then at his left, also red and raw, though not quite as bad. Could he really play? Could he follow his mother's lead and call for that impossibly powerful passion that would overcome such excruciating pain?

Finally, he shook his head. "I can't right now. I don't think I should aggravate my hands."

Clara gave him a doubtful stare and turned to the front, muttering something about preparedness.

After two other agents entered, Nathan looked out the window. The fourth agent pulled away the airstairs while one closed the door from the inside with a thud. Without bothering to look at the passengers, the two agents sat in flight attendant seats up front and buckled in.

Nathan buckled his own belt and signaled the others to follow suit.

"Psst!" Daryl lifted her shoulder bag, slid out a mirror, then pushed it back in.

Nathan glanced at the agents. A half partition stood between them and the passenger seats, likely obstructing their view of Daryl.

Giving her a nod, Nathan settled back. Would the Earth Blue mirror do them any good? Could it give glimpses of the future or transport them somewhere if need be?

A click and a slight hum sounded from the plane's PA system, then Victor's voice came over the speaker. "We'll be taking off in a minute. You might want to use the facilities. You'll find one in the front and one in the back."

After the ladies finished their bathroom trips, Nathan journeyed to the back, not wanting to face the agents. He used the toilet, washed his face, and looked in the mirror. With mussed hair, bags under his eyes, and whiskers showing in the usual places, he looked pretty bad.

As soon as he sat down, Kelly lifted the armrest between them and leaned against his shoulder. "Better get some sleep," she said. "It's going to be a long flight, and you'll need your strength."

He looked at Daryl. She had already snuggled up to Kelly from the other side. A slight buzz indicated that she had already fallen asleep.

Settling back, he took in a long breath. The aroma of roses was gone, replaced by the odor of sweat and dirt. Was it his or Kelly's? He glanced at her hair, tangled and oily, certainly not what most people considered attractive these days. Yet, something about her looked right. After toiling, fighting, and sweating with him day after day, both her odor and her appearance painted a portrait of a warrior.

He closed his eyes. Yes, more like Joan of Arc than Marilyn Monroe. And that was just fine.

As his brain eased toward sleep, he tried to remember the last time he dozed off. With all the crazy time changes and wild adventures, constant shots of adrenaline had kept him going for countless hours. Now, it felt like his brain was sinking and spinning in a slow whirlpool. Images of Kelly, Daryl, Scarlet, and so many others swirled and blended, then broke apart again.

After a few minutes, he opened his eyes. Although everyone was still seated, something was different—a presence, a touch, a smell. He inhaled. Yes, it was roses.

He looked at the aisle. A young woman in a red dress knelt there, her cheek against his arm. Her hair, redder than Daryl's, smooth and silky, gave off the scent of gardenias, mixing with the roses to create a garden paradise of aromas.

Nathan's heart thumped. How could Scarlet be here? She was dead ... or was this a dream, another realistic phantasm that issued a challenge to his mind? Could he really tell the difference anymore?

He leaned toward her and whispered, "Scarlet?"

She jerked her head up and looked at him, her eyes widening with her smile. "My beloved awakes!"

"You mean ..." He could hardly squeeze the words through his throat. "You mean, this isn't a dream?"

"It is a dream, my love." Still on her knees, she turned his hand over and showed him his palm—smooth, pink, and clean. "I have searched and searched for you in the dream world, and at last I have found you!"

"But you died. I threw your body into Sarah's Womb."

She lowered her head and her voice. "I did die, Nathan. I gave my life energy to your mother and the power of my physical presence to you. You now carry my eloquence and my voice, though your gift of music has always been your own."

"So you're like a spirit? You can still visit me in my dreams?"

Looking at him again, she nodded vigorously. "I wanted to visit you earlier, but either you have not slept or you have been in other worlds."

"Both, I think."

She patted his arm lovingly. "But now you are here, and I can help you."

"Help me? Do you know what's going on?"

"Oh, yes. Now that my physical body is dead, I am much freer to view whatever I wish. I once could see only through a mirror, dark and limited, but now I can see anything in this domain."

"This domain? You mean Earth Red?"

"Yes, my love. But I am no longer your supplicant. Although I once lived and breathed to serve you, now you are left with only memories and dreams. I can no longer show you potential futures through mirrors or transport you while you are driving on the highway or ..." She covered a giggle with her hand.

"Or change you and Kelly into safari clothes and send you into another world."

Nathan smiled with her. "What can you do now?"

"I can only offer you wisdom." She straightened her body and unbuttoned the top of her dress, revealing a dark void. "I have already given you my heart."

He looked over at Kelly. She slept soundly with Daryl still nestled at her side. Up front, the two agents stared straight ahead, apparently unaware of Scarlet's presence.

Scarlet laughed. "They won't bother us. They are merely part of your dream. Yet, when you awaken, you must be wary. These men might not be what they appear to be."

"Who do you think they are?" Nathan lowered his voice. "Why are they going with us?"

Keeping her own voice sharp and lively, Scarlet looked at them. "I have not learned all I need to know, but if they are officers of your government, their words do not match what I would expect. One spoke to the other about Sarah and the foundation points, so I think they are well aware of our secret worlds."

"Cult members? Part of Sarah's Covenant?"

"I am not familiar with this covenant of which you speak, but I am certain these men have not been straightforward with you about what they know. I advise caution. You must learn if these agents are here to help you or hinder you."

"If they want to stop me, then why go through all this trouble to fly us out there?"

"An excellent question. And I would add another: Why would a friend stay silent when he purports to convey the instrument of salvation? Would he not speak of it gladly and not hide behind a mask?"

Nathan met Scarlet's piercing gaze. After a few seconds, he gave her a nod. She was right. A friend wouldn't hold back anything. If these agents were really on his side and trying to save the world, they wouldn't be so quiet and secretive. Something was definitely wrong.

She took his hand and enfolded it into hers. "Wisdom often has many facets and many applications, my love. Remember what I have told you. You may well need these words again."

"So what do I do about those guys? They have guns. Even if I could take both of them out, there's still Barker to deal with. He's in the cockpit."

"The man you call Barker seems familiar to me. He dreamed for a short while, and I listened to his unguarded thoughts. In his dream, he was dressed in a grim reaper's black cloak, and he waved a bloody scythe, cackling about harvesting the fields of the innocent in order to rescue the world." She scrunched her brow. "I found it rather melodramatic, but he took himself quite seriously."

"That sounds like something Patar would say. Could those two have teamed up for some reason?"

"I know so little about these agents, it would be foolish to speculate without further investigation, but it would not be the first time a stalker has persuaded high-level people to render him aid."

"That's true," Nathan said, "but the gray-bearded guy I got the card from wasn't a fan of the stalkers. He didn't want Mictar to get your mirror or figure out how to use Quattro, but I guess he could've gotten together with Patar, and maybe that would explain why they're staying quiet. They plan to wait until everyone is together. Then they'll try to kill the other supplicants to stop interfinity."

"On that point, wisdom must guide you, for my knowledge is too limited to provide all the answers."

"There's still the biggest question." Nathan ran a finger along his right palm. "My hands aren't really like this. If I'm supposed to play music that will set the cosmos in order, how can I do it when I can barely bend my fingers?"

She kissed the center of his palm. As she lifted her head, she brushed a tear from her cheek with her finger and let it fall on the spot she kissed. "I do not know, my love, but from watching you for so long, I have learned something about you, a quality in your character that you might not even recognize yourself." Her eyes wide and sparkling, she paused, apparently waiting for the obvious question.

Nathan obliged. "What quality is that?"

She spoke the words with reverence. "You are willing to change your mind."

As her sweet breath caressed his face, Nathan let her words sink in. Was she right? He did change his mind sometimes, but it usually took a lot of persuading. "Well, maybe, but how's that supposed to heal my wounds?"

"Such willingness heals many wounds. It reaches out to everyone you touch and helps them see what real love means. Love has nothing to do with emotions, but everything to do with sacrificing yourself for the sake of another."

"How is that supposed to—"

"Speak no more, my love." She covered his mouth with her hand. "For now, you must rest. I feel that danger awaits you when you arrive. London's fog will be more than a reminder of Mictar's misty world; it will surely bring you face-to-face with the pale beast who would destroy the cosmos."

Her skin felt soft and cool, raising again the aroma of flowers. As the images in his mind darkened, he whispered, "When will I see you again?"

Her voice sounded like a song. "Whenever weariness overwhelms your mind, whenever fatigue drains your body, whenever sorrows weigh down your heart, come into my world, and I will catch you in my embrace."

After what seemed like a few seconds of darkness, Nathan blinked open his eyes. Jet engines hummed in his ears and the smell of coffee replaced the scent of wildflowers. He swiveled his head toward the window. Kelly and Daryl were gone.

He lunged forward and looked all around. Clara was also gone, as were the two agents up front.

Laughter rose from the back of the plane, obviously Daryl's. Nathan got up and walked that way, trying to steady his nearly numb legs as he rubbed his bleary eyes.

Near the lavatory, a curtain had been drawn across the aisle, blocking his view. He slowed his pace and looked out the windows. The sky looked strange. From the east, fingers of orange invaded the purplish canopy. The moon, veiled in an odd white mist, appeared to be twice its usual size as it glided along with the airplane.

As he approached the back, the curtain snapped open, revealing Clara. Her brow lifted, and she called out, "Nathan's coming!"

Daryl peeked past her, grinning. "Sorry for being so loud. My dad and I are trading *Back to the Future* quotes."

"Your father's with you?" He gave Clara a hug and looked around the flight attendant's food-preparation area. Kelly stood at a counter pouring coffee into a large Styrofoam cup. "Who's flying the plane?" he asked.

"Dad is." Daryl showed him a phone handset attached to the wall by a cord. "He hasn't flown trans-Atlantic in years, but since he doesn't trust the three stooges enough to take a nap, we're making him some high-octane coffee."

Clara moved back to allow Kelly to come through. "One cup of wake-up juice on its way," Kelly said as she walked toward the front.

"Can you see all right?" Nathan asked.

She glanced back, smiling. "No problem. It's kind of hard to make a wrong turn."

"Where are the stooges? In the cockpit?"

"One is," Clara said. "The other is in the front lavatory. He's been there a while. I learned their names while you were asleep. You met Mr. Barker. The other one in the cockpit is Dobbins, and the guy snoozing in the john is MacKinnon."

"Dobbins and MacKinnon. Got it." Nathan stretched into a yawn and rubbed his eyes. "How long was I asleep?"

Clara looked at her watch. "About five or six hours."

He laid a hand on his stomach. "I guess the growling down below should have told me it was a long time."

"We have food," she said. "Nothing real appetizing, but it'll do in a pinch."

He looked at his watch out of habit, but since he couldn't remember what world he had last set it on, the six fifteen reading probably meant nothing. "So how long till we get to London?"

"Victor said it normally takes about seven or eight hours, but he's flooring it, so we only have an hour or so remaining. Since we're heading east, we're gaining time fast, so it will be morning when we get there."

"I guess I'd better eat here. We won't have time for a restaurant." He looked toward the front of the plane. Kelly had already delivered the coffee and was starting back, but she stopped at the lavatory and set her ear close to the door.

Nathan watched for any sign that Kelly heard anything before turning back to Clara. "How long has MacKinnon been in there?"

"Maybe an hour," she said. "We think he's sleeping. He looked really tired when he went in."

He looked at Clara, then at Daryl. "He's supposed to be on duty."

"I told my father," Daryl said, "but he didn't seem to care. Dad acted kind of weird, but we weren't about to go in there to check on the guy, and Clara said not to wake you up."

"I'll check on him." Nathan strode toward the front.

"I can't hear a sound," Kelly whispered as he drew near. "Not even breathing."

Using his knuckles, Nathan tapped on the door three times, then waited. No answer.

Kelly pointed at the "Occupied" sign. "It's not lit, so it's probably unlocked."

He glanced at the sign. "Then how do you know he's still in there?"

"We've been taking turns watching. I guess he could've slipped by us, but where would he have gone?"

Nathan nodded and took a quick look at the cockpit entry before pushing the lavatory door open a crack. Inside, the agent sat on the toilet, fully clothed. He leaned against the back wall, his head tilted and his mouth hanging open.

Stepping in, Nathan grabbed the agent's wrist and checked for a pulse. Nothing. With blue lips and a motionless chest, there was no doubt about it. Trying to stay calm, he looked back at Kelly. "Better get Daryl's father on the horn. MacKinnon's dead."

"Are you sure?" She tried to look past him. "Are there any wounds?"

"I'm sure." He opened the agent's jacket and checked his shirt for bloodstains. "I can't see anything obvious, but he's definitely not breathing."

As Nathan stepped out, Kelly hurried to the rear of the plane, touching the seats on each side along the way. He stared at the cockpit door. Should he knock? Maybe it would be better just to alert Victor instead of letting the other two goons know what was going on.

Daryl jogged toward the front, while Clara and Kelly followed at a slower pace.

"There's a phone up here," Daryl said. Breathless, she picked up the handset and punched a button. A second later, her brow shot up. After clearing her throat, she put on a nonchalant expression and added a matching voice. "Well, hello there, Mr. Barker. May I speak to my dad? ... No, I just wanted to ask him a question." She leaned against the cockpit door and rolled her eyes. "Do you mind if I ask him myself?... Well, yeah, you could say it's personal.... Thanks." Now tapping her foot, she looked at Nathan. "He said Dad was talking to Heathrow. He'll be with me in a minute."

The cockpit door opened, knocking Daryl to the side. Dobbins, his jacket off and his white sleeves rolled up to his elbows, stepped out and reached for the lavatory door.

Nathan slid in front of the handle. "Your partner's in there."

"You sure?" Dobbins looked pale and weak as he glanced at the dark "Occupied" sign.

"Yeah. I already looked. I guess he didn't lock it."

"I'll go to the back." Dobbins staggered that way, bracing himself on a seatback every few rows.

"Dad?" Daryl peeked into the cockpit. "You got a second?"

Nathan looked over her shoulder. Inside, Victor and Barker both wore headsets and seemed quite busy as they fiddled with dashboard instruments.

"Not really," Victor said without looking back. He pointed out their windshield. "Do you see what we have to deal with?"

At the horizon, bright streaks of light shot up from two sources. To the left, at about eleven o'clock in Nathan's field of vision, the top arc of the sun appeared, the first glimpse of dawn. Then, at about one o'clock, another sunlike sphere came into view. Moving faster than its twin, the second sun revealed its entire disk before the first had shown its top half, but it seemed separated from the horizon somehow, as if drifting to the left.

"Two suns?" Nathan asked.

Victor took off his headset. "Apparently, but if it were true in reality, I don't see how our planet could survive either the gravitational imbalance or the radiational shock. In any case, Heathrow is reporting widespread panic in London. We don't have to worry about airline traffic, but getting to Buckingham Palace could be a nightmare."

Daryl stepped farther into the cockpit. "Are we looking through a portal, maybe? Like, we can see the other sun, but it's not really there?"

"Precisely." Barker pointed toward the left-hand window. "And we can see one of the other Earths."

Nathan squeezed in with Daryl and looked through the window. The huge moon he had seen hovered in the brightening sky, and the mist that had veiled it earlier now appeared as clouds, partially covering blue oceans and continents of green and brown. "So is that Earth Blue or Yellow?" he whispered.

"Judging from the rapid sunrise," Barker said, "my guess is Yellow. Our most recent analysis calculated a time-passage ratio of four-point-seven-to-one compared to that of our Earth." He pointed at the sun, now well past the other. "Still, it's difficult to know. The other Earth is not spinning at the same rate as ours, so our perception of their relative positions is confusing and perhaps skewed."

"How do you know so much about this?" Nathan asked. "If you're a government agent, then—"

"Nathan." Daryl nudged his ribs. "MacKinnon?"

"Oh, yeah! MacKinnon."

Victor slid his headset back on. "Is it important?"

"Well," Daryl said, "it's a matter of life and death." She looked back at the lavatory. "Or I guess it's just a matter of death."

Victor nodded at Barker. "I think you'd better see to that."

"Agreed."

As Barker took off his headset, Nathan and Daryl backed out of the way, joining Clara and Kelly in the aisle.

Daryl pointed at the lavatory. "Uh ... he's in there. But he's no longer with us, if you get my meaning."

"Not unexpected." Barker opened the door, peered inside,

then closed it again. "Dobbins has likely suffered a similar fate."

Nathan spread his arms in front of the ladies and backed them away. "You knew he was dead?"

"No, but I knew he would die." Barker pulled the box of mints from his pocket and shook it. "They're slow-release, but they always work."

18

THE ASSASSIN

"You killed your own partners?" Nathan asked. "Why?"

"Working with them was the only way to get this flight off the ground." He withdrew a wallet from his jacket and flipped it open, revealing an FBI badge. "It's phony, but it looks real enough to the unpracticed eye."

Clara pushed Nathan aside and stood toe to toe with Barker, her hands firmly planted on her hips. "Enough of this twaddle. Exactly who are you?"

He smiled as he rubbed his cheeks and chin with his hand. "It's quite convenient to wear a beard most of the time. All I have to do is shave to get a quick disguise."

"Better cool it, Clara," Nathan said, pulling her back. "I know who he is now, and he's not afraid to use his gun." As he glared at Barker, a million questions stormed through Nathan's mind, but one stayed at the forefront. How could this be the bearded gunman? He had died in the observatory. Unless . . .

He pointed at Barker. "You're the Earth Red version, aren't you? It was your Earth Blue twin who died. You were the crazy gunman who chased me in Chicago and at the observatory."

"Good thinking, but not exactly correct. I was the gunman in Chicago who tried to shoot you from the drawbridge, but, unfortunately, I was arrested. It took my people some time to get me out of jail, so my twin, as you call him, was responsible for the other encounters."

Nathan bit his tongue. It would do no good to retaliate now, but he also couldn't be too soft. He had to keep his voice firm. "So what's this all about? Why did you try to kill Clara and me, but now you're killing FBI agents to help me get to London?"

"If you knew what was going on behind the scenes, you would understand. This isn't about you at all, and it never has been. My goal has been to protect Sarah's foundation from an assault by Mictar or anyone else. Since you were one of the few who could contact the supplicants through the mirrors, we wanted to eliminate you. If Mictar obtained one of the mirrors you used, he would have reached through it to one of the supplicants, and the power he would have gained would have made him unstoppable. But since you have successfully eluded him, and since interfinity is at hand, it's crucial that we help you get the job done."

"But why kill the agents?" Nathan asked. "Weren't they helping, too?"

"I cannot allow anyone to know where the foundation points are." He withdrew his gun. "Understand?"

Nathan stared and the barrel and nodded. After they stopped interfinity, Barker was going to kill them all. But what could he do? He had to cooperate. Otherwise billions of people would die. "There's one problem," he said. "Mictar probably does know the coordinates. I took your twin's encoded card and a page from the Interfinity Labs report that had the points. I'm sure he'll figure it all out."

Barker seemed unmoved. "That is problematic but not insurmountable." He waved his gun toward the passenger seats. "Strap in. We'll be arriving soon."

Nathan picked up the violin and laid it on his lap as he sat down, while the others settled into the same seats they had chosen before. As he buckled his seat belt, he glared at the gunman, reliving the trial of floundering in the river while this assassin tried to shoot him and Clara in the cold, murky water.

As Barker turned to go, Nathan called out, "Wait. I have one more question."

Barker pivoted. "What?"

"How did you find out about the supplicants and foundation points in the first place?"

Barker slid the gun back into his holster. As he leaned against a partition between the passenger's cabin and the exit door, an odd expression passed across his face—winsome, dreamy, maybe even childlike. "As a teenager, I often dreamed about a girl dressed in red. She said she was seeking her beloved and thought I might be him. She told me about a land of mist and white-haired beings, about Sarah and how her Womb separates the three worlds, and about how beautiful music strengthens the fabric of the cosmos. She told me she would pray for me and sing songs of supplication to her heavenly father if only I would repent of my wicked ways and follow the faith of my parents.

"Since I was firmly entrenched in my rebellious years, I turned her down more times than I can count. Then, she stopped visiting my dreams. She had told me many times that I would forget the details of her world when I awakened, but I didn't forget. I remember every word to this day. Although I never learned her name, I knew she was real, and I had to find her."

The plane dipped, signaling its descent. Victor's voice sounded over the PA system. "We'll be landing in about ten minutes, and we might hit some bumps. Make sure your seat belts are good and tight."

Nathan checked his belt again, as did Kelly, who was once again at his side. He watched as her hand gripped the strap and pulled. She seemed tired, lethargic. Ever since they had returned to Earth Red, she had stayed pretty quiet, lacking her usual pluck. The loss of her vision must have drained her energy.

Barker picked up the phone and pressed a button. "Markey, I'll be there in a minute ... Yeah. I'll hurry."

After hanging up, he stood at the front of the aisle, like a flight attendant giving safety instructions, and spoke quickly, barely pausing between sentences.

"I talked to hundreds of people about my dreams. Most of them thought I was crazy, but I eventually located two others who had similar experiences, and we formed Sarah's Covenant, based on the only name the girl in red ever mentioned. I have since learned that my counterpart on Earth Blue had dreamt about a boy in blue, so he traveled the same path and was seeking the same goals.

"Not long ago, we placed an Internet ad in both worlds promising financial aid for interdimensional research, which is how we learned of the two Dr. Simons. They answered our ads when they lost their government grant money and were forced to seek financial help from outside sources.

"Since we funded Interfinity Labs, my cohorts joined the board of directors, and when we needed to keep secrets from the other members, we communicated with each other by code. You see, we believed in the fourth world, the Quattro world, long before anyone else discovered it. We borrowed a device that Dr. Gordon was working on that allowed us to locate and transport to that world. That's when your father entered the picture. Gordon hired his firm to track us down, and when he discovered us, he traveled to the Quattro world himself. He actually helped us learn the foundation points of Sarah's Womb, but that story would take too long to tell."

Barker took a deep breath and reached for the cockpit door. "We were going to confess everything and cooperate with Dr. Gordon, but when Mictar and Patar showed up, that threw our plans into turmoil. The cosmic wounds flourished, and we had to save the worlds and once again conceal the secrets we had learned. We decided the best way to do that would be to kill everyone who could contribute to the coming of interfinity, including Mictar once we were finished using him, and dispose of everyone who knows about Sarah's foundations."

"Including yourself and your cronies?" Nathan asked.

He lifted his box of orange candies again and gave it a gentle shake, his features sagging as he looked at it. "Even us." Turning abruptly, he ducked into the cockpit and closed the door.

Kelly grasped Nathan's wrist. "So after we save the worlds, he's planning to kill us all."

"Sounds like it."

The plane tipped down into a steep descent. It dropped suddenly, then caught the air again and bounced heavily. Nathan looked out the window. The other Earth had dimmed somewhat in the brightening dawn, but it had grown larger, now four times the size of the moon. Below, roads and highways were jammed with cars and trucks, barely moving at all. But where could they go? Did they think the countryside would provide protection from this looming planet in the sky?

Clara opened her purse and pulled out a nail file. "It's not much, but there's only one of him and five of us."

"True," Kelly said, "but he's not stupid. He's got to know he's outnumbered."

Nathan looked at the cockpit door. Barker had to have something up his sleeve, some card he hadn't played yet.

The plane began bucking wildly. It banked to one side, then the other, as if slapped by a furious hand.

"Where's the barf bag?" Daryl yelled. "I'm going to be sick!"

Nathan reached around his seat and yanked one from the pocket in back. "Got it!" He threw it into her lap and grabbed his armrests. "Hang on!"

Victor's voice pierced the roar and rattle. "We have opposing weather patterns, and they're stirring up some violent clouds that seem to be converging on London. Odds are it's only going to get rougher."

"Never tell me the odds!" Daryl shouted.

Nathan looked at her. The fear in her eyes said she hoped for her father to answer with another *Star Wars* quote, but he didn't respond.

His teeth clacking with every word, Nathan spat out, "You said you wanted to be around when I made a mistake. Well, this could be it, sweetheart."

Daryl forced a trembling smile. "I take it back."

Kelly's fingers tightened on Nathan's arm. "We made it through a worse flight," she said, her voice calmer than her grip. "We can make it through this one."

Nathan stared into her eyes. Although still glazed, they seemed at peace. He then looked at the violin as it bounced on his lap. "You're right," he said, stretching out his thumb to hold it down. "But I can't play 'Amazing Grace' this time."

"Maybe not, but I can sing it." She tilted her head up and began to sing, "Amazing gr —"

The plane bucked hard to the right, thrusting her body against Nathan's. She gasped. Nathan pushed against her, trying to get upright again, but the force was too strong.

Then, as if recoiling, the plane rocked back, angling just as far to the other side. Daryl coughed into her bag.

"I think I'll sing it in my head," Kelly whispered.

"Great." Nathan grunted out his words. "We'll need it."

He again looked out the window. Dark clouds swirled above the airplane, eerie and unearthly, almost alive in their frenzied dance. The ground drew close. The airport runway raced underneath the wings, but at this angle, a wingtip would surely strike the pavement before the wheels would. Was Victor really qualified to fly this jet? Was Barker? Maybe the conditions were just too much for them. If only —

A jolt rocked the plane. The wing scraped the runway, shooting sparks into the air. The wheels banged down. Everyone bounced violently then jerked forward as the plane decelerated abruptly. Nathan clutched the violin with one hand and his stomach with the other, thankful that he never got a chance to eat anything.

When the plane had slowed to a gentle taxi, Kelly flopped back in her seat, while Daryl crumpled her barf bag. "Don't ever talk me into one of these adventures again," Daryl said. "If we survive, I'm taking up Scrabble. That's all the excitement I need."

Clara reached across the aisle, holding the nail file. "Take it. You'd use it better than I could."

Opening his hands, Nathan shook his head. "Not with these. I already hurt them again hanging on to the seat."

As the plane rolled toward the terminal, rain pelted the windows. Barker stalked out of the cockpit, fishing for something in his pocket. "Word is that all roads are too jammed for travel. We'll have to go by chopper."

Nathan glanced at the IWART clipped to his belt. Now would be a good time to check on his parents and Francesca, but not while this crazy assassin was listening.

A gust pushed the plane to the right, lifting the wing slightly. Barker braced against the lavatory, still digging in his pocket. Finally, he withdrew a small chip and pulled his cell phone from his other pocket.

"This chip," he said as he slid the back panel off his phone, "contains the code for the latest foundation coordinates for all three worlds. Although you will be quite close with the coordinates you have, without the new data, you won't be close enough. And since only I know how to retrieve the codes, you'll have to wait until we arrive at the palace before you get them."

Nathan whispered to Kelly, "That's his ace in the hole. He made sure he let us know that we need him."

"Right," she said, also keeping her voice low. "I picked that up."

After inserting the chip, Barker put the phone back together and slid it into his pocket. When they rolled to a stop, the engines died away, but the plane rocked in place, pounded by the storm.

Barker opened the side door. Wind and rain swept inside, whistling and swirling. He backed away and retrieved a large blue-and-white umbrella from the cockpit. "Time to go."

Nathan popped open the overhead luggage compartment, picked up a dark blue blanket, and peered out the window as he wrapped the violin. Two men rushed toward the plane, pushing a stairway. Nearby, a large helicopter sat on the tarmac, its blades slowly turning above its camouflage-coated frame. "C'mon," he said, reaching for Kelly's hand. "We're in for another rough ride, but we don't have much choice."

Daryl grabbed two more bags from the backs of other seats. "I might need these."

Barker handed Nathan the umbrella. "One at a time. The guy down there will bring it back when you get in the chopper."

As he took the handle, Nathan looked back at Kelly. "I'll see you in a minute."

She gave him a tight-lipped smile and nodded, but said nothing.

After tucking the violin under his arm, he stepped onto the staircase, opening the umbrella as he passed through the door. Cold wind assaulted his body and knifed through his sweatshirt with moist slaps. He hustled down the stairs and to the helicopter, ducking under the blades, though they were well above his head.

He handed the umbrella to a tall, skinny man wearing fatigues, then climbed aboard. A helmeted pilot sat up front, but he stayed quiet as he jotted something on a clipboard.

Nathan snatched the IWART from his belt and tuned it to Earth Yellow. "Francesca, are you there?"

"Yes, Nathan! Oh, thank God you called. It's the final

day, and we can see another Earth in the sky. Everyone is panicking."

"Same here. I'm in London, but I still have to take a helicopter to Buckingham Palace. We have a howling storm going on, so we'll need some extra prayer."

"I will pray for safety and speed, Nathan."

"And to get us out of a jam. We're kind of at the mercy of an assassin who plans to kill us when the job's done."

Francesca said nothing for a moment, then whispered, "Amber wants to speak to you."

"Oh ... okay." Nathan cleared his throat and tried to calm his nerves. Whatever Amber had to say would probably rattle him again.

A quiet voice lilted from the tiny speaker. "Nathan?"

"Yes, Amber. I'm here."

"Nathan, I heard what you said about the assassin. This healing of the cosmos might well cost the lives of several sacrificial souls. Do not fear the path of martyrdom. Greater men than you have died to save countless others. That is what heroes do."

Nathan held down the button and paused for a few seconds before speaking. "You're right, Amber. I don't know what else to say, but you're right."

After another moment of silence, Francesca spoke again. "I will talk to you soon. Take care."

He pulled in his lower lip for a second before continuing. "I love you, Francesca."

This time the pause seemed interminable. Had she heard him at all? Finally, her sweet voice came through loud and clear. "I love you, too, Nathan. If I don't see you again on one of these Earths, I'll see you in heaven."

Kelly climbed aboard, brushing water off her pants as she sat next to him. "Good thing this helicopter's big," she said as she buckled her belt. "In the rain, my eyesight is worse than ever."

Trying to push down his emotions, Nathan switched to the Earth Blue setting. "Yeah. Good thing."

She touched his shoulder. "You okay?"

"Not really, but I'll be all right." He buckled his own belt and pressed the IWART's talk button again. "Dad, are you there?"

He waited through a few seconds of silence before trying again. "Dad? Mom? Either of you there?"

Again, silence. Nathan left the IWART on the blue channel and reclipped it. "I don't get it. Even if they had to run to use the bushes, they'd do it one at a time. Someone should be listening."

"I agree," Kelly said. "It doesn't look good."

"Brrr!" Daryl hopped into the helicopter, sat on a bench opposite Nathan and Kelly, and quickly buckled up. She shook her hair out, slinging droplets all around. As she pulled her wet, oversized pant legs away from her skin, she nodded toward the door. "Clara's on her way. I figured this was taking too long, so I bolted for the chopper without the umbrella."

Soon, Clara joined them, along with Barker, who sat up front with the pilot while Clara slid onto the bench next to Daryl. The blades whipped against the wind, and the engine whine raised such a racket, Nathan could barely hear himself think.

The helicopter lifted off and immediately surged to one side. Daryl reached across the gap between the benches and took Nathan's hand. "Not to be forward or anything," she shouted, "but I could use a little old-fashioned comfort right now."

Nathan patted his side of the bench. "We have more seatbelts." He had to yell just to hear his own voice. "Wait for a lull in the turbulence and jump across."

Rolling her eyes upward, apparently trying to sense smooth air, Daryl poised her hands over her belt. Then, in a flurry, she unlatched it, leaped to Nathan's bench, and buckled in. She hooked her arm around his and pressed close. "My father has to stay in the airplane," she said directly into his ear. "I don't know what they're going to do to him." She paused for a moment, then added in a trembling voice, "And I don't know what I would do without him."

Keeping a hand on his violin, Nathan tightened his arm around Daryl's. He kissed her on the top of her wet head and whispered, "Your father did what heroes do."

Kelly grasped his arm from the other side and leaned her head against his shoulder. The warmth of both girls' bodies felt good—soothing and filled with love. Knowing they depended on each other calmed him down. If he shivered or trembled, they would feel it and maybe lose their nerve. For their sake he had to be a rock and a pillow at the same time.

As he willed his muscles to relax, both girls nestled closer. He breathed a sigh of satisfaction. Even though he had to force it, they definitely felt his peace, and soon he felt it, too.

With the helicopter continuing to bounce, Clara sat on the opposite bench, clutching her belt. Other than her white knuckles, she seemed relatively calm.

"You all right?" Nathan shouted, now able to smile with ease.

She gave him a thumbs-up. Her own smile seemed calm. She always was a tough one to scare.

After several more minutes of rough riding, the helicopter descended onto a huge green lawn, but with the metal frame obscuring their view, not much else was visible. At least the rain had stopped, but the bending trees gave notice that the wind still howled outside.

Barker jumped out and opened the passenger door. "Get down," he said over the wind. "The London police are cooperating by cordoning off the area, but I don't know how long they'll believe that a boy with a violin is going to save the world."

"I'm not sure I believe it myself." Nathan glanced at his hands but said nothing more. Carrying the violin, he jumped out into a ferocious gale. Above, the clouds had cleared, revealing again the Earth hovering in the northern sky, now at least twenty times bigger than the moon.

Kelly and Daryl leaped out and splashed to the grass beside him. Daryl pointed to the south. "Looks like the squeeze is on."

Nathan followed Daryl's hand. Another Earth loomed over the horizon, not quite as big, but obviously growing. "We're on Earth Red. The other Earths are supposed to miss us."

Barker pulled out his cell phone and opened it. "What makes you think that?"

"I watched a simulation at Interfinity Labs on Earth Yellow. It showed Blue and Yellow colliding and us skipping past them."

"Don't count on it," Barker said. "The paths shift all the time. There's plenty of dissonance going on to bring Earth Red back into a collision course."

While Nathan helped Clara step off the helicopter, Barker punched in a few numbers and put the phone to his ear. After a few seconds, he shouted, "Any updates? . . . Good. I'll go with the codes I have."

"Who's providing the data?" Nathan asked. "And why doesn't he just give you coordinates instead of musical codes?"

"My source is an old friend of yours who refuses to provide the coordinates directly. He is suspicious of recording devices."

Nathan pointed at himself. "An old friend of mine? Who?"

Barker kept his eyes on his phone. "Patar."

"He's in league with you? I can't believe it."

"Trust me. He's no friend of ours." Barker's face turned grim. "Look, we can either talk about his morality while the worlds collide, or you can let me program this phone to get the data. But if I were you, I wouldn't get up on a high horse about killing a few people to save a few billion others."

Nathan jerked the blanket off the violin. He said he couldn't believe it, but he knew it was true. Patar wanted the supplicants killed and had said so multiple times. Yet, he seemed to have softened, especially after Abodah died. He went out of his way to help Jack, didn't he? And his manner with Amber was tender as well. Still, it made sense that he would help Barker. They both displayed a weird sort of cold heroism in wanting to save all three worlds without regard to the sacrifices they made along the way.

In a fresh blast of air, the helicopter lifted and rose into the gale. Kelly and Daryl pushed back their whipping hair, and Clara turned away from the gusts. Soon all was clear.

While Barker punched numbers into his phone, Nathan turned slowly in place. Buckingham Palace sat at the far end of the pristine lawn, and a pond bordered the grass on the opposite side. A few trees stood about, all thrashing in the cold wind.

In the distance, ropes spanned the streets, and bobbies stood guard every few yards. Hundreds of people bent over the lines, trying to catch a view of the happenings on the palace lawn, but they didn't seem anxious to get any closer.

Above, the two Earths continued to rise from each horizon, growing larger by the second. It seemed that if they kept the same heading, they would collide at the top of the sky. Not physically, of course, or the gravitational pull would have already forced all three worlds to zoom together at breakneck speed. No, this collision would be different ... but how?

A chill crawled across his body, the foreboding heaviness that signaled a stalker's approach. Nathan searched the trees for Mictar. Seeing no sign of the stalker, he yanked the IWART from his belt and gestured for his three companions to come together. When they gathered, he lifted the device and showed Daryl the screen. "Check it out. Are those right?"

Holding her hair back again, she squinted at the numbers. "North, fifty-one point five zero zero; west, zero point one four six." She looked up at him. "Yep. He deposited us right on the money."

"So what happens now?" Nathan asked. "Am I supposed to play your codes and get Kelly to interpret?"

Barker held up his phone. "I'm almost done. I'm programming it to use the musical stream as a ringtone, so you won't have to play it for her."

"How have you interpreted the codes in the past?"

"We used Kelly of the Blue world. Her father has always been lax on security, so it was easy to break in and play the tunes while she slept. She talked in her sleep, so she was an excellent resource before Mictar killed her. Since then, we haven't been able to update the coordinates."

Nathan looked up again. The two Earths moved ever closer together. The distance separating them was now less than the diameter of either one. "Okay. Let's get on with it." His own words echoed hollow in his mind. This was like sitting for a test he hadn't studied for. How could he possibly pull this off without healthy hands?

Clara pulled a notepad and pen from her purse. "I'm ready. Fire away."

Extending the phone toward Kelly, Barker pressed a series of buttons. The speaker played a string of notes, starting with the codes from the plastic card, the musical key that had programmed her brain earlier.

She bent closer to it, but after a few seconds she shook her head. "It's too windy," she shouted. "I'll have to hold it up to my ear."

Barker's brow furrowed. After looking all around, he drew his gun and lowered the phone as if making ready to toss it underhand, but a black streak splashed against his chest, and a second struck his face.

Nathan spun. Mictar stalked toward them, one hand carrying his black violin and bow and the other poised to strike again.

19

RETURN TO THE WOMB

Barker fired his gun—once, twice, a third time. With each bullet, Mictar halted for a moment, grimacing. Dark blood dampened one sleeve and a pant leg, and a red streak across his cheek gave evidence of a graze wound. Still, he marched on.

Now half blinded by the spreading blackness, Barker emptied his clip into the stalker's body. Mictar doubled over and thrust out his arm, but no new bolts came out.

Collapsing to his hands and knees, Barker sputtered, "Shepherd! Take the phone. Push star seven seven seven to get the ringtone."

Nathan ran to him and pried the phone from underneath his hand. Barker dropped to his belly, panting through his words. "Save the world, Shepherd. I ..." He let out a long breath and said no more.

"Star seven seven seven," Nathan said as he shoved the phone into Kelly's hands. "I'll try to keep Mictar away."

While Kelly pushed the buttons and lifted the phone to her ear, Nathan stood between her and Mictar. The stalker, now on his knees, glared at him but stayed silent.

Nathan grabbed the IWART and shouted into it. "Dad! Mom! Are you there?"

A stream of static buzzed through the speaker along with a garbled voice. "I'm here, son. Your mother is at the spot and is ready to play."

Pressing the button, Nathan shouted again, still competing with the roaring wind. "We're waiting for new numbers. Hang on."

"Understood. I'll stand by for your instructions."

Nathan switched to Earth Yellow. "Francesca! Can you hear me?" He waited, looking up at the converging planets. His mother stood on one of the spinning spheres, her twin on the other, both with violin and bow at the ready. Would anyone on those worlds ever believe that two women with violins were their only hope for survival?

He looked back at Mictar. Did he dare attack? How long before the stalker's throwing hand was back in business? With his eyes riveted on Kelly, Mictar seemed content to wait through his rapid healing process while she interpreted the new codes.

"Nathan?" A voice spurted through the IWART's speaker, interrupting Nathan's thoughts. "Nathan, I'm sorry I couldn't answer right away. Solomon is hurt. He had to fight off some local guards, and one of them shot him."

"How bad is it?"

"I don't know. It's a chest wound. The bleeding's pretty bad, but he's conscious and talking. When the guards saw the Earths in the sky, they panicked and ran, so they won't bother us, but we have no way to call for help."

"We don't have any choice," Nathan said. "Give him the IWART. You have to play, and I'll give him the new coordinates when we get them."

"That's exactly what Solomon said." Francesca's voice faltered. "He's ready to die to protect me."

"He is?" Nathan's throat pinched his voice into a squeak. "That's cool, Francesca. That's very cool."

"Nathan?" The new voice was definitely male—strained and shaky. "Francesca's playing the key now. I'll await your instructions."

He looked up again. The two Earths drew closer together,

but now a dark form materialized, a cylinder that hovered about two hundred feet above the ground, like a black pipe lying on its side. It sprouted three cylindrical branches, one of which lengthened and snaked slowly toward them. Yet, it wasn't really moving at all. Air molecules seemed to burn in place and blacken, becoming part of the cylinder as it stretched downward.

It stopped at least a hundred feet in the air, and the end stretched wide, like a mouth ready to swallow anything lying below. The wind suddenly calmed. The air felt eerily alive, as if every particle carried an electrostatic charge.

"We have the coordinates!" Daryl yelled. "It can't be more than a hundred yards away!"

"Find the spot, tell the others their numbers, and make sure they're playing. I'll be right with you." Nathan tossed her the IWART. It sizzled as it passed through the supercharged atmosphere.

She snatched it out of the air with one hand. "Gotcha, boss."

Still holding the cell phone, Kelly ran to his side. "Did Mictar hear the coordinates?"

He shook his head and pointed at the stalker, who was now struggling to his feet. "It doesn't make any difference. The creep will just follow us."

The cylinder's branch drew closer, now no more than fifty feet high, but the center point hovered over another part of the lawn, a section closer to the palace. Kelly blinked at it. "What's that dark thing?"

"I'm guessing Sarah's Womb is searching for the foundation point, too. It's almost like she can't quite stretch that far."

Holding a hand over his bleeding stomach, Mictar sneered. "Pitiful! Sarah calls for healing from a quack who doesn't even know her illness." He straightened and pointed his bow at Nathan. "Go ahead and try, fiddle boy. Play the magic song and see if your bloody hands can heal Sarah's wounds."

Nathan looked at his palms again. They seemed more raw and blistered than ever, completely incapable of playing even a simple tune, much less a world-saving symphony.

"And don't forget," Mictar continued as he waved his black violin, "I will be right behind you to corrupt every note you play."

The sky darkened again. Screams echoed all around. The crowd broke through the police blockade, some running toward them and others just scattering. A cacophony of screams, police whistles, and car horns filled the air.

Squeezing the neck of his violin, Nathan backed away. For some reason, the stalker seemed more malevolent than ever. This was the monster who killed Nathan and Kelly Blue, consuming their eyes along with their vital energy and leaving them limp, lifeless, and staring into the endless void through empty sockets.

As a familiar lump grew in his throat, he reached for Kelly's hand. "C'mon. Let's catch up with Daryl and Clara." They turned and ran. With the air still electrically charged, popping sounds rushed past his ears. The sounds of panic magnified. Screams pierced his brain, raising images of Felicity, blind and alone, still clutching her walking stick while leaning against her morbidly etched tombstone. The ugly girl no one cared about still awaited her hero.

Nathan swallowed the lump. He couldn't be everyone's hero. It was all he could do just to stumble along on this crazy path, this impossible task that called him to play in concert with two virtuosos in different dimensions. At the moment, he felt more like Nero than a hero. Would he be playing a fiddle while Rome burned to the ground?

Across the field, Daryl walked slowly, her gaze locked on the IWART. Clara stayed at her side, looking on and apparently checking the numbers on her notepad.

Above, the cylinder branch still hovered, crackling, sizzling.

Now the size of the palace itself, its mouth undulated as if buffeted by an unfelt wind.

When they arrived, Daryl stopped and pointed at the ground. "I think this is the spot. Earth Blue's numbers didn't change, so your mother is playing at the right location, but Earth Yellow's did change by a little bit, and I couldn't get hold of Solomon Yellow to let him know."

Nathan looked up. They stood right under the center of the dark mouth. Within the tube, all was blackness. "Keep trying."

He lifted the violin and bow into playing position, but even curling his hand around the bow sent horrific pain up his arm, and pressing his fingers against the strings did the same. He couldn't play this thing. It was impossible.

After turning the switch to the Earth Yellow position, Daryl raised the IWART to her lips. "Yo! Solomon! Are you there?"

Kelly pointed at the unit. "Call the observatory and see if anyone's heard from them."

"Gordon Red can't talk to the Yellows."

"Just do it," Kelly said. "It's a hunch."

"Whatever you say, Miss Interpreter." Daryl set the switch to Earth Red. "Dr. Gordon. Can you hear me?"

After a few seconds, a breathless voice replied. "Yes, Daryl. I'm glad you called. Tony of Earth Yellow has been in contact with Solomon Yellow by cell phone. Solomon's IWART stopped transmitting and receiving. He says a dark cylinder appeared in the sky and blocked out all light. The only thing they can see is the glow from the IWART's screen. Francesca is already playing 'Foundation's Key,' but it appears to be making no difference."

"So do their GPS functions still work?"

"They do. Solomon mentioned that specifically. The satellite signals are coming through."

"Are you still in contact with Tony?" Daryl asked.

"Yes. The transmitter you and he put together is still operational."

"Perfect! Get these new changes to them, pronto. Add point zero zero one to the north coordinates and subtract point zero zero two from the west coordinates."

"Hold on."

While they waited, Clara nudged Nathan. "Better start playing, or Mictar will beat you to the punch."

Nathan looked into the field. Mictar shuffled toward them, now stronger, his violin in one hand and his bow in the other. Grimacing, Nathan took a deep breath. He had no choice. It was time to dig deep and go for it.

He pushed the bow against the strings. The note wasn't quite right, but it was close. It hurt like crazy, but maybe he could go on. Just as he pulled the bow back, the IWART interrupted, making him stop.

"Tony is passing the information along," Dr. Gordon said. "And the Earths seem perfectly in sync with time passage now, almost as if they've been tied together."

"Yeah," Daryl said. "It looks like Sarah has sent branches out to the three Earths. It's almost like she's making a last ditch effort to get them to dance together."

The sky grew darker. The black cylinder drew closer, hovering now maybe thirty feet above the ground. As if gagged by the stifling air, the sounds of fear subsided. Mictar, now almost veiled by darkness, stopped and lifted the black silhouette of a violin. With his bow held high, he looked like a ghost, the revenge-seeking phantom of the orchestral opera awaiting the conductor's first wave of his baton.

Clara stood behind Nathan and laid a hand on his shoulder. "You can do this," she said as she massaged his muscles. "It's time to be the hero I know you can be. Release these people from their prisons. Give Sarah the melody she needs to heal the wounds and call the worlds into their dance."

Nodding, he tried again. This time the first three notes sounded fine. As they rose from the strings, they seemed to pop like tiny firecrackers ignited by the supercharged air. An electric shock surged up his arms, stiffening them. Pain seared across his palms, but he had to go on. The fourth note spewed out flat, and the fifth died out before he could finish the stroke. His heart thumping, he looked back at Clara. "It's just not right. I have to start over."

Mictar's shadowed arms flew into action. The sound of his violin pierced the calm—angry, dissonant, hate-filled. As if set on fire by the mysterious air, strings of sparks flew out from the black violin. Like a vacuum, the black cylinder slurped them upward into its void.

Daryl swallowed hard. "Better go now, Doc. We have a 'Devil Went Down to Georgia' fiddle duel about to take place, and the Devil's getting warmed up."

The cylinder lowered farther, now within reach just over their heads. Daryl tossed the IWART into her bag and withdrew candles and a book of matches.

As she lit one of the candles, Mictar eased closer, now only ten feet away. He sawed his violin. Screeching notes flew out, like discordant demons with wings of fire. Again, the cylinder sucked them into its dark grasp.

Joining Clara at Nathan's back, Kelly massaged his other shoulder, whispering, "Nathan, God has given you your talent. You can do this. You can play through pain." She paused for a second, then added in a quavering voice, "Even if you don't believe in me, I will always believe in you."

Like a lightning bolt, her words shot straight to his heart. Heat boiled from within and surged through his limbs—pain, sheer pain. Lifting his head, he let out a guttural cry. Then, bending toward his violin, he played. Again the first three notes sounded perfect. Sparks flew, red and sizzling. The cylinder swept them upward as it continued to descend.

Nathan played the fourth note, then the fifth. Each wracked his hands with pain, but Kelly continued to massage both body and heart. "Roll the stone away, Nathan. Reach down deep and call forth the passion, the breath of God that heals the wounds."

He played on. Kelly's words were like magic, so profound, so penetrating. Was she interpreting his music? Was she reading his mind, plunging deeper into his thoughts than he could himself?

Finally, the cylinder lowered to the ground, enveloping everyone in the field, including Mictar. Darkness shrouded Nathan's vision. Even his violin disappeared. A single candle interrupted the void, illuminating Daryl's face, now taut and wide-eyed.

But where was Mictar? His foul music played somewhere to Nathan's left, but how far away? What might he do to win this new battle?

As he continued playing, the aroma of roses filled his senses, and the bite of cinnamon and vanilla laced his tongue. His sparkling notes cast an intermittent red glow over his hands before being lifted into the empty sky.

The wonderful words continued, as sweet as ever. "You are the gifted one, my love, and you are playing the celestial waltz."

Scarlet? But he couldn't utter her name, not while playing. Not with all this pain. And he couldn't see if the red-haired angel had appeared. It was just too dark. But that voice wasn't Scarlet's. It was Kelly's, though it seemed bathed in pure peace and contentment.

With pain scourging his mind, he stroked the strings with every ounce of passion he had. Mictar responded. Sparks shot upward, red from Nathan's violin and a jumble of red, blue, and yellow from Mictar's, giving away his position. He was close, maybe within reach, but the blackness made it difficult to know how close.

Nathan watched the sparks shoot upward into the darkness. His stream mingled with Mictar's, the two seeming to fight as they ascended. High above, they stopped and mixed into two new streams descending from higher levels, each coming in at a steep angle, a blue stream from the left and a yellow one from the right.

"I hear more violins!" Daryl pumped her fist. "Rock on, Francesca!"

Goose bumps covered Nathan's skin. His mother had arrived with her greatest weapon, and little Francesca, his darling from the Yellow world, had taken up her bow. The battle was on. The breath of God had taken center stage. Mictar didn't stand a chance.

Nathan again bent his body and dug deep. Heat flowed from his belly and ripped through his limbs. His hands felt like they were on fire, but he didn't care. Let the fire burn. Let the blood flow. This performance was for his Lord; no holds barred, nothing left unplayed.

As if given birth by the music itself, the words returned, still spoken in Kelly's gentle voice, still carrying wisdom beyond her reach.

"Now you are in Sarah's Womb, my love, a place of comfort and healing. As the trio of gifted musicians mend her wounds, she will rise again. She will separate the worlds and guide them in their dance through time and space. Everyone in her grasp will feel her healing touch — the touch of her creator, the greatest of all healers."

The mingling of sparks descended, a cyclone of color, like fireworks that wouldn't die. As the storm reached the ground, Nathan's stream continued to fly toward it, angling into a horizontal flow. The swirl looked to be the size of the top of Sarah's Womb, the hole the great violin spanned with its golden strings.

As if drawn by a gravitational pull, Nathan walked toward the swirl. Kelly kept a hand on his shoulder while Clara's hand slid down to his waist. Daryl kept pace at his right, her candle in hand, while Mictar's sparks flowed at his left, still mixing with Nathan's.

When he reached the edge, he halted and gazed across its expanse. The storm of sparks illuminated everything within an arm's reach. On the other side of the storm and to his left, his father and mother stood, his mother playing her violin with bloody hands. Cerulean walked up behind them, his arms crossed over his chest and his brilliant blue eyes shining. A dark tunnel lay behind them, their path to this central point.

Far to the right, Francesca Yellow stood in a simple white dress, Amber at her side. While Amber shed an aura of glowing gold, Francesca seemed to radiate white. With her dark locks draping her luminous shoulders, Francesca truly looked like an angel. As she played her violin, sparkling tears ran down her cheeks and dripped into the swirl, adding a new color to the musical storm—pure white, like diamonds mixing in with the rainbow streams. She, too, stood in front of a tunnel, apparently her passage from Earth Yellow.

Below, a dark void spread out beneath the sparks, bordered by a perimeter wall that acted as a circular boundary for the cyclone, keeping it from expanding further.

While his hands continued to blaze, Nathan stared at the amazing sight. This vertical chamber must have been the larger cylinder that hovered in the sky, while the three paths to the central point were likely the branches that had stretched to the three Earths.

Clara stood at the very edge of the sparkling storm and shouted at Nathan's father on the other side. "Solomon, Mictar is somewhere close. He is wounded, but he is interrupting the music. I'm not sure how much longer Nathan can go on." She looked back at Nathan for a moment, her expression a blend of feigned confidence and worry, then turned back to the cyclone. "Any suggestions?"

Nathan's father's voice boomed from his Earth Blue position.

"There is a narrow ledge that goes around the hole. I tried to come around, but I could barely keep my feet on the path, and those sparks are like live wires."

Daryl pushed her candle into Clara's hand. "I'll make sure that cocky zombie takes his final bow." With her fists clenched, Daryl rushed toward the source of the foul music.

"Daryl!" Kelly cried. "No!"

Two seconds after Daryl disappeared, a loud thud sounded, then grunts and groans. Nathan lifted his bow and looked, but a new voice—low, masculine, and familiar—sprang up from Francesca Yellow's direction. "Play on, Nathan! You must not stop."

His bow hovering over the strings, Nathan looked toward the source of the voice. Patar strode toward them over the top of the storm. His sandals seemed to absorb the sparks, and a dimmer path appeared in his wake. Something protruded from the top of his trousers' pocket, something plastic. When he hopped down to their side, he pushed the plastic out of sight and looked Nathan in the eye. "Now that Mictar is down, you are free to complete the healing! You cannot stop now! Not for Daryl, not for anyone!"

Kelly tapped Nathan's shoulder. "Keep playing. I'll help Daryl." She ran into the darkness. Clara followed, carrying the candle. Its glow illuminated the struggling trio on the ground. Arms, hair, and fists flew, along with growls and shrieks, but it was impossible to tell who was getting the upper hand.

"Stay back, Clara," Nathan yelled as he stepped toward the fray.

Patar stopped him with a rigid arm. "You must play the key, Nathan Shepherd! Forsake the few you love and rescue the un-lovable masses. This is true sacrifice. You were called to this task, and you have suffered a great deal to get here. Do not turn from your sacred duty now." He lowered his arm and turned toward Mictar. "I will deal with my brother at the proper time."

Nathan raised the bow and watched, shaking so hard he could barely stand. Patar walked toward the candlelight slowly, too slowly. Nathan began "Foundation's Key" again, but the driving fire in his hands had cooled. The notes sounded wrong—flat and lifeless.

As Patar drew close, Mictar threw Daryl to the side but hung on to Kelly, her back against his chest and his arm around her waist. "Not another step, brother!" Mictar sat up and laid a hand over Kelly's eyes. "Or you know how much she will suffer."

Nathan cringed. He played, but just barely. His mind screamed at Patar to stop Mictar. But would he?

Patar pointed at his twin. "Do not think that your threats will stop me from exacting justice, brother. You killed my mate and many others, so you must die."

Now on her hands and knees, Daryl crawled to Nathan. Her face marred by deep scratches and her hair matted by blood, she looked up at him with pleading eyes. "Don't ..." She coughed and spat. "Don't trust Patar. You have to save her yourself."

Nathan pulled Daryl to her feet, but she couldn't stand on her own. As he lowered her back to the ground, he whispered, "I have to let her go. I have to sacrifice what I love and keep playing." Again he stroked the strings with his bow, and again the notes sounded pitiful, cursed by fear and hatred.

Patar set his hands on his hips. "What do I care about that girl's pathetic eyes? They are of no value in her own world. Why should they be of any value to me?"

"You surprise even me," Mictar said. As light spilled out from behind his hands, Kelly screamed and thrashed her arms and legs. The stalker held on tight, his body seeming to radiate a light of its own. Kelly struggled, but she seemed weaker. Then, her screams fell silent.

20

BLINDNESS

Nathan dropped the violin and charged. He pushed Patar to the side, grabbed Kelly around the waist, and pulled, but Mictar held fast.

As smoke rose from Kelly's eyes, Nathan grunted through every word. "Give ... her ... to ... me!"

Mictar's evil face grew brighter than ever. "She is no good to you now. She will be blind and helpless, an invalid you will have to feed and dress. She's as good as dead."

Nathan peeled Mictar's lethal hand back, revealing Kelly's charred sockets, but he couldn't pry her free. "She's more valuable blind than I am with sight."

Mictar snorted. "That is saying very little."

"If you let her go, I'll ..."

"You'll what?" Mictar turned his hand and dug his pointed nails into Nathan's wrist. "Are you offering to take her place again? You lack creativity."

"Creative or not, that's my offer."

"Be gone, fool. Your mother has already provided the catalytic element, and your little harlot has given me enough energy to feed Lucifer. So why would I need you?" Mictar planted a foot on Nathan's chest and shoved him backwards. Still holding to Kelly, Nathan flew away and tumbled across the ground while she slid to a stop nearby, writhing and moaning.

Clara leaped for Kelly and gathered her into her arms. Kelly reached for her face with her fingers. They passed over her eye sockets, for a moment interrupting the rising strings of smoke. "My eyes!" she screamed. "They're on fire! I can't see!"

Crawling on hands and knees, Daryl scooted closer. She grabbed Kelly's wrists and forced them against her chest. "Just relax, honey," Daryl said, weeping. "Don't touch your burns. Just take deep breaths. We'll take care of you."

Nathan struggled to his feet, holding his head. He wobbled, unable to figure out what to do next. One thought crowded out all others: Kelly was hurt, and he had to help her.

Boosted by Kelly's energy, Mictar rose to his full height. His skin glowed white, and his eyes shone red.

"Clara!" Nathan's father called from beyond the storm. "Is everyone okay?"

"No! I think Nathan's all right, but Kelly's not."

"Should the Francescas keep playing? The swirl is dying."

Patar shook his head. "They can stop. They have already provided substantial healing, but the foundation points have likely shifted. We will have to employ the final option if we are to complete the task."

Picking up his violin, Mictar glared at Patar. His glow pulsed in a heartbeat rhythm. "Are you such a fool that you think I have no plan to stop this final option of yours?"

Patar turned back to him. "Let us say that I am such a fool."

With several quick strokes, Mictar played a violent run of dissonant notes.

Kelly called out, her voice a lament as she translated the music. "I come. Release Lucifer and let him roar!"

Like flying embers, the notes shot toward the spinning storm, hesitated a moment over the swirl, and then zoomed upward into the cylinder. Mictar followed, leaping into the cyclone and soaring around and around, ever upward until he was out of sight.

"Whoa!" Daryl called. "That can't be good."

Patar's eyes blazed as red as his brother's. "Mictar has called for his allies in my world to start the Lucifer engine. Come! We must leave this place."

Nathan staggered to Kelly and lifted her away from Clara. Her arms fell limp. Although she was breathing, she showed no other signs of life. "What about Kelly?" he asked. "How can she be healed?"

"Her physical eyes have burned," Patar said. "They can never be restored, but if you will finally heed my words, you will be able to gain the power to recover her lost energy."

Patar helped Nathan shift Kelly's body to a better carrying position. "The storm of music will end soon," Patar continued. "Then we must follow my brother and ascend the Womb's canal to the great violin. That is where the final step must take place. If, indeed, the Lucifer lion begins to growl, that passage might close."

In the distance, the cyclone slowed its spin and formed an inverted funnel that channeled the sparks straight up. As tiny lights vanished in the upper reaches, the edges of the swirl contracted, and the darkness grew thick again.

In the light of the few lingering sparks, Nathan caught only brief snapshots of his parents, Francesca Yellow, and the supplicants. His father eased around the hole, his back to the wall as he carefully guided his feet along the narrow path. Nathan's mother followed, as did Cerulean. On the opposite side, Francesca and Amber did the same, each one spreading her arms for balance.

"Son!" Solomon called as he arrived hand in hand with his wife. "Is she alive?"

Nathan nodded, but he couldn't speak. With Kelly near death, he barely managed enough strength to breathe. It was as though his spirit weakened in proportion to her dwindling life force.

His father held out his arms. "Give her to me. I'll carry her for you."

Shaking his head, Nathan refocused on Kelly. Now with only a candle flame flickering across her lovely face, she seemed ghostly. She had saved his life so many times, but now she was helpless. His heart ached, and he let the passion flow. He had to give it all back, every ounce of love she had shown him, even after he responded with doubt and distrust. Now if only she would wake up and live, he would show her the love she de-served—pure, holy, unconditional.

Squaring his shoulders, he lifted Kelly higher. "I have to carry her."

"I understand, son, but don't take it too far. Let your loved ones help you bear your burdens."

"Right, but not just yet."

His mother pushed back his hair. "I see it in your eyes, my son. You have found the passion, haven't you?"

"I think so, but is it enough? Will Kelly ever—"

From somewhere high above, a long note sounded, sung at a high pitch. Another joined it, and soon, a choir of several voices screeched a horrible tune, if it could be called a tune at all.

Patar laid a hand on Amber's shoulder. "Are you ready?"

Her face looking paler than usual, Amber nodded. "I am ready."

Patar reached for Cerulean. "And you?"

The male supplicant's blue eyes shone like radiant sapphires. "I have cradled my beloved's dream image of herself, but I have not yet found her living body. Although my friend Jack still searches for her, I have little hope that he can find her." Cerulean bowed his head and folded his hands at his waist. "Still, if you command this step, I will take it."

With an arm around each supplicant, Patar walked toward the spot where the sparks had spun. "Come, everyone. Although our three players have given us more time, we must make haste before Lucifer roars."

Still cradling Kelly, Nathan followed. Daryl shuffled along at his side, carrying her bag and candle once again. "I feel like Edward Scissorhands gave me a facial, but at least my legs are okay."

Nathan winced. "I hope you don't get scars."

"Me, too." She held the candle close to her eyes. "I'm not exactly vain, but how often does the world get to see a face as gorgeous as mine?"

He gazed at her half-hearted grin. Obviously she was trying to lighten his mood, but it wasn't working.

When Patar and the two supplicants stopped at the edge of the hole, Patar looked up.

Solomon arrived next and faced him. "What do you have in mind?"

"Elevation. We have to rise into the heart of Sarah's Womb."

"But how? We can't fly."

Patar turned to Solomon and gave him a condescending stare. "By now, my friend, you should have learned that the rules of physics are not the same in my world, but your ignorance matters little at the moment. I will guide us from here."

Nathan shook his head. Patar never was one for polite talk. Still, all the caterwauling flowing down from the misty world was enough to make anyone irritable, especially considering the danger it signaled.

Francesca Yellow raised her hand. "If you don't need me, sir, I would like to return. My husband is badly wounded."

"Very well." Patar nodded toward the tunnel leading to Earth Yellow. "Follow the path. It will lead you back to the foundation point."

"I'll go with her," Clara said. "I've patched up our Solomon a few times."

After Francesca and Clara made their way around the hole

and then through the tunnel, everyone gathered at the edge. Patar looked again into the darkness above. "Most of you have seen images of the dream worlds and Sarah's central Womb, but now we are standing underneath what you saw. Though your vision is inadequate to perceive it, the violent shaking of the cosmos has ripped apart the barrier that separates the dream worlds. Yet they are still held together by a force I cannot discern. I would have thought they would fly apart."

"Even Earth Red's?" Nathan asked. "It wasn't supposed to crash with the other two."

"How little you know." Patar formed a cylinder with his hands. "The three worlds, both the real and the imagined, are linked in an interdependent bond. If any one of them is lost, the others would be thrown out of balance, as I am sure you learned."

Daryl nodded. "You mean Earth Red's loss of analog communication."

"Very good. And the more they diverge, the worse their conditions. They would eventually perish in a fashion more excruciating than what they would have experienced from interfinity."

"What would you call that?" Daryl asked. "Extrafinity?"

Patar glowered at her. "I assume you think that to be a clever quip. Perhaps you will also deduce the reason the dream worlds hold together."

"Uh ... no. I haven't figured that out yet."

"Then leave the cleverness to me."

Daryl leaned close to Nathan and whispered, "Wow! This guy is really fluorescent."

"Fluorescent?" Nathan repeated. "What do you mean?"

"He's bright, but irritating."

Patar pointed at the floor. "The approach of interfinity caused Sarah's Womb to expand in three directions, and the harmonic music created a new floor here, though a hole remains that leads to her infinite depths. There are two other floor levels above us; one for the dream worlds, and one at the top for my world. Since the visible realm is codependent with the invisible, if the dream worlds were to split, your extrafinity would occur. So we must complete the healing of both."

"By playing the big violin?" Nathan hoisted Kelly a little higher, sweating now as her hot body pressed against his. "But how? We almost got killed the last time we tried."

"You will see." Patar waved an arm toward the void. "Come. We will ascend to the next level. Who will lead the way?"

"Are you kidding me?" Daryl said, setting a hand on her hip. "Why don't you take the first step?"

"Because, Miss Fluorescent, I must buoy anyone who has trouble ascending. The level of dreams is the center of mass, and all are drawn to it, whether from below or from above, but not all travel there at the same rate."

"When I walked around the ledge," Solomon said, "I didn't feel an upward pull."

"You must get closer to the center. It will require a leap."

Amber walked to the edge. "I will go first. They trust me." She jumped out over the hole and immediately began to rise. Within seconds, she vanished into the upper darkness.

Nathan's father and mother joined hands. "Shall we?" he asked.

"By all means." Turning to Nathan, she leaned close to the hand that gripped Kelly's shoulder. She breathed on his knuckles, then gazed at him lovingly. "The breath of God never fails, my son. Whether by music, by love, or by resurrection from the dead, he will restore everything to its proper place."

After backing up a step, they jumped and lifted into the air. Nathan and Daryl did the same, with Daryl still holding the candle, the only light they had, save for Cerulean's faint glow.

As he ascended, Nathan looked down, barely able to see over Kelly's body. Below, Cerulean and Patar drifted upward at the same rate. The blue-haired supplicant stared straight at Nathan—poised, confident, fearless.

Nathan pulled Kelly's face next to his. Her skin, cold and damp, smelled of burnt flesh, and her hair smelled worse. Still, her breaths, though rapid and shallow, gave him hope. He had to revive her. And he had to do it without letting the supplicants die. His only hope was to play the big violin. But how? Even though he had succeeded with the normal one, Sarah's instrument was a completely different story. Every note caused an earthquake, and without a bow, it seemed impossible.

Daryl held out her candle, illuminating the dark barrier surrounding them. "That wall isn't more than a few feet away. This part of Sarah's Womb is kind of a tight squeeze."

"I noticed. I think there are mysteries here we'll never solve."

Soon, the wall sloped and drew farther back. Their upward ascent slowed until they reached a point where the wall ended with rough edges at the top, as if someone had ripped away the perimeter. They stopped and hovered in place, floating next to Amber, who looked around with narrowed eyes.

Nathan followed with his own gaze. With lights from various dreams illuminating the expanse, several images took shape—a football field with stadium lights, a sunlit meadow with a girl flying a kite, and a cemetery, barely visible under a half moon.

"Very strange," Amber said. "The three dream worlds are now in view of each other, and it is a simple matter to travel between them."

"How?" Nathan asked. "Wouldn't the dream people hit some kind of boundary if they tried to go around this hole? Hasn't that always been there?"

"Yes. That barrier likely still exists, but look." Amber pointed up. "The bridge is complete."

Nathan lifted his head. Above, the vine Amber had stretched between the two spider trees was still there, and now another vine had been tied to the middle of that one, bending it toward a third spider tree. Who could have anchored the Earth Red dream world to the other two?

Still holding the candle, Daryl reached up and grabbed the vine with her free hand. "Get ready," she said. "I'm going to haul us to the side." She reached around Nathan's shoulders, keeping the flame clear of his shirt and Kelly's hair, and pulled toward the edge of the hole.

As soon as their feet passed over the floor, gravity took over. Nathan dropped to the ground with a thud but managed to balance Kelly and stay upright.

Daryl, too, landed heavily, groaning as she steadied herself. "If we pull this off, the three worlds had better come up with the biggest honkin' gold medal in history."

Standing well out of reach of the tree, Nathan looked back at the core. Like a circus acrobat, Amber swung easily to the side on her own.

Daryl held out her candle. "Pretty dark in this dream world."

"Yeah," Nathan said. "I want to check out the cemetery."

"To find Felicity?" she asked.

"Right." He looked down at Kelly. "When Kelly went with Felicity into the sandbox, she might have learned more about where she really was. I wish she were awake to give me more clues."

Daryl shrugged. "If wishes were wardrobes, we'd all be in Narnia."

Nathan gave her a smile. She was still doing her best to cheer him up. It helped, but Kelly's body weighed down his spirits as well as his arms.

When Patar arrived, still floating in the center, he grasped the vine and examined the knot that fastened one to the other. "Amber, did you do this?"

Amber walked back to the edge of the hole. "Nathan and

I tied two spider trees together, but someone else added the other vine."

Rubbing a hand along the fibrous line, Patar raised his brow. "Who but a supplicant could have conceived such a brilliant plan?"

"I'll bet I know who." Nathan turned to his father. "Dad, I could use that help now, if you don't mind."

"Glad to." Solomon grabbed the vine and swung to the ground. While he held out his arms, Nathan shifted Kelly into his grasp.

"Thanks. I hope this won't take long." Nathan dug into Daryl's bag, withdrew a candle, and set the wick to her flame. "Let's look for Felicity."

"When I found her," Solomon said, "she was leaning against a tombstone."

"Same for me, but if I'm right about what's going on here, this place might not be safe, so maybe you'd better stay with Mom."

Still floating at the vine, Patar frowned. "Time is of the essence. Even now these vines are stretched to the limit and are ready to break. If the real worlds are in such a state, the people are surely suffering, and it will only get worse if Lucifer wakes up."

Nathan pointed at Patar. "Just stuff it! If you wanted someone who'll ignore the cries of a lost and frightened girl, then you got the wrong guy." He shifted his finger to the cemetery. "I'm going out there to find Felicity, or whoever she is. If God won't hold the cosmos together long enough for me to find her, then maybe it's not worth holding together." He laid a hand on Kelly's brow. "There's one thing I've learned through all this; every single person is worth more than I can imagine, and I'm not about to pass one by with the excuse that I'm too busy with a higher calling."

Cerulean pulled on the vine and jumped to the ground.

Looking back, he bowed to Patar. "Allow me to go with them. This is the Blue dream world, and I am confident that my aid will shorten the delay."

"Very well. Amber and I will stay with the others. I concur with Nathan on one point. This place is not safe. With the breach in these walls, the danger to these Earth-dwellers is high. All living captives have likely escaped."

Nathan walked on a path of twisted vines as he led the way past the first tombstone, checking the other side before moving to the next. With only the partial moon and his candle providing light, seeing proved difficult. Several oaks with low-hanging limbs and dangling gray moss cast humanlike shadows over the gravesites. As a soft breeze swayed the branches, it seemed that dark ghosts waltzed across their resting places.

Nathan cupped a hand around the flame, though it never flinched, even when a light rain began to fall.

"Shouldn't we call her?" Daryl whispered. "I don't think we have to worry about waking the dead."

Nathan lifted the candle close to her bleeding face. "It's not the dead I'm concerned about, but with Cerulean here, we should be okay."

"I will call," Cerulean said. "She will heed my voice."

"What happened when you dove into that chasm?"

"She disappeared into a dream-ending cyclone, and Jack and I eventually rose back to the dream level. When Patar called me to return to help the musicians, I left Jack to continue the search."

"Patar called you?" Daryl asked. "What is he, the head honcho in charge of supplicants?"

Cerulean seemed ready to answer, but he just shook his head. "There is no time to dwell on this topic. Come, I will lead the way." He stepped to the front, cupped his hands around his mouth, and called out, "Felicity, my beloved, harken unto me. It is I, Cerulean."

They followed the winding path, still checking both sides of every grave marker. Soon, a human form appeared ahead, female, but too dark to identify. Nathan caught up with Cerulean and extended his candle. "Can you tell who she is?" Nathan asked.

Cerulean stopped and called out, "Felicity, do you fear our approach?"

A weak voice replied. "I smell death."

Nathan ran ahead and looked at her through his candle's flame. Her hair and dress dampened by the steady rain, her walking stick clutched in a thin hand, and her eye sockets still vacant, she looked as pitiful as ever. "Felicity, listen carefully. You are the dream representation of your real self. We're looking for that real person. Have you seen someone sleeping around here?"

Felicity said nothing. She just crossed her arms and gave him a stern look.

When Cerulean arrived, he took her hand. "You have no need to fear. If we find whom we seek, we will not leave you here alone. In fact, you may go home with us. Death will never stalk you again in these gardens of decay."

"I did see someone," she said, her fingers throttling her walking stick, "but the last time I trusted you, I fell. When I woke up, I was by myself again."

"That is because you allowed fear to overwhelm you." Cerulean lifted her hand to his lips and kissed her knuckles. "Now you have another opportunity."

"Why should I believe you? Your claim that I'm a dream is ridiculous." She tapped the side of her walking stick against her head. "I know when I'm dreaming. I'm always floating in an empty place all alone."

"Always?" Nathan asked. "Haven't your dreams changed at all?"

She aimed her stick in his general direction. "Now that you

mention it, my most recent dream was pretty strange. But the story really starts before the dream. A while back, I felt something odd with my walking stick. Someone had pulled a vine from one of the spider trees and pushed it through the wall. The next time I was awake, I decided to try the vine trick at a different tree. I managed to dig a hole in the wall and poke the vine in, but then the tree grabbed me, and I fell asleep.

"That's when my strange dream started. I was floating in darkness, as usual, but then I saw something. Yes, *saw*. It was the tiniest speck of light. I floated toward it, but on the way, I passed by a vine that I could only feel. It was tight, and I could move around by pulling on it. So I pulled hard to make it spring me toward the light."

Nathan watched her animated facial expressions. He wanted to hurry her along, but he didn't want to risk missing an important clue.

"That worked," she continued. "The light came through a tiny hole in a wall that had the end of a vine poking through, so I pulled on it until I had reeled out several feet. Then, I bent my knees and pushed off the wall, but I didn't have enough slack in the vine to get all the way to the other one, so I sprang back.

"I was able to pull out a little more vine, so I tried again. This time when I pushed from the wall, I reached as far as I could. I grabbed the other vine and stretched both far enough to tie one to the other. It felt good to accomplish something, even if it was just a dream.

"I was just floating there, holding on to the vine and enjoying the fact that I finally had something to anchor me in place, when, after a while, sparkles of light rose from underneath me, red, yellow, and blue. They were beautiful. I liked watching them, but they stung when they touched me, so I pulled over to the wall and flattened myself against it. They rose into the dark sky and made tiny explosions, but it didn't last long.

"Another kind of sparks came from below that attached to

the wall and ate through it like acid. The wall tore apart, and I fell to the ground and hit my head. I could still see, but I kind of staggered around for a while, and I was so dizzy I just had to lie down. When I did, the dream ended, and I woke up back here." She took a deep breath and let it out slowly. "Weird, huh?"

"Very weird," Nathan said, "but if you'll show me where you saw someone, I think I can explain it all."

Felicity extended her walking stick and sighed. "I suppose my life can't get any worse." She turned and began tapping the stick on the path. "The person's either asleep or unconscious. I felt long hair, so I think it's a girl or a woman. She's big enough to be an adult."

Nathan waved for the others to follow. After about a minute, she slowed and sniffed the air. "She is close."

"Which direction?" Nathan asked.

She pointed with her stick. "That way, but I will not go. Death is also in that direction."

21

THE REAL FELICITY

Nathan laid a hand on Cerulean's back. "You stay here with Daryl and Felicity. If I run into trouble, I'll give a shout."

"Very well. But you must hurry. We still have much work to do. Patar will not be happy."

"Trust me, I know." Nathan turned and stepped off the path. Now searching in the heart of the cemetery, dozens of tombstones loomed before him; some small, barely more than a foot high, and others tall and ornate, rising higher than his head. Anyone or anything could be hiding behind them, maybe even this "death" Felicity had smelled.

Again cupping his candle, Nathan stalked closer to one of the larger stones, a head-high obelisk with a marble cross on top. Rain fell loudly on the gray stone, making every spatter sound like a breaking twig or the unguarded footstep of an approaching enemy.

Something moved ahead, a shadow on the other side of the stone. Nathan crouched and skulked to the obelisk, glad now for the rain's concealing noise. Pressing his back against the stone, he peeked around the edge. A body lay on the gravesite, curled and unmoving; it was obviously female, though darkness concealed any details. A tall figure stood near the body and held a short stick in one hand.

Nathan looked back at the path. The others had disappeared among the shadows, leaving him to handle this guy by himself.

That stick didn't look like much of a weapon. A surprise attack with a swift kick in a vulnerable spot should take him out. But was he an enemy? He couldn't jump a guy without finding out first. And maybe he was just part of the dream. Either way, he had to act now.

With a quick lunge, he jumped from behind the stone, wheeled around to the front, and leaped for the girl's body. Straddling her as he extended the candle, he squinted through the curtain of rain. A white-haired man stood only a foot or two in front of him, his eyes wide. In one hand he held a sonic paralyzer, and in the other, a small book.

Nathan gulped. "Tsayad!"

The paralyzer flashed on. A red light pulsed at the top, and an ear-splitting wail rocked Nathan's brain. The stalker shouted a string of harsh vowel sounds, but Nathan didn't need Kelly to interpret. After being pushed into Sarah's Womb, Tsayad had a score to settle.

Nathan jumped and landed a hard kick against Tsayad's chest. The stalker flew backwards, and his paralyzer clanked to the ground near the body. The girl stirred. Her face toward the ground, she moaned but said nothing.

With a quick stomp, Nathan crushed the end of the sonic rod. As the noise died away, the girl continued to squirm, again moaning softly.

Tsayad climbed to his feet and let out a shrill whistle. Two more figures emerged from the shadows, each one holding a paralyzer.

The rods flashed on, and twin squeals ripped through the air. Nathan dropped his candle and covered his ears. Just as he took in a breath to yell for help, another loud noise erupted from behind him, a deep bass that sounded more like a foghorn than a voice.

Cerulean strode their way, his mouth open in song. The

notes varied, but they stayed deep, rich, and resonant. They seemed to muffle the squeals, making them tolerable.

A stiff breeze swirled. One of the smaller tombstones lifted from the ground, followed by another. Weeds and turf flew into the growing cyclone, along with several trees. The three stalkers stood with their legs set wide, trembling as they braced against the storm. Although they obviously feared Cerulean, two held their sonic rods aloft as if daring anyone to come nearer. The supplicant had canceled the sound, but one touch from a rod would still carry a paralyzing jolt.

Daryl ran to Nathan's side, her hair whipping as she shouted, "Felicity's waking up! I mean, the real Felicity."

"I know!" Nathan shouted back. "Where's the dream version?"

"Right next to me!" Daryl dug both heels into the ground and hung on to Felicity. The wind picked the girl off the ground and stretched her out horizontally, like a banner flapping in the wind. The ferocious pull dragged both her and Daryl toward the awakening body.

"Let her go!" Nathan yelled. "She needs to wake up!"

"If you say so!" Daryl released Felicity's hand. With her vacant sockets wide open and her mouth gaping in a silent scream, she flew into the wind. She made a wide circle in the cyclonic flow, then vaporized into a stream of gray mist and splashed over the body.

Pulling in broken tombstones and shattered trees, the whirlpool compressed into a tight funnel and spun toward the sleeper's scalp. Like a corkscrew, it drilled through her skull and disappeared.

As the light faded, the girl rose to all fours, shaking her head, but if she said anything, the cacophony of battling noises drowned her out.

With the dream at an end, darkness flooded the area. Nathan's candle lay on its side a few steps away, but its flame had dwindled to almost nothing. Another candle flame floated nearby, but it shed only enough light to illuminate the hands that held it: Daryl's.

Nathan reached down to help the girl. He found a forearm and slid his hand underneath.

Daryl's meager candle flame bobbed toward the sleeper and settled opposite Nathan. "She seems pretty groggy," she shouted. "We'll have to give her a boost."

The paralyzers switched off, dousing their lights. When the sound died away, Cerulean stopped singing and hurried toward them, his dim blue glow revealing his location. Breathing heavily, he added his strength as all three lifted the girl to her feet.

"Don't worry," Daryl whispered. "We've got you. You're going to be all right."

With Cerulean now supporting her body from behind, Nathan tried to see the girl's eyes, but the blue light wouldn't penetrate the curtain of hair that had fallen over her face.

"Can you tell who she is?" Daryl asked.

"I think I know, but I didn't want to say it out loud until I was sure." Nathan gently pushed back her hair, but even then shadows kept her features hidden.

"She is my beloved," Cerulean said. "I need not see her face to know."

Nathan waved at the flickering flame. "Daryl, bring it closer, please."

"Right here, Captain." She pushed a candle stub between Nathan's finger and thumb. "Not much left, though. Don't burn yourself."

"Thanks." Nathan laid a hand on the girl's cheek. "Daryl, can you hear me?"

"Of course I can hear you. I'm right here. I just said don't burn—"

"I don't mean you." As he held the candle closer to the girl, his throat caught. The glow rose to the eye level of her feminine face, freckled, with red bangs draping her forehead. Her lips trembled, and tears trickled down her cheeks. He set the glow near where her collar would be. It was missing.

His tongue dried out as he tried to speak the words. "I was talking to Daryl Blue."

Daryl Red squealed. "It's really her! It's really Daryl Blue!"

"Is she conscious?" Cerulean asked.

"I'm conscious." Lifting a hand to her head, Daryl Blue groaned. "But I'm so confused. Am I awake or dreaming?"

"Awake," Nathan said. "But we'll have to convince you of that later. Can you walk?"

She blinked three times. "I'll try." As she set her feet firmly, she smiled. "Is that you, Nathan?"

"Yeah. It's great to see you again."

After testing her legs, she looked at him, her brow tightly knit. "Dark have been my dreams of late."

"Is that a movie quote?" Nathan asked.

"Yeah. *Lord of the Rings.*"

"I remember. Then Gandalf says, 'Your fingers would remember your old strength better if they grasped your sword.'" He patted his hip where a scabbard might have been. "But I don't have a sword to give you."

"I do ... sort of." She pulled free from Cerulean and stooped. "I found it while I was floating in that dark place."

"We should go," Cerulean said. "The stalkers fear me, but they might summon enough courage to strike from the darkness, and we have lost too much time already."

"Hold your horses just another minute." Daryl Blue straightened, lifting a long object in both hands. "It's that crazy bow you used to play that crazier violin."

"Perfect," Nathan said. "Just what we need."

Daryl Red pushed her shoulder under Daryl Blue's arm. "Lead the way, blue eyes. I'll help this gorgeous redhead."

After giving Cerulean the candle, Nathan picked up the bow and searched for any sign of the direction they should go.

Cerulean turned in a slow circle, the candle dimly lighting his worried expression.

"What's wrong?" Nathan asked.

"The two Daryls have met in the dream world. I do not know what the consequences will be, but we can expect a drastic change. Do you feel the breeze?"

As a cool wind swept across his forehead, Nathan's mind rang with the memory of Amber's warning, and a cold lump formed in the pit of his stomach. "Maybe it's just a new dream getting started."

"It is not." Cerulean waved a hand. "We must go. Stay close to me. I think the stalkers will feel the same uneasiness, but we should take no chances."

He led the way, and the two Daryls followed. Nathan trailed the group, keeping watch for any sign of a white-haired head. With every step, the breeze grew, though no new lights illuminated the area—no fresh images arose from the mind of a sleeper in the real world.

In the distance, the other dreams dimmed. The football field warped like a curtain blown by a strong gust. The sunlit meadow fragmented, as if cut into jigsaw puzzle pieces.

Cerulean marched with longer, quicker strides. Daryl Blue, now walking on her own, breathed heavily, but she and Daryl Red kept pace. Nathan cast one last glance behind him, then kicked into a jog. The wind whipped his shirt and hair, causing both to swirl like one of the cyclones that signaled the end of the dreams. He tucked the bow under his arm and pointed it forward, lowering the wind resistance, the only way he could hang on to it at all.

Seconds later, they reached the ruptured core. Patar stood near the edge, his feet spread and his body leaning into the wind. He shouted above the whistling storm. "Your rescue mission has had disastrous results. Every dream is collapsing, and all are being swept into Sarah's Womb."

Nathan looked around. His parents, Amber, and Kelly were nowhere in sight "Why? And where is everyone?"

Patar glared at the two girls as they drew near. "Like similar poles on two magnets, she and her twin carry repelling energy forces, and they are creating an environment that makes this realm incapable of maintaining dreams. With every imagination ending simultaneously, the winds pulled the others into the Womb." He pointed upward and twirled his finger. "The cyclone took Amber and your family to a higher level, though I cannot tell how high."

Nathan stared into the darkness. The chaotic choir had silenced, leaving behind only an eerie hum. Somewhere up there, his father carried very precious cargo. Yet, no matter how hard the wind blew, there was no way he would ever let Kelly fall.

"Maybe it isn't the two Daryls meeting," Nathan said. "Could the Lucifer machine be causing this?"

As if taken by surprise, Patar stared at him. "I do not know. Mictar is the master of the devilish engine."

"So what do we do now?" Nathan asked. "Follow the others?"

Patar blinked at the strengthening wind. "We have no choice. We must release ourselves into the flow, Cerulean first and myself last."

Cerulean raised both arms, then, as if swimming with a river's current, lifted into the air and disappeared.

Shifting the bow back to his shoulder, Nathan walked right up to the edge. Just as he started to lean into the flow, the floor crumbled beneath him. He fell backwards, but the cyclone lifted him into its grip.

Everything turned black. As his mind swirled, a sense of flying took over, overwhelming all feeling except the bow pressing against his body. Rushing wind whistled past his ears, then the sound of one of the Daryls calling his name.

Someone grabbed his hand and pulled. Long hair brushed against his face, and a warm body pressed close. Then a weak whisper blew into his ear. "I'm scared."

"Daryl Red?"

"You got it. But I'm feeling like Felicity. I'm as blind as a radar-challenged bat."

He wrapped an arm around her and tried to silently radiate comfort. For some reason, this rocketing ascension felt safe, similar to one of their drops from the misty world. But with the hum of the Lucifer machine growing louder, that feeling quickly melted away.

Soon, the sense of rising eased, and the rush of wind ceased. Nathan blinked. Darkness surrounded him — not a hint of light anywhere. He pushed his toes down but felt nothing below, just empty space.

Warmth from Daryl's body drew trickles of sweat, plastering his shirt against his skin. Although her trembling continued, she made no sound. A new breeze swept over Nathan's body, soft and cooling. A sweet aroma rode its current — the smell of roses, subtle, yet leaving little doubt. He took in a long draft. Scarlet's presence? Before, he had noticed the aroma from within, as if the scent of roses welled up from his own lungs, but now it drifted all around.

A gentle laugh floated by, but it was more than a laugh. It was musical, like the tinkling of chimes blown by the wind. Nathan craned his neck to listen, but another sound drowned out the laughing song. Daryl's rapid breaths passed over his cheek, hot and damp.

He relaxed his arm and felt for her elbow. "Are you all right?"

"I think so." She blew out a longer, calmer breath. "Where is everyone?"

He searched the darkness in the area where her hand should have been. "Do you have a candle?"

"No. I thought you had one."

Nathan closed his eyes, trying to remember when he had set down his candle. Was it when he started jogging back to the central core, or when he got there and couldn't find Kelly or his parents?

"I see a light!" Daryl whispered sharply.

"Where?"

She turned his head. "There!"

He squinted into the black canopy. A dim glow, small but steady, drew closer. It seemed to be the familiar aura of a supplicant, bluish, though not as shimmering as before. "Cerulean?" Nathan called. "Is that you?"

"Yes." Cerulean's face came into view. At his side, he held Daryl Blue by her arm. "We are both well."

Daryl Blue laid a hand on her forehead. "That crazy tornado scrambled my brains. I can't tell which way is up."

Patar's voice pierced the darkness. "You have good reason to be confused, for there is no longer any floor beneath us by which you may orient yourself." A few seconds later, his white-capped head appeared, then his body. "Since there is no floor beneath us to pull us downward, you feel no gravity, and that is a disorientating sensation."

"You're telling me," Daryl Blue said. "Back when I first fell into this place, I felt the air rush by, then after about five minutes of gut-wrenching terror, I slowed down and fell the opposite direction for maybe a minute. Then I stopped again and fell for only thirty seconds or so." She moved her hand up and down to demonstrate. "I bobbed like a screaming, redheaded yo-yo for an hour. Once I settled into floating around like a seasick guppy, I was so dizzy I just slept most of the time."

Patar gave her a grim nod. "And a similar disorientation will affect the three Earths, assuming they survived. Without an intact core and an anchor in the foundation, they will drift apart. Sound waves will become so corrupted that no human will be able to survive the brain-splitting frequencies."

"So what do we do?" Nathan asked.

"We must continue to follow my plan to restore the foundation, heal the cosmic wounds, and draw the three worlds back to their anchor points." He looked up, his brow deeply furrowed. "With much of the floor beneath us crumbling, we will ascend to the great violin, though I have no idea how long it will take. Once there, we will attempt to call everything back into order. It could well be too late, but we must try."

"I can understand why we're not falling," Nathan said, "but what makes us ascend?"

"Just as we drew together around Cerulean's natural aura, we will drift toward the light in my world. At some point gravity will come into play again, likely somewhere still out of reach of the violin, so we will have to devise a way to continue when our upward movement ceases."

Nathan gazed into the darkness above, searching for any sign of Amber's glow. Since she and the others lifted off first, they were likely somewhere up there. He blinked. For a moment it seemed that a yellow light flickered, but it was only a pinpoint if anything.

A low moan sounded from somewhere below, a stretched-out lament, almost like a song. Nathan looked down and saw nothing. Those three stalkers likely were ascending, too, but would they cause trouble? Would they dare do anything with Patar and Cerulean around?

Daryl Red reached out and clutched Nathan's sleeve. "I don't know about you guys, but I'm ready to go psycho. The proverbial light at the end of the tunnel had better show up soon."

"I know the feeling," Daryl Blue said. "Dropping like that was ..." Her voice suddenly fell to silence.

Nathan looked into her sad eyes, two glistening orbs barely

visible in the blue glow, squeezed half closed by her fear-tightened features.

He set a hand on Daryl Blue's shoulder and gave it a gentle squeeze. "I have to tell you something."

As he took in a breath, every eye turned toward him. The silence seemed to thicken the air. Even the moaning quieted. "I ... uh ... I misjudged you, Daryl, and I said some pretty bad things about you to Kelly."

Without a blink, Daryl's eyes stayed focused on his. Cerulean's glow strengthened, shining a brighter light over her pain-streaked face.

"So," Nathan continued, "I apologize for my stupidity. You're a true hero, and I hope you'll forgive me and help me finish what we started."

Gentle laughter drifted again through a freshening breeze. Daryl's red bangs brushed back. The lines in her forehead slackened. She threw her arms around Nathan's neck and pulled him close. "Of course I forgive you!" she cried as she rested her head on his shoulder. "I was worried you wouldn't forgive me for being such a coward."

The aroma of roses returned, this time in his own breath as well as in the surrounding air. Words streamed to his mind, but they were much too eloquent, way beyond his normal ability. He had to speak them in his own way. "You faced your worst fear and forestalled a world disaster. I don't call that cowardice, Daryl. You suffered a lot more than I did. I really owe you everything."

Daryl hugged him closer. "Paid in full!"

He breathed in deeply, enjoying the aroma as well as the warmth of her embrace. Now he couldn't stop the words from slipping through. "If there is any debt between us, it is cancelled. We now owe nothing to each other but love."

She pulled back, sniffing as she stared at him. "You ... you love me?"

He glanced at the other Daryl, then met Daryl Blue's stare. "Of course I love you. You're like the sister I never had, a really cool sister. I'd do anything for you." As he let a smile break through, he pointed at himself with his thumb. "Next time, though, let me take the fall. I'll play the part of the guy in *Vertigo*."

"You and your movies!" Daryl kissed him on the cheek and whispered into his ear. "You've got yourself a sister, buddy, for better or for worse."

Daryl Red piped up. "Well, if that goes for me, too, then your big sister says we need to figure out a way to get this freight elevator moving faster. I mean, it smells nice, but the Spartan décor makes the Flintstones look stylish."

Nathan turned toward her. "Any ideas? With the smartest girls from two Earths putting their heads together, you ought to be able to come up with something."

Daryl Red leaned her head against Daryl Blue's. "My brain sprang a leak. How about yours?"

"Drained dry. I think my IQ dropped to single digits."

"There is a way to accelerate our ascension," Patar said. "One of our songs carries such power, but it is obscure, and I have not sung it in a long time. It left my memory ages ago."

Cerulean nodded. "I have heard you speak of it, but I have never heard the song itself."

"Can you remember the tune?" Nathan asked Patar. "Maybe the words will come back to you. I mean, we can't just wait until doomsday to get up there, or doomsday will come too soon."

Patar lowered his head. "My mind is not like yours. Once a memory has been purged, it will not come back. I am not as human as I appear to be. I am—"

The moaning voice returned, this time carrying a cadence, the familiar vowel sounds that marked a stalker's song.

Keeping his voice low, Patar translated. "I see you, you vile supplicant. Are you drawing me into your clutches to slay me?"

Nathan stared down again. A tall, slender figure floated slowly closer. With Cerulean's glow washing over his upward-turned face, his identity became clear. It was Tsayad.

Cerulean sang a string of vowels, similar to the stalker's, yet far more beautiful in tone.

Patar continued providing the translations. "If you bring evil intent, I will surely sing you into ashes."

Tsayad held up a book, the same music book he carried when Nathan first met him, and spat out a barrage of vowels.

"I heard you mention the song of ascent. It is in this book, and since I also desire to safely rise to my home, I offer it to you in exchange for safe passage."

Tsayad slowed to a stop, now only a few feet below them.

Cerulean extended his hand. "Give it to me. Otherwise I cannot be sure it is really there."

Tsayad hugged the book against his chest. "Do you think me fool enough to come near you? I would have used it earlier, but my ascent would have taken me past your destroying hands. You have grown far too powerful. That is one of the reasons I was hoping for replacement supplicants. They would have been easier to control."

"You are wise to fear my touch," Cerulean said. "Do you have a suggestion that will break the impasse?"

"The boy has a violin bow. Have him extend it toward me, and I will lay the book over it. Then he can raise it to your level."

"When I sing it," Cerulean said, his sounds still translated by Patar, "will everyone rise along with me?"

"While we were trapped in the void, it worked for the two who were with me, and they were no closer to me than I am to you. After a few seconds, we fell back, but I assume with the lack of gravity we will not experience that problem."

Cerulean turned to Nathan and nodded. Nathan lowered the tip of the bow to the stalker's level. Leaving the book open, Tsayad turned it over and laid it face down.

Without gravity, Nathan had no trouble lifting the laden bow. Cerulean slid the book off, then, turning away from the stalker, he began to study the two facing pages in the light of his own aura.

As two other stalkers joined Tsayad, he sang again. "I trust you to complete the words you have spoken," he said. "We have heard that a supplicant cannot lie."

"You have heard correctly." Cerulean kept his stare riveted on the book.

Nathan leaned toward Cerulean, but the page was too dark to read. The musical notes looked like vague smudges on blurry lines, and extra marks, like hieroglyphics with wild swirls, filled the gaps between the staffs.

After a few seconds, Cerulean looked at him. "You would not understand this music, Nathan. It is more than mere notes; it carries meanings that transcend simple sounds in the air. As a supplicant, I can give it poetic voice in your language, so we will not require an interpreter."

"What should the rest of us do? Just watch and listen?"

Cerulean's smile dressed his face in a mysterious aspect. "For the power of heaven to pull you upward, all you have to do is surrender to its call."

While Daryl Blue looped her arm around Nathan's, Daryl Red locked arms on his other side, and Nathan held the bow upright in front of them. Letting the songbook float in their midst, Cerulean completed the circle, and Patar stood on the outside of their gathering, looking as somber as ever.

Cerulean tilted his head upward and, glancing at the book every few seconds, crooned in a strong baritone.

O let the winds arise and bear
The faithful ones who heed the song.

With hearts of love we draw the breath
That gives us wings and makes us strong.

As soon as the last note died away, a fragrant breeze kicked up from below. Nathan breathed in the aroma, expecting the usual touch of roses, but it carried a blend of wonderful smells—vanilla, sage, horsehide, jasmine—just about every scent he had ever loved.

With the wind blowing through his clothes, his sweat dried, cooling his body, but he couldn't tell which way they were going. Were they falling? The rising air seemed to indicate that, but the slightest feeling of weight said otherwise. Apparently this rush lifted them higher and higher.

About ten feet below, three white-topped heads were the only clue that the stalkers ascended as well. Above, a golden light came into view, getting bigger and brighter by the second. Soon, Amber's form clarified, and in her glow, Nathan's parents quickly took shape. Kelly was still cradled in his father's arms. His mother and Amber had bent their knees fully, keeping their dresses in place as they rose.

When Nathan's group caught up, the breeze strengthened, lifting everyone at the same rate. Nathan handed Daryl Red the bow and extended his arms. "Mind if I take her again?"

"Not at all." His father transferred Kelly to him. "She's breathing fine. She's been talking in her sleep, but I can't understand what she's saying. Something about Scarlet."

"I'll bet Scarlet's talking to her in her dreams. I'll try to—"

Something slid down Nathan's arm, like a snake slithering from shoulder to hand.

Daryl Blue cried out, "The rope!" She wrapped her fingers loosely around the line and let it slide through her hand. "We must be getting close."

Light appeared above. Soon, the golden strings of Sarah's violin shimmered in the glow, and the upper chamber materialized, including the ceiling's rocky promontory that held the staircase leading down from the stalkers' world.

When they reached the rim, they slowed to a stop and bobbed on the rising wind, which bubbled around them and spread out to the sides, as if the Womb had become a boiling pot. Nathan glanced around. On one side of the core he spotted Mictar, standing only a foot or so to the right of the strings that spanned the void. As the wind brushed against them, a faint sound emanated, a sweet hum, barely audible in the midst of the noise coming from the upper reaches.

The flow pushed Nathan toward the opposite edge of the hole, but with his body floating just high enough to keep his torso elevated above the rim and with Kelly in his arms, he couldn't reach for the side.

A hefty tug jerked him upward, then plopped him down on his bottom at the edge of the hole, leaving his legs dangling. He twisted and found Daryl Blue hanging on to the rope and the back of his sweatshirt.

"Tarzan's got nothing on me," she said, grinning.

With the ground vibrating beneath him, Nathan laid Kelly down, and Daryl helped him scoot her safely away from the edge. The others swam with the current, Daryl Red still clutching the huge bow. When they all reached the edge and climbed to solid ground, the three stalkers bubbled to the surface and body-surfed the breeze to the side on which Mictar stood.

As Nathan helped his father to his feet, his mother knelt at Kelly's side and dabbed her grimy cheeks with the hem of her dress. The low hum from above grew louder. Now it carried a thrumming beat that drilled into Nathan's body and made his heart quiver.

Across the void, Tsayad lifted his head and sang out a stream of vowel sounds, wretched notes that seemed to burn in the air.

"He calls my people," Patar said. "They have no basket by which to descend, but they could create problems with their voices. If the healer plays the violin, they are sure to try to corrupt the music."

Nathan searched for a hidden door but saw nothing. "I heard there's a secret passage. Can they get down here that way?"

"I created that for Abodah and my children. No one else knows of its existence."

"What's shaking the ground?"

"I deduce that two influences are at work—Sarah's violin is being brushed by the wind, and Lucifer's engine is being stirred by Mictar and his allies. You must play the strings before Lucifer is fully awakened."

Nathan looked at the opposite bank. Mictar, tall and pale, walked to the edge of the void; then, as though wading into a pond, he stepped into the bubbling current. While the upwelling breezes filled out his clothes and swung his ponytail, he lifted his violin and began to play. The strings squealed. The hum from above strengthened and rose in pitch. The door in the upper promontory opened, revealing a pair of stalkers, one man and one woman. As if conducted by the sway of Mictar's bow, they sang along with the horrible noise.

Glass shattered and fell to the ground. Nathan looked up. Barely visible through a gap near the upper walls, he could see the image of one of the three Earths. Wide cracks shot out from it, breaking the crystalline wall and sending shards down through the gap.

As the ground continued to shake, Patar took the bow from Daryl and propped it in front of Nathan. "It is time to do battle."

Cerulean stepped to the edge. "Amber and I can end this conflict. Mictar is no match for us."

"He has gained great power from Kelly's life forces," Patar said, "and his violin is far more powerful than you know. If, however, you wish to try, then go. Even if you are killed, you will sink into the Womb and join Scarlet in healing the wounds."

"No! I'm going to do it." Nathan wrapped his fingers around the bow. His palms still blazed with pain, but it didn't matter. Kelly lay near death on the ground, her eyes burned out. Even if she could survive outside of this world, because of that foul beast, she would never see again. It was time to settle this once and for all. For Earths Red, Yellow, and Blue, and for Kelly, he would go to war with that monster, and he would prevail.

"How're you going to get out there?" Daryl Blue asked. "That current's pretty stiff."

He lifted his arms. "Tie the rope to my waist. I've done this before; I can do it again."

While his father wrapped the line around Nathan's body to form a makeshift harness, his mother took each Daryl by an arm. "We have to work the finger board. Come with me. I'll show you how."

With the knot now fastened, Nathan gave his father a nod. "I'm going to get a running start, but I'll need you to give me a push every time I swing back here."

"You got it. Now go out there and give it all you've got."

"I will, Dad." Nathan almost added, "Just like you've taught me." But he already knew. They both knew.

His father glanced upward. "Uh-oh. More trouble. One of those stalkers is trying to cut the rope with a piece of glass."

22

FRIENDS FOREVER

Nathan looked up at the staircase. The female stalker continued to sing while the male sawed away at his lifeline. "I can't worry about that now. Let's just hope it isn't sharp."

After taking a last look at Kelly, he gripped the bow with both hands and charged toward the void. When he reached the edge, he leaped out. For a brief moment, he dropped, but the rope tightened, and the updraft lifted him as he passed over the center just out of Mictar's reach.

As the arc took him higher, he shifted his body to a horizontal position and pointed his head toward the golden strings. He glanced at the fingerboard. His mother and the two Daryls were in position. His hands aching, he stretched the bow downward and played the first note. As he passed over the strings, the sound roared past his body, sending an electrical shock across his sweat-dampened skin. The sensation shot from head to toe and stung his hands mercilessly, nearly making him drop the bow.

He gripped it tighter. Playing every note would be excruciating, but he had to go on. He suddenly lowered a notch. The stalkers in the stairwell must have cut through part of the rope. He was probably dangling by only a few fibers now, but there was no use looking, even if he could.

Swinging back with his feet pointing toward his father, he stroked the proper string. This time he had already passed by, so the shock didn't affect him, but a loud rumble echoed in response, shaking the ground. His mother fell off her string, but Daryl Blue was there to help her up while Daryl Red jumped to the next position.

Though his shoulders slumped a bit, Mictar played on. Soon, a louder, deeper roar sounded from above. Resembling a dark waterfall, a black stream poured out from the open door leading to the staircase, knocking the two stalkers from their perch. The female stalker fell only inches from Nathan and clawed at him as she passed, but missed. Like thick oil, the river of blackness flowed, covering the two stalkers and plunging them into the void in spite of the upward breeze.

A hefty push on his shoes sent Nathan flying toward the strings again. He had to pull in an elbow to avoid the spilling blackness, but he passed it without harm. As he swung by, he glanced at Mictar. An evil, confident smile spread across his face.

Nathan took in a breath and stretched the bow down. He couldn't worry about what the stalker was doing. Concentrating on the violin meant everything, and with another shock about to surge through his body, that was quite enough.

Again he played a note. Again the sound jolted his frame. But he just gritted his teeth and pressed on. No matter how bad the pain, he couldn't let anything stop him now.

Back and forth he went. His mother and the two Daryls jumped from string to string, falling down after every note as the violin's ground-shaking music rattled the chamber. His father's shoves kept him swinging, each carrying an emotional boost as well as a physical one.

The wind from below eased to a gentle draft. Mictar sank lower, but he didn't seem to mind. When he had descended about ten feet, he began to rise again, now standing on solid ground, a flat black surface.

As soon as the new foundation reached the top of the former hole, he stopped playing and lowered his violin. The black stream stopped flowing. A final few drops spilled to the new floor and hardened in place, and the roar from above ceased.

Nathan played the key's final note, and as he swung back, he called out, "Dad. Catch me. I'm done."

Strong arms grasped his legs and turned his body upright. Nathan tried to stand, but his legs shook so hard, they barely gave enough support. While his father hurriedly untied the knot, his mother and the Daryls rushed his way.

"What's going on?" Daryl Red called.

Patar stood between Cerulean and Amber, his arms crossed as he stared at Mictar. "My brother has used Lucifer to fill Sarah's Womb with physical darkness. Sarah can no longer coordinate the great dance, so no matter how much healing the great violin's music brought to the Earths, they will no longer be able to hear her song, and they will drift away. Unless we employ our final strategy, all three are surely doomed."

"Final strategy?" Nathan asked. "You mean, kill the supplicants?"

Mictar let out a loud cackle. "And where will they go, dear brother? I fear that lodging vacancies for dead supplicants are no longer available. Sarah's Womb cannot echo their songs, so their deaths will do nothing to stop my plans."

Patar didn't flinch. "And you plan to let two Earths perish while you uphold Yellow with your dissonant choir."

Mictar played a fast, squealing measure on his violin. "I am especially fond of Francesca of that world. Since her husband is dying, she will become my pretty plaything, a ballerina who dances to my merry music."

Nathan balled his fists. Gritting his teeth, he whispered to Patar, "Can't Cerulean take him out? He and Amber together could—"

"No," Patar said. "*You* take him out."

"Me? But he's so powerful now. When he got done with me, I'd be just another eyeless rag doll."

"He *is* powerful—too powerful for the supplicants. That is why you must be the one." Patar grabbed Nathan's shoulder and jerked him around. "Will you now heed my words? I have overheard you extolling the virtues of faith. Is it not time for you to demonstrate with your actions what you so easily spew from your lips? You know you lack the power to defeat my brother. It is when you realize that your own strength is inadequate that real faith begins."

Nathan looked at Kelly. Daryl Red held her in her lap, whispering into her ear. With her eyelids open, Kelly appeared to be awake.

He threw the bow down. After giving his parents one last glance, he took a deep breath and charged toward Mictar. As he approached the stalker, he kept his eyes wide open, staring right at his red orbs. His fists balled, he leaped, but with a lightning-fast spin Mictar dodged and grabbed Nathan's hair. He spun Nathan in an orbit around his body, kicked him in the groin, and threw him to the ground.

Pain throttled Nathan's mind. He could barely breathe. The stalker jerked him up by his hair again and suspended him several inches off the ground. "Take a last look at your friends. The harlot has merely lost her sight, but you will lose your life and soul. I will breathe it in, and you will die."

"Patar!" Daryl Blue screamed. "Don't just stand there! Help him!"

Patar crossed his arms over his chest. "Nathan has chosen his own path. His sacrifice is noble, and we must let him complete it. I will stop anyone who tries to interfere."

Nathan's father dashed ahead, but Patar grabbed his collar and threw him to the ground, then planted a foot on his chest. "Solomon Shepherd, do not play the fool. You should know by now that I understand these matters far better than anyone. No one else can stop my brother; not me, not you, and not the supplicants. If you will stand with me, I will let you rise."

Solomon nodded. As Patar pulled him to his feet, Nathan's mother joined them, clinging to her husband as she watched Nathan through tear-flooded eyes.

Mictar let out another loud laugh. "How appropriate. An audience of cowards will watch the death of the only one brave enough to challenge me."

"Nathan?" Kelly cried out, her blank sockets wide open. "What's happening?"

"He is sacrificing himself for your sake," Patar said. "When it is over, I will deal with my brother."

Mictar lowered Nathan until his feet touched the ground. With pain still paralyzing him, he couldn't fight. He couldn't even clench a fist.

"When I take this gifted one's life," Mictar said, "you and ten supplicants would be no match for me."

Kelly reached out, wiggling her fingers as if trying to grasp the air. "Nathan," she cried, "come back to me. If you die, I don't want to live."

Taking in a pain-filled breath, Nathan coughed and let out his words in a rush. "I wish I could, Kelly. I wish I—"

Another kick silenced him. Mictar laid a hand over his eyes. "Now suffer and die."

Nathan took in another breath and tightened his muscles. Maybe it would happen quickly. Patar wouldn't save him. He didn't care about the death of one soul if it would help him save the Earths. He had made that clear many times.

Light flashed through Nathan's eyelids, bringing a slight stinging sensation. Horrible pain would surely follow, then death. Maybe the next sight he would see would be his Savior standing with open arms, but what would Jesus say? Did he make the right decision? Did he leave anything important undone?

As the pain increased, a new surge of heat pushed up through his throat, then into his mouth. The scent of roses, stronger than ever, burst from within. There *was* something left undone, something more important than life itself.

He gulped in another breath. "Kelly," he called, trying to keep his voice steady, "can you hear me?"

"Yes, Nathan." She wept through her words. "Yes, I can hear you."

"Kelly"—he licked his parched lips—"Kelly Clark, please forgive me for not telling you this before. It doesn't matter what you did in the past. I love you, and I hope I'll see you in heaven."

Her wail pierced his heart like a stabbing dagger, and his name stretched out in a pain-racked lament. "Nathan!"

"Oh, dear God," his mother cried. "Dear God, help him!"

The sound of a violin drifted in and out of Nathan's mind, then a piano. But how? Was he already traveling down the road toward death? Squeezing his eyes shut, he tried to let his other muscles go lax, but scalding pain sent stiffening shock waves from head to toe. He heaved in quick breaths and puffed single-word prayers between jolts of agony. "Give ... me ... strength ... to ... endure ... Defeat ... this ... monster ... in ... my ... place."

As pain overwhelmed every physical sense and darkness filled his mind, whispers filtered in—Scarlet's voice, gentle, like a breeze cooling the flaming tongs. *Take courage, my beloved. Your faith will bring life everlasting. This test of fire will merely burn away the dross and transform you into the strongest steel. But you must heed what you have been taught. Remember the words Patar spoke to you when you faced doom in a jetliner.*

The voice in his mind transformed into that of the stalker, calm and soothing. *Fear not, son of Solomon, and open your eyes. I bring you a gift that will protect you from my brother and equip you for the battles to come.*

Nathan gasped for air. How could he heed those words? How could he open his eyes and expose them to the flames?

Kelly's lament returned. "Nathan, I can't see you. I'm back in my nightmare, and I can't wake up. Help me wake up." Sobbing, she added, "Oh, dear God, I want to see Nathan again."

Clenching his fists, Nathan opened his eyes to the blinding light. Pain flooded his body. He let out a roar, but he couldn't fight. He was too weak, too wracked with pain.

"What?" Mictar shouted. "What are you doing?"

The stalker sounded confused and irritated. His hand lifted, and he pushed Nathan away. Nathan fell to his back, his eyes stinging, but he could see. In fact the chamber seemed to blaze with light.

"Nathan!" his mother called. "Beams are shooting from your eyes!"

Mictar fell backwards and landed on his seat. His own eyes flashed. Pressing his palms against his cheeks, he screamed, "What did you do to me?"

Patar strode to Mictar and crouched at his side. "Days ago, I transferred one of my powers to him. He reversed the flow and absorbed much of your energy. Now your power will continue to leak until you perish."

His eyes bulging, Mictar's face thinned. He clutched Patar's pant leg. "Brother! You can help me! You can seal the breach! It is within your power."

"Yes," Patar said. "It is within my power." He jerked his leg free and turned. "Come, everyone. Join me at the center of Sarah's Womb, and bring the girl. We must be quick."

"You knew!" Daryl Red cried, still cradling Kelly. "You knew all along that Nathan could reverse the flow."

"I knew he *could*, but I was unsure if he *would*. He had to ignite that power from within."

While Nathan struggled to his feet, his father scooped Kelly out of Daryl's arms and ran toward his son. His mother followed, waving for the two Daryls to hurry. With each moment, his vision clarified further, and new energy surged through his body. It seemed that every point of the floor he scanned began to sizzle as if electrified by his gaze, eating away at the physical darkness.

Kelly swung her head back and forth as though looking around. "What's happening?" she called. "Is Nathan dead?"

Solomon held Kelly upright and pushed her into Nathan's arms, then supported his back. Nathan held her up from behind with one arm around her waist. With the newly found strength, he didn't need his father's support, but it felt good all the same.

Patar withdrew a bag from within his shirt, the plastic Nathan had seen earlier. He dumped the contents into his hand—two eyeballs with vessels and nerves still attached, very much like the eyeballs he had recovered for Jack.

"I removed these from Scarlet's body, which once floated in Sarah's Womb, though I know not where her physical form dwells now." Patar drew back Kelly's hair, stretching her brow upward and forcing her lids open. He inserted the eyeballs, taking great care to put the dangling strands in first. Then, still holding her hair, he pulled down on the skin just below her eyes.

"Proceed," Patar said, "while I keep her new eyes exposed."

"You mean . . . ?"

Patar nodded. "Look at your skin."

Nathan stared at his palm, now bloodier than ever. Red light emanated from his pores, pulsing in time with his heartbeat. He slid it toward Kelly's face. "Do I just lay it over her eyes?"

"Yes. Do it now, while the energy channels are open."

Nathan covered her eye sockets with his hand, the same hand he had used to revive his mother. But what could a mere touch do? When he had revived his mother, Amber had told Kelly to push on her chest and say something like, "In the name of the

Father, the Son, and the Holy Ghost, restore the breath of life," but Kelly already had breath, so did that make a difference?

"So do I say anything?" he asked.

Patar shook his head. "You have already spoken the words of life. Just let your love for her pour through. The stone over your heart has rolled away. The music of your soul has been set free, and now nothing can prevent the flood of holy passion from flowing through your gifted hands."

Nathan pressed his hand down. Light flashed around the edges. For so long he had feared such a sight, an eye-covering hand that radiated energy, but now it gave him a different kind of shiver—excitement and joy.

Kelly cried out and tried to shake her head, but Nathan kept his hand firmly in place. Her legs stiffened. She gasped, then let out a loud groan, giving voice to her physical torment.

Feeling the energy draining, Nathan looked at Patar. He could barely speak, but he managed, "How ... much ... longer?"

"When the light in your hand fades, the surgery will be complete."

Keeping one eye on his glowing skin, Nathan watched his surroundings. Again, with each look at the floor's physical darkness, new sizzles arose, followed by white vapor. His mother clasped her hands over her mouth, tears flowing. His father kept him propped up, whispering, "You can do it, son. I know you can do it."

Mictar lay in a fetal position, writhing as his body continued to wither away. Light flowed out from beneath him in a pool that spread out over the floor, raising more sizzles and thick vapor. He moaned but spoke no audible words. Tsayad and the other two stalkers cowered near the former edge of Sarah's Womb.

Nathan offered his parents a nod, but he still couldn't speak. It seemed that his entire body erupted, spilling everything within—love, faith, joy, courage, peace—everything that gave him life, or at least made life worth living.

He lifted his eyes skyward and cried out, but formed no words. His wild groan echoed, filling the chamber. Gasping for breath, he lowered his head. The light around his hand dimmed. Kelly squirmed in his embrace, her muscles flexing.

As she stood upright, he withdrew his hand. She turned toward him, blinking. "Nathan?" She wrapped her arms around him and hugged him close. "Oh, Nathan! You're alive! Thank God you're alive!"

Nathan enfolded her in his arms and wept. She, too, cried, and in the midst of their gentle sobs, the music of a violin and piano continued in a soft and gentle tone.

Casting a faint glow, Amber glided to Mictar and knelt at his side. As she laid a hand on his quivering shoulder, she looked up at Patar. "Father, shall I end his misery?"

Nathan raised his brow. *Did she say, "Father"?*

"Yes, child," Patar said. "He is truly a miserable creature."

Amber turned back to Mictar. Pursing her lips, she began a wordless song. Filled with rapid shifts in key and abrupt swings from high to low octaves, it seemed fitting—a violent tune, void of melody, void of order.

As she sang, Mictar convulsed, shrinking with every rhythmic thrash.

Kelly whispered, "It's so sad."

"What's she saying?" Nathan asked.

"She called him her uncle and said she loves him, but now … Oh, my!"

"Can you tell me the words?"

Moving away from Nathan, she sang softly. Though her voice was no match for Amber's, every nuance of emotion came through.

You shunned the way of faith and trust,
Rejecting love and song,

So now I grind your bones to dust;
I rescue right from wrong.

Mictar's body twisted. His skin peeled, exposing crumbling flesh that flaked away from gray bones. The three other stalkers fled into the darkness.

Now stand before the righteous king,
The judge of all the earth,
And hear his verdict play and sing,
Declaring blight and worth.

Finally, a puff of air rose from the heap of shattered bones, taking a stream of dust in its wake as it rose into the darkness and disappeared.

Amber scooped a handful of Mictar's remains and, looking at Nathan, sang again, this time with her own words and a beautiful tune.

To dust and ash we all must turn,
The final dance of life.
For this I live, for this I yearn,
To be my savior's wife.

To waltz with him, to sway and spin,
To dance upon the stars;
I leave behind this world of sin
And kiss away my scars.

She let the dust sift between her fingers, leaving a bone fragment in her palm. Clutching it tightly, she rose and looked at Patar. "Father, is it time for our final dance?"

As streams of vapor rose all around, Patar laid a palm on top of her radiant blonde head. "Soon, my child. Very soon."

With Lucifer's roar silenced, and Sarah's violin now quiet, Nathan took Kelly's hand and spoke in a normal tone. "Can you see?"

"Just fuzzy shadows, like it's been on Earth Red, maybe a little worse. I'm not sure."

"Well, I guess it's better than having no eyes at all."

"How are your wounds?"

He looked at his palms. They were bloodier than ever, raw and swollen. "Uh ... they're not so good either, but they'll never stop me from doing what I have to do."

She offered a smile, but it seemed weak and halfhearted. "Is there anything left to do?"

"You bet." Daryl Blue slapped her shoe against the sizzling black surface. "We have to figure what's cooking on this floor and empty Sarah's Womb."

"I hear Daryl," Kelly said, her smile growing. "I'm glad you could stick around for this adventure."

Daryl Red joined Daryl Blue at her side. "Kelly-kins, look closer. You're not seeing double."

Kelly squinted, then squealed. "Daryl Blue's alive!"

"About time you noticed, girl!" Daryl Blue ran to her and gave her a gentle hug. "It's so good to see you again. I just wish ..." Her voice fading, she lowered her eyes and stepped away.

"To have Kelly Blue back," Kelly finished.

"Yeah. And there's no Nathan Blue, either. Maybe if we get these worlds dancing again, I can stay with you guys."

Patar walked to the center of the floor, holding the hand of a supplicant on each side. "Those of you who can hear the music, come and join us in the dance."

Nathan perked his ears. Again the duet drifted in, still soft and slow. "Do you mean the violin and piano?"

"Yes, I discerned its meaning only moments ago. Sarah's captives have flown from her protective Womb. They awaited the playing of the great violin, the song that would loose their chains."

"Who are Sarah's captives?" Nathan asked.

"Those who died at Mictar's hand. Scarlet also dwelled in

the dream world as a disembodied spirit, and Lucifer's darkness forced her to flee. Two of the captives wish to play a farewell before they journey to heaven's gate."

Amber joined hands with Cerulean to complete the circle. "Our dance is for our family alone," she said. "Your partner will be whomever God has given ears to hear this new song of ascents."

Solomon took Francesca's hand. "We don't hear it."

Amber gave him a radiant smile. "You have danced the great song together for years, so you have no need to join us."

"I hear it," Kelly said. "The violin is especially beautiful."

Nathan turned toward her. "I was going to say the piano was really good."

"I don't hear squat," Daryl Blue said. "Just you guys yakking."

"Same here." Daryl Red sat on the floor. "But we'll watch from the sidelines and groove with your moves."

Nathan reached for Kelly's hand. "It's bloody. I hope you don't mind."

"Why should I mind?" She showed him her palm, still imprinted with the heart-shaped smudge. "Love made him bleed, so love makes us bleed."

He pressed his palm against hers and intertwined her fingers. "Do you know how to dance?"

"If you lead," she said, pulling his arm around her waist, "I'll follow."

Nathan looked into her eyes, now reddish-brown, a visible blend of hers and Scarlet's personality. Kelly's words brought back Amber's solemn counsel: *Whenever someone dances with another, he is saying that he agrees with every aspect of his partner's purpose—the partner's beliefs and the principles by which he or she lives. If the music is greater than that of both partners, each one gives up his own path to follow the music's universal call.*

With their hands still joined, Amber, Cerulean, and Patar

began swaying, in similar fashion to how Amber and Francesca had danced when they entered the dream world, yet this time the dance was slower, more somber. With downturned expressions and glistening eyes, they seemed to be in mourning. Amber released Cerulean's hand for a moment and tossed the bone fragment into the center of their circle. The sizzles grew louder, apparently eating away the floor around the bone, and the rising vapor thickened.

"Shall we join them?" Nathan asked.

Kelly's smile seemed to brighten the chamber. "By all means."

Listening to the music, he picked up the rhythm and stepped into a slow waltz. Again, the crackling sound of dying darkness heightened, and another voice joined in, humming the violin's melody.

Nathan turned toward the sound. Only a few paces away, Scarlet walked toward him. Semitransparent, her red hair and dress flowed as though she were strolling on a breezy day. She stopped and spread out her arms. As if commanded to appear by her gesture, a piano materialized on one side along with a girl seated on a bench, her fingers on the keys. On Scarlet's other side, a male teenager stood with a violin. Both played their instruments with great emotion, dipping and swaying with each impassioned note.

As he turned Kelly so she could see the musicians, Nathan stared at their faces. With vacant eye sockets and scorched skin, there was no doubt who they were. "Nathan and Kelly Blue," he whispered. "They were two of Sarah's captives."

While her family sang sweet, wordless harmony, Scarlet's hum transformed into words, vibrant and lovely.

The veils that blind our hearts and minds
Are symbolized by veils of earth.

When darkness shields our fleshly eyes,
It paints a portrait, dark and dearth.

The blinders force our steps askew;
We bump and bruise our hands and eyes.
And shedding blood reveals our need
To beg for stripping false disguise.

Beautiful and ghostlike, Scarlet glided toward the trio of dancers. Cerulean and Amber released hands and allowed her to join in. Although their physical fingers couldn't touch Scarlet's, the three supplicants seemed bonded, now dancing in perfect cadence as she continued.

To heal our injured eyes and hands,
We step in time with borrowed song.
A song of heaven, sung in threes;
Uproot what blinds, the anchored wrong.

So dance in time with healing verse
And peel away the blinding doubt;
Your partner thirsts, forgive the past,
And let it rain to end the drought.

She stepped away from her family's waltz and, still swaying, she touched Nathan and Kelly, looking at each of them in turn.

To all who dance forgiveness steps,
The reaching hand, the tear-stained face,
Release the captives from their bonds.
Let love erase the past disgrace.

Then, she backed away and turned toward the musicians, lifting her hands.

Ascend on high O captive ones,
And rise above the solemn sound;

Your joy will make the angels laugh
And lift your souls to higher ground.

When her final note echoed and died away, Nathan and Kelly Blue joined hands and faded until they and their instruments disappeared.

Patar, Cerulean, and Amber stopped but stayed in their circle. Nathan stopped as well, keeping his fingers locked with Kelly's and his arm around her waist. With a radiant smile, Scarlet leaned toward him and whispered, "I will see you in your dreams, my love. Try to remember me when you rise from your slumber."

She ran to join her family, taking her place between Cerulean and Amber. Once their hands joined, Patar and his two living children became less solid, eventually fading into luminescent ghosts.

As if energized by their transformation, the sizzling amplified once more. At the center of their circle, a hole appeared and grew at a rapid rate. The perimeter expanded past their feet and they slowly descended. Bright light shot up from below, encompassing them and making their bodies glitter as if hundreds of silvery fireflies had alighted on their clothes. Their bodies caught fire, though they were still recognizable within the flames.

"Do not fear," Patar called. "Let Sarah enfold you and lead you home. Everyone's gateway to his or her proper home has already been prepared."

As the hole widened, the two Daryls shot to their feet, Daryl Red still carrying her bag by its shoulder strap. Nathan guided Kelly to his parents, and they joined the Daryls in a huddle near the hole.

Shielding his eyes from the brightness, Nathan stood at the edge and backed away as it expanded toward him. "What about the Earths?" he shouted. "What do we do to heal them?"

Patar's voice rose from the depths, strong, yet somber. "You were right all along, Son of Solomon. If the supplicants were to die, their sacrifice had to be willing. I commanded you to carry out the task I feared to do myself, and for that, I am sorry. Now that they have joyfully acquiesced to their father's will, our descent into the Womb, enabled by the energy gained by your sacrificial act, will heal every cosmic wound."

His voice faded. Light exploded from the void and shot into the air like a geyser. It splashed against the ceiling and ripped a wide crack in the stone. The promontory that held the staircase plummeted. Rocks and dirt rained down. Everyone backed away as the debris cascaded into the hole.

"Look!" Kelly said, pointing upward. "The three Earths aren't on the walls anymore."

Nathan stared through the widening crack. The curved walls in the upper chamber were now just blank crystal without a sign of the planets anywhere.

Kelly bounced on her toes. "That means they're healed, right?"

"You can see that far?" he asked. "I can barely see the walls myself."

Grinning, she nodded. "Perfectly. Better than ever." She grasped his wrists and turned them palms up. "And I see the most wonderful pair of hands in the world—healed, just like the wounds in the cosmic fabric."

He lifted a hand closer to his eyes and flexed. His palm and fingers, void of any hint of injury, moved without pain. He looked at his other hand. It, too, was now free of wounds.

Kelly stared at him. With firelight illuminating her crystal-clear orbs, her vision seemed to penetrate his mind. He opened his eyes wider to let her in. If she wanted to read his thoughts again, that was fine. He let them flow. *You are a treasure. I have been willing to risk my life to save the world, but if you were the only one alive in any of the three Earths, I would give my life for you, without question.*

Kelly trembled. She pressed her lips together but said nothing.

Daryl Red shook Nathan. "Hey, we'd better do what the head paleface told us. I think this place is about to blow."

The crack continued to widen above them. Stalkers peered over the side, shielding their eyes and backing away from the encroaching gap. Rocks and pebbles continued to fall, most landing on the floor instead of in the void.

"Join hands everyone!" Nathan called. He took Kelly's hand as well as his mother's. When they all had formed a line, he shouted, "Jump!"

They leaped into the hole. Nathan closed his eyes to protect them from the blinding light. A rushing wind met his body and seemed to buoy him. He couldn't look to see how everyone else was doing, but the pressure of a clutched hand on each side let him know that at least two were still with him.

Soon, the light grew dimmer. Nathan opened his eyes. He floated with Kelly, the two Daryls, and his parents next to the interconnected vines.

"I guess some of the dream world ground survived," Nathan said. "The trees are obviously still here."

Still holding to his wife's hand, Nathan's father grabbed a vine and vaulted with her to the edge of the hole. Once they settled, he reached for the others. "Hurry. If my guess is right, the walls of the Womb will be restored soon."

Kelly swung to the side, followed by Nathan and the Daryls. Nathan's father withdrew a small pocket knife, reached as far as he could into the column of light, and sliced the vine. As the vines retracted toward the three trees, the light gathered at the perimeter of the central core. It darkened and solidified, recreating the dream world's barrier.

Now in complete blackness, Nathan found a cool hand and grasped it. "Is that you, Kelly?"

"Yep, but I'm blind again."

"No worries. I think we all are."

"Tut, tut," one of the Daryls said. "We will soon have light."

A match ignited. It seemed to float in the darkness toward a candle. "I know this isn't a real world fire, but it'll do in a pinch."

As soon as the flame crawled down the wick, Daryl Red blew out the match. "And I have something else in my bag of goodies."

"I already got it," Daryl Blue said. She lifted a mirror and set it under her chin. "Let's see if this will take us home."

Nathan looked at the reflection—an image of the telescope room at the observatory. But which one was it? Red, Blue, or Yellow? The details were so small, he couldn't figure it out.

Daryl Red took the mirror and laid it on the ground. "Let's just do a Mary Poppins and jump right in." She handed the candle to Nathan. "I'll go first if you don't mind. This place is messing with my phobia."

While Nathan held the candle low, Daryl stepped on the mirror. Her foot sank. Smiling as she lifted her arms, she shouted, "Geronimo!" and disappeared into the image.

Daryl Blue did the same, echoing the shout. Nathan's parents followed, then Kelly.

Now alone, Nathan looked all around. Somehow he knew a visitor would drop by.

In a dazzling aura, Scarlet walked his way. Her dress, now a sparkling red gown, flowed behind her as she drew near. She smiled as she stopped and took his hand. "When you finally lay your head to rest after these days of danger, I will be there to ease your mind."

"You're physical," Nathan said, lifting her hand.

She laughed gently, her breath making the candle flame

quiver. "Only because you see me in the light of this world. I am real, to be sure, but not physical. We will not truly touch one another again until I see you in the everlasting city."

Nathan firmed his chin and nodded. He gazed at her lovely face, then at the mirror. In the image, his parents and Kelly looked back at him, but they slowly faded.

"I have to go."

"Of course you do." She kissed him on the cheek, letting her lips linger for a moment as she whispered, "Thank you for releasing me from my prison. I always knew you would."

Backing away, she waved, tears flowing. "You will always be my beloved."

He set both feet next to the mirror and swallowed hard. "And I will never, ever forget you."

Nathan blew out the candle and dropped it on the ground. Scarlet disappeared. Bending his knees, he leaped onto the glass and plunged through darkness. One second later, light flooded his vision. As he stood at the center of the telescope room, several sets of eyes stared at him.

Kelly ran up and wrapped her arms around him. "Welcome home!"

He returned the embrace. "So is this Earth Red?"

"Yes!" She drew back and pointed at her eyes. "And I can see perfectly!" She turned him toward the other waiting travelers. "And look who else made it. Clara!"

Clara marched toward him, her gray hair a mess and her dress torn in several places. "And you wouldn't believe what happened to me," she said raising her fingers and counting them down. "I patched up Solomon Yellow, who now seems like a new man, much more like your father; I found a surgeon in India for Gunther who said he could remove that explosive chip from his skull; and I kissed a precious baby good-bye—little Nathan. Then, Francesca showed me her mirror, and the channel was tuned to this station." Taking a deep breath, Clara spread out her arms. "I jumped in, and here I am."

Nathan laughed, feeling so much joy he thought he might explode.

"And I'm home, too." The voice came from the computer speakers. Nathan looked up. Daryl Blue stood in the middle of the ceiling mirror's image, waving. "I don't have Nathan or Kelly to keep me company, but I think a gorgeous, blue-haired hunk is going to visit me in my dreams. Things could be worse, you know."

Nathan and Kelly waved. "Good-bye, sweetheart," Kelly shouted. "I love you."

The screen flashed and went blank. From the computer desk Dr. Gordon called out, "I've lost communication. The radio telescope isn't picking up anything."

Nathan's father walked toward him. "Then the portals are all closed? The wounds are healed?"

"That's my guess." Dr. Gordon closed his laptop firmly. "As far as I'm concerned, my research is complete. I think I'll practice my viola and audition for an orchestra."

Something beneath Nathan's feet moved. He stepped off the mirror square that had somehow traveled with him. As if sprouting from the ground, a man rose from the glass, a bearded man holding a crumpled hat in his hands.

"Jack!" Nathan patted him on the shoulder. "How'd you get here?"

A wide smile lifted his smudged cheeks. "I was wandering through the dream worlds, still looking for Felicity, and suddenly the whole place exploded with light. I just floated in nothingness until I heard a voice, a beautiful, laughing voice. She said, 'You have no home, so I will send you to those who will understand your plight.' Then ..." He stepped off the mirror and bowed gracefully. "I showed up here."

With a firm kick, Nathan slid the mirror across the floor

toward Dr. Gordon, who rose from his chair and stepped right on the glass. "I heard from your father, Daryl. He's fine and on his way back to Chicago."

Daryl clasped her hands. "Thank the Lord!"

Dr. Gordon and Nathan's parents walked to the center of the room, joining Nathan, Kelly, Daryl, and Jack.

Nathan scanned the company. Everyone looked exhausted. His father's clothes, frumpy and still covered with spider-tree webbing here and there, smelled as bad as they looked. His mother, though smiling as brightly as the sun, had bloodstains on her forehead and chin. Long red marks striped Daryl's cheeks, though they didn't seem as deep as they did before. Maybe they would heal without leaving scars.

"Well," he said, "I think just about everyone's accounted for."

"Except Simon Blue," Daryl said.

Nathan snapped his fingers. "Right. I wonder if we'll ever find out what happened to him. I didn't agree with him all the time, but I think his heart was in the right place."

"True," Kelly said, "and we don't know what happened to Gordon Yellow, either." She looked up at the ceiling. Now only their reflections appeared. "I wonder if we'll ever see any of our friends in the other worlds again."

Nathan took Daryl's hand, then Kelly's, and gazed into Kelly's sparkling eyes. "I don't know about that, but I'm looking forward to just kicking back for a while and getting to know the friends I already have."

Daryl pressed a palm against her chest and gave him a dreamy look. "Oh, Nathan, you're such a romantic. Are you sure you don't want to watch *Pride and Prejudice* with me?"

He laughed and linked arms with her and Kelly. "Just get me some popcorn, a tall Dr Pepper, and maybe a few Hershey's Kisses, and I'll watch just about anything."

ECHOES FROM THE EDGE

BEYOND THE REFLECTION'S EDGE

BRYAN DAVIS

BESTSELLING AUTHOR OF DRAGONS IN OUR MIDST®

THE FIRST SIGN

Nathan watched his tutor peer out the window. She was being paranoid again. That guy following them in the Mustang had really spooked her. "Chill out, Clara. He doesn't know what room we're in."

She slid the curtains together, casting a blanket of darkness across the motel room. "He parked near the lobby entrance. We'd better pack up and leave another way." She clicked on a corner table lamp. The pale light seemed to deepen the wrinkles on her face and hands. "How much more time do you need?"

Nathan sat on the bed nearer the window, a stack of pillows between his back and the wall, and tapped away at his laptop. "Just a couple of minutes." He looked up at her and winked. "Dad's slide rule must've been broken. It took almost an hour to balance the books."

Clara slid her sweater sleeve up an inch and glared at her wristwatch. Nathan knew that look all too well. His tutor's steely eyes and furrowed brow meant the Queen of Punctuality was counting the minutes. They were cutting it close, and they still had to get the reports bound at Kinko's before they could meet his parents at the performance hall for the company's quarterly meeting. And who could tell what delays that goon in the prowling Mustang might cause? His father had noticed the guy this morning before he left, and he looked kind of worried, but that could've been from the bean and onion burrito he had eaten for breakfast.

Nathan frowned at the spreadsheet. "This formula doesn't make sense. Dad's trying to divide by zero."

"Can you call and ask him on the way? We have to hit the road."

Nathan pushed the laptop to the side. He knew how his father would respond. He'd just grin and say, "Dividing by zero reflects my creativity." Nathan laughed. Dad knew a lot more about math than he ever let on; he just concentrated on spying and research and let Nathan do the number crunching.

As Clara peered out again, he looked over her shoulder. The driver of the black Mustang was parked under a tree, sloppily eating a sandwich as he watched the front door of the motel. An intermittent shower of leaves, blown around by Chicago's never-ending breezes, danced about on the convertible's ragtop.

"Don't worry about him," Nathan said. "He's too obvious to be a pro."

"True enough. But you don't have to be a pro to frighten an old lady."

As she turned toward him, he gave her the goofiest clueless stare he could conjure. "I'm not an old lady!"

He waited for Clara's infectious laugh that had brightened a hundred mornings in dozens of strange and lonely cities all over the world. But it didn't come. A shadow of worry passed across her face, draining the color from her cheeks.

He squinted at her. "Something else is bugging you."

For a moment, she just stared, a faraway look in her eyes. Finally, she shook her head as if casting off a dream. "Did you pack the mirror your father gave you?"

"I think so." He jumped up and walked over both beds before bouncing to the floor in front of the shallow closet. A towel-wrapped bundle sat on top of his suitcase at the very peak of a haphazard pile of clothes. Carefully unfolding the towel, he revealed a square, six-by-six-inch mirror with an ornate silver frame. His father had entrusted this mirror to him just yesterday, calling it a "Quattro" viewer and warning him to keep it safe.

Nathan pondered the strange word that represented his father's latest assignment, something about retrieving stolen data for a company that used reflective technology. Dad had been tight-lipped about the details, but he had leaked enough clues to allow for guessing.

He gazed at his reflection in the mirror, the familiar portrait he expected, but something bright pulsed in his eyes, like the split-second flash of a camera. Clara's face appeared just above his blond cowlick, suddenly much closer.

He spun his head around. Strange. She was still near the window. When he turned back to the mirror, her image was no longer there.

As she walked up behind him, her face reappeared in the glass. Nathan glanced back and forth between the mirror and Clara. The inconsistent images were just too weird.

The opening notes of Beethoven's Fifth chimed from his computer—his custom sound for new email. Still holding the mirror, he leaped back to his computer and pulled up the message, a note from his father.

Your mother is rehearsing with Nikolai, and that reminded me to remind you that she's going to call you to the stage to play your duet for the shareholders. She'll have your violin, all tuned and ready to sizzle. Since it's the Vivaldi piece, you shouldn't have any problem. Just don't mention your performance to Dr. Simon. Trust me. It will all work out.

Two words embedded in Nathan's mind, *Trust me*, the same words he had heard so many times before. With all the narrow escapes his father had engineered over the years, what else could he do but trust him?

Clara flung a pair of wadded gym socks that bounced off his chin. "Where is your tux?" she called as she searched through his crumpled clothes.

"I hung it on the shower rod." He patted a shiny motorcycle helmet sitting on his night table. He had hoped to ride their Harleys through town. With Clara in her new dress and him in a tux, they would've looked as cool as ice. But, no, they had to hitch a ride in the company limo. With their chauffeur, Mike, at the wheel, they'd be better off in a hearse. He wouldn't do more than thirty, even in a forty-five zone.

Clara disappeared into the bathroom and returned in a flash, brushing lint from his tux. "Aren't you going to help me?"

"Sure." He picked up his elastic exercise strap and karate belt and threw them into the suitcase. They were essential items. Since his dad was planning to rent an RV for a month-long trip out West, with all that driving, he had to do something to stay in shape. They'd have a whole month with no wild getaways, no running from crazed neo-Nazis, no dodging bullets from Colombian drug dealers. Sometimes those scrapes with death gave him a rush, and decking a thug or two with a well-placed karate chop was always a thrill, but ... He gazed at his motorcycle helmet and let out a sigh. It was probably better to avoid trouble than to dance with it. That's what his father always said.

Clara peeked out the window again. "The driver just got out, and I think he saw me."

"Here we go again." Nathan slapped the suitcase closed and zipped it up. "You got an escape plan?"

She snatched up her own suitcase. "There's an emergency exit down the hall. I'll call Mike and tell him where to pick us up when we find a place that's not so dangerous."

Nathan tucked the computer under his arm and grabbed the strap of his red backpack. "Yeah, like ground zero at a nuclear test site."

Forbidden Doors

A Four-Volume Series from Bestselling Author Bill Myers!

Some doors are better left unopened.

Join teenager Rebecca "Becka" Williams, her brother Scott, and her friend Ryan Riordan as they head for mind-bending clashes between the forces of darkness and the kingdom of God.

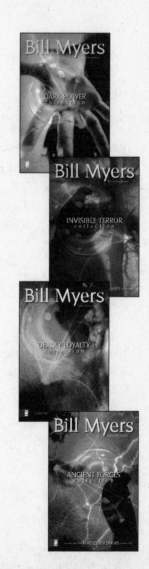

Dark Power Collection
Volume One

Softcover • ISBN: 978-0-310-71534-4

Contains books 1–3: *The Society*, *The Deceived*, and *The Spell*

Invisible Terror Collection
Volume Two

Softcover • ISBN: 978-0-310-71535-1

Contains books 4–6: *The Haunting*, *The Guardian*, and *The Encounter*

Deadly Loyalty Collection
Volume Three

Softcover • ISBN: 978-0-310-71536-8

Contains books 7–9: *The Curse*, *The Undead*, and *The Scream*

Ancient Forces Collection
Volume Four

Softcover • ISBN: 978-0-310-71537-5

Contains books 10–12: *The Ancients*, *The Wiccan*, and *The Cards*

The Shadowside Trilogy by Robert Elmer!

Those who live in lush comfort on the bright side of the small planet Corista have plundered the water resources of Shadowside for centuries, ignoring the existence of Shadowside's inhabitants, who are nothing more than animals. Or so the Brightsiders have been taught. It will take a special young woman to expose the truth—and to help avert the war that is sure to follow—in the exciting Shadowside Trilogy, the latest sci-fi adventure from Robert Elmer.

Trion Rising

Book One

Softcover • ISBN: 978-0-310-71421-7

The Owling

Book Two

Softcover • ISBN: 978-0-310-71422-4

Beyond Corista

Book Three

Softcover • ISBN: 978-0-310-71423-1

Pick up a copy today at your favorite bookstore!

Visit www.zondervan.com/teen

ZONDERVAN®
.com

Share Your Thoughts

With the Author: Your comments will be forwarded to the author when you send them to *zauthor@zondervan.com.*

With Zondervan: Submit your review of this book by writing to *zreview@zondervan.com.*

Free Online Resources at

www.zondervan.com

Zondervan AuthorTracker: Be notified whenever your favorite authors publish new books, go on tour, or post an update about what's happening in their lives.

Daily Bible Verses and Devotions: Enrich your life with daily Bible verses or devotions that help you start every morning focused on God.

Free Email Publications: Sign up for newsletters on fiction, Christian living, church ministry, parenting, and more.

Zondervan Bible Search: Find and compare Bible passages in a variety of translations at www.zondervanbiblesearch.com.

Other Benefits: Register yourself to receive online benefits like coupons and special offers, or to participate in research.